PRAISE FOR *CHEF'S KISS*

"It's hard to say which aspect of TJ Alexander's novel is sweeter: the slow-burn romance or the drool-worthy desserts."

—*Time*, "100 Best Books of the Year"

"Like a dish of comfort food you'll want to devour."

—*The Washington Post*

"One of the most intricate and satisfying queer romances in years. Fans of Casey McQuiston will be wowed."

—*Publishers Weekly* (starred review)

"A luscious dessert of a novel, a romantic comedy as classic as it is modern, as satisfying as it is groundbreaking."

—Camille Perri, author of *When Katie Met Cassidy*

"An utter delight, filled with sumptuous food, and adorable banter. This is the first time I've read a book with a nonbinary love interest, and I was cheering for Ray and Simone the entire time . . . The ultimate feel-good read!"

—Jesse Q. Sutanto, author of *Dial A for Aunties*

"Beyond the delicious recipes and the playful banter between the charming leads is a story about the sometimes difficult realities of the queer experience, and Alexander effortlessly tackles heavier topics without ever losing sight of queer joy and the happily ever after these characters deserve!"

—Alison Cochrun, author of *Kiss Her Once for Me*

"Start with two charming, lovable main characters, add a lot of laughs, and finish with a healthy pinch of spice and you've got *Chef's Choice*. I devoured every morsel of this delicious romance."

—Amanda Elliot, author of *Best Served Hot* and *Sadie on a Plate*

"A total delight, filled with queer joy and found family and so much warmth. Luna and Jean-Pierre stole my heart. Jean-Pierre is a tour de force of grumpy depressed European queer chaos and I would personally die for him."

—Cat Sebastian, author of *The Queer Principles of Kit Webb*

"Like Luna's beloved cheese plates and charcuterie spreads, this appetizing romance has something to delight a wide variety of readers. A first choice for contemporary romance collections."

—*Library Journal* (starred review)

PRAISE FOR *SECOND CHANCES IN NEW PORT STEPHEN*

"In a world that feels increasingly dark, this book is a light . . . sexy, hilarious, heartwarming, and gloriously queer."

—Camille Kellogg, author of *Just As You Are*

"From start to finish, this hilarious and tender rom-com stole our hearts! It's joyfully queer, laugh-out-loud funny, and scratches every small town and holiday romance itch possible. (And did we mention the hot single dad???) Five second chance stars!"

—Julie Murphy and Sierra Simone,
authors of *A Merry Little Meet Cute*

"A small-town romance with a great big heart. You'll be rooting for Nick and Eli as they find the courage to change, to seize second chances, and to love each other."

—Jenny Holiday, *USA Today* bestselling
author of *So This Is Christmas*

TRIPLE SEC

ALSO BY TJ ALEXANDER

Chef's Kiss
Chef's Choice
Second Chances in New Port Stephen

TRIPLE SEC

A NOVEL

TJ ALEXANDER

EMILY BESTLER BOOKS

ATRIA

NEW YORK LONDON TORONTO SYDNEY NEW DELHI

EMILY
BESTLER
BOOKS

ATRIA

An Imprint of Simon & Schuster, LLC
1230 Avenue of the Americas
New York, NY 10020

First Emily Bestler Books/Atria Paperback edition June 2024

EMILY BESTLER BOOKS/ATRIA PAPERBACK and colophon are
trademarks of Simon & Schuster, LLC

Simon & Schuster: Celebrating 100 Years of Publishing in 2024

For information about special discounts for bulk purchases,
please contact Simon & Schuster Special Sales at 1-866-506-1949
or business@simonandschuster.com.

The Simon & Schuster Speakers Bureau can bring authors
to your live event. For more information or to book an event,
contact the Simon & Schuster Speakers Bureau at 1-866-248-3049
or visit our website at www.simonspeakers.com.

Interior design by Lexy East

Manufactured in the United States of America

1   3   5   7   9   10   8   6   4   2

Library of Congress Cataloging-in-Publication Data is available.

ISBN 978-1-6680-2198-9
ISBN 978-1-6680-2199-6 (ebook)

to all sluts everywhere—cheers

TRIPLE SEC

PART ONE
OLD-FASHIONED

CHAPTER 1

Mel Sorrento stared at the black velvet box sitting on the Carrara marble bar top and tried not to roll her eyes.

It wasn't the guy's fault, or the fault of the engagement ring that probably cost something like fifty grand. Mel was just tired of this bullshit. Love. Marriage. Putting unethical gemstones into champagne flutes. All of it.

"So, okay," the guy said. There was a fine sheen of sweat along his prematurely receding hairline. He was chalk white, his eyes darting around like he expected to be caught red-handed at any moment. "I told her I was going to the bathroom. She can't see me, can she?" His head swiveled toward the back of the lounge, where the emerald velvet booths were more shadow than candlelight.

"No, you're fine." That was a tad optimistic. He actually looked like he was on the verge of fainting. Mel poured the guy a glass of ice water. Proposals usually didn't go well if the question-popper passed out in the middle of it.

"Oh, thank you." The man reached for it, but his hands must have been as sweaty as the rest of him, because he fumbled it badly. It landed with a terrific crash, broken glass mixing with crushed ice, the water making a mess of cocktail napkins and menus alike. "Fuck! I'm sorry."

"No worries." Mel swept up the glass with a rag and, without missing a beat, moved the ring box before the pool of ice water reached it. She cast an apologetic smile at the patrons seated at the bar, craning their necks to see what was going on. Jessica, her fellow bartender, swept by in a blur, doing her damnedest to serve everyone while Mel was otherwise occupied. Mel mouthed a silent thanks as she delivered glasses of water to guests on Mel's side; Jessica waved it off with a tap to her own wedding band. She knew the score: proposals took precedence.

The ring guy, meanwhile, moaned like his guts were being torn up. "Maybe this is a sign that I shouldn't ask her tonight. Would she really want to marry a guy like me? What if she says no? God, if she says no—"

"Take a breath, friend." Mel caught his panicked gaze and held it. She was a good bartender, which meant she could stick an engagement ring in a glass, clean up a mess, and be someone's therapist all at the same time. Possibly, at some point, she'd even mix a drink. "What's your name?" she asked.

"Darryl."

Yeah, he looked like a Darryl.

"Everything's going to be okay, Darryl," she said. That was a stretch, but who cared. "You're here in this beautiful place on this beautiful night and you're going to ask the beautiful—what's her name?"

"Pauline," he said with an exhausted sigh.

"You're going to ask Pauline something you've been wanting to ask her for a while now, right?" Mel swept the broken glass and ice into the beat-up champagne bucket she kept behind the bar for that exact purpose. Glassware accidents came with the territory. Mel would know; she was at Terror & Virtue six nights a week, and the only reason it wasn't seven was because they were closed on Mondays. "Pauline's going to gasp and cry, and it'll all be so wonderful, you'll completely forget the part where you were nervous."

She tried not to think about how she'd proposed to her now-ex: a frank discussion over morning coffee while rain pattered down the windows of their fifth-floor walk-up. She hadn't been nervous because there had been nothing to ask, only the assumption that she and her then-girlfriend were on the same page. What a crock of shit that turned out to be. A few years after the vows, they weren't even in the same book, let alone on the same page. Hence the divorce.

Darryl leaned on the bar like he couldn't keep himself upright. "You think so?" His gaze went to the ring box. "And that won't get, like, lost or anything? I've been carrying it around for so long, I'm kind of afraid to let it out of my sight now."

"Trust me." Mel gave him a conspiratorial smile. "It'll go off without a hitch. I've put hundreds of engagement rings in drinks."

"Hundreds?" Darryl's face fell. "I didn't know it was that . . . common."

"Well—" Mel couldn't help but give an assessing look at their surroundings: a bastion of carefully constructed opulence, the kind of cocktail bar that asserted itself as romantic and classy with prices to match. Terror & Virtue was a perennial darling of all those Must Visit lists for good reason: it was tailor-made for an impressive date or a public proposal. "It's not *un*common." Did Darryl really think he was the first man to stick a diamond ring in a glass of champagne? Or rather, ask a capable bartender to do it for him?

"I want this to be special," Darryl said. He sounded more like a whiny child than a man about to propose to his girlfriend, but at least he wasn't hyperventilating anymore. "Is there something else you could do? Something more interesting?"

Mel tamped down the annoyance that rose inside her. This job paid well, but she deserved to be compensated extra for shit like this. She pasted on her best customer service smile and tried to think of something, anything, that would get Darryl out of her proverbial hair so she could deal with the rest of her guests.

Thankfully she was saved from having to come up with a suitably romantic idea. Daniel—best friend, coworker, roommate, a real triple threat—appeared with his serving tray, nimbly skirting around a palm tree in a huge brass pot and stopping right next to Darryl. He picked up the last order Mel had managed to complete—two Keelhaulers, a tiki-style confection of rum and papaya served in a golden pineapple and topped with a ludicrous sugared-fruit skewer. His eyes fell on the velvet box.

"I didn't know you two were getting so serious," he said, tossing the sweaty guest a wink to let him know it was all in good fun. "To-night's a big night for you, eh?" His round face and sharply trimmed goatee gave him an air of friendly benevolence that guests always gravitated toward.

"Darryl here would like to propose in a unique way," Mel said. "What do you think we can do for him?" She took advantage of Darryl's head being turned to lift a flute and make a slashing motion across her throat, indicating to Danny that the usual game plan would not cut it.

Daniel hefted his tray on his shoulder. "Oh my god, well, first off, congratulations," he said to Darryl, free hand making his usual over-the-top gestures that tended to accompany his speech. "You've got nothing to worry about. Mel here is going to take good care of that ring." He stopped gesturing long enough to put his hand on Darryl's shoulder and leaned in like they were old friends sharing secrets. "Why don't you put it on a garnish? That way, your special someone won't have to fish it out from the bottom of a glass. Who wants that? Ugh, all sticky." He made an exaggerated face of disgust.

Somewhere behind her, Mel heard another guest give a loud snort. She dutifully did not acknowledge it. One thing at a time.

"That might work." Darryl turned back to Mel. "Do you think that's special enough?"

She schooled her face into what she hoped was a grave mask of professionalism. "Pauline will love it." She knew she had no business promising any such thing; she could only pray this guy wasn't going to get shot down in front of a packed house. Why did people do this— put themselves out there to be humiliated in public? "What does she usually drink? I'll make you something bespoke."

People liked hearing the word "bespoke." It made them feel fancy.

As predicted, Darryl's eyes lit up. "That would be great. She, uh, I don't know? She likes fruity drinks?"

Mel couldn't imagine marrying someone who didn't know her usual order, but to each their own. "I have just the thing. Don't even stress."

Daniel piped up. "I will personally deliver the precious cargo to your table. For now, why don't you visit the men's room, splash some water on your face, take a couple yogic breaths, then we'll get this show on the road."

"Yeah. Yes." Darryl took Daniel's free arm in a grateful grip. "Thank you." He nodded to Mel across the bar. "And thank you for all your help. You're right. It's going to be fine." He released Daniel and walked toward the restrooms, shaking his hands like fans, as if he were working out a cramp.

Mel gave Daniel a mild glare. "Now I've got to make an elaborate garnish, so thanks for that." She grabbed the ring box and put it in her pocket for safekeeping. It barely weighed anything. Hard to believe something so small could cause such a big fuss.

"What are you complaining about? If she says yes, we'll get a huge tip. You know how it goes." He blew her a kiss and disappeared into the crowded lounge, tiki drinks held aloft.

Mel shook her head while she dumped the bucket of glass and ice into a nearby garbage can. She needed something long and pointy that the engagement ring could slide onto. A sprig of fresh rosemary would be ideal—she could skewer a couple plump blackberries dusted with edible gold glitter on it, do a riff on a Ramos fizz for Darryl and his (fingers crossed) bride-to-be. Hopefully Pauline liked the combination of summer berries and orange flower water.

Mel collected her ingredients, measuring them out with the ease of someone who'd done this a thousand times. As she clapped her

Boston shaker shut and began her dry shake, she sized up the crowd. As usual, there were plenty of men in expensive suits leaning over flickering candles to speak in low murmurs to the women who accompanied them. Typical for their clientele: tech bros and finance guys, a few influencers, money to spare and show off, painfully heterosexual. Her gaze landed on a guy in a striped tie seated at the other end of her section.

Oh, great. Haircut was back.

Of all the Terror & Virtue regulars, Haircut was the worst. So named for his only defining characteristic—an unfortunately tight undercut that made him look like a right-wing motivational speaker—he came into the bar once or twice a week, always on a date, and never with the same woman. He was a lousy tipper. Five bucks on a ninety-dollar tab? Fuck off with that cheap shit. Mel couldn't stand assholes who only tipped a dollar per drink like this was some college bar with a watered-down happy hour. Mel loaded her ice and began shaking in earnest, but even over the racket she made, she could hear Haircut talking to tonight's unlucky plus-one.

"Yeah, I've never been here before either," he said. "It sure is something, huh?" Mel counted down in her head: three, two, one . . . He reached for the woman's hand right on cue. "I'm so glad I brought you. A special place for a special lady."

As far as first date lies went, Mel supposed it was mild. But why couldn't he just tell his dates he came here all the time? Did he want to seem more fun and spontaneous than he really was? Or was it a ploy to lull the women into thinking they might get a second date? Whatever the reason, Mel found the whole thing sleazy. Play the field all you like, but don't play dirty—that was her feeling.

She strained the fizzes into a pair of chilled highballs, then finished them with a light top of soda water. Berries, herbs, and—what the hell, Darryl wanted different—a swan hastily constructed from lemon peels, and they were ready to go. Right on cue, Daniel reappeared to place them on his serving tray.

"Ring," he said.

"Ring," Mel confirmed. She got out the velvet box and removed the engagement ring, not bothering to note its carat count or shape or style before slipping it onto one of the rosemary sprigs. "Darryl's in position?"

Daniel nodded. "He may or may not have thrown up in the men's room, but he's back at their table." He shook a box of Tic Tacs in his hand, indicating he'd handled the worst of it.

"Then go, go, go!" Mel made a shooing motion toward the lounge. She watched him disappear behind one of the curtain swags. Finally, she could fill some pressing orders. Mel plucked a ticket for two swizzles, loaded each glass with pebble ice, and reached for the Amaretto. She was in the middle of rinsing out her jug when she heard a shocked squeal, followed by half the lounge clapping.

Another successful performance, Mel thought. Another chance to be a background player in someone's magical night out, a footnote in the grand tale of their love story. All the usual horseshit.

Another snort of laughter brought her out of her thoughts. Right, there were other guests to see to.

She turned to the snorter seated in her section, the one she'd been ignoring for the entire Darryl saga. "I apologize for the wait. Can I—?"

Mel forgot what she was going to say the moment she laid eyes on her.

She had seen lots of beautiful women in lots of bars over the course of her career. That, by itself, barely even registered anymore. And this woman was beautiful, sure—honey-blond hair spilling over her shoulders, generous curves, peaches-and-cream complexion, lipstick so red, it looked like maraschino cherries—but Mel's attention was arrested by the way she held herself, like she was seated on a throne and not a tufted barstool. When her gaze fell on Mel, she smiled in a way that made Mel feel like everyone else in the packed bar had vanished.

"That's all right," the woman said in a loud voice. (Mel loved loud talkers. They made hearing orders over the din of a crowded bar so much easier.) Her fingers played idly with her necklace, sliding the pendant back and forth on the delicate gold chain, but her hand stopped mid-slide under Mel's gaze. She was wearing a navy suit tailored to her plump frame, with an Art Deco–ish brooch pinned to the lapel. Delicate silver flowers sat on a curved stem, quivering as she moved. Corporate, but not stuffy, which was odd for T&V. "Quite a night, hm? Full of excitement."

"Sure is," Mel agreed, even though so far it had been like any other night. She cleared her throat and went through the motions: the requisite glass of ice water placed perfectly in the center of a cocktail napkin bearing the T&V logo, the menu arranged alongside. "Have you visited us before?"

It was a standard question that Brent, the shift manager, liked them to ask. It gave the bartenders a chance to walk the uninitiated through the menu, get a sense of what the customer would like, build a rapport. The fact that this woman seemed so comfortable made Mel think this wasn't her first time at Terror & Virtue, but Mel had never seen her before. And this wasn't someone she would have forgotten.

"No, I'm a complete virgin," the woman said. She smiled wider. "Please tell me you serve drinks here, because if it turns out this is a pizza joint, boy, will I have egg on my face."

The laugh tumbled out of Mel before she could swallow it. Putting people at ease was supposed to be *her* job. "You're in luck. We happen to offer a cocktail or two. I can make some recommendations if you like." She braced her hands on the rail and leaned in. It was a pose she sometimes adopted to make the guest feel heard and understood. It also had the secondary use of showing off Mel's toned arms where her shirtsleeves were rolled up to reveal her tattoos. Brent insisted the bartenders wear a staid uniform of crisp white shirts, black bow ties, and suspenders, but allowed the more "colorful" staff to lean into the contrast. Customers got a thrill out of seeing someone with a dozen piercings and a shaved head dressed like an old-timey train conductor, and Mel was in a position to deliver.

The woman's eyes—a deep hazel that reminded Mel of Central Park in autumn—tracked over Mel once more. She placed one fingertip on the black leather menu and pushed it aside unread. "My name's Blair," she said, extending the hand toward Mel, "but my friends call me Bebe."

Mel stared at the offered hand—shell-pink manicured nails kept short; delicate fingers that didn't look like they'd ever seen a day of manual labor—for half a second before wiping her damp hands on a dry bar towel and taking it in her own. It wasn't her fault she was slow on the uptake; guests didn't normally bother introducing themselves. "I'm Mel," she said. She kept the handshake polite but firm, and the soft hand in hers responded in kind. "Pleasure to meet you, Blair."

"Ah-ah." She held up her free hand, a single admonishing finger stuck in the air. "I'd like to think we're all friends here."

Mel couldn't speak for her brain, which was currently blue-screening, but certain parts of her were definitely on board with being "friends." She could feel an embarrassing flutter-clench between her legs. This woman was clearly sent from some alternate dimension specifically to torment unsuspecting lesbians who were just trying to get through a damn shift.

"Of course," she managed. "Pleasure to meet you, Bebe."

Those red lips spread into a pleased grin. "Now, that's more like it." She reclaimed her hand from the overlong handshake and leaned back.

Okay, that was flirting. Right? Mel normally hated it when customers tried to flirt with her, but *normally* those customers were fintech dudes with all the personality of a wet napkin. She considered shutting Bebe down with a polite but unmistakable brush-off like she'd done a million times before ("Aw, thanks, but right now I'm only interested in making your drink."), but something made her hesitate. Maybe it had just been too long since she'd held the attention of a beautiful woman. Maybe it comforted Mel to know that if she wanted to get back in the game, she could. Not that she'd ever want to. Not in any way that mattered.

Then again, maybe she was imagining the tension between them. Desperate to get back on script, Mel asked, "So what can I get you?"

"I'm an old-fashioned kind of girl," she said, although if Mel's expert ability to guess someone's age was correct, this "girl" was a few years older than her, probably mid- to late-thirties. "I know most places do their own spin on an old-fashioned, but would you do me a favor?"

There was a pause in which Mel guessed she was meant to actually answer. "Anything."

Bebe's eyes widened in delight. "Would you make it for me the way you like it? It's always a treat to taste a professional's . . . interpretation." She looked down at the marble bar top, then back up at Mel, her eyelashes working overtime.

Okay. Definitely flirting.

Mel hummed a doubtful tone. She made a mean old-fashioned, but she also knew a trap when she saw one. "Might be best for you to tell me what you like so I can give you exactly what you want. You're the guest, after all."

"What I want most is to be surprised," Bebe said.

"I can't even get a hint?" At this point, Mel's well-honed bartender senses were tingling. She grabbed a lounge ticket for a gin and tonic plus a glass of prosecco, an order she could fulfill in her sleep, let alone while chatting with Bebe. Jessica and the two barbacks could only cover so much ground. She shouldn't be dragging out this interaction, no matter how welcome it was. And yet— "Favorite labels, preferred flavor profiles . . . ?"

Bebe's lips quirked up playfully. "Shall I look up Merriam-Webster's definition of 'surprise' for you?"

"All right," Mel said, finishing her prosecco pour and placing it alongside the G&T on a salver. "But if you hate it, it's on the house."

Mel liked whiskey well enough, but she always gravitated toward tequila—her drink of choice being the reliable paloma with a hint of rosemary-infused syrup. If Bebe wanted Mel's personal version of an old-fashioned, she was going to get Mel unfiltered.

Orange blossom bitters and vanilla sugar muddled together, reposado and mezcal stirred fast and loose, one huge orb of ice in the glass, loud as it chimed against the sides. A pour from up high, more dramatic than was strictly necessary, but fuck it. Stirring the jug with the elegant silver bar spoon. A quick dip of a taster straw into the liquid, a burst of smoke-tinged sweetness on Mel's tongue: not too bad. A flamed lime peel—not easy to pull off if you didn't know where to pinch—and garnished with a single Luxardo cherry that sat on top of the ice, a vaguely erotic, dark red nub.

Mel placed the finished drink in front of Bebe. "Here you have a twist on the Oaxacan, which is a twist on the old-fashioned, which itself is a twist on the Holland gin, and so it goes, on and on and on, all the way back to the beginning."

"And what do you call this one?" Bebe placed her hands flat on the bar on either side of the glass like it was a full-course meal that she was preparing to enjoy.

"Well, I invented it on the fly this very second, so it doesn't have a name yet." Mel shrugged. "Sorrento's Stab in the Dark?" She'd have to remember to grab her ratty notebook that she kept shoved behind the register and write that down during the next lull.

Bebe laughed. It sounded like glitter. "That's good, I like that." She placed her fingertips on the glass, her eyes not leaving Mel's for a second. "Sorrento. Italian?"

"Got it in one." Probably obvious with her swarthy Mediterranean looks, but she lifted her forearm to show Bebe the outline of Italy's boot anyway. "Great-grandparents came from here," she said, tapping the coastline, "near Pompeii." The tattoo had been an impulsive decision, like all the decisions she'd made in her early twenties; she didn't feel much of a connection to her family, didn't have any real pride in her heritage. Maybe she'd just been after a sense of belonging.

"Pompeii," Bebe said, still not breaking eye contact. "I love a good disaster, myself." She lifted the glass and took a sip.

Mel was helpless, caught in her gaze, watching her throat move as she swallowed. She felt nervous in a way that was rare for her these days, at least when it came to work. Her mixology prowess was the one thing she should be sure of, but Bebe had her questioning even that.

She dipped her chin at Bebe's glass. "How is it?" Her small taste test had passed muster, but everyone was different. What Mel thought was tasty could easily be a train wreck on Bebe's palate.

Bebe's lipstick left a red imprint on the rim of her glass. A single word purred from her mouth: "Delicious."

Mel was a grown-ass woman who couldn't remember the last time she'd blushed, but damn if the entire surface of her skin didn't feel like it was on fire now. "Good. I'm glad."

"You should put this on the menu. I'm serious—it's amazing." Bebe took another sip, this time closing her eyes in bliss at the taste.

Mel suppressed a wince. "They're pretty strict about menu curation here." If she dared suggest it, Brent would pitch a fit and say they already had a perfectly good old-fashioned on offer, a bestseller, why mess with success, blah blah blah. She busied herself with rinsing her bar tools instead of getting angry about her stifled creativity. Someday, if she ever opened her own place, she could enjoy free rein over the offerings.

Bebe hummed in commiseration, then turned her voice toward levity. "Probably for the best," she said, offhand. "I doubt anyone else could make this the way you can." She took another, deeper sip of her cocktail, her eyes watching Mel.

Something was crackling between them. Mel loathed the idea of love, of course, but she did subscribe to the idea of chemistry. Some bodies were drawn to each other. That was science, that was gravity, that was stars and planets and space trash. Maybe it wouldn't be the end of the world to go home with a beautiful woman at the end of her shift. Just once.

All thoughts of that possibility were interrupted by someone raising her voice slightly louder than the combined hum of the room.

"No, I really think I should go." There was an edge of panic in those words.

Mel's head whipped up, her bartender senses now sounding alarm bells.

Haircut's date was on her feet, struggling to get into her jacket while Haircut blocked her path to the exit.

"Come on. One more drink? It's early. You've got time for one more quick drink," he said.

Damn it. Terror & Virtue had a high-class reputation, but that did not make it immune from the kinds of disturbances that plagued any bar. Part of Mel's job was to keep the peace—break up fights, cut off people who'd had too much, and, most pressingly, keep the clientele safe. Usually from pushy guys like this.

The woman next to Haircut was looking around for help, but no one else seemed inclined to step in. No one else seemed to notice, too wrapped up in their own conversations. Mel geared herself up to intervene, even though it might mean a stern talking-to later from Brent, who always thought there were "better ways" to deal with problem customers, like pretending everything was fine and selling more drinks. Her shoulders went back, and her jaw went tight.

"Excuse me," a guy shouted from the other end of the bar. He was waving around his Amex. "I need to settle up now."

Mel's eyes darted between the guest and Haircut, trying to gauge which needed dealing with first, but then a soft hand touched her tense forearm, arresting her attention. Bebe wasn't looking at her, though. Her eyes were narrowed in Haircut's direction, giving Mel a view of her profile with its strong chin and aquiline nose.

"Let me take care of this for you," she said. Her eyes met Mel's again, full of steely determination. "All right?"

Mel nodded silently, taking the guest's credit card while keeping an eye on the situation. Bebe slipped off her stool and sashayed over to Haircut. The guy was now crowding his date so that she was forced back onto her seat, his hand on her arm. Mel could hear him speaking in a low, cajoling tone that sent rageful fire up her spine. Bebe came up right behind him, a full head shorter than he was, and tapped him on the shoulder.

"Harold! Is that you? Oh my god, it's been forever and a day."

Haircut—Harold? What?—spun around, his mouth flapping open and closed. He looked confused, though his gaze still found the time to linger along Bebe's neckline. Gross.

"I'm sorry," he said, "I think you've mistaken me for someone else."

Mel listened to all this while running the Amex as fast as she possibly could. She'd never known a credit slip to print so slowly. She watched the show unfold in the giant mirror that made up the back wall of the bar as she waited.

"Fucking Harry, always with the jokes. Feels like we're back in law school." Bebe slapped him a couple of times on the arm. "How've you been? Here, let me get you a drink. Hello? Bartender?" She squeezed her way between Haircut and his date (who seemed as taken aback by this turn of events as he was) and made a show of flagging down Mel. "When you have a minute."

Mel delivered the Amex slips slowly, approaching even slower to buy them all some time. She could see Bebe nudging the other woman with her elbow, urging her to take the opening and get out of there. Haircut's date gave Bebe a bewildered look but caught on quickly. She headed for the door, walking backward.

"I'll let you two catch up. Have a good night!" she told Haircut as she peaced the fuck out.

"What can I get you?" Mel asked, distracting him further. "Another Manhattan?" His usual.

"Uh." Haircut turned to her, then his disappearing date, his face going red with frustration. "Hold on! Wait!" But she was already gone. Haircut rounded on Bebe, who was looking up at him with a wide, pleasant smile. "Lady, you've got the wrong guy, seriously. I didn't go to law school. I got my MBA."

"Oh?" Bebe examined him closely. "Wow, I'm so sorry. How embarrassing! You must have one of those faces. My mistake." She floated away from the glaring man and back to her seat, tossing a secret smirk in Mel's direction. Haircut grumbled something into his glass. It was still three-quarters full, so Mel could reasonably abandon him as a customer for the moment.

Which was good, because she had a ticker tape parade's worth of tickets to get through, thanks to Bebe being so distracting. Daniel and a couple other servers were stationed at the end of the bar, pointedly waiting for their tables' orders, not to mention all the people seated at the bar itself in need of second or third rounds. She lost herself in the rhythm of mixing for a few minutes—a handful of Naked Victor Hugos, their citrusy champagne cocktail; two of the aforementioned boring old-fashioneds; and a boatload of T&V's signature drink, the Robespierre Club.

Better to concentrate on work, she thought, than alluring and mysterious women affecting heroic rescues. What was she thinking? How could she seriously consider taking a customer home? Mel hadn't picked up anyone—ever. Fuck, that was depressing. Nine years of marriage and nothing to show for it. Even her ex-wife had that girlfriend, the one who'd started showing up on her Instagram four months (four!) after the papers were signed. *She's so **easy** to be with*, one caption had said.

Not that Mel was bitter about it.

She stabbed a gilded cocktail stick through an olive and dropped it into an extra dirty martini. It sank to the bottom like a stone. She deposited the drink in front of the guest who'd ordered it and wished him a less-than-heartfelt cheers.

Another ten or fifteen minutes, and Mel had caught up on all her other work. She had no excuse not to check in with Bebe again. She wiped her hands on a clean bar towel and made her way over to where Bebe was sitting with her near-finished drink still in hand. "Can I get you another?" Mel asked, nodding at it.

"Yes, please." Bebe smiled. "You might have turned me on to a new favorite, Mel."

Hearing her name in that mouth, with that velvety voice, made Mel's whole body throb. That sharp gaze settled on her, so she kept up the chatter, more self-conscious of the silence than she normally would be as she gathered up her tools. She cut her eyes toward Haircut, several seats away, grumpily pulling out some bills to fling on the bar before he took his leave. "How did you know how to handle that?" Mel asked with a subtle chin jut in his direction. "Most people wouldn't have bothered. Or they would have let me deal with it."

"I have a lot of talents," Bebe said. "And I was in a better position to aid and abet the escapee."

True enough. Mel had been prepared to act, but there were weird power dynamics between the server and the served that complicated things. She was surprised Bebe was aware of that. Her hands were soft enough to make it unusual.

"Well, thank you. It was masterful," she said.

Bebe beamed at her, then her expression softened into something more thoughtful. "Listen, if I'm way off base here, please tell me, but would you be interested in coming to a little get-together at my place next week?"

"A get-together?" Mel echoed. Not exactly the vague fantasy she'd been harboring of a one-night stand, but maybe Bebe was the kind of person who liked to draw these things out.

"A dinner party. Low-key, a few friends. I love throwing dinner parties." Bebe took the cherry from the top of her giant ball of ice and popped it into her mouth, chewing slowly. Mel tried not to pass away right then and there. "I think you might fit right in."

"I work nights, unfortunately," Mel said, indicating the bar with a wide sweep of her arms.

"Did I say 'dinner party'? I meant brunch." Bebe didn't even bother hiding her cat-with-the-cream smile. "Are you free next Sunday at one?"

Mel regarded her for a moment. She really was something else. "I could be," she hedged.

"You should be. Picture it. Frittatas. Fresh biscuits. More mimosas than you can shake a stick at." She put a fingertip to her chin. "Or would it offend your professional sensibilities to drink one of my lowly concoctions?"

"Mimosas don't offend me," Mel said, "as long as they're done right."

Bebe made a perfect O with her red lips. "You'll have to let me in on all the secrets of the trade. You know, so I don't offend you. Here." She dug into her purse and retrieved a small white card. "You can text me at this number."

Mel took the business card from where it was slotted between her fingers. A quick glance told her that Bebe's full name was Blair B. Murray, and she was an attorney at Kipling and Beech, LLP. When had she last gotten someone's phone number? It was so outmoded, but then again, Bebe had said she was old-fashioned. Mel shook her head, already knowing she was hooked.

"All right," she said, feeling the thrill of possibility in her belly.

She slipped the card into her pocket. It felt heavier than any ring could. "Looking forward to it."

"Same here." Bebe smiled, the most genuine smile Mel had ever seen inside Terror & Virtue. Even in the artful shadows, it looked bright as day.

As Mel was about to stir Bebe's fresh drink, a new figure came into view at the corner of her eye. Whoever it was sat right next to Bebe, hovering just inside her personal space. The run-in with Haircut had Mel on edge, so she wanted to make sure this newcomer wasn't going to bother Bebe.

She barely got a glimpse—loose copper curls, elfin features, a creamy cable-knit sweater that reminded Mel of a lighthouse keeper from 1887—before Bebe flung herself into the person's arms.

"Darling!" Bebe kissed that unsmiling mouth. "You made it." She turned to Mel with breathless delight. "Mel, this is my wife, Kade. They drink gin. Could you mix up something for them?"

CHAPTER 2

"And then what happened?" Daniel asked, swiping away a smudge of hot sauce from the corner of his mouth with the thinnest napkin in the world. His breath made clouds in the winter air.

Mel sighed and stabbed her plastic fork at the tacos in the paper boat she held. (Her taco-handling skills didn't pass muster, so she always opted for the coward's cutlery, as Daniel called it.) "I made them a French 75 with thyme. What else could I do?"

Neon lights from the dot matrix signage illuminated Daniel's disappointed face. They were standing on the sidewalk next to Julio's, their favorite late-night taco truck, one of their only options for getting a decent bite to eat after work. Even in the December cold, the sidewalk was jammed with other bar and restaurant workers grabbing food. Their own secret after-hours club in the middle of Alphabet City. Terror & Virtue closed at 2 a.m. on Fridays, but once the last lingering customers cleared out and the staff wrapped up their cleaning tasks, it was closer to four. The subways were hit-and-miss by that time, so Mel and Daniel tended to make their way home on foot instead of waiting for a train.

"If I were in your shoes," Daniel said, "I would have said something." He tilted his head and took another huge bite of his taco.

"Like what? 'Hey, what the hell, paying customer? I thought you were into me, but it turns out you're married?'"

"You can get some clarification without being rude! Like—" Daniel adopted a high-pitched voice. "'So what's the vibe here? I'm getting a vibe.'"

"I do not sound like that."

Daniel ignored her. "So was the rest of your shift, like, super awkward?" he asked before eating more.

Mel considered Daniel's question while she shoveled a bite of birria into her mouth. The sudden appearance of Kade had thrown her for a loop, no question. She'd nearly forgotten to put ice in her shaker for the French 75. Once she'd fallen back into the groove of tending bar on a busy Friday night, though, the awkwardness had taken a back seat. She remembered the snatches of conversation she'd overheard between Bebe and Kade while she worked: normal couple stuff about their schedules, things that needed doing that weekend, Bebe's plans for the brunch party. Kade seemed to be the more tight-lipped of the two, sipping their drink quietly while Bebe chattered away.

From an outsider's perspective, Bebe and Kade looked like total opposites. Loud and quiet; curvy and lean; friendly and introverted. It made you wonder how they'd gotten together.

Not that it was any of Mel's business.

They'd been pleasant, unrushed, and lovely. And they'd tipped well, around 25 percent. Really, Mel had no reason to complain.

The only moment that had even approached dicey was when Bebe and Kade had been preparing to leave. Kade was helping Bebe get into her soft-looking camel coat. Bebe had caught Mel's eye as she was rushing to finish off a large order. Mel had paused, lemon in one hand and a reamer in the other, ready for a pat farewell. *Thank you for coming, so nice to meet you*, that sort of thing.

Instead, Bebe blew a kiss in her direction and said, "Mimosas! Don't forget, I need professional help. You have my number."

Mel had shifted uneasily, glancing at Kade to gauge whether Bebe's spouse—wife—would be rubbed the wrong way by this show of familiarity, but their face remained as impassive as ever.

"Looking forward to it," Mel had managed to say before the couple swept out of the bar.

She shook her head, trying to dislodge the image burned into it: Kade guiding Bebe through the crowd with a hand on the small of her back, both of them glancing over their shoulders as if they wanted one last look at Mel.

"It was . . . strange," she finally told Daniel, "but not awkward. They were both perfectly nice." She ate the last bite of taco and tossed the container into a nearby can, wrapping her black coat around her more tightly. "It's my fault, I guess. Picking up signals that weren't really there."

Daniel made an unsure noise as he wolfed down the last of his al pastor. "I don't know. Must have been powerful signals if *you* noticed them. Most signals go right over your head," he said with his mouth full. "Remember that girl who tried to hit on you during Fleet Week?"

"That wasn't my fault," Mel protested. "Who tries to pick someone up on the subway? You make eye contact with me on public transportation, I'm gonna assume you want to fight."

"She was literally wearing her dress whites. There's no bigger billboard declaring 'fuck me for my service' than that."

"From a distance, I thought she was a chef," Mel mumbled. She rubbed a hand over her face. "My eyes are going. I'm officially old."

"Early thirties is not old." Daniel wound his scarf around his neck now that the danger of taco drippings had passed. "My point is, if you were getting signals from this Bebe lady, they must have been powerful ones. Who knows what the deal is? Maybe it's a sham marriage. Maybe she's got a permanent hall pass."

"Fuck off," Mel said. "That doesn't happen in real life."

"It absolutely does."

"Only for your hookups," Mel shot back.

"Okay, Scarlet Letter." Daniel folded his hands in front of his chest as if in prayer. "Remember the commandment: thou shall not hate on thy friends' sluttiness. Saint Channing Tatum did not gyrate on all those laps in the Magic Mike franchise for you to come at me for sucking more than one dick a week."

Invoking Saint Tatum was sacred in their shared household, so Mel lifted her hands in the air, indicating the subject was dropped.

They began walking south along the avenue, breath misting in the frigid early-morning air. It was dark, save for the light spilling from the windows of the all-night diners and the Christmas lights blinking from the bodega awnings. Mel stuffed her cold hands deep into her coat pockets. T&V didn't close for the holidays or do anything so pedestrian as offer Christmas specials, so it was easy to forget that people were celebrating something out in the real world.

Mel made it ten blocks before asking, "Do you think I have to go to this dinner party still? Brunch party? Whatever?"

"Not if you don't want to." Daniel stepped over a suspicious-looking puddle in the middle of the sidewalk. "You can always make up some excuse. No big deal."

A huff of breath left Mel's lips: "But if I flake now, it'll look like I only accepted the invitation because I thought it was—you know. A flirty invitation. And I'm declining because now I know she's not available."

"Isn't that exactly what's happening?"

"Yes, but I can't let them think that I thought it was a flirty invitation!"

"Who cares what they think? If you ditch this party, you'll probably never see them again, so what difference will it make?"

Mel chewed on that, and her lower lip.

"If I go, it could be awkward," she said. "If I don't go, I'll have to live in shame. There's no winning."

"Do you want my advice?" Daniel asked as they turned down their street.

Mel snorted. "Oh, so you're a relationship expert now? I can't recall, are things with Jackson on again or off again?"

"Excuse you! For your *information*, Jackson and I have a good thing going."

"So good you hook up with other dudes every other week," Mel said with a laugh. In an apartment as small as theirs, it was impossible not to notice the rotating cast of characters that Daniel brought home. Not that Mel was judging—really, she didn't care, and she was *definitely* not jealous. "I know when *I* have a good thing going, I go to great lengths to check my Grindr profile on the daily."

She expected Daniel to take a potshot right back at her, rhythm of the patter and all, but when she glanced over at him, his lips were pursed like he'd eaten a whole lemon. Daniel Quince was constructed almost entirely of witty retorts, thick skin, and show tune lyrics, so seeing him exhibit real hurt was an unpleasant shock.

"You know what?" she said, backpedaling. "That's none of my business. Sorry. Tell me your advice." She nudged her shoulder into his arm. "Bless me with your wisdom, Prophet Quince."

When Daniel cracked a smile, Mel knew all was forgiven. He never could hold a grudge, even when Mel ate the last of the Oreos he liked to hide on top of the refrigerator.

"I think you should go to the party," he said. "Several reasons. One: it's free food."

Mel gave a half shrug at that. Valid.

"Two," Daniel continued, "from the brief glimpse I got, I can tell you that woman's outfit was not off-the-rack. So if for no other reason than to see how the other half lives, you should show up. She might own, like, a jaguar or something."

"I don't really care what kind of car someone drives," Mel said.

"No, not the car. The jungle cat."

"How would *that* be a good thing? Do you want me to get mauled?"

"No, I just think it would be a cool story. I'd dine out on that anecdote for decades." He stuck his fore-, middle, and ring finger into the air in a fan. "Three: if you're worried that a couple of strangers will judge you for changing your mind, then go! Prove that you're totally normal and didn't think some fancy woman was hitting on you. If brunch sucks, you can leave." He made a pair of legs out of two fingers and mimed them prancing along an invisible floor.

"Maybe." Mel trudged up the stoop that led to their building's front door, Daniel right behind her. "I'll take it into consideration." Even though Daniel was essentially repeating back to her the arguments she'd already made to herself—albeit a tad more in-depth—she still wasn't sure. Ever since the divorce, she rarely felt sure about anything.

Mel climbed the stairs to their apartment with a weight in her chest. This could be any night of any week of the last two-plus years: coming home before dawn with Daniel, knees and back aching from a long shift, a long taco-induced nap that stood in for a real sleep schedule, and then up around noon to do it all over again. It wasn't how she'd pictured her life at thirty-three; she was supposed to be more stable, more of an adult. There had been a vague shape in her imagination that included a wife, a house with a yard, maybe a dog. A modest goal, if not a dream.

She unlocked the door and let herself and Daniel into the cluttered living room. Daniel had inherited the apartment from his grandmother, and it was still decorated with Granny Quince's memorabilia, draped gossamer scarves and trailing pothos in macramé hangers, photographs of a young Granny with a beehive hairdo, sharing cigarettes with Warhol and Baldwin. Mel usually didn't mind the decor, but tonight it felt like she was living in someone else's museum. Guilt followed hot on the heels of the thought; Daniel had invited her to live with him out of the kindness of his heart after her divorce. He didn't actually need a roommate, what with the place being rent-controlled, and the second bedroom that Mel was using could have easily been his home gym or something equally luxurious.

Daniel unwound his scarf with a big yawn, hanging it on the antique coat stand that Granny had won from Truman Capote in a poker game, according to family legend. "I think I'm going to turn in. Unless you want to watch a movie?" On nights when they arrived home still keyed up from a busy shift, they often watched something—the Marx Brothers or *Singin' in the Rain* for the millionth time. Once in a while, that new queer mockumentary with the hot older lesbian.

Mel shook her head as she shrugged out of her coat. "Nah, go get some sleep. I'll see you later."

Daniel kissed his fingers and tossed the sentiment in her direction. He headed down the hall to his bedroom, shedding pieces of his T&V uniform as he went. Mel resisted the urge to pick up after him. It was his place, after all.

She collapsed on the ratty burnt-orange-and-umber striped corduroy sofa and rubbed her palm over her shorn head. The buzzed hair was getting long enough to be annoying; she would have to clean it up if she was going to make an appearance at the brunch party.

Was she really going, though? She let her arm flop to her side with a sigh. Maybe Daniel was right. A free meal in fancy digs was a good enough reason to wake up early (for her) on a Sunday.

Plus, Bebe and Kade were a cool couple. Working at Terror & Virtue meant Mel saw all sorts of couples. Most seemed to barely tolerate each other, let alone enjoy each other's presence. Mel had noticed the way this couple leaned into each other, the way Bebe lit up when Kade murmured something into her ear. It would make for a nice change of pace, to befriend a pair of interesting people.

Besides, how many other chances to make new friends was Mel going to get? It was almost impossible with her work schedule. And since her ex had kept most of their mutual friends in the divorce, Mel's circle had dwindled to Daniel and—actually, that was about it. Everyone she knew from work was a casual acquaintance at best. They were the kind of people she might share a drink with, but nothing more.

She owed it to herself to try, didn't she?

"I should go," she said aloud. On the wall, the sun-faded photo of Granny Quince seemed to stare into Mel's soul in love bead–tinged judgement. "I will go," Mel amended. "I'm going."

She lifted her hips and dug her phone and Bebe's business card from her back pocket. Better to get this over with now before she changed her mind.

> I make an excellent mandarin cordial
> if you're really interested in upping
> your mimosa game

There. She'd done the thing.

Did the text sound too flirty? No, she wouldn't obsess over it. It was friendly. Just a reference to their previous conversation.

Mel put her phone on the battered coffee table. It wasn't even 5 a.m., so she didn't expect a response. Normal people were in bed.

Her phone buzzed loudly, making her jump. She grabbed it and saw that Bebe had already double-texted. Full sentences and everything. Interesting.

> I am more interested than I could
> possibly say. Can you share the recipe
> or will you bring a batch? I assume
> it's a trade secret, so I lean toward the
> latter, but your choice.

Followed immediately by:

> Here's the address. Can't wait to
> see you!

A map pin was attached, indicating some corner in—ugh—Tribeca. Mel clicked on the tab showing photos of the location. Sure enough, it was a high-rise condo, the kind with floor-to-ceiling windows and views all the way to the Delaware fucking Water Gap.

Well, now she had to bring the cordial. Otherwise the doorman might not let her past the lobby. She tapped out a reply.

> Consider it brought

CHAPTER 3

Mel stood in a hallway so plush, she was certain Bebe and Kade would open the door to find her ankle-deep in the carpet. The trains had been a mess due to weekend construction, and she worried her arrival was too late to be polite or fashionable. Behind the door, she could hear the faint sounds of a party already in progress: soft instrumental music, the murmur of voices, the clink of glass stemware on a marble surface (a sound Mel heard in her sleep, she was so familiar with it), and cutting above it all, Bebe's loud laughter.

Knocking would be a good, normal thing to do. The doorman had already called up to announce her arrival, so Mel couldn't stand in the hall forever. She hefted the old plastic milk jug full of mandarin cordial in her arms. It had been the only container in her apartment big enough to transport it. Maybe she should have bought a case of mason jars, something classier than a rinsed-out gallon of Cream-O-Land.

Screw it. She knocked.

The door swung open to reveal Kade. They were wearing what Mel could only describe as a costume of loose black trousers topped with a sweeping wrap cape the color of an arctic sea. A large geometric pendant hung from their neck. Their feet were bare and pale, their red hair pulled back into a short ponytail with a few curls framing their face. The overall effect was that of a time traveler from the future, if the future had been imagined by someone in the 1950s. Mel really dug the look, actually. She felt out of place in her ripped jeans and steel-gray sweater, but she resolved not to second-guess her fashion choices.

"Oh hello. Mel, right?" Kade said, their gaze falling to the jug Mel held clutched to her chest. "And you brought . . . liquid."

"It's cordial," Mel said.

Kade nodded, their sharp chin bobbing exactly once. "It's certainly a very friendly gesture."

The joke was so at odds with Kade's stony demeanor that Mel gave a shocked laugh. Then she noticed that Kade was staring at her like she'd grown two heads.

Okay. Not a joke.

"That's not— I mean it's, uh—" She shook the milk jug a bit, hoping the slosh of the bright orange liqueur would explain itself. It didn't; Kade kept staring. "Literally cordial. The kind you drink?"

"Ah." Kade's eyes flicked over her once more. They opened the door wider and gestured for Mel to enter. Mel gave a half smile, half grimace and stepped inside. So much for endearing herself to Bebe's wife.

She let Kade take her jug and her winter coat and watched them spirit both away.

Mel took stock of her surroundings. Daniel had demanded a complete rundown of her hosts' condo, after all, and he'd be pissed if she skimped on the details. The place was, as suspected, ridiculously swanky. The front door led directly into an expansive kitchen/living room/dining area with high ceilings and an entire wall of windows overlooking the river. This one room alone could probably fit Mel and Daniel's whole apartment inside it, and if the floating staircase was any clue, there was a lot more to see. Mel tried to take in what she could from her spot, noting an eclectic mix of paintings on the walls and sculptures displayed on various pieces of furniture. If she squinted, she could be inside some high-end SoHo gallery.

The brunch guests were as artsy as the surroundings, with a range of ages and styles and accents. They all looked perfectly at home among the expensive finishes. Mel overheard someone by the break-fast bar say something about Munich in the winter. Everyone nodded knowingly and made noises of commiseration.

What the hell was she doing here? These weren't her people. They'd never worked for tips a day in their lives; she would bet her last hard-fought dollar on it. They likely never even considered the exist-ence of people like her. There was no fucking way she could fit in with this crowd, let alone become friends with Bebe and Kade.

As she stood there contemplating a strategic retreat with some excuse (sudden onset migraine? Daniel texting from the ER? She'd left the stove on?), Bebe came barreling toward her with a huge smile on her face. She was wearing a canary-yellow sundress. In the middle of winter. Clearly, she had no plans to leave the comfort of her home today. Mel didn't blame her; if she lived in a place this nice, she'd never leave either.

"You made it!" Bebe raised her arms, then stopped short. "Are you a hugger?"

The question wasn't really a surprise, coming from Bebe. She had texted Mel the day before to ask if she had any dietary restrictions and what her pronouns were.

"I'm not opposed," she said, trying to sound chill.

"I'll take it." Bebe threw her arms around Mel's shoulders. The embrace brought her mouth alongside Mel's ear. "So glad you came," she said right into it. She smelled like cinnamon. It made Mel feel slightly feral.

She squeezed Bebe around her soft waist, wanting to return the gesture. Should she say something complimentary, too? "I like your perfume," she said as they broke apart. "It's nice."

"Oh, it's not perfume. Kade's sensitive to artificial scents, so none of that for me." Bebe's smile made her nose crinkle. "It's the coffee cake. I always get messy when I'm in the kitchen. There's probably a metric ton of spices in my hair." She shook a hand through her loose blond waves, laughing.

Mel felt a little better knowing that, at least in this respect, her hosts were down-to-earth. No caterer or maid service at this party. "Well, you smell great."

Cool. And normal.

If Bebe thought it was a weird thing to say, she didn't show it. Her smile only grew as she grasped Mel by the wrist. "Come on, let me introduce you to everyone."

The group consisted of a handful of people, not counting Bebe and Kade. Bebe strode right into their little circle to disrupt the current conversation.

"Everyone! This is Mel," Bebe announced in her booming voice. "She's a wonderfully talented mixologist and she was kind enough to bring us a replacement for our boring old orange juice." Bebe nodded over to the open-concept kitchen, where Kade was already dutifully measuring out the cordial into champagne flutes.

A murmur of excitement went through the group. Mel felt her face heat; she hadn't felt this on display since winning a spelling bee in third grade. Being the center of attention, even the positive kind, tended to make her skin itch.

Bebe threaded their arms together and led Mel around the circle, introducing her to each person in turn. Mel was terrible with names and worse with faces—at work, she could rely on guests' credit cards and seat locations to provide her with the relevant info. In a real-life party, she was adrift.

The only thing the guests seemed to have in common was an unreasonable level of attractiveness. There was Callen, who was Bebe's financial adviser (okay, fancy), and his husband, CJ, who was in ceramics, whatever that meant. (Did he make them? Import them? Mel didn't ask.) Both were white, older, light-haired, and had names that started with C, which was really unfair. CJ had a small scar through his upper lip, though, which Mel noted as he shook her hand and declared himself charmed.

"Are you here all on your own?" Callen asked. "No plus-ones?" He craned his neck as if looking for some invisible partner who might be standing behind Mel.

She tried to take the nosiness in stride. "Yep, flying solo. Totally single."

Callen looked pointedly at Bebe. "I *see*."

"Ignore him. He's an incurable gossip," Bebe said, and led Mel to the next guest in the rotation.

Dez was a white woman with a career in academia and an accent of vaguely European origin. Next was Cilla, who was so gorgeous they could have been a model, but who actually worked in the mayor's office doing something with small-business outreach. They had several pieces inked onto their forearms, the whorls expertly shaded onto their dark skin. Mel felt a surge of relief at not being the only tattooed person at this party.

Last was Sawyer, who was just—some guy.

"Sawyer is a visual artist," Bebe said while Mel searched his face for a birthmark or piercing or literally anything to distinguish him from any other white guy. No dice. "He and Kade shared studio space once upon a time."

"Kade is an artist?" Mel now knew more about the other guests than she did Bebe's partner, apparently.

"You weren't aware?" Sawyer gestured with his water glass at the paintings and sculptures arranged around the huge room. "They're pretty prolific. You must have seen a Kade St. Cloud piece at some point, unless you're living under a rock."

This one was kind of judgey. At least that was a memorable trait. Mel forced a brittle smile onto her face. "No rock, just the LES. Guess I don't dip my toes into the art world much."

"Everyone has their bubble," Bebe said diplomatically. She unhooked her arm from Mel's to pat Sawyer on his pale, featureless cheek. "That's why I still invite you to these things, Sawyer: to get you out of that studio. Otherwise, you might start to think that's all there is to life, hm?"

The admonishment, though subtle, was not lost on Mel.

Sawyer seemed to pick up on it, too. He ducked his head, his shoulders rounding forward in classic chagrin. "Sorry, Mel. I shouldn't have talked down to you. I love Kade's work so much, it's hard for me to imagine someone not knowing about it."

Bebe nodded in approval, then cut her eyes to Mel. It seemed some kind of response was in order.

"Uh. That's okay," Mel said. There was some kind of power dynamic going on here, she thought, one she didn't totally understand. She'd never received such an apology for a small slight. Was Bebe an actual wizard at negotiating these kinds of things? This was the second time in their short acquaintance that Mel had witnessed her take control of a situation where someone was behaving badly. Maybe it was a lawyer thing.

Whatever it was, probably best to keep the conversation moving. Mel turned to one of the sculptures perched on top of a mid-century cabinet. "So Kade made all of these?" She didn't know much about fine art, but she had an eye for aesthetics that came in handy when crafting a cocktail that was as visually striking as it was drinkable. (Fucking Instagram, everything had to make a good photograph these days.) The piece on the cabinet, a jagged shard of plaster about the size of a coffee mug, looked like an abstract knife caught in a downward slice, the point of it balanced on its plinth. It looked totally badass, though Mel was pretty sure that wasn't a word people used for high art. "What's this one called?"

"'Lovers Number 12.' It's a series," Sawyer said helpfully.

Mel was taken aback. She had assumed the shape was meant to evoke something interesting like movement or violence, not love. That was the blandest thing in the world. She realized with a quick look around the room that many of the other sculptures were built along the same lines, and probably belonged to the same series. "I like it," she said, "but what's it supposed to mean?"

Sawyer opened his mouth, but Bebe beat him to the punch. "I imagine the artist themself is the only one who can truly answer that. Darling?"

Kade appeared with a mimosa in hand. Their gaze was fixed on the sculpture, cool and aloof. "Please don't make me talk about my pieces," they said with a sigh. "It's so tedious."

Mel had the distinct impression she'd made a misstep. "Sorry. I didn't mean to put you on the spot."

Bebe laughed, her hand coming up to catch Kade's arm. "They're just embarrassed," she said to Mel. "If I were a genius, I'd be inviting people to fawn over me left and right, but not Kade."

"If I'm a genius," Kade said, "then no one would need me to explain my work. It would speak for itself. The fact that it doesn't shows I still have a long way to go." They sipped from their flute but said nothing about the flavor of Mel's cordial. The only reaction Mel could perceive was a slight raise of their brows when they swallowed.

Maybe her work spoke for itself, in their view.

"How is it?" Sawyer asked, reaching out and taking Kade's glass. Mel watched as he took a sip. Must be close friends, she thought, if they were cozy enough to share drinks like that. Sawyer smacked his lips, then looked over at Mel. "You made this yourself? Bebe said you were talented, but this is *beyond*." He handed the glass back to Kade, who nodded as they took it.

Mel could feel her cheeks getting warm. No one thought her skills were anything out of the ordinary when she was behind the bar and charging twenty bucks a glass. The guy was probably trying to play nice after that initial snafu. "It's nothing really. Some mandarin— stuff. Whipped it up at home."

Bebe gave a put-upon sigh. "Why am I such a magnet for self-effacing geniuses?" Before Mel could protest—she wasn't a genius; she was barely a real adult—Bebe floated off toward the kitchen.

Sawyer also drifted away, sitting right next to CJ on the sofa and snuggling into his side with the kind of familiarity that surprised Mel. CJ paused in saying something to Dez, turned, and placed a brief, tender kiss on top of Sawyer's head before returning seamlessly to the conversation at hand. Mel looked at Callen, who was standing right there, but if he noticed the gesture of affection his husband had bestowed on someone else, he didn't seem bothered.

They were all old friends, Mel reminded herself. Very old friends. Not to mention kind of—artsy. It was just a touchy-feely crowd. A little kiss on the head wasn't anything but paternal. Probably.

She prayed no one noticed her reaction; the last thing she wanted was Bebe thinking she was too uptight to hang with these folks.

Where was Bebe, anyway?

Bebe clapped her hands, drawing everyone's attention to her in the kitchen. "Time to eat!" Bebe recruited Callen and CJ to assist her in transporting the food to the table, while everyone else meandered to a dining table that sat under a satellite-looking light fixture. There were four chairs on each long side of the table. Kade had evidently mixed everyone a mandarin mimosa, leaving a flute at each place setting, save one, which Mel assumed would be theirs. Sure enough, Kade took that seat as the guests claimed the others. Mel lingered and watched, trying to figure out where she was supposed to sit.

There was some nominal chaos and appreciative gasps while Bebe and the husbands delivered food to the table: pans of fresh biscuits, a tureen of sausage gravy, a vegetable-studded frittata, slabs of coffee cake arranged in a towering pyramid, a fruit platter that could sink a battleship, and more crispy bacon than Mel had ever seen in her life.

"Wow," Mel said, adding to the awed murmurs of the guests. "This looks amazing." She reached for an unclaimed chair at the end of a row, but Bebe stopped her with a light touch to the small of her back.

"Oh, that's CJ's seat," she said brightly. "Why don't you sit over here by me?"

Mel let herself be led around the table, confused as to how, as a complete newcomer, she had earned a spot next to the Empress of Brunch. "Don't you want to sit next to Kade?" she asked, even as she dropped into the chair.

Kade, she now saw, was seated opposite her, eyeing her coolly and sipping at their drink. Mel couldn't decide if they were bored or plotting a murder; both seemed equally likely.

Bebe waved a hand through the air as she took her seat on Mel's right. "I see them every day. Much as I love them, dinner parties are about mixing it up." She pointed out Callen, who was on Mel's left, far from his husband, CJ. "See? It's fine."

Well, if that was a Bebe Murray dinner party—brunch party, whatever—rule, then Mel would comply.

Bebe swept her gaze up and down the table. "Don't bother with formality, people! Dig in, dig in." She reached for a plate of bacon and its accompanying pair of serving tongs. "Do you eat meat?" she asked Mel.

Mel's stomach rumbled so audibly that she felt compelled to respond loud enough to cover it up. "Yeah! I mean—please." She lifted her plate so that Bebe could load it up with way more bacon than was sane. The strips looked magazine-perfect, wavy and glistening and crisp.

"I do it in the oven," Bebe whispered, leaning in like she was sharing a secret. "Perfect every time. No spatter. Plus it cooks while the biscuits bake. Bacon infusion, yum." She plonked one of the fluffy country-style biscuits on Mel's plate as well, this time without asking.

"Wow, you're like Martha Stewart or something," Mel said. "Once in a while I'll throw a handful of frozen vegetables into some ramen; that's about the extent of my home cooking."

"Really?" Bebe boggled at her, gravy ladle frozen in the air. "But you have such an amazing palate! Those drinks you make— I would think you'd be a force of nature in the kitchen, too."

"Some skills don't translate, I guess," Mel said with a hint of sheepishness. She moved her plate under the ladle, which was in danger of dripping thick peppery gravy, and Bebe finished topping off her biscuit. The sausage gravy flowed over its side, pooling around it in homey luxury. "Besides, I spend most of my waking hours behind the bar. When I get off work, I'm so beat I usually grab whatever's easiest. Not a lot of time to be domestic."

Bebe served herself a piece of frittata, humming in thought. "Domestication is overrated, anyway. That's why I tend to collect feral strays." She looked across the table at Kade and winked.

Mel followed her gaze. Kade was sitting placidly with a chunk of melon speared on their fork. The only acknowledgment they made was a wry lift at the corner of their mouth in Bebe's direction. Cilla asked them something that Mel couldn't make out over the hum of chatter. CJ and Dez spoke to each other from across the table about their favorite brunch spots in Brooklyn, and Sawyer roped Callen into a debate on local taxes, of all things. Mel was left with Bebe as a conversation partner.

Before she'd left for the party, Mel had coached herself on a few topics that she was pretty sure normal people would deploy in a situation like this. "So, Bebe, you do legal work, right? What kind of law do you practice?" She popped a piece of bacon in her mouth.

Bebe laughed and cut off the tip of her frittata slice with the edge of her fork. "Employment law. Mostly representing employees who've been screwed over by their companies. Contract breaches, wage theft. On a good day, I take the bad guys to court and make them pay. But most of the time there's no good or bad, and it all comes out in the wash. Very dry stuff, you don't want to hear about that."

"No, please, it sounds interesting," Mel said. She wasn't even lying, really. Office jobs were exotic to her; she'd never worked a nine-to-five. Some folks weren't meant for fluorescent lights and PowerPoint presentations. And Mel wanted to get to know Bebe, which meant she had to get to know her work—that's what friends did, right? Learned about each other's lives and commiserated?

Bebe put down her fork and turned in her seat to face Mel more fully. She wore a warm smile that matched her sundress. Mel was once again overwhelmed by the sensation of being alone with this woman, despite being surrounded by people. There was something about her attention that made Mel feel like she was the most special person in the world.

"I promise you," Bebe said, low enough that Mel had to lean in a little to hear her better, "the only person who finds my job fascinating is me. Even Kade can only take it in small doses, and they adore me. If I get on a roll telling you about my cases—minus confidential information or identifying details, naturally—you will be bored to tears. And that's the last thing I want." She toyed with the stem of her flute, twisting it between her fingertips. "Can I make a suggestion?"

"Of course." Mel ate a bite of the biscuit and gravy. Then she stopped and stared down at her plate, her hand coming to shield her mouth to stop any happy screams from escaping. It tasted heavenly, the homemade biscuit flaky and buttery, the gravy rife with nuggets of sausage. Forget law; Bebe should hang it all up and make brunch for a living.

"Let's do a lightning round, get the boring stuff out of the way in under twenty seconds," Bebe said. "That way, we can move on to the more interesting questions."

Mel, still in rapture over the biscuit, could only nod. She swallowed and immediately began forking up another bite. "What counts as boring? Work? Family?"

"Bingo. 'Where you from? What was your childhood like?' The basics."

"That last one isn't basic," Mel pointed out. "Most people go to therapy for years trying to cover that ground."

"Have you?" Bebe asked.

Mel refused to blink. She would not let this fast-talking, biscuit-making beauty railroad her. "Is this the lightning round? Are we already in it?"

"Oh! Here, this will help." Bebe took a cell phone from a pocket in her dress and set it face up on the table between them, swiping to a timer app. "So we're agreed on twenty seconds? I probably only need eight, to be honest."

"How about the fastest time for covering the boring stuff wins a prize?" Mel said. This felt good. Bold and fun, but friendly. She was making friends.

"Yes!" Bebe's eyes sparkled. "Winner gets to ask the first real question. Deal?" Her fingertip hovered over the timer button.

Mel licked her lips, already thinking about what she'd ask. Because she had no intention of losing.

CHAPTER 4

Mel went first, reminding herself not to mention the divorce. This was a party, and her divorce, while probably the biggest life change she'd ever experienced, was not a fun topic. She took a deep breath and started speaking as soon as Bebe pressed the timer: "Bartended my whole life; not really in touch with my folks; no drama or anything, just drifted apart; grew up on the Jersey Shore; moved to New York at twenty"—no need for further details there—"childhood was fine and a little boring!" The final syllable coincided perfectly with the beep of the timer. Twenty seconds.

Bebe's turn was even more impressive: "Born in Austin, law school in Boston, got the job I wanted, parents in Jakarta, I was the apple of their eye as a kid, still am, BOOM! Seven point three-five seconds." She proudly brandished the phone.

"Jakarta?" Mel said, stunned.

"They like the heat." Bebe shrugged. "But forget all that. We're past boring now. I get to start asking the real questions." She wiggled in her seat as if gearing herself up.

Mel smiled despite herself. All that enthusiasm was infectious. "Okay, go ahead. I'm an open book." She took another bite of her food and hoped that Bebe wouldn't ask about past relationships.

Bebe took a sip of her mimosa, staring at Mel over the rim like she was seriously contemplating her line of questioning. She certainly had the dramatic flair for a courtroom, though Mel's knowledge of that world was based solely on early seasons of *Law & Order*.

Finally Bebe set her drink down and asked, "What's your biggest dream?"

"Oh," Mel said, covering her discomfort with a sip of her drink, "so we're not messing around here, huh?"

"Nope." Bebe popped her lips on the word. "Come on, spill. Do you want to see the northern lights? Run with the bulls? Hike the Appalachian Trail? What?"

Mel smiled down at her glass. "Nothing that cool, I promise."

"So there *is* something." Her soft hand made the lightest smack of contact against Mel's biceps. "Whatever it is, I want to hear it. Rules are rules, Mel."

Mel downed her drink and poured herself another. "Okay." She'd had a few; she could stand to be honest at this point. "I want to open my own bar."

Bebe's mouth fell open in undisguised delight. "Really? That's amazing!"

"Is it?" Mel took a healthy sip of her fresh mimosa. "It's a ton of work for not a lot of reward, usually. Plus I'd need capital, a business plan, investors. Not to mention the real estate and permits and—"

"Okay, while I appreciate the realistic outlook, I'm more interested in the non-nightmare part of your dream," Bebe said, her smile growing. She leaned closer, her chin propped in her hand. "What would it be like, your bar?"

Mel told her. She described a menu that was hers from top to bottom, a veritable journey through her bartending career, all the drinks she'd ever poured into a glass with her blood and sweat metaphorically mixed in. She noted especially the low- and no-alcohol options. Prices would be as reasonable as she could make them. Wherever it was located, Mel would make sure it offered community space because a bar, in her dream world, should be more than a place to get a drink. She wanted book clubs and knitting circles and activists rotating through on a regular basis. She wanted queer people to feel like they were being catered to, not merely tolerated. If she could ever open her own place, it would be a complete reflection of her. It would be everything she wanted in a bar: good ventilation, comfortable seating, no frills.

And it would have a fucking ramp, because honest to god, how did anyone with a cane or wheelchair live in this city without going absolutely apeshit on all the establishments that didn't give them access?

"Well, actually," Bebe broke in at that point, "the issue of ADA codes in New York is pretty fascinating if you—" She glanced at Mel's face and saw her incredulous look. "Sorry. Lawyer brain. Switching over to 'bowled over by your amazing vision' brain." She mimed turning a key next to her ear.

"Yeah, right." Mel pitched her voice into a goofy register. "My vision."

"Hey, Mel," Cilla piped up from across the table, "if you plan on opening your own bar someday, you should definitely check out Food Fest. Are you going?"

"Uh, no. Not this year," Mel said. She'd almost forgotten the other people at the party. "But I've been before."

It was technically true. Tickets for the weeklong event started at nine hundred bucks, way too much for a bartender who'd blown all her savings years ago on a farmhouse wedding upstate. (Her ex-wife had insisted on the farmhouse.) To help pay off the credit card bills, Mel had picked up a gig serving Finger Lakes Riesling at one of the many Food Fest stalls. Her experience with the event was limited to an endless stream of out-of-towners demanding more generous pours and leaving her sad tip bucket empty. She guessed that at nine hundred a pop, people thought they were entitled to as much free booze as they could put away. Toward the end of the first day, the Javits Center had been heaving with drunk people. The restrooms were a war zone.

Fights broke out over taxis. It was a total shitshow. Mel had barely escaped with her shoes free of puke.

"Isn't it fun?" Cilla asked with a pleasant smile. "Anyway, you should look into entering the cocktail competition."

Mel almost choked on her mimosa. "The what?"

"The cocktail competition at Food Fest," they repeated, absorbed in cutting into their piece of frittata. "They're making an effort to include more mixology in the lineup. The winner gets two hundred thousand dollars."

Mel nearly choked again, this time on a bite of coffee cake. "*How* much?" Then, realizing that no one else at the table had so much as batted an eye at the number, she cleared her throat and said, in a much more level tone, "Not bad for a day's work, I guess."

"That's not all," Cilla said, politely skipping over Mel's embarrassing reaction. "The winning cocktail becomes *the* Official Drink of New York for an entire year." They spoke in unmistakable capital letters. "Which means it'll be on the menu for lots of hoity-toity official events and fundraisers, that kind of thing."

"So the mayor will have to try it?" Bebe's red lips quirked into a grin. "Are cocktails vegan?"

"Who cares about the mayor?" CJ scoffed. "Everyone who's anyone in this town will be drinking it by the bucketful. The prize money is nice, I imagine, but it's the potential investors that are really valuable." He lifted his brows at Mel meaningfully, then made the international "money" gesture by rubbing his fingertips together.

Mel's thoughts were in a whirl, but they were interrupted by Callen, who chimed in once more. "Adam Lavender is going to be one of the judges, I think. He owns that place in Toronto—dear, what was the name of that bar? We had those edible woodland dioramas with the moss that was actually cake?"

"Ill Intentions," CJ said.

"That's it! Oh, he's a genius."

"I've heard of him," Mel offered. That was putting it mildly. Everyone knew who Adam Lavender was. He'd practically invented molecular mixology. Or reinvented it. Put it on the map, for sure.

Half the cocktails in Manhattan lounges were rip-offs of Lavender originals. Mel couldn't imagine having him drink something she'd made. "He's really judging the competition?"

"Oh yes. We insisted on a big name," Cilla said. "The city and the Fest are expecting a lot of attention for this competition. The theme is supposed to be 'The City That Never Sleeps,' so I bet you'll get a ton of coffee-flavored drinks." They made a face.

Mel knew that look; it was the look of someone who'd had one too many espresso martinis at some point in their life and lived to regret it.

CJ groaned. "Boring! Everyone knows how to make an Irish coffee. A child could do it."

"Well, we probably shouldn't allow a child to try," Kade said, making a rare comment instead of focusing on eating their fruit salad as they had been for the last several minutes. "I imagine we'll see an awful lot of everything-bagel seasoning, unfortunately. The judges will be picking seeds out of their teeth after every sip."

The dry tone was so cutting, Mel felt her face heat. She mentally excluded bagel-flavored anything from her list of possible ingredients.

Not that she was going to enter the competition. But if she did—

"What would you make, Mel?" Bebe asked. She swept her hair over one shoulder as she turned to pin her with a look. "You're the professional here."

All eyes trained on her, making it impossible to think. "I'm not sure," she said. What screamed New York in a glass? A Bloody Mary with pizza seasoning in the tomato juice? A dirty martini with a kosher pickle instead of an olive? A tribute to Harlem—both the cocktail and the place—with a pineapple shrub and cayenne pepper? Could you try to encompass all of Queens and Brooklyn with a wild mixture of spirits imported from Asia, Latin America, and the Caribbean? Probably not, but damn if it wouldn't be fun to try.

Not that she planned on trying.

Mel felt a gentle nudge at her ribs, dispelling her ill-conceived daydreams. She turned to find Bebe leaning close, her elbow still winging out to the side. "Something to think about."

Before Mel could protest that she wasn't going to think about it because she had no intention of entering some bullshit competition, Bebe turned to Dez and asked her about her last trip to the Poconos. The conversation moved on, and Mel was left feeling—some kind of way.

She poked at the remaining bits of food on her plate. Almost a quarter of a million dollars was more money than she'd ever dreamed of having in one lump sum; even with her paltry rent and minimal expenses, her savings account was practically nonexistent. Money like that might actually get her concept off the ground, a bar of her own. A place where she had creative control over curation, where she wouldn't have to sling a bunch of shitty fizzes just because the owner had signed a deal with some liquor label that was desperate to be top shelf.

She guessed it wouldn't hurt to look into the competition. See what the rules were. Professional curiosity, nothing more.

Brunch came to a close once everyone had eaten their fill, and the guests drifted back into the living area. Some people were already getting into their coats and saying their goodbyes.

Mel figured she should use the bathroom before she left. Her personal rule of one glass of water per one alcoholic beverage was great for keeping her head clear, not so great for her squirrel-sized bladder. CJ was in the downstairs bathroom, so Bebe pointed the way up the stairs. Mel left her, Kade, and Dez all chatting about plans they had for a shopping excursion.

As Mel ascended the stairs, teal and pink walls came into view, the candy colors a big contrast from the downstairs' muted earth tones.

Soon the murmur of conversation below her fell away, and she found herself in the quiet world of Bebe and Kade's private life. There were three framed black-and-white photographs on the wall of the hallway that showed the two of them artistically posed with their faces close together. Mel let herself contemplate them for a moment, then padded down the hall, nudging open doors as she went. She found what must have been two guest bedrooms—although one bedroom looked kind of lived-in: a blank sketchpad open on the desk under the window, a pair of socks crumpled on the floor. Maybe Kade used it as an office? At any rate, no attached bathrooms in those.

Finally, she reached the largest bedroom.

It was an incredible space, all done in dreamy creams and light blues with a velveteen wallpaper behind the upholstered headboard. Mel's eye was drawn helplessly to the bed, which dominated the room, impressive especially given the constraints of most New York apartments. It could probably fit the entire Knicks starting lineup. Mel's fingertips itched to touch the silky-looking comforter.

She opened a door that turned out to be a walk-in closet before finally finding the bathroom. It was as well-appointed as the rest of the place, and Mel used it quickly. As she made her way back, Mel could hear low whispers in the living room. Her steps slowed at the top of the staircase. She thought she heard her name—but that was ridiculous. Lots of things sounded like "Mel." Tell. Sell. Well.

Fell.

Mel cleared her throat before she could be accused of eavesdropping.

"So it's settled?" Bebe's voice carried, even at a whisper. "I'll ask her?"

Mel's hand froze on the banister. Maybe they *had* been talking about her. Or possibly Dez, the only other "her" at the party.

"It's fine with me." Kade's deep rumble was so quiet compared to Bebe. "But don't be too disappointed if it doesn't pan out, Love."

So Kade had a cute epithet for Bebe as well. Maybe they weren't the immovable glacier that Mel had assumed.

Wait. Rewind. Disappointed about what? Mel frowned to herself. She couldn't picture Bebe allowing anything to disappoint her.

"I promise in the unlikely event that things don't go as planned, I will manage," Bebe said with a throaty laugh. Then her voice got quieter, but only a little. "Come here, you." Mel could hear the sounds of two people kissing. A soft, distant smack of lips meeting again and again.

Okay. Overhearing a couple's conversation was one thing. Listening in on their make-out session was approaching creepy. Mel made a show of coughing into her fist, hoping it would give Bebe and Kade plenty of time to break it up while Mel clomped down the stairs.

She nearly ran into Kade, who was coming up the stairs. They both made apologetic eye contact, then did that awkward dance of trying to get out of each other's way.

"Sorry—" Mel said.

"Sorry," Kade muttered.

"I'll just—"

Kade finally managed to duck around her. "It was nice having you here," they said, painfully sincere. "I hope you had a good time." They headed up the stairs before Mel could even thank them for the hospitality.

She turned instead to Bebe, who was beaming up at her. "Thanks for inviting me. This was really great," Mel said. She crossed the living room, gesturing at the coatrack that held only her lone jacket. "I should get going. Shift starts in a few hours."

"Of course, here, let me get that for you." Bebe beat Mel to the rack, holding her coat open so she could more easily slip into it.

"Full service," Mel joked as she turned around to stick her hands into the sleeves. "You're getting a five-star review for sure."

"Listen, before you go, I wanted to ask you—" Bebe lifted Mel's coat over her shoulders, then waited for Mel to turn around and face her. "Would you like to have lunch sometime next week?"

"Lunch?" Mel parroted. Her foolish brain registered the words and computed them as a date, even though she knew that couldn't be what was being offered.

"Kade and I would like to take you somewhere. If you're available?"

Right. Kade. Bebe's wife. See, brain? Not a date.

Bebe's smile turned gentle. A lock of honey-blond hair fell across her eyes, and she swiped it away with her hand, her gaze never leaving Mel. "I thought lunch would be best, seeing as you work nights and probably need to eat before you go in, but if I'm wrong about that—"

"No, no—you're not wrong." Mel should have felt vindicated by the invitation. Clearly she'd comported herself well at brunch if this cool couple wanted to take her out for another meal. And yet her first reaction—instinctual and unwelcome—was that she hadn't done enough to deserve Bebe's friendship. She was still struggling not to be attracted to her, for a start.

Mel steeled herself. She had to get over this mental block that kept telling her to retreat from everyone. She was divorced, not dead, damn it. She could have lunch with new friends. She could even have a tiny crush, so long as she didn't act on it. No harm in that. "Lunch is perfect. Any day, really."

"Yeah?" Bebe's eyes were bright. She gave a pleased wiggle. "Wonderful! It's been so lovely getting to know you today. I thought, 'Why not keep it going?'"

"Yeah," Mel said. "Let's . . . keep it going."

"Oh, you have no idea how happy that makes me." Bebe's hand slid over hers and squeezed for less than an eyeblink before falling away. "Do you like Mediterranean food?"

"Sure. Who doesn't?"

"I'll text you all the details." And with one final grin and a swirl of fabric, Bebe swept toward the door to see Mel out.

CHAPTER 5

Mel sat on her rickety bed in her tiny bedroom and stared at the Food Fest website she'd pulled up on her ancient, battered laptop. The site was as sprawling as the event itself, a confused jumble of typo-riddled information. The weekend had grown over the years to cater to both food- and bev-industry pros and civilian looky-loos. In the days since she'd had brunch at Bebe's place, Mel had been refreshing the page constantly, waiting for the promised application to appear. Today, it finally had.

The website took ages to load. She ran her eyes over the section on the new cocktail competition, or, as the Fest was touting it, "The New Era of New York Mixology." The judges were pictured at the top of the page with Adam Lavender as the headliner. Mel jotted down the other names in her notebook; she'd google them later if she decided to actually apply. The janky forms and slapdash website made her think that it would be a nothingburger of an event. Might not be worth her time.

She glanced at the clock on her computer. Her lunch with Bebe and Kade was happening in less than an hour. Mel knew she should get out of her ratty pajamas and into real clothes, but she couldn't stop studying the cocktail competition's FAQ. It wasn't like she could just throw her hat in the ring willy-nilly. There were forms to fill out, work history to submit, and a nominal entry fee, all probably designed to deter anyone who wasn't a serious competitor. Even after jumping through those hoops, it was still up to the Food Fest beverage committee whether you'd be accepted. The prize money was tempting, but did Mel really want to do so much paperwork?

She brushed the frayed end of her hoodie string over her lips in thought. The deadline to apply was still weeks away. Plenty of time to decide whether to put herself out there for potential humiliation or possible glory. She slammed her laptop shut and scrounged around in her clean laundry pile for something to wear that said, *I'm cool and casual and can be coolly casual friends with a cool couple*. In black, obviously.

The restaurant was tucked away in the basement of a Greenwich brownstone, the kind of hole-in-the-wall you'd never know was there unless someone led you. It wasn't fancy in the least, which was a weight off Mel's mind. The menu was on a flat-screen TV bolted to the wall. The seating was aggressively informal, with low couches and huge floor pillows arranged around secondhand coffee tables. The guests were a mix of NYU students and people in ripped jeans. Everyone was eating with their hands, which made Mel nervous. She hoped she didn't spill anything on her shirt like she was wont to do with her tacos.

They claimed a squat round table surrounded by enough jewel-tone pillows to build a fort. Mel watched Bebe extend her hand to Kade, who took it wordlessly and assisted her in keeping her balance as she dropped gracefully into a cross-legged seat atop a purple satin number. The skirt of her aqua dress poofed out all around her like a princess sitting on a lily pad. Okay, that looked doable. Mel positioned herself above a royal-blue pillow and began to descend in jerky stages. She was almost to the ground when she realized Kade was standing right next to her with their hand reaching out to her, a gesture she'd completely missed.

"Uh," she said. "Sorry, I didn't realize—" Why was she so awkward?

"It's fine." They tucked their hands into the hoodie-like pocket of their earth-toned—caftan? Mel wasn't sure what to call it. Drapey smock thing—and dropped onto a forest-green pillow as smoothly as a cat.

Bebe leaned over the table. "Isn't this place wonderful? I took Kade here on our first real date."

Mel tried to school her expression into something approaching polite interest, but she knew her eyebrows were inching sky-high. "Oh? So it's . . . special. For you two." She groped for something more to say while she scanned the menu. "What do you mean by 'real'?"

"We were both aware it was a date," Kade said, "as opposed to all the previous time we'd spent together, where we hadn't yet agreed to add a romantic aspect to our relationship."

"What they mean is, we were fucking around at first before we figured it out," Bebe said cheerfully. "Took a while to make it official. Not to toot my own horn, but I made a very convincing argument. There was a PowerPoint presentation and everything. The title page said 'BENEFITS OF A ROMANTIC ARRANGEMENT WITH ME' in big letters." She made a box with her hands to illustrate. "Eleven years later, and here we are. One thing about me? My arguments are iron-clad."

"She was very thorough." Mel imagined she heard a tinge of dry wit in Kade's otherwise emotionless tone.

"How did you two meet, anyway?" Mel asked. That was a polite question, the kind you asked couples.

"Mutual friends," Kade said at the same time Bebe said, "A party." They shared a look across the table. Then Kade grinned the tiniest, most microscopic grin, and Bebe burst out laughing.

"A party with mutual friends," she clarified, "though I wish we could tell you it was more exciting. Like they saved me from dying in a taxi that was stuck in the middle of a blizzard or something."

Kade lifted an alarmed brow in their wife's direction. "You wish you had almost died in a taxi?"

"Of course not. Though if you were the one saving me, I wouldn't say no." She swatted their arm playfully. Kade rolled their eyes, though their hand sought out Bebe's knee and gave it an affectionate squeeze. "Anyway," Bebe continued, "that's the short version of our story. What about you?"

"What about me?" Mel asked, unrolling her silverware from the paper napkin.

"You mentioned at brunch you're not currently seeing anyone, I think?" Bebe was good at a lot of things, but pretending she didn't know something she definitely knew was not one of them. Her voice went all high at the end, trying to force the statement into a question.

Mel's smile faltered. "Yeah, I've been single for a while. Went through a divorce a couple years ago." She turned her head and pretended to study the menu on the wall some more. "I don't like to talk about it." That was an understatement. Even admitting the existence of the divorce felt like a failure.

"Okay," Bebe said. "Consider it untalked about." She gestured at the menu board. "Everything here is excellent. We usually get a handful of small plates and share. How does that sound?" The server arrived with a carafe of tap water, and Bebe busied herself filling Kade's glass, then her own.

"That's fine with me." Mel was happy to lean on Bebe's expertise. She reached for the water, but Bebe didn't relinquish it, filling her glass for her instead. "Oh, thank you."

Those bright eyes twinkled at her—much as Mel tried to ignore them. "My pleasure. You're our guest, after all."

Bebe placed the food order for the table. She also handled the server's questions about allergies and the party's preferred spice level, saying, "No food allergies, but—oh, Mel." She turned to her. "Kade and I like it hot. How about you?"

Mel gaped like a goldfish for a moment. There had to be another way to phrase that.

"The harissa is delicious, but very spicy," Kade broke in, no doubt to move things along. Mel was grateful. "Should we tell them to put it on the side?"

"I can handle spice," she said, which was true. She wouldn't be eating at Julio's taco truck twice a week otherwise. She tipped her head to look up at the server. "It's not 'melt your face off' level, is it?"

"No," said the server. "We try to keep our guests' faces . . . intact."

Mel grinned. She liked bantering with other service workers. Hopefully, it was obvious she was one of them. Otherwise she'd cringe to death. "Then bring it on."

Once the order was placed and the server had vanished into the back, Bebe turned the full tonnage of her gaze on Mel. "Have you had a chance to check out that Food Fest competition yet? It sounded right up your alley, the way Cilla described it."

Mel fiddled with her paper napkin, creasing it into different shapes. "Yeah, I took a look at the website." Aka, read every word of text available regarding the brief, the rules, the dates, the deadlines, and the application process. "Still not sure it's for me, you know? I'd have to take off an entire Saturday, which is our busiest day. Plus, who knows if I'd even get picked to compete?"

"Well, if you decide to go for it," Bebe said with a smile, "we're willing guinea pigs for anything you want to test."

Kade nodded in agreement. "We're excellent at drinking."

"Thanks." Mel tried to temper the confused furrow of her brow at that comment with a genuine grin. "That's—very sweet."

The food arrived: a pot of fragrant mint tea, mounds of hummus in different flavors, steaming stacks of fresh pita bread, spiced lentils, herby baba ghanoush, some sort of yogurt dip, a white bean spread topped with a thick swirl of the aforementioned harissa, fat pearls of couscous mixed with pistachios and dried cherries, a simmering tagine of lamb and vegetables, rice studded with star anise and cardamom pods, a whole grilled fish with its head still on, resting atop a glossy bed of green leaves, and more kebabs than Mel could shake a kebab stick at.

She was in the middle of a tricky maneuver, trying to slide a skewer's worth of roasted chicken and bell peppers into a taco-folded piece of pita, when Bebe put down her own hunk of bread and cleared her throat.

"Now might be a good time," she said to Kade, who was methodically working their way through the bowl of hummus, swiping up exactly one third of the dip and leaving the rest looking like a pie chart.

Kade hummed in agreement but did not stop eating.

Mel lowered her kebab-on-bread to her plate. "A good time for what?" she asked.

"Well, I have a question for you. And right off the bat, let me say I don't want you to feel pressured into giving me an answer right now," Bebe said. "We want to communicate clearly and openly so there's no confusion." Her palms were flat on the low table, framing her plate like she'd done with her cocktail the night she'd come into Terror & Virtue.

"'We'?" Mel cast a glance at Kade.

"My presence is merely to confirm my knowledge of the situation. Feel free to pretend I'm not even here." Kade drank from their comically small teacup and returned to excavating the hummus.

"Ohhh–kay." Mel looked back and forth between the two of them. Were they about to recruit her into a cult? Or some kind of pyramid scheme? Or maybe a combo cult/pyramid scheme? "What's this all about?"

"I would like to ask you"—Bebe made a gesture that was half jazz hands, half muppet shimmy—"on a date!" She froze in a ta-da stance, arms thrown wide, her smile sparkling brilliantly. Mel was reminded of the Beauties on *The Price is Right*, introducing the latest joint health supplement onstage. That made her wonder if Bob Barker was still alive, which meant her brain didn't register what Bebe was saying until an embarrassing amount of silence had passed.

"A date?" was all she could say.

"Yep." Bebe was still frozen, her grin taking on a pained sort of determination. "A date. What do you say?" The server dropped off yet another plate, this time piled with sweets, before exiting the scene after everyone had murmured their thanks.

Mel didn't know what to say, so she blurted out the first semi-reasonable explanation that came to mind. "Like . . . as friends?" she asked.

For someone who was supposed to be effectively invisible, Kade sighed really damn loudly. "I told you we should print up pamphlets," they said to Bebe. "It would save us all some time."

"We don't need pamphlets, Darling. We just need to talk. Talking is good." Bebe dropped her arms and turned back to Mel. "Like a real date. Kade and I are polyamorous, which, for us, means that we sometimes date people outside our marriage. And I would like to take you out on a date. As my date. Who I would be dating. If you wanted to go out on a date with me."

"Extremely thorough, Love," Kade murmured.

Bebe beamed at them. "Thank you. I thought so." She turned the full force of her shiny personality back to Mel. "No pressure, though. Entirely up to you." She played with the pendant on her necklace, swishing it back and forth on its chain. It occurred to Mel that the gesture might actually be a nervous one. Slightly comforting, that thought.

Mel was sure her mouth was hanging open. It was likely she had not blinked in minutes. Of all the things she had considered might happen this afternoon, being propositioned by one half of a poly couple was not one of them. It sure beat the hell out of being invited to participate in a multilevel marketing scam. She had a healthy distrust of patterned leggings.

And the more Mel—slowly—thought about it, the more everything Bebe was saying made sense. Memories of the brunch party, like the way some of the guests seemed more affectionate with each other than Mel had expected, filtered through her head. Things started clicking into place.

Of course Bebe and Kade were poly. *Of course* they hosted interesting dinner parties with other poly people. *Of course*—

"Oh!" Mel stabbed her finger across the table at Bebe. "You *were* flirting with me the night you came into T&V!"

"Yes." Bebe picked up a rosy cube of Turkish delight between her fingertips. "I thought that was obvious, actually." She tossed the candy into her mouth and chewed.

"You could see it from space," Kade put in. "Positively blatant, and I wasn't even there for the worst of it, I'm told."

"Ignore them," Bebe said to Mel. "Do you need a minute? You seem surprised." She began playing with her necklace again.

"Yeah, sorry to be so slow on the uptake, but this isn't exactly a situation I've ever found myself in before," Mel said. She chugged her water. Dry mouth.

Bebe smiled wide, seemingly delighted, and said, "I thought so. That's why I decided not to beat around the bush."

Mel turned on her fluffy pillow to face Kade more fully. "And— you're okay with this? You're, like, totally fine with your wife going out on dates with other people?" It felt like the decent thing to do, to confirm.

Bebe made a sound like she'd spotted a basketful of puppies. "That's so sweet of you to ask! See, Darling, I told you, it's good to have you along for these conversations." She reached over and patted Kade's knobby knee.

Kade placed their hand over Bebe's, but kept their gaze on Mel. "This arrangement," they intoned, "makes us both happy. Much happier than we would be as a strictly monogamous couple. So yes, I am . . . *totally* fine." The emphasis made it sound like this was the first time such a plebian word had passed their lips.

"We're very open. In all senses of the word," Bebe said. "I won't be offended if you're not interested. If you want to keep things platonic, that's fine. We could be friends. The kind that don't go on dates." She picked up her teacup and took a small sip. Her eyes peered at Mel over the rim, glittering like jewels.

Mel took another drink of her water solely for something to do that wasn't gawking. She drained the glass, clearing her throat as she placed it back on the table. A real adult would have questions, she thought. That would be the responsible thing, asking more questions.

"Do you have, um, many other . . . people you date? At the moment?" Amazing work. A totally coherent query.

Bebe shook her head, smiling. "No, it's been a while, actually. Dez—you met her at brunch? She and I were an item a year or so back, but then she met someone who wasn't into the whole open thing so—" She made a gesture that indicated something unraveling. "Logistically, it didn't make sense anymore. But we're still friends."

Mel considered the logistics, then realized she had no idea what those logistics were.

"If I did decide to—date—you, how does it, you know," she said slowly, "work? I mean, what are the rules?"

Bebe sucked her teeth. "'Rules' implies some kind of crime has been committed if you don't follow them precisely. It's very stifling."

"You're a lawyer," Mel pointed out. "Shouldn't you be all about rules and regulations?"

"I know, it's kind of funny." Bebe tore off a piece of her pita and scooped up more food. "We all truly contain multitudes, don't we? At work, I'm a stickler. With my lovers, I prefer a more . . . fluid framework."

Lovers. Mel repeated the word to herself silently, her lips forming the word. "It's only—if I were going to do something like this"—big if—"I would want everything to be written down. You know, to make sure everyone's on the same page."

"That could be arranged," Bebe said, "as long as you're open to amendments."

"Things change," Kade clarified. "Situations evolve. We try to keep that in mind, but yes. We could write down our expectations. You might even call them guidelines." They locked eyes with Mel, their gaze impassive. "For instance, anything that happens between you and Bebe will be your own business. I won't be involved in any way. In case that is a concern for you."

"Ah. Right." It hadn't been a concern, exactly, but there had been a tiny voice in the back of her head that had wondered— "So if this were television, it wouldn't be, like, a Special Guest Appearance by me in the sweeps week episode of your relationship?" She waggled her hands around her face, trying to illustrate the opening credit sequence that was happening only in her own imagination.

"I . . . have almost no idea what you're talking about," Kade said. The corner of their mouth hooked downward. "I don't really watch TV."

Mel tried again: "I meant, you're not looking for a threesome sandwich with some Mel meat." More crass than she'd meant to be, but in for a penny.

Kade's face didn't move a muscle, though their faint distaste at the phrasing was palpable via the tilt of their head.

Bebe leaned over the table. "Correct, Mel. No sandwich. Kade's consent is the extent of their involvement. Unless that's something you'd like to negotiate?"

Her tone was professional. Not salacious in the least. So why did Mel's entire body feel like it was on fire? She hoped the heat in her cheeks wasn't creating too obvious a blush to any onlookers. At the risk of going even redder, there was something Mel knew she needed to ask.

"Is 'date' just the word you're using for sex? Is a fling all you're looking for here?"

Bebe didn't even blink. If anything, her smile only widened. "I would have said I was only interested in having sex with you if I was only interested in having sex with you. I pride myself on being intentional with my word choice." She ate an olive in a way that Mel could only describe as needlessly sensual. Even her careful discarding of the pit on a provided saucer held a tinge of the erotic. (Or maybe Mel just really, really needed to get laid.) "Not that there's anything wrong with a purely sexual arrangement. God knows I had plenty of them when I was younger. Oh, remember some of those play parties, Darling?" She shot a smile at an amused Kade before returning to the subject at hand. "But that was then, and these days, I find I enjoy myself more when there's some connection. Romance, or something approaching it. Ideally, we'd spend time together, see where it goes." She held Mel's gaze fearlessly. "Is that a problem for you?"

"Well," Mel said, unable to stop herself from glancing at Kade, who was refilling their teacup with ceremonial precision, "I'm not sure."

Honestly, she wouldn't really mind if it was just sex Bebe was after. She'd felt drawn—chemically, just chemically—to Bebe from the start. But a date? Mel had been on a mere one and a half dates since the divorce: the one being an ill-conceived attempt by Daniel to pair her up with a friend of a friend (boring; she hadn't bothered to get in touch for a second date, and neither had the blond) and the half being an invitation from a woman who tended bar down at the Empire State Lounge. Mel had accepted, thinking it was a date, but it had turned out to be a Group Thing an hour in. So, not the best track record.

Mel licked her lips. "What would this date involve?" Going on a date was a fairly low-stakes proposition, but going on a date with a married woman was not something she had on her post-divorce bingo card.

Bebe shrugged. "Maybe dinner and a movie? The traditional first-date foray."

"Because you're so old-fashioned," Mel said, feeling unmoored.

"Exactly." Her smile didn't contain even a hint of irony.

Mel once again looked over to Kade, hoping to make eye contact so she could deploy an "Are you seeing this?" sort of look, but they were completely absorbed with mopping up the last of the harissa-laced white bean dip with their flatbread.

Clearly, she was on her own.

Mel's tongue was stuck to the roof of her mouth. Her lower body was locked in a battle with her brain, wanting nothing more than to get closer to this woman, while the part of her that was supposed to be smart scrambled for reasons why she shouldn't.

"I—" She faced Bebe fully once more. "I'd like some time to think about it. Can I get back to you?" She was proud of how even-keeled the words came out. Like she wasn't sweating through her winter layers and composing exactly what she'd say to Daniel when she got back home.

Ugh, he'd been right about the hall pass. He was never going to shut up about that once he knew.

"Of course!" Bebe said. "Take all the time you need, really. I know it can be a lot."

Kade signaled the server. "We'll take the check," they said.

They left the restaurant together and stood outside on the freezing sidewalk in that awkward way people in New York did when they weren't sure if they could say goodbye there or if they were—horror of horrors—going to walk in the same direction. Kade solved the issue by saying they would flag down a taxi at the corner. They disappeared into the crowd of pedestrians, leaving Mel alone with Bebe for a moment.

"Well." Bebe clasped her clutch in front of her demurely. "Thank you for coming. And for hearing me out."

"No, yeah, thank you for—lunch," Mel said. She hated goodbyes. Should they hug? Shake hands? Indecision wasn't very punk rock. She did what felt most natural and leaned in to give Bebe a kiss on her cheek. She still smelled like cinnamon. "I'll be in touch," she said as she pulled away, hands stuffed in her pockets.

Bebe lifted a perfectly manicured hand to her cheek where Mel had kissed her. She looked extremely touched by the gesture, her eyes shining and buoyant. "I look forward to it."

A cab honked its horn at the corner. Kade was holding the door open.

"Bye, Mel," Bebe said with one last smile. Mel watched her sashay off into the cab.

CHAPTER 6

Mel couldn't find Daniel in the apartment when she arrived home, so she headed to the roof. He often went up there so he could smoke a joint without triggering one of Mel's migraine headaches. When Mel emerged from the emergency access door, she found him leaning against the lip of the roof, cupping his hands around the joint to keep it from going out in the harsh wind. He was wrapped in thick layers against the cold, with a knitted beanie pulled down low on his forehead.

Mel made her way across the uneven gray rooftop and stood next to him at the waist-high balustrade. She leaned her forearms on the gritty surface and stared at the back of the brick building next door. They didn't get much of a view from up here, surrounded by taller buildings on almost every side.

"How'd lunch go?" Ever the gentleman, Daniel was already going through the intricate ritual of snuffing and secreting the roach away in an old Altoids tin.

"I need your help," Mel said. She glanced over at him from the corner of her eye. She was closer to Daniel than anyone else on the planet, and she needed his input on this. "Bebe and Kade are poly."

Daniel's eyebrows journeyed to impressive heights. "You know I'm a very helpful guy, but I'm not sure what I'm supposed to do with that."

Mel slumped against the wall with a scowl. "Bebe asked if I wanted to date her. Me. Date her. As in romantically. Kind of. And I have no idea what to do." If she had hair, she'd be pulling it out.

Daniel didn't say anything right away, but rather dragged a fingertip through the air, sketching out a straight vertical line.

"What are you doing?" Mel asked.

"Who, me? Oh, I'm just keeping score. That's one point to Quince for correctly calling it from miles away," he said in an old-timey radio announcer voice. "For the folks at home, once again, that's Quince one, Sorrento zilch."

Mel pushed away from the low wall to groan at Daniel's antics. "You did not call it! You weren't even close to calling it."

"I told you that night she came into the bar, you should have asked about the vibe!"

"That is completely different from predicting that she wanted to include me in her poly—thing." Mel made frantic circles with her hands to illustrate what was still an ill-defined concept.

"I suspected. Now you have confirmation—like I knew you would—and you're all shocked? It's 2024. Get with the program. Basically everyone's poly." Daniel tucked the tin into his peacoat pocket and rubbed his hands up and down his arms. The wind picked up, whipping the loose end of his scarf around his shoulder. "So what did you tell her?"

"Nothing yet." Mel turned back to stare at the depressing brick wall. She could still make out the faint lines of an old advertisement for boot polish stenciled on the building. "I told them both I would give it some thought, but I have no idea what I'm going to say."

"Both?" His eyes—bright pink like they always got when he smoked—blinked slowly. "The wife was there, too?"

Mel nodded. "To confirm everything was on the up-and-up," she said.

"That's thoughtful."

"Is it?" Mel groaned and tugged her coat tighter around her frame. "I thought it was weird. I mean, I wouldn't have ever initiated something like this when I was married. How can someone be okay with their wife just . . . seeing other people?"

Daniel shrugged. "Do you think they were lying?"

Mel chewed on her cold lip, thinking about Kade's inflectionless comments over lunch. "No, Kade seemed perfectly fine. Though it's hard to get a read on them. Tough nut to crack, I guess."

"Then you have to take what they say at face value," Daniel said.

"Yeah." Mel dropped down to the ground so she could lean back against the wall, out of the worst of the wind. "The whole thing seems way too complicated to me. Do I really need this kind of drama in my life? Relationships are hard enough."

This was not the path Mel had thought her life would take. Since the divorce, she'd pictured herself as a lone wolf, and being with Bebe—and, in some capacity, everyone else Bebe was partnered with—was the opposite of that.

Daniel shimmied onto the ground to sit beside Mel. "Do you like her, though?"

Mel hugged her knees under her chin. "I think she's great. Funny, smart, gorgeous, weird sense of humor." She chewed on her lower lip. "This could be ideal, actually. I could dip my toe in without a ton of pressure. It's not like we can progress past a certain point when she's already married to someone else." As Mel said it out loud, it all started to sound more and more appealing. The only thing that nagged at the back of her mind was— "Am I really the kind of person who can be in an open relationship, though? And at this point in my life? Who does that?"

"Well." Daniel cleared his throat. "I have."

Mel squinted at him. "What? When?"

He picked some ash off the front of his shirt. "I'm in an open relationship right now. Technically."

Mel stared at Daniel. "What do you mean, you're in an open relationship?"

"Jackson and I," he said slowly, like he was speaking to a child. "We both see other people."

"That's different." Mel waved her hand around with a scoff. "You two aren't serious. You're casual. It's normal to casually date other people in that situation."

"This is obviously a foreign concept to you, so let me be clear: Jackson is allowed to fool around with other folks, I'm allowed to fool around with other men, but that's it. We're not dating anyone else; we don't get serious with anyone else. Because we are serious with each other. Because we're in love."

Love? Her head throbbed, and she rubbed at her forehead with the heel of her hand. "When did you two decide this?"

"Like, five months ago."

"And you didn't tell me?" Mel had assumed they told each other everything.

Daniel gave her a wild look. "The mere mention of love pisses you off these days. You're not the easiest person to talk to about this stuff."

Mel's mouth dropped open. "I'm easy! I'm incredibly easy!" Her voice echoed off the buildings around them. Quieter, she mumbled, "I'm sorry if I wasn't . . . receptive. It's a surprise, is all."

"I get it." Daniel wagged his head side to side. "But it's what makes me happy."

Mel thought about that. Happiness—true, soul-shaking, life-affirming happiness—seemed like a far-off goal. Something that happened to other people. But if she could have her job and her little apartment and her old-timey movies with Daniel and sex with a beautiful woman who was already getting her emotional needs met by someone else—would that be so bad? Bebe said she wanted some kind of connection, which was fine. She'd never mentioned how *deep* the connection had to be. Mel could have a nice time with someone and keep it on the surface-level. Not superficial, but . . . fun. Light! Nothing serious.

She turned to Daniel, wildly grateful she had someone to talk to and that that someone was him. "These guys you sleep with while dating Jackson—it's just sex? Nothing else?"

Daniel nodded. "That's the idea, yeah."

"So, nothing romantic? Just fucking. A purely physical thing."

"Well, sure, but I don't treat these guys like garbage," he said. "We talk, get to know each other at least a little bit. There's got to be *some* trust. No one wants to go home with an organ harvester." He shrugged. "We might grab something to eat on the way to his apartment or mine, but I wouldn't call it romantic. More like basic decency."

Mel let her head fall back against the rooftop balustrade with a thunk. "See, that sounds perfect to me. Polite. No strings. But Bebe said she wants to go on dates, so that's a slightly higher bar."

Daniel hummed. "I may be stoned out of my mind, but can I just say? I want you to be happy. If dating someone, even as an experiment, might help—why not give it a try? And if not a new relationship, there's got to be something you can do to shake things up."

Mel thought about her laptop, probably still whirring on her bed. "There is one thing," she said. "You know how I'm always saying I want to open up my own place if I ever win the lottery?"

"Yeah. Our big 'How We'd Spend Our Lottery Winnings' talk. You behind the bar, me managing the staff, also me on all final decor decisions." Daniel nodded to himself. "Though we really should start playing the lottery if we ever want that to actually have a chance of happening."

"Forget the lottery. There's this competition at the next Food Fest," Mel said, and the whole story spilled out. After she finished explaining the logistics, she sighed. "I don't know if I should enter, though. I mean, with the *thousands* of bartenders in this town? The chances of me even getting in are slim."

"Are you kidding me?" Daniel stared at her. "Mel, you should absolutely enter. Think of how much closer we'd be to that bar of our own with that prize money."

Mel shrugged. "It costs like fifty bucks alone to apply."

Daniel lifted his butt off the ground so that he could reach his wallet. "I'll give you fifty bucks. Shit, we can make fifty bucks in an hour on a good night. You're really going to let fifty bucks stop you?" He tried to open the billfold the wrong way, making a distressed noise and holding it out to her.

Mel shoved the wallet away. "All right, all right, put your money away. I'll enter. And if I don't get picked, I'll chalk it up to a losing lotto ticket."

He put his hand on her knee and patted it. "That's the spirit." He stood up shakily and pocketed his wallet. "Let's go. You've got a competition to enter, and I'm going to take a hot shower and pretend I'm in a '90s shampoo commercial."

"Okay." Mel laughed as she stood as well.

"My hair is going to feel delicious," Daniel said mostly to himself. He turned and ambled to the rooftop door. Mel followed him inside.

As she sat on her bed listening to Daniel singing in the shower down the hall, Mel opened her laptop yet again. She had some time before her shift started. Maybe she could get a head start, or at least download the forms and begin the process of filling in the easy stuff. Mel got to work—and soon found herself surrounded by scratch paper, a pen behind her ear and another between her teeth. She was on a roll, tearing through her employment history, describing some of her favorite obscure drinks, writing a goddamn *personal statement* on her mixology philosophy. Forget the entry fee, no one in their right mind would spend this much time yakking about cocktails unless they were completely obsessed. Which, Mel figured, she was.

Distantly, she heard the shower shut off. Daniel appeared in her open doorway wearing a towel around his waist and another wrapped around his head. "Shouldn't you be leaving for work soon?" he asked.

Mel glanced at the clock on her bedside table. "Yeah, in a minute. I'm just uploading these forms." Plus entering her credit card info to cover the fee. Then it would be done.

"Hell yeah! You're doing it? Entering that competition?" Daniel flew over to her bed, dripping slightly on her bedclothes as he climbed onto the mattress to join her. He peered at the entry screen on her laptop. "Look at you."

She gave him a wry look. "Want to do the honors and press the submit button?"

He wrapped a damp arm over her shoulders, ignoring her affronted screech of laughter. "No way. This is all you. Go for it."

With a dramatic flourish, Mel raised a finger in the air and brought it down on her trackpad. The website reloaded, taking its sweet time before showing a confirmation message. Now all she had to do was wait and see if she was chosen to compete. She let out a long breath.

"Hey." Daniel squeezed her tight against his side. "Proud of you."

"I'm . . . actually proud of me, too." A giddy feeling of accomplishment welled up inside her. "I'm fired up. I could run a mile. I could fight a bear."

Daniel hummed. "Could you go on a date with a really hot rich lady?"

Mel's smile morphed so that her lips were pushed out in thought. "I mean. Maybe? Yeah. Yeah, why not?"

A high squeal of delight left Daniel. He squeezed her once more, then leapt from the bed, nearly losing the towel around his waist in the process. "Get it, girl. I've got to get dressed and eat, like, two bowls of Lucky Charms." He left the room with a blown kiss. "Keep me updated! On both fronts," he called as he made his way down the hall.

Mel shook her head fondly and took out her cell phone. The last text from Bebe stared back at her.

We had such a nice time with you at lunch. (Kade says hi!) Looking forward to hearing from you, but AGAIN no pressure. ☺

There was a voice in the back of her head hissing that she wasn't that kind of person, that she'd never be able to handle any kind of relationship again, let alone a poly one.

That voice was a real bastard. Mel hated that voice. She'd ignored it successfully in the past: when she'd first shaved off all her hair, every time she made another tattoo appointment, each new piercing—the little voice had piped up. It wanted her scared. It wanted her to care more about what other people thought about her than what she thought about herself.

If she'd listened to that voice in the past, she'd probably have a practical bob, a job she hated, and a husband in the suburbs. Gross.

If she was going to go for this, there were worse reasons than spite. She texted a response to Bebe. Short and sweet.

> No pressure on YOU but . . . let's meet up for drinks? Super casual. Mondays are my only free evenings, sorry. But at least that should make scheduling easy 😊

Her thumb stabbed at the send button about five times before it actually worked. She'd never admit it, even to herself, but her hands were shaking a little.

Okay. Done. She'd done the thing. The voice in the back of her head was fuming, which was a good sign she was on the right track. Fuck that guy.

Her phone buzzed in her hand. She hadn't even had a chance to take a full breath before getting Bebe's reply. Was the woman glued to her phone 24/7? Mel checked the message.

> !!!!! That sounds great! Let's say a week from Monday? That gives us some time to hammer out the details. Guidelines, as Kade would say. Oh, we're going to have fun together, I can already tell 😊😊😊

Mel was certain she was grinning at her phone like a teenager. Who knew getting out of a rut would feel so good? First the competition, now Bebe. Mel was a winner, and she was going to prove it.

GUIDELINES FOR POLY LIVING
WITH BEBE & MEL

1. Communication in everything.

2. Be respectful of boundaries. Everyone gets to decide for themselves what they want to hear about their partner's other partners and what they are willing to have shared of themselves.

3. New partners may be added to anyone's personal roster so long as all involved are informed beforehand with an open discussion in mind.

4. For the health and peace of mind of everyone involved, we all agree to be tested regularly.

5. Though a married, cohabitating couple will naturally have some joint obligations that cannot be avoided, all involved agree that there will be no "power ranking" of couples in the arrangement, i.e., one partner will not be held as superior or more important than the other when it comes to scheduling, distribution of affection, etc.

6. Bebe agrees to keep the arrangement with Mel casual, as defined by:

   a. No commitments more than three weeks in the future

   b. No use of the L word for any reason

   c. No endearments

"But I give all my favorites some kind of cutesy name," Bebe protested, her hand hovering over the legal pad where it held the pen. "Kade is 'Darling,' for example. I'm not allowed to do that with you?"

Even through the FaceTime call, Mel was not immune to that pleading gaze or the pouting lips. "Okay," she said, "but it can't be something really silly, like 'cupcake.' That's a no-go for me."

Bebe smiled at her. "What about 'sweetheart'?"

"Hm." Suitably nonthreatening. Not too over-the-top. "'Sweetheart' is fine," Mel said. She lifted a finger in the air. "But *just* that. Not 'sweet cheeks,' not 'sweetie pie,' not fucking 'sweet pea'—"

"All right, all right." Bebe wriggled her shoulders and put pen to paper. "Consider the guidelines amended."

   c. No endearments except for "sweetheart." Variations on "sweetheart" not permitted.

CHAPTER 7

The Monday of the first date rolled around, and so did Mel's stomach.

First dates were the worst. It was like having a job interview where you were also expected to be hot. Mel dabbed a careful pinkie around the waterline of her right eye, pulling a face in the mirror so she could more easily fix her makeup. She normally wore heavy eyeliner and colorful eye shadow to match her vibrant tattoos while working. Guests expected her to look put-together, albeit in a punk rock way. Tonight, Mel had opted for a pared-down look.

She tossed her gel pencil onto the bathroom counter with a sigh. She still wasn't sure what the hell she was signing up for with Bebe. Sure, during the course of their conversations about guidelines, Bebe had patiently explained some of the more pressing stuff about dating a poly woman. They'd already exchanged proof of all-clear STI screenings, for example, which Bebe had covered with her own money. Mel thought it was kind of overkill for a first date, but Bebe had been firm.

"It's one of Kade's only asks," she'd said when they'd talked on the phone that weekend, "and it's for your protection as much as ours. I hope you understand."

Couldn't argue with that. Mel hadn't seen a doctor in years, so getting an all-expenses-paid checkup was a great deal. She needed to work on her cholesterol, apparently, but otherwise a green light from the doc.

Mel gave herself a coat of setting spray and headed to the kitchen. Her stomach needed something to chew on besides her nerves.

Daniel came into the kitchen and stopped short. "What are you doing?"

She thought it was obvious, but she answered anyway. "I'm pre-eating."

"What? What is that?"

"It's eating before you eat."

"Yes, I gathered. But why do you need to do that?"

"Because the bar I'm taking her to only serves small plates. Like, miniscule." Mel held her thumb and forefinger about a quarter-inch apart. "If I don't eat something now, I'm going to be hungry later. Or worse, I'll order too many things and rack up a huge bill. So: pre-eating."

Daniel stared at her. "You know that sounds absolutely unhinged, right?"

"Yes," Mel said, chowing down a granola bar and tossing the wrapper in the garbage can. "But you're going to steal the idea the next time you have a date, aren't you?"

"One hundred percent."

"Can you do me a favor?"

"Anything for the woman who has shown me the wonders of pre-eating."

"Will you help me brainstorm some ideas for a new drink later?" She gave a self-effacing shrug. "I have a couple things in mind but I'm not in love with any of them yet."

"Are you kidding?" Daniel grinned widely. "Yes, please, storm my brain all you want! As if I'd ever say no to any drink you made." He winked.

Mel did not wink back. She wasn't a winker.

After her snack, Mel pulled on some clothes she figured were suitable for a first date: her "formal" white patent leather Docs, a slinky black top that showed off the scrollwork tattooed on her collarbones, and a pair of black jeans that were warm enough for the long, wintry walk to the subway station. She was glad for the freezing weather; it meant she could cover any fashion faux pas with her jacket, plus the cold mitigated her tendency to sweat when nervous. She left with plenty of time to spare, then dawdled on the sidewalk outside Bebe's building, not wanting to seem too eager.

When she arrived at Bebe's door on the dot, Bebe greeted her wearing a velvet wrap top the color of celery and metallic gold trousers. She was still barefoot, and she held a poofy makeup brush in one hand. Her smile was electric, and Mel couldn't stop herself from returning it.

"Hi!" She invited Mel inside with a sweep of her arm. "Come in, come in. I'm still working on my final touches. Sorry about that. Work kept me longer than I thought it would."

"No worries." She was already familiar with the perils of dating a high femme. Mel unwrapped the chunky knit scarf from around her neck as she entered, and Bebe took that and her coat.

"Want to graze a bit before we go?" Bebe gestured to the breakfast bar, where a plate overflowing with shards of hard cheese, spiced almonds, and bright green grapes had already been picked at.

Mel's mouth must have fallen open in shock that seemed more negative than it was, because Bebe filled the silence with a snit in her voice. "Look, you're the one who wanted to keep our destination tonight a surprise. I have no idea if we're eating a full dinner or if it's going to be one of those tapas situations, and either way, I like to have a little nosh beforehand."

"No, I—" Mel turned to her, knowing that her grin had likely reached manic proportions. "I totally get it. I already snacked before I came over, actually."

Bebe blinked. "Really?" A pleased smile bubbled up, spreading across her lovely face. "So we're both on Team Snack-Ahead? Oh my god, it's like an O. Henry story." Bebe waggled her makeup brush and floated up the floating staircase. "Give me five minutes?"

"Take your time," Mel called after her. She plucked a grape from its bunch. The condo was quiet, only the distant sounds of Bebe getting ready upstairs mingling with the hum of the luxurious central heating. Mel wondered where Kade was. Maybe they made themself scarce when Bebe had a date planned. Or they were out on their own date.

Mel decided that wasn't any of her business, and even thinking about it might cross some line. She ate some cheese instead.

When Bebe descended ten minutes later, she was wearing sensible low-heeled ankle boots, her camel coat, and pink earmuffs that made her look like cotton candy. "Okay!" She tucked her clutch under her arm. "I'm ready for whatever you want to throw at me. Not to sound like a lush, but after the day I've had? I hope it involves alcohol."

Mel eased off the high stool that she'd occupied while grazing, a smile on her lips. "Tough day at the office slaying employment law dragons?"

"You don't know the half of it." She reached for the grazing platter and popped a green grape in her mouth. "Let's just say class action lawsuits are a huge mess. Especially when it involves a gigantic company that doesn't want to pay its workers for the time they, you know, *worked*. Also, how do you systematically fire every pregnant employee you've had in the last seven years and not expect me to notice?" She ate another grape, chewing angrily. "It's not like you would've even paid for their maternity leave. You're going to be that big of a dick to avoid a minor scheduling hassle? I'm going to bleed these fuckers dry."

"Restaurant industry?" Mel guessed.

Bebe stopped mid-chew to stare at her. "Is it that obvious?"

"It's a small world. We all talk. Plenty of businesses operating like that in this town."

"Well, by the time I'm done with them, there might be one fewer."

That made Mel laugh. They left the condo in good spirits, heading on foot toward the bar that Mel had chosen for their date.

"Am I going to be in suspense the whole way or can you at least give me the name of our destination?" Bebe asked as they walked. She threaded her arm through Mel's, a gesture that made Mel feel like a Victorian gentleman. She didn't hate it.

"Have you ever been to a speakeasy called Loose Lips Sink Ships? Some people call it LLSS for short. The die-hard fans, anyway."

Bebe's eyes went wide with eagerness. "And are you one of those die-hard fans?"

"Well . . ." Mel thought on that, her mouth in a thoughtful pout. "I wouldn't go that far."

At Bebe's questioning look, Mel elaborated: "It's usually right up there with Terror & Virtue on the annual Best Of lists. They make this lavender negroni—it's damn good. You'd like it."

"Hm," Bebe said. Her eyes narrowed on Mel's face.

Mel felt pressured to sell her date-night spot harder. "Very cozy booths, too. You can fit two people. Barely."

Bebe's face pinched. "Will I be able to get in and out without an undignified struggle? Booths aren't the most friendly to people who aren't rail-thin."

Mel hadn't thought about that. Which wasn't very cool of her. "I think you'll be fine." She attempted to recover. "You'll like the special entrance. The only way in is through this old florist shop. They've got a guy in there selling roses all night long, straight from central casting, and you have to give him the password to be let in."

Bebe's face smoothed slightly. "That does sound kind of fun. What don't you like about it?"

"What do you mean?"

"You said you weren't a die-hard fan. So it must not butter your biscuit completely. I'm just curious."

Mel licked her lips and tried to put on a winning smile. "It's bad form for bartenders to shit-talk each other's places."

Bebe simply waited her out, her head cocked, the barest smirk on her lips. Mel felt a surge of sympathy for anyone who found themselves cross-examined by her in court.

"Okay, so the whole speakeasy thing—'oh, it's a cute little secret to find your way inside' or whatever," she said, miming the voices of a million Yelp reviews. "I *get* it, but what's that saying to your clientele who have historically not been welcomed into certain establishments? The whole point of speakeasies back in the day was to keep those folks safe from cops. Now it's this—I don't know, it's more about exclusivity. That rubs me the wrong way, I guess."

"Hm," Bebe said. This was a different *hm* than the previous one. Mel might have tried to dissect it, but she was on a roll.

"And then once you make it through the secret door, you've got to walk down the steepest, darkest staircase in Manhattan—totally not accessible—and the staff always look bored, like they're too cool for school, and sure, most of the drinks are good, but their martini is—how do you fuck up a martini that badly? I'm all for being spirit-forward, but that thing is an abomination." She turned her head and caught Bebe's amused look. "Uh, but other than that, it's a great place."

"Oh yeah," Bebe drawled, "sounds like a real winner." She stopped walking and nudged Mel to the side so they weren't impeding the flow of pedestrians. "Are you sure this is where you want to take me?"

"Yes. Sorry. Ignore my professional criticism," Mel said. "Seriously, you'll have a good time. I promise. It's actually a lot like T&V, and I know you like T&V."

Bebe's eyes went wistful. Now that they weren't in motion, they could face each other, and Mel could see every flicker of feeling across Bebe's lovely face. "Oh, you really are an actual sweetheart," she said, "but I want to know what *you* like."

Mel could feel her brow collapsing in consternation. "Why?"

"Because I like you! I want to know everything about you." Bebe took Mel's bare hands in her gloved ones. "I appreciate you picking a place you think I'd enjoy, but I was kind of hoping I'd get a peek behind the Mel Sorrento curtain. Why don't you take me somewhere you'd go if you weren't trying to impress anyone?"

That drew Mel up short. She covered her surprise with a shaky laugh. "You don't want to go to those places, trust me. They're kind of trashy."

"I love trash. I mean, I love high-class, too, but only because I have the world's worst case of FOMO. Why do you think I go to both tiny cash-only mezze cafes and places like T&V? I want a full life." Bebe leaned in, her lips brushing the shell of Mel's ear. "And I want you to have fun tonight."

Mel vacillated for half a second. Her plans for squeezing into a too-small booth next to Bebe were dissolving, but Mel didn't miss them too much. "Fine," she said, turning around and heading north instead. Bebe's hand was a welcome weight in hers. "Don't say I didn't warn you, though."

Sal's was the last of a dying breed, a true dive bar in a part of town where rents were too high for anything except the most expensive joints. Sal had lucked out, though—or rather his grandfather of the same name had when he'd bought the tumbledown Chelsea building in the '50s. With little overhead and a cash-only business, they could afford to keep slinging giant cups of cheap beer and fried clams. The bar itself was dark and dingy, with tattered panties of all colors, eras, and fabrics hung from the low ceiling. In more recent years some jockeys, boxers, and briefs had entered the fray, which Mel supposed was as close to equality as you could get at Sal's. (The women's room was a disgusting pit, never a roll of toilet paper to be found, so Mel always used the men's.)

As Mel led Bebe into the dank, basement-level bar, she wondered if she had made a huge mistake. Sure, Bebe had practically begged to be brought here, but Sal's was not the kind of place anyone should take any woman ever, unless said woman, like Mel, had a misplaced nostalgic fondness for New York's bad old days.

Mel turned to ask if Bebe wanted to go somewhere else—somewhere with fewer health code violations, perhaps—but Bebe was wide-eyed and marveling at the sight of the various underpants hanging from the drop-tile ceiling.

"This is amazing! I would've never known this place was here, and I must have walked past it a dozen times over the years." She leveled a look at Mel. "I'm guessing they don't serve craft cocktails."

"Frankie might mix you a screwdriver if you ask nicely, but yeah,"

Mel said, taking her by the elbow to steer her toward the bar. "It's definitely a beer-and-a-shot kind of joint."

Back when she'd just turned twenty-one and was working her way up as a barback in un-trendy pubs, Mel couldn't afford many luxuries. If she wanted to have a drink after a long day, this was one of the few places she could go. Sal's had been a haven for the after-hours crowd because the place stayed open until Frankie, the longtime bartender, decided it was time to go home. Which was usually lunchtime the following day.

"Well, I'm delighted. Thank you for bringing me here," Bebe said. She sounded like she meant it. Her eyes kept darting around the walls to see all the old posters that had been hung in decades past: rock-'n'-roll acts that had come through back when the neighborhood still had a decent venue; pay-per-view boxing matches that Sal had put on the dusty TV; handwritten notices that declared credit cards, debit cards, checks, and money orders were not accepted here and never would be.

Mel was glad to see Frankie was still behind the bar. He must've been pushing seventy at this point, but he was still on his feet, working the taps, pointing at the various guys in Rangers jerseys who stood three deep, shouting their orders back at them. Frankie was huge, easily six foot five, so he spotted Mel over everyone's heads.

"Melanie!" He always called her by her full name. Like an uncle or something. "It's been a while, kid! How ya been?" Frankie scowled at the dudes crowding around the bar, shooing them to the sides like he was parting the Red Sea. "Make a hole. Let the ladies in."

Bebe's eyes went wide. Apparently this brand of chauvinism startled her. "Oh, we can wait our turn."

"Nonsense. Melanie knows she and her friends don't wait. Push these numb nuts aside, all right?" Frankie was already popping bottle caps. "It ain't me being sexist, I swear. I just like her better than these losers."

Mel ignored the angry grumbles of the barflies and shouldered her way up to the rail. "How's tricks, Frank?" She gave him a fist bump.

"Terrible," he said. "Got to retire soon."

"Oh my god." Her heart fell into her Doc Martens. "Really?"

Frank shrugged. "Sal wants to sell. Says it's too much work at his age. This time next year, this'll probably be a Citibank or some shit."

That was depressing. Mel knew nothing in New York stood still, but to lose an institution like Sal's hit her right in the gut. She looked over at Bebe, who appeared equally stunned, even though she'd only learned about Sal's today.

"Aw, come on," Frankie said, laughing. "Why be sad over this? There's worse things." And he launched into a laundry list of problems. The weather was lousy. He was getting a knee replacement next month. The fucking mayor was going to run the city into the fucking ground while the rats ran circles around him. All the while, Frankie was busy readying two shot glasses on the bar. He only paused in his diatribe to ask, "Tequila?"

Mel hooked a thumb at Bebe. "She's a whiskey drinker."

"Nice! Same here." Frankie gave the glasses a cursory wipe with a rag.

"Pour yourself one, too, Frank. On me," Mel said, pulling out a few bills. "To celebrate a legend's retirement."

Frankie went soft around his crow's-footed eyes. "Aw, thanks, kid." He got out one more shot glass.

"Hey, can I get a Stella?" a guy at the end of the bar asked.

Frankie smacked the rag down on the bar. "Can't you see we're having a moment here? Keep your fucking shirt on. What's on that shirt, anyway?" He peered over the bar, spying some sports logo that Mel didn't care enough about to recognize. "Look at this prick. A Devils fan? Seriously? Get outta here with that garbage." He pointed to the door, and sure enough, a bouncer even bigger than Frank appeared from the gloom to escort the spurting, would-be patron away.

The Rangers crowd ate it up. Beer sloshed to the floor from all the sloppy plastic cup–clinking. A decent ploy to ensure more sales, Mel thought with an impressed nod at Frankie.

Bebe clutched Mel's arm. At first Mel thought she might be alarmed by the antics, but one glance at her face and she knew Bebe was thrilled to pieces.

"This," Bebe said, "is the best bar in the world."

"Right?" Mel smirked. They did their shots with Frankie and then took their beers to a small table over by the wall where the noise of the sports fans wouldn't be too distracting. Now out of Frank's earshot, Mel continued: "Don't get me wrong, the tap lines haven't been cleaned since the Reagan administration and you might get a UTI from just walking by the women's restroom, but other than that, it's great." She looked around the scuffed walls fondly, noting the old Christmas tinsel someone had strung up for the holidays years ago and never taken down.

Bebe grinned and sipped at her beer—a bottle, Mel's usual here. (She wasn't joking about the tap lines.) "So Sal is selling, hm? New signage, a little sprucing up, could be perfect for, say, a cocktail bar."

Mel groaned. "Don't joke. You heard Frank. Sal's looking for Citibank money. Even if I win the cocktail competition, I bet that cash would barely cover a down payment on the building. I'd need to know someone rich who could be talked into investing." Then, realizing how that sounded, she hastened to add, "I didn't—that wasn't me trying to come on to you, financially."

"Hey, getting hit up with a business pitch is not the weirdest thing that's ever happened to me on a first date," Bebe said, bubbly.

"This is not a pitch!" Mel was horrified by the thought.

"I know, but even if it were, it would be firmly on the charming end of the scale." She tapped her fingers to her cheek, drumming and humming. "You're burying the lede here, though. Did you decide to enter the competition?"

"Oh. Yeah." Mel scratched the back of her neck. In all the first-date excitement, she'd forgotten to tell Bebe. "I turned in the paperwork. Still got to wait and see if they accept me."

"Mel! That's great! I bet you'll—" But whatever Bebe was going to say was drowned out by a pair of white dudes in Yankees caps at the table behind her. Their agitated voices rose from a heated murmur to an all-out screech in seconds. Bebe, her brow furrowed in annoyance, planted her hand on her chairback and twisted to get a better look at the interruption.

Mel could see the two guys over Bebe's shoulder. One guy swayed to his feet, red-faced, and shouted, "You watch your fucking mouth, Barry, or I swear to god—"

The other guy, Barry, followed suit, standing so abruptly that he almost knocked his chair over. "No, you clean out your fucking ears and listen, man! Listen!"

Both of them presented a slurred, stumbling picture that could only mean one thing: day drinkers. Mel could spot someone six hours into a bad decision as easily as she could taste the difference between sweet vermouth and angostura bitters.

"Maybe we should move over there," she murmured to Bebe, cutting her eyes to an empty table against the opposite wall, far from the maddening bros.

Bebe turned to give her a perplexed look. "Why should we move? Give me two seconds." She pushed her chair back and stood, dusting invisible lint from her clothes as she did so. Before Mel could hiss a warning, Bebe had already inserted herself in the argument. The guys stopped shouting long enough to stare at the unexpected arbiter. She planted a hand on each of their shoulders and stood between them.

"Hey, fellas," she said. "What's going on here?" Both guys opened their mouths to speak simultaneously, which Bebe cut off at the pass. "One at a time. Barry, is it?" She pointed to the guy who'd almost knocked over the chair. "You go first."

Mel looked around wildly for help. Frankie caught her eye from across the room; he had the handle of a baseball bat in one hand and the other on the leaf, ready to make a rare appearance on the other side of the bar if the situation warranted it.

But it never got that far. Because Bebe was some kind of asshole-whisperer.

"Tucker's being a dick!" Barry whined. He stabbed a finger in the aforementioned Tucker's direction.

"You're the dick!" Tucker said.

Bebe's fingers tightened on their shoulders, keeping them from going for each other's throats. Or falling down drunk. It looked like it could've gone either way, really. "This isn't a playground, gentlemen.

Talk to me. What did Tucker say that made you so angry?" she asked Barry.

Mel turned back to Frankie and held up two fingers in a peace sign. "Water," she mouthed. "Big ones."

Frankie seemed disappointed as he returned the bat to its hidden spot beneath the bar, but he dutifully started filling up a huge cup from the spigot.

Barry sniffed. "He was saying I should never have proposed to Denise. Fuck you, man, I love her!"

"Tucker." Bebe's head swiveled to speak to him. "Were you shit-talking Denise?"

"She's no good for him, man," Tucker lamented. "She treats him like shit."

"She does not!"

"Dude, all she talks about is how much of a slob you are. And she backs the fucking *Jets*, man."

By then, the water cups were full. Mel scurried over to the bar and grabbed them, depositing them on Tucker and Barry's table. Bebe smiled at her in thanks, but the other two didn't register her presence.

"Barry, is that true?" Bebe asked.

"It's not her fault her folks have season tickets—"

"No, I mean have you noticed Denise being critical of you instead of supporting and uplifting you?"

Barry's glassy eyes blinked. "Sometimes, I guess. But not all the time!"

"So you've decided that you want to remain committed to Denise because the good times, for you, outweigh the bad, is that right?" Bebe patted his shoulder. "And Tucker, you worry about your friend because you love him and want the best for him, right?"

Tucker bit his lip and nodded hard. "That's my boy," he said.

"Do you think you can continue to support and uplift him without criticizing his decision to be with Denise? Because he's grown, and he's going to do what he wants to do."

"Yeah!" Barry said. "I am grown!" He reached down, fingers grasping for his beer, but Bebe nudged the water into his hand. He gulped it down.

Tucker looked pained. "But she—"

"You don't have to agree with him," Bebe said. "You don't even have to like Denise. But you have to respect your friend's choices. It would be kind of shitty if you didn't, right? Especially since that's what you worry Denise is doing."

A chagrined look overtook Tucker's red face. He actually ducked his head like a chastened schoolboy. "Yeah. Okay."

"And Barry?" Bebe turned to him. "Your friend was willing to go out on a limb, knowing you'd get angry, to tell you his concerns about your relationship. If he's saying there's red flags, sit with that. Pay attention to how Denise treats you and how she makes you feel. The pros might outweigh the cons now, but maybe that will change. And if it ever does, you'll need friends who will be there for you." She squeezed his shoulder.

Tucker nodded, still not looking up. "Sorry I got in your face, man," he mumbled to Barry.

"Nah, it's fine. I get it."

Oh my god, Mel thought to herself. *Are they going to hug?* Sure enough, Bebe stepped away, and the two men crushed together, arms beating across each other's backs, Yankees caps in danger of falling from their heads. A smattering of applause came from the other customers who'd been watching the drama unfold. Mel collapsed back into her chair in relief.

Bebe floated back toward Mel and retook her seat with a small, self-satisfied smile. She went to take another drink of her beer but stopped halfway to her mouth when she noticed Mel staring. "What?"

Mel leaned back and crossed her arms over her chest. "Do you have some kind of superpower for defusing bar fights?" Or maybe Bebe exuded some kind of calming pheromone that made jerks rethink their actions and made lesbians hot under the collar.

"Oh, that?" Bebe shrugged and sipped at her bottle. "It's one of those things I happen to have a knack for. A girl's got to cultivate talents." Her gaze traveled from Mel's face to the wall behind her. "Speaking of—" She pointed. "Want to play?"

Mel twisted in her seat and looked at the tattered dartboard that hung on the wall. "I could go a few rounds," she said, turning back. She was great at darts and knew the ins and outs of this board in particular, having played at Sal's tons of times over the years.

The gleam of competition entered Bebe's eye. "Let's make it interesting. Same game as before. Winner gets to ask any question?"

That gave Mel pause. She wasn't up for providing answers about her divorce, for example. "Within reason." The guidelines said they could have boundaries, after all.

"Deal," Bebe agreed, and Mel went to get the slightly bent darts from Frankie.

Bebe was good, but Mel was better. She racked up point after point, while Bebe struggled to keep up. It felt nice to be winning at something, Mel thought. A good confidence booster, even though Bebe groaned dramatically every time Mel hit the bullseye.

"You're a shark!" she said, using the neck of her beer bottle to point accusingly. "I've been set up. You didn't tell me you were a professional dart-thrower."

"You didn't tell me you're such a sore loser." Mel couldn't help her smug grin. She took up her position at the scuffed line on Sal's floor and hefted a dart in her palm. One more decent throw and the game was hers. "Looking forward to asking you all about that once I win."

Bebe leaned against the wall right next to the dartboard with a huff. "Now you're just being mean," she said, lifting her beer to her lips in the most sullen way possible.

Mel gave her a "sorry-not-sorry" shrug and lifted the dart above her shoulder. Her tongue stuck out of the corner of her mouth as she contemplated the bullseye. Victory was going to be very sweet. "Might want to move," she told Bebe.

"Why?" Bebe dragged her wet bottle down the middle of her chest, leaving a damp trail on the skin bared by her wrap top. Mel's gaze followed it closely. "You haven't missed yet. Planning to start now?"

Mel swallowed her comments about safety being first. "You're trying to distract me."

"Me?" Bebe's eyes flew wide in faux innocence. "How dare you. My character is unimpeachable." She played with her necklace, drawing Mel's attention inexorably to that slice of skin.

"Suit yourself." It wasn't like Sal's ancient darts were even remotely sharp anyway. Mel lined up her shot once more.

Right before the dart left her hand, Mel saw Bebe out of the corner of her eye, leaning casually forward to give Mel an eyeful of her truly excellent cleavage.

The dart flew wide, hitting the very edge of the board with a dull thunk. Zero points. Bebe didn't even turn her head to check the score. Her grin was sly as a panther's.

Mel shook a finger at her. She could barely hold in her laugh; it was all so ridiculous. "You did that on purpose!"

"I don't like losing." Bebe pushed off the wall, sauntering closer. "And whattaya know?" She finally contemplated the dartboard, sipping her beer. "Looks like I win."

"You cheated."

"I strategized," Bebe said archly. "There's a difference."

That made Mel's eyebrows shoot up and her lip curl in a half smile. "Wow. You're a real take-charge kind of gal, aren't you?" She retrieved the errant dart and deposited the set back on the bar.

"I guess so. Out here in the real world, at least." Bebe gave her a mysterious glance as she meandered back to their table.

Mel followed. "What do you mean by that?"

Bebe retook her chair, sitting sideways and crossing her legs at the knee. Her gold metallic trousers swished and clung to her, giving Mel a great visual of her round thighs, one half of her plump ass. "I have this personal theory," she said as Mel sat. "I believe that generally— note that word, *generally*—personalities do a complete one-eighty when it comes to sex. If someone is commanding and domineering in their day-to-day life, for example . . ."

"Like a high-powered lawyer who mediates bar fights for fun and cheats at darts," Mel drawled. "For example."

Bebe raised her near-empty beer bottle in acknowledgment. ". . . then that person is likely, in my view, to be submissive in bed."

Mel waited for Bebe to land the rest of the punch line, but even when nothing else was said, she laughed. "What? Are you serious?"

Bebe nodded firmly. "Sex is where we get to act out all the little dramas we're not allowed to indulge in public. When people take their clothes off, they want to be the opposite of how they're always expected to be."

"Is this your roundabout way of telling me you're a bottom?" Mel asked.

"Oh, Sweetheart, there's nothing roundabout about it." Bebe's eyes danced. The lights caught on her hazel eyes, bringing out the green and blue flecks. "I'm a champion pillow princess. I've made bottoming an art form. I can drape myself over a mattress and let you do whatever you want to me like *that*." She snapped her fingers. "So here's the question I get to ask as the darts champion: Do you agree with my little theory?"

Mel pretended to think about it, humming. "I don't know. You really think most people fall along these lines?"

"In my experience," Bebe said. She smirked and lifted a hand to her necklace, playing with the charm.

Mel wondered if the necklace had been a gift from Bebe's wife. Before she could think better of it, she asked, "Even Kade?"

Bebe made a sound that Mel couldn't place at first, but only because she'd never heard a grown woman giggle before. "Oh, absolutely. Especially them."

That was—food for thought. Kade came off as so quiet, so serious, a bit passive in an aloof sort of way.

Mel couldn't help but smile. "So your sample size is two, and both happen to support your idea, huh?"

"Oh, at my age, my sample size is way bigger than that," Bebe said. "But you're dodging the real question!"

"Which is?"

"Do you think my excellent and well-researched theory applies to you as well?"

Mel tried to keep her composure, but it was a near thing. She was sure if she were wearing something skimpier, Bebe would be able to see her shoulders and chest turn a splotchy, anxious pink. "Do you ask all your first dates how much of a top they are?"

"Only the ones with good forearms." Bebe dipped her gaze to where Mel was leaning her elbows on the table, her sleeves pushed up to expose skin and tats. Mel hesitated, thinking of whether she fell along the lines of Bebe's theory herself. In her everyday, professional life, she was a people pleaser because she worked in the service industry. Was she only like that because of her job? Or was she a different kind of person deep down?

After considering it for a moment, she shook her head. She loved tending bar, and the reason she was so good at it was because her personality lent itself to making sure everyone was having a fun time.

According to Bebe, that meant she would be the opposite of that, sexually. Which sounded . . . bad.

Mel's beer was not halfway finished, so she didn't even have the excuse of being tipsy when she opened her mouth and said out loud on a first date, "So if I'm the consummate service worker in my real life, does that mean I'm supposed to be self-centered in bed?"

Bebe's eyes lit up. "I don't know. Are you?"

Mel thought about that. Sex with her ex-wife had been—fine. Basic. A little boring. But they'd been together since they were seventeen, for crying out loud, and they both worked in the bar and restaurant industry, so their schedules didn't leave much room for alone time. Mel's expectations for sex had been fairly low. As long as one of them got off, she considered it ticked off the chore list. Which was kind of depressing. But definitely not self-centered.

"I . . . don't think so," she said slowly. "At least, I don't think I have been."

"Would you like to give it a try?"

Mel barked a laugh. "What? Being inconsiderate?"

"Sure." Bebe shrugged.

"But that's—it's a bad thing. Especially in bed. Why would you want to sleep with a self-centered person?" Mel felt she might be torpedoing her chances with Bebe, but better to hash things out honestly before getting too involved.

"Didn't you listen to my whole spiel? Sex is playacting. It's doing all the things you're not 'supposed' to do, quote, unquote." She made bunny ears with her fingers. "It might be kind of fun to go off the rails. As long as we're both on board, I say hurrah." Her voice dropped to a whisper as she leaned across the table. "You could toss me around, use me, treat me like I'm a toy. The more I talk about it, the more I'm convinced." Bebe fanned herself with one hand and took a long drink of her beer. Her cheeks were, in fact, taking on a bright rosy hue.

"You'd really be into that?" Mel asked. It seemed impossible that this was happening to someone like her, a normal person on what she'd thought would be a normal first date.

Bebe smiled, tipped her bottle to her lips, and drained the last of the beer. "One way to find out." She kept her eyes on Mel as she placed the empty on the table with a firm click. "Want to get out of here?"

That was—quick. One drink, two if you counted the shot, and they were off to the races. Was this moving too fast?

Or maybe it was moving at exactly the right speed for a low-stakes hookup.

Mel took her wallet out of her back pocket and tossed a few bills on the sticky table.

"Yeah," she said. "I do."

Her place wasn't too far of a walk, and she was about to offer it as their next venue when Bebe stood and said, "I know a great spot a few blocks away if you're up for an adventure."

Mel paused, her wallet halfway back to her ass. She'd assumed Bebe had meant—well, when someone said, "let's get out of here," it was usually followed by the "your place or mine" discussion, wasn't it? She was rapidly understanding, though, that nothing with Bebe was the usual.

"It'll be fun. I swear." Bebe was already putting on her coat, getting a hand beneath her fall of hair to lift it free of the coat collar. "You showed me this place; let me show you a place of my own."

To hell with it. Mel peeled herself out of her chair and waved goodbye to Frankie, who was too busy hollering at the game on the TV to pay her any mind.

CHAPTER 8

They spilled out of the bar and into the cold night air, laughing at each other, leaning on each other. Mel's hand sought Bebe's and found it already reaching for her. Their fingers threaded together as they made their way down the damp sidewalk. Sleet had fallen while they'd been inside Sal's, puddles along the street reflecting a spectrum of neon lights back at them. Their breath misted and mingled together like a wintry dance.

For the first time in a long time, Mel felt good. This was the kind of magical night she'd only had once in a blue moon in New York, where the grinding pulse of the city suddenly felt like it was beating in tune right alongside hers. Or maybe that was Bebe, pressed against her side, warm and happy. This was the kind of night where nothing could go wrong.

They were still laughing when a man stepped out of a brightly lit doorway directly into their path, a roil of loud, pumping music following him.

"Oh!" Bebe stopped short and brought herself upright. She tugged at Mel's hand, guiding her somewhat behind her. "Gary." Her tone was so cold and professional, Mel hardly recognized her voice.

The man—Gary—looked up from his phone screen. There was something familiar about him that Mel couldn't place. He was white, middle-aged, with a full head of hair that was dyed an unfortunate shade of brassy blond. His navy suit was perfectly tailored, but there was a splotch of something that looked like mayo on his lapel. Dear lord, she hoped it was mayo.

"Blair Murray," he drawled. His gaze traveled over her in a way that Mel did not like one bit, lingering on her tight green top where her coat was unbuttoned. "I suppose you're having a night on the town?" His sharklike eyes shot to Mel, then to their joined hands.

"Yes, we are," Bebe said, her voice going bright with fake cheer. She turned to Mel. "This is a colleague of mine, Gary Willis."

"Colleague might be a bit generous," Gary sneered. He stuck out his hand. "Mrs. Murray and I often spar from opposite sides of the courtroom."

Mel took his hand, not knowing what else to do. "Mel Sorrento," she said. His handshake was like a thousand other alpha male bros she'd dealt with in her life; it was like he was trying to crush her fingers in a vise. But Mel's hands had a strength honed over years of twisting open liquor bottles and manipulating her bar tools, so she crushed right back. He winced as the bones of his hand clicked loudly.

"Charmed." He tore his hand away. Mel tried not to smile too smugly. "I have the distinct feeling that we've met before."

"Doubt it," Mel replied. "Unless you've been to Terror & Virtue." As soon as the words left her mouth, she knew that was why he was familiar. He looked like so many other white, middle-aged guests that Mel hadn't remembered him at first.

Now it was coming back to her: single-malt, neat. The priciest bottle they'd had, probably to impress the other guy who'd been with him. Bad tipper.

Unfortunately, Gary Willis made the connection as well. His eyes widened slightly. "That's right. You're one of the bartenders

there, aren't you?" He sounded more overjoyed than the simple rec-
ognition required. "I was there a few nights ago. Very classy place.
Very nice."

"Thanks," Mel said. "I try."

"So what are you up to tonight, Gary?" Bebe asked. "I would have
thought you'd be tucked away in Westchester at this hour." She tipped
her head back and stared above their heads. Mel followed her gaze to
the illuminated sign for the place Gary had just exited: a gentlemen's
club that boasted "three floors of entertainment." Kind of a cliché for
a sleazy lawyer.

"If you must know," he said with a haughty poke of his nose into
the air, "I was having a scotch with a client."

"There's mayo on your jacket." Mel pointed at the stain. It always
felt nice to take a jackass down a peg.

Gary pawed at his suit coat, staring at the offending splotch.
"Lobster sliders," he muttered. Then, more loudly: "It was the lobster
sliders."

"Club soda will get that right out," Bebe chimed in.

Gary cut a glare in her direction. "Never mind my jacket," he
said. "I'd ask what your plans for the evening are, Mrs. Murray, but it
doesn't take a detective, now, does it?" He leered at Mel in a way that
made her skin crawl.

"Lucky for you. Evidence has never been your strong suit." Bebe
threaded her arm through Mel's.

He sputtered for a moment, his white face turning an angry pink.
"Well, enjoy your flavor of the month from atop your high horse. I'm
sure you have a judge or two waiting in the wings?"

Mel sucked in a breath. Fear snaked up her spine. This guy knew
about Bebe's poly lifestyle? That couldn't be good.

Bebe, though, seemed unperturbed, waving a hand with a scoff.
"Please. I have standards." She flicked her gaze up and down his
form. "But if you want to believe I'm sleeping my way through the
system, more power to you. Tell your wife I said hello!" Bebe swept
past him, guiding Mel along with her. "Don't mind him," she whispered into Mel's ear. "He's only cranky because he's representing the

losing side in that class action thing I was telling you about. Well, soon to be losing. And losing big, I promise you."

Mel waited until they'd turned the corner before she spoke. "Is that going to be a problem? That he saw us on a date?"

"Why would it be a problem?" Bebe said breezily.

"I don't know. Can't you get disbarred or whatever if you're caught acting—" She bobbed her head side to side, trying to shake the word loose. "Immoral?"

Bebe stopped in the middle of the sidewalk and laughed, throwing her head back. The streetlights caught her hair and painted the line of her throat gold.

"Mel, if we could be disbarred for having extramarital affairs, there wouldn't be a single practicing lawyer in all of Manhattan. Gary's been cheating on his wives since he was a clerk. That's why he's on his fourth one. He doesn't have a leg to stand on—and neither do the rest of these losers who think they're slick."

"Oh. I guess I thought—there're so many regulations in your field," Mel mumbled. "I was worried I had gotten you in trouble. Like, lost you a case or something."

Bebe took Mel's hands in both of hers, bridging the small gap between them. "Nothing could make me back down from a case, especially not Gary," she said, achingly fond. "Seriously, it's fine. I don't hide the way I live my life. If I did, that would give people like him all the ammunition they need to threaten me. You can't blackmail someone if everything's out in the open."

"I guess that makes sense," Mel said, though the sensation of danger was still wrapped around her like a tourniquet. She glanced down the street, but Gary Willis was out of sight, lost in the steam that seeped from the manhole covers. His grating voice echoed in her head, though. *Flavor of the month.* "He seemed to imply that you lose interest in your dates pretty quickly."

"Even if that were true, there's nothing wrong with that," Bebe said, glancing over at her. The cold wind ruffled her fuzzy pink earmuffs. "But in this case, it's definitely not true."

Mel nodded to herself. "So if you're ever interested in someone new, you'd tell me, right? That's part of the guidelines?"

"Exactly. Same goes for you, don't forget. If anyone ever catches your eye, just let me know. I'd be your biggest cheerleader. I'd give excellent references." Her eyes danced.

Mel laughed. "I'm not in the market, believe me. One plate is plenty to juggle, in my book."

"Never say never, that's my motto." Bebe squeezed against her side. "But hey, don't let Gary rile you up. He's not worth it."

True. It would be a shame if she let one random, unsettling encounter ruin what was shaping up to be a spectacular first date. Mel shook off the feeling of unease and turned up the wattage on her smile. "So where are you taking me, exactly?"

Bebe tugged her along the sidewalk. "This way! It's not much farther."

They walked a few more blocks into a ritzy part of downtown that had been gentrified about three times over in the last decade. Bebe led the way to one of the few remaining buildings that retained a façade from the previous century. "Ever been here?" she asked as they went through the revolving door.

"Can't say I have." Mel's brow arched skyward as they entered the sleek lobby of the Empire Excelsior Hotel. It was like something out of another century. The domed ceiling was covered in frescos, and everywhere you looked, bellhops in tiny red caps pushed brass luggage racks at a fast clip. "I've got to admit," she said, "I did not think you'd take me to a hotel on a first date. Bold move."

Bebe rolled her eyes. "We're not here to get a room." Still holding Mel's hand, she led her through the obstacle course of guests and suitcases.

"What are we doing here, then?"

"You'll see," Bebe said, and pushed open an unmarked door bound in tufted black velvet with a single porthole window.

Bebe's hand slipped out of Mel's to press lightly on the small of her back, guiding her inside.

The Excelsior's bar was dark and decorated in a baroque style similar to the lobby. It was also teeming with the late-night crowd, out-of-towners enjoying their evening in the city. A martini kind of joint. Mel had a lot of respect for hotel bars—they did volume, and she'd worked at enough to know how rough one busy convention weekend could be—but they weren't exactly on her bucket list.

She looked back over her shoulder at Bebe, her mouth pulled into a small frown. "Another bar? One date and we're already in a rut."

"Not for long." Bebe guided her deeper into the room. "Don't worry. I know a guy."

The guy was actually a woman named Ronica. She made a mean Manhattan and was meticulous in her back-up work. Mel knew this because they'd worked together years ago at another hotel bar, a Scandi-inspired place that had since been turned into one of those movie theaters that served food and beer. As Mel and Bebe approached, Ronica looked up from the coupe she was drying, her long lashes fluttering in surprise.

"Mel! It's been a minute." Then she spotted Bebe right behind her. "And Bee! You two know each other? Small world."

"We're actually just getting to know each other, funny enough," Bebe said.

Ronica made an impressed, high sound that had them all laughing. She reached a hand across the bar toward Mel in a gesture of both welcome and congratulations.

"Hey, Ronnie. Christ, it's good to see you." Mel curled her fingers into Ronica's and let them part on a snap. "How've you been?"

Ronica tossed her head to get her short twists out of her eyes. "Been fine. Been fine. Heard you're working at T&V these days."

Mel shrugged. "Yeah, it's okay. How's this place been treating you?" She glanced around, noting the business-class clientele. Ronnie was the only Black person in the room, which, Mel knew from previous conversations with her, was not particularly fun.

"Could be worse." Ronica gave her a knowing look. "Could also be better."

Mel wished she could offer her a heads-up if T&V had any openings, but she wasn't sure if that environment would be much of an improvement. "And how do you know . . . Bee?"

"I met Bebe through some people. Real swinging cats." Ronica winked.

"I tell you, this city is actually the size of a postage stamp when you're poly," Bebe said with a put-upon sigh that was all for show.

Mel whipped her head to Ronica. She'd known her for years and had never suspected Ronnie was anything but monogamous. "Oh, so you're—?"

"Nah, not really." Ronica laughed. "Or, like, under the right circumstances. I dated someone who was for a while."

"Ah. Right. Cool." Mel bobbed her head, feeling foolish. It felt like everyone in Manhattan had more experience with open relationships than she did. Maybe those nine years of marriage had put blinders on her.

She had so much catching up to do.

"So, listen, Ronnie," Bebe said, breaking the chain of Mel's thoughts, "I was hoping, if tonight's not too inconvenient for you . . . ?"

Ronica was already digging a wad of keys out of her pocket. "It's all yours. No one else is using it."

"Using what?" Mel asked, looking between them.

Bebe either didn't hear or was doing a great job of pretending she hadn't. "You're a lifesaver, Angel." She pocketed the jangle of keys and tossed Ronica a wink. Mel wondered if she should be jealous that her date was flirting with someone else right in front of her, but it seemed like Bebe would flirt with a wooden post if the opportunity arose. Mel couldn't find it in herself to be offended. In fact, she was kind of impressed.

Bebe spun on her heel and headed for the gilt elevator bank. Mel followed, her heavy Docs making a racket on the marble floor of the lobby.

"Are we breaking into the Presidential Suite or something?" she asked.

"I told you, we're not here for a room." Bebe pressed the call button and turned to wiggle herself right into Mel's personal space.

Their faces were inches apart. Mel's hands went to Bebe's hips without a second thought. "I'm way more interesting."

"I'm starting to see that," Mel said. Hotel guests and bellhops swirled around them, but she couldn't take her eyes off Bebe, a force of nature with lipstick to match.

The elevator arrived, and Mel allowed herself to be pulled inside. A few other people squeezed in with them, but not before Bebe placed one of Ronnie's keys into a slot in the panel, turned it, and pressed the button labeled *R* that lit up at the very top.

"The roof?" Mel whispered in Bebe's ear once the elevator doors shut. "What's up there?" According to the small brass sign next to the button, the rooftop lounge had closed hours ago and wouldn't open again until the following afternoon.

Bebe twirled the key ring around one finger. "Us, in a few minutes."

Mel wished the elevator wasn't packed with couples from Ohio in that moment. She wanted to kiss the smug look off Bebe's face. Or watch it get smugger. It was a toss-up. She leaned against the mirrored wall and waited patiently for the ride to end.

The Excelsior rooftop was completely deserted. A winter covering of huge glass panels made up a temporary dome that evoked being inside a botanical garden. Various lounge chairs had been stacked in a far corner near a forest of unplugged heat lamps. Only the pool lights were switched on, the underwater glow illuminating the steam coming off the heated surface of the water.

"Okay, this is pretty cool," Mel said.

She wandered around the pool's edge, peering with professional curiosity at the rooftop bar. It was shut down and clean as a whistle. The gleaming surface of its stainless bar top winked in Mel's direction.

Bebe floated to her side. "Hey, you're not thinking of throwing together some drinks for us, are you? You're off the clock, Sweetheart."

Mel laughed. "I couldn't even if I wanted to. Bottles are locked up by now." She gestured to the modern lines of the bar's floating shelves that served as a backdrop. "See? All empty."

"Just as well. I don't need another drink. But I might need a

swim." Bebe sauntered over to the edge of the pool, her boots clicking on the cement of the deck. She stuck her hand in the water and
swirled it around. "It's like bathwater." She gave Mel an impish smile
over her shoulder. Her honey hair shone in the weak light. "What do
you say? Fancy a dip?"

"I don't know." Mel looked around the empty expanse of the roof,
feeling exposed. "You're sure Ronnie won't get in trouble for letting
us up here?"

"It's fine. I've done it a couple times before," Bebe said. Mel
wondered who she'd brought those times, but quickly dismissed the
thought. Who cared when this was so casual? "According to Ronica,
they don't have security cameras up here. The owners are real cheap-
skates."

"Sounds about right." She eyed the pool. Despite the glass enclosure keeping them out of the wind, the air was chilled. The heated
water would probably feel great, but— "I didn't exactly bring a bath-
ing suit," Mel pointed out.

Bebe shrugged. "I'm fine with swimming in my undies if you are."

And with that, she began stripping right there. First her coat,
which she draped over a nearby stack of chairs, then her ankle boots,
which hit the deck with twin thuds. Her wrap blouse had a hidden
clasp at her hip, which Bebe undid expertly. She pulled the green
velvet blouse off, revealing a silky peach bra embroidered with vines.
It looked like its price tag could rival that of a large family sedan. It
also looked about as well-engineered as a sedan, fitting Bebe's ample
tits like a glove.

Mel looked down at her own small breasts. She was absurdly glad
she hadn't gone braless under her shirt like she sometimes did when
she was off the clock, but she worried her plain black bralette would
be boring by comparison. Fuck, it didn't even match her gray boxer
briefs, did it?

Bebe tossed her shirt at Mel, and Mel had to claw her way through
tons of soft velvet instead of worrying about the state of her own
underwear. "Come on," Bebe called, "let's get in the water!"

"Okay. Fine." Mel tossed Bebe's shirt on the stacked lounge

chairs and started unbuckling her belt. "But if we get arrested for this—"

"Don't worry." Bebe turned and looked at Mel over the curve of her creamy shoulder. "I know a great lawyer." And with that, she cannonballed directly into the deep end.

Mel finished shucking off her jeans and boots as Bebe surfaced with a rapturous exhale. Water sluiced off her head and was flung in droplets from the ends of her hair as she tossed it back. She looked even better wet, which was—yeah, this was trouble.

"The water feels amazing!" she called. Her voice echoed in the emptiness of their glass enclosure.

Mel tried not to stare but got tangled in her drapey shirt for a long, frustrating moment. Finally, she stripped down to her very boring, very mismatched underwear and shivered her way over to the pool steps to dip in a single toe. The water was warm compared to the frigid winter air, like Bebe had promised.

"Get in before you freeze to death," Bebe said as she doggy-paddled over. She even made that look sexy somehow. With her hair flowing all around her and her skin flushed, she looked like a Dutch master's painting brought to life. And just as expensive.

Once Mel got into the water up to her chin, she felt good and relaxed. The goose bumps on her limbs were still there, but they were caused less by the cold air and more from anticipation as she swam-walked over toward Bebe. Mel took a big breath and ducked her head below the surface, letting her buzzed hair get wet. When she resurfaced and opened her eyes, she found Bebe staring at her—her arms, specifically, which were raised to rub the water off her head. Mel took a moment to bask in the attention. She'd always thought of her arms as her best feature, well-toned and covered in a celebration of ink. It was nice to be reminded of it.

"Wow." Bebe's eyes ran over Mel's clavicle and down her right arm, tracing the lines of her intricate sleeve. "That is gorgeous work."

"Thanks." Mel rotated her arm so Bebe could see the brightly colored citrus fruits that encircled her biceps. She'd gone for a cocktail-inspired sleeve once she'd had the money to do a larger piece. "My guy did a good job."

"If I didn't already know you were devoted to your craft, this would tell me the whole story. Look at that, berries and cherries and—oh, I love the way the ice holds all those tiny reflections." She floated closer, nodding at Mel's arm. "May I?"

Mel didn't hesitate for a second. "Sure. Here." She held out her arm and allowed Bebe's fingers to touch her slick skin.

She prodded at a juicy wheel of lime, then ran her fingertips along the cascade of cocktail makings, ending with the Nick and Nora glass inked on her forearm. "I've always admired tattoos," Bebe said, "but I could never think of anything I would want for myself permanently. Classic indecision, you know." She grinned at Mel. "And I'm also terrified of needles."

Mel laughed at that. "You don't strike me as the kind of person who's terrified of anything."

"I'm scared of lots of things. Needles. Spiders. Not knowing if the dog is going to die at the end."

"That's . . . a very specific fear."

"Some of us never got over *Where the Red Fern Grows*, all right?" She smiled that nose-scrunching smile of hers and let her touch linger for one more moment at Mel's wrist before letting her hand fall away into the water. "I'm glad you came here with me," she said.

"I'm glad, too." And it was true, not some pat nicety. She ran her tongue over her teeth, tasting the thrill of it. "Really glad," she added.

Bebe's smile turned mischievous then. She moved backward in the water until the bottom fell away and her feet were left kicking. She lifted a dripping hand from the water and beckoned Mel with one finger.

Mel paddled toward her, the swirl of water around her body tickling at her ribs. She floated closer until they were face-to-face, then nose to nose. She pushed and Bebe went easily, no resistance until Mel had her backed up right against the metal pool ladder that rose from the deep end. Bebe reached behind herself and grabbed hold of the ladder's bars, sitting on one of the rungs. Her hair, dark with water, was plastered to her skin. Mel picked a slick strand from where it had curled on the swell of her breast and heard the sweet hitch of Bebe's gasp.

"You're the most gorgeous thing," Mel murmured.

Bebe's white teeth bit into her plump red lower lip. "I'm aware," she said.

Of course she was.

Blood pumped through Mel's body. Everything with Bebe was so hot and wet and visceral. It made Mel feel powerful to be on the verge of kissing a woman as sexy, as self-assured as Bebe. The excitement of their bodies pressing together, half in the water, half exposed to the air. The thrill of knowing they were doing something that could get them in a lot of trouble—on multiple levels, actually, if this whole poly thing ended up being more drama than it was worth—but they were going to do it anyway. Because Bebe was tipping her face closer and closer to Mel's, because Bebe was making the most delicious low whine of want, because Bebe wanted her as much as she wanted Bebe.

Their mouths met in a messy crash that made Mel's pulse spike. Bebe was as soft and open here as the rest of her, plush lips parting in invitation, her tongue like velvet against Mel's. Mel groaned, reaching for handfuls of Bebe's hips and holding on tight.

Their lips parted with a slick pop. Bebe looked at her with mischief in her eyes. "Any interest in taking this onto dry land?" she asked. "Chlorinated water is not the sexiest fluid in the universe."

"Good idea," Mel said, dipping in to steal another kiss. The sound of her own voice was alien, all gravel and greed.

Bebe smiled into the kiss. Despite the mutual decision, they remained where they were for long minutes more. Mel couldn't help herself; she never wanted to stop kissing this woman.

Maybe Bebe's pet theory was right. Mel could be a little selfish. In the right circumstances.

Her hands wandered over Bebe's skin, finding the shelf of her soft hips, moving along her ribs—ticklish, if the high squeak she made into Mel's mouth was any indication—then farther upward until she was palming her heavy breasts through the wet silk of her bra.

"You can take it off," Bebe said, her breath coming in gasps. Her eyes were glassy when they found Mel's. "You can be a little mean, too. If you like."

Mel's fingers were already scrabbling for the catch behind Bebe's back. "What's 'a little mean,' uh, mean?" It seemed polite to ask. What had Bebe said at Sal's earlier? Something about making sure expectations were aligned?

Bebe licked her lips, and whether it was calculated to drive Mel insane or just an unconscious move, it had the same effect either way. "Take what you want. Objectify me. It's all good." She leaned forward the scant inch needed to take Mel's bottom lip between her teeth and give it a quick nibble. "Ooh, maybe tell me I'm bad. That could be fun."

"I'm not great at dirty talk," Mel said. "I mean, I've never really tried it."

Bebe took this cheerfully. "Well, this is the perfect time to give it a whirl. I'm a great audience." She pressed closer to Mel, her back arching off the ladder's slats.

That gave Mel's fingers enough room to complete the job on her bra. Mel peeled away the soaked peach fabric from Bebe's skin and placed it carefully on the edge of the pool deck. "Is that so?"

Bebe hummed in assent. "I can hear all sorts of wild shit and not bat an eye. I definitely won't laugh." Her words turned into a gasp as Mel mouthed along the velvet slope of her tits. "Or, if I do, it'll be because I'm so impressed with your foul-mouthed skills."

Mel considered this as she teased one of Bebe's nipples with the edge of her teeth. Couldn't hurt to try something new. That was what this whole experiment with Bebe was about, right?

She ran her tongue over the reddened nib, letting the tip of her barbell tongue piercing drag against Bebe's flesh. "My mouth can do fouler things than talk," she promised.

Bebe made an approving sound high in her throat.

They got out of the pool via a combination of fumbling and chaotic determination, the both of them dripping wet. Mel wriggled out of her thin bralette, then wrapped Bebe in her arms so they could keep kissing. The air of the domed rooftop was cold compared to the warm pool, but Mel felt like she was on fire. She could barely believe she was doing this—about to have semipublic sex on a first date. It wasn't like her. It wasn't like anything she'd ever done.

Maybe, for a few brief minutes, she could pretend to be someone else. Reckless and needful.

She spun Bebe around and clasped her hands to her soft shoulders. Bebe gave a breathless *oh* of surprise as she found herself facing forward, her back leaning against the line of Mel's whipcord body. The curve of her backside pressed into the bowl of Mel's hips like a temptation. "So you like doing it from behind?" she asked with a light laugh.

Mel made a noise that she could only classify as a growl. She dipped her head to kiss the back of Bebe's neck, nosing aside her wet hair to reach skin. Bebe went pliant in her arms with a faint whimper.

Mel dragged her lips up to the shell of Bebe's ear. "You're trouble," she said right into it. She could feel Bebe shiver through every inch of her plush body.

"I can't help what I am," Bebe said, teasing.

The stainless steel, all-weather bar was only a few yards away. The barstools were simple, a flat seat of metal. Mel eyed the setup, doing some quick math, then began frog-marching Bebe in that direction.

"Up you get," Mel said, and bullied Bebe against the bar. "I have an idea."

"Oh my." Bebe breathed a little heavier. She placed one knee on the closest stool. Mel put one hand on Bebe's bare, damp back, right between her shoulder blades and gave a gentle push, but Bebe resisted bending over the bar. She turned her head and smiled at Mel over her shoulder. "Wait a minute, what do I get if I go along with this tawdry little idea of yours?" Her hips wiggled side to side as she backed her plump ass right against Mel.

Being mean was not just allowed. It was clearly encouraged.

Mel swatted Bebe's enticing bottom. Bebe arched her back on a gasp, facing forward once more. She folded at the waist so that her upper body was laid across the bar like a particularly interesting menu. Her legs were splayed with one knee still on the high stool, the toes of her other foot curling in midair.

"You get what I give you," Mel said in a stranger's voice, "which is nothing if you're not good."

Bebe pressed her cheek to the bar top. Her hot breath made a damp spot on the cool metal a few inches from her lips. "But we've already established I'm trouble," Bebe argued. "I'm not given to being good."

Mel smacked her ass again, though this time she let her hand stay on the round curve, rubbing over the soaked fabric possessively. "You're going to have to try," she said. She hooked her fingers into Bebe's panties and played with the silk, tugging experimentally this way and that. For a second, she thought about taking them off entirely, but it made Bebe look more naked somehow to be left wearing that tiny scrap of clothing.

"You make a c-compelling argument." The shake in Bebe's voice, the breathlessness—it had Mel's pulse racing. Even though the threats and teases were nothing more than pretend, the effect was very real. "I'll be good," Bebe said, and pressed herself onto the bar top.

Mel took a moment to admire the line of her back, the way her legs trembled. She pulled the gusset of Bebe's panties to one side and enjoyed the view there as well. Her sweet little cunt was flushed pink and was shiny with slick. Mel wanted to taste her so badly. Then she remembered there was nothing stopping her.

She braced her hands on Bebe's thighs, nudging them wider. The bar was the perfect height, as Mel had so expertly calculated.

The first touch of her tongue was tentative, a light brush against the folds there. Bebe jolted against the bar with a cry and Mel's confidence gathered strength. She dove in and licked with no mercy. Bebe was delicious, earthy and hot on Mel's tongue. Sweat was beading on the delicate skin of her inner thighs despite the cold air, and Mel tasted that, too, craving the salt. Bebe made an unhappy whine at that, wriggling in an effort to get Mel's mouth back where she needed it most.

Mel bit into the flesh of her thigh. Not too hard, but hard enough to make Bebe gasp and freeze, save for her shivers. "Stay still," Mel murmured while she licked at the red marks left by her teeth. Her tongue piercing dragged over Bebe's skin, smoothing and teasing in equal measure.

"I'm *trying*." Bebe was not trying one bit. Bebe was, in fact, still moving her hips in that hypnotic way she had. Like she needed to be touched more than she needed air.

"Not hard enough." Mel drew two fingers, middle and pointer, along the seam of her cunt, up and down, up and down, collecting the slick wetness on her fingertips. She would normally take this part slowly; despite the pantomime they had going, Mel didn't want to hurt Bebe even a little. But all plans for caution went out the window when Bebe thrust back against her hand with a low moan.

"Yes, yes, give me those hands," she said. Her forehead was pressed against the bar so that she was speaking into the surface of it, but Mel could hear her clear as day. "Your hands—oh my god, please."

"Greedy." Mel spanked her thigh, right where the bite mark was already fading. The clap of her palm on flesh echoed across the rooftop. Bebe shook and made a noise so obscene, Mel wished she could bottle it. Instead she thrust her two soaked fingers into Bebe so she could hear it again.

"I *know*," Bebe said between heaving breaths. "I'm greedy, I can't help it." She turned her head so her cheek was pressed to the bar once more. Mel could see her mouth, open and panting, lipstick somehow still perfectly in place. Her hips, though, were another matter, continuously rebelling and pushing back so she could fuck herself on Mel's fingers.

Mel circled her thumb over Bebe's hard nub of a clit, making it as wet as the rest of her. "You're a brat, is what you are." Bebe fluttered around her hand at that, all of her reacting at once, bodily and vocally. Mel was shocked by the force of it, but recovered well enough to sound smug instead of awe-inspired. "You like that? You like being a little brat?"

Bebe nodded frantically. Her lips opened in a wide, silent O. It was intoxicating, seeing someone as smart-mouthed as Bebe lose all her words.

Maybe Mel was better at this stuff than she thought.

She crowded up against Bebe and leaned over her naked back so she could put her mouth right against her ear. Her hand picked up speed, fingers thrusting faster. "You done being difficult? You going to be good for me?" More nodding and abortive movements, but Mel used the weight of her body atop Bebe's to keep her still. "Be good and come for me."

For once, Bebe did as she was told. Her whole body went haywire under Mel, arms curling under her chest, legs flailing, head snapping back. Mel avoided getting hit in the nose at the last second, pulling herself upright to watch Bebe writhe through her orgasm. Her fingers and thumb worked her through it, massaging single-mindedly while Bebe cried out. Finally, the throbbing around Mel's fingers subsided, and Bebe lay boneless on the bar, gasping for air.

Gently, Mel slipped her fingers from the clench of Bebe's body. Mel's gaze wandered over her, and she smiled as she caught sight of Bebe's toes trying and failing to find purchase on the ground before giving up and hanging there limply.

The back of Bebe's thigh was too much for Mel to handle. Working on instinct, she shucked her wet boxer briefs down her legs and stepped out of them, not wanting to get hamstrung at an inopportune moment. She took Bebe's now-still hips in her hands and pressed herself up against Bebe's leg. Bebe, for her part, sighed happily.

"There you go," Mel said. "You relax and let me do what I want."

Bebe opened her eyes to the narrowest of slits and looked back at Mel. A small smile flirted at her lips. "Go ahead," she said. "Not like I could stop you in the state I'm in."

That fired up something primal and snarling in Mel's brain. She rubbed herself along the warm, damp skin of Bebe's thigh, humping like a teenager, like an animal. She'd been so focused on Bebe, she hadn't realized how turned on she was herself. Mel could feel a drip of fluid trailing down her own inner leg. It felt so good, grinding her clit against Bebe, leaving her skin all slick and fragrant. She was a different person like this; she was on a totally different planet.

She didn't expect to finish—it took a lot, sometimes—so when it happened, it hit Mel out of nowhere. Her fingers dug into Bebe's soft hips, the center of her fucking hard against that velvet skin, coming in waves. Somewhere in there, she was pretty sure she laughed. Not surprising, given how ridiculous the whole thing was. Who fucked on a roof on the first date? *Me, that's who*, Mel thought to herself with something like pride.

She braced one arm at the lip on the bar and tried to catch her breath. "That . . . ," she said, and then couldn't imagine saying anything that could encompass the whole thing.

Bebe turned over on her back with a groan. "I know," she said, still sounding winded.

Lucky for them, the pool had an outdoor shower meant for rinsing off before and after swimming. Once they could stand on their own power, Mel helped Bebe up and led her over to it. They took turns sluicing off sweat and other stickiness under the freezing spray, shrieking at the chill. Bebe flicked cold water at Mel, and Mel grabbed up her hands, and then they were both under the cold stream, kissing each other with teeth.

"You're as hot as a furnace," Bebe said into Mel's mouth. "With you here, I could stand this for hours." One of her knees buckled then, but she was saved from taking a fall by clinging to Mel's arms. "Well, shit." She laughed at herself. "Guess I should sit down. I'm still like jelly."

It was all Mel could do not to preen.

They helped themselves to some fluffy hotel towels before Mel led Bebe to a lounge chair, insisting on giving her an arm to lean on. "Such a princess," she muttered fondly as she laid her out on the clean white canvas.

"Give me a few minutes to catch my breath," Bebe said with a wrist thrown across her forehead, "and I'll be right back to my usual self."

"No rush." Mel left her soaked underthings where they sat on the pool deck and instead pulled on her dry jeans and shirt. "I have business to attend to, anyway."

"What do you mean?" Bebe took her arm from her forehead and sat up a little, watching Mel move behind the bar. "I thought you said the liquor was locked up."

"It is." Mel rummaged beneath the bar, looking for— "Aha!" She stood with the spray bottle of industrial-strength cleaner in her hand, brandishing it like a weapon. "Can't leave this place in the state it's in. We bartenders have a code."

Bebe's nose wrinkled. "Does the code state that you must clean up after yourself if and when you fuck on someone else's bar? Because that's a pretty specific code." She got up and grabbed a few fluffy white towels from the cabana and wrapped herself in them, warding off the cold.

Mel spritzed down the bar top and began wiping it off with a clean rag she'd located in a neat stack. "It's implied." She scrubbed at a particularly lurid smear until it disappeared into the scent of lemon and pine. "What kind of professional would I be if I didn't sanitize this for the next shift? I wouldn't be able to live with myself."

Bebe laughed, stretching in her towel cocoon. "See, this is why I like you. Come here." She opened her arms and beckoned Mel with a flap of her fingers. "I'm getting cold again. I need my radiator."

Mel smirked, tossing the rag into a nearby bucket. "You could also get dressed."

Bebe dismissed this idea with a huff. "Nonsense. I demand at least three minutes of cuddles." She flapped her fingers again.

Mel rolled her eyes but still shuffled over to the lounge chair. Bebe scooted over to give her a sliver of room, and somehow they managed to both fit on the damn thing by wrapping their limbs around each other like sweaty squids.

It would be easy to fall for this woman, Mel knew. It was dangerous, how easy it could be. Good thing Mel was keeping her eye on the ball. Not letting anything get out of hand. As untethered as she was.

She pressed a kiss to the top of Bebe's head and held her closer.

CHAPTER 9

Dating casually was easy. All Mel had to do was pretend to be a completely different person forever.

Not that dating Bebe was a chore. They went to interesting restaurants that Bebe seemed to sniff out like a bloodhound; they went on long walks along the East River when the weather cooperated; they told each other about how work was going and laughed at each other's funny stories. And the sex—Mel really looked forward to that. It was like a part of her had been unlocked, and every hour spent in bed with Bebe gave her another chance to indulge in it. Bebe didn't complain that all their dates ended with them sleeping together—and in fact was very vocal about how much she enjoyed herself, both during and after—so Mel didn't feel too bad about it.

Still, it didn't feel natural. Not to Mel, who had only been with one other person in her entire life. And they'd been serious from the jump. Mel was fighting every instinct she had to treat Bebe the same way.

She was chewing on the rising discomfort as she came home from yet another date with Bebe. It was a Monday, which meant Mel wasn't working. Neither was Daniel, and she found him sprawled on the sofa in pajamas watching *Casablanca*.

"Weren't you supposed to hang with Jackson today?" she asked as she locked the door.

"He got called in to cover for someone. Sad trombone." Jackson worked at a white-tablecloth mainstay up in Midtown. Daniel ate a palmful of popcorn, not taking his eyes off Bogart's flashback. "You're not sleeping over at Bebe's tonight?"

Mel had done that a couple Mondays in a row. And Sundays. And they had been wonderful sleepovers with the condo all to themselves. (Kade had made themself scarce and was, Mel assumed, staying with another partner.) But tonight . . .

"Nah," she said, hanging up her coat. "I don't want to get too comfortable, you know?" She made her way to the sofa and waited for Daniel to lift his legs so she could sit down.

His legs settled heavy across her thighs. "What do you mean? I thought things were going well with her."

Mel snorted and stole a handful of his popcorn. "They are. Too well." Bebe was—so chill. If Mel wanted to meet for lunch because it was the only free time she had that week, Bebe said yes. If Mel wanted to sleep over in Bebe's huge, amazing bed, Bebe said yes. If Mel wanted to fuck against those huge plate-glass windows in Bebe's condo to see what this exhibitionism thing was about—

Well. She'd definitely said yes to that. Multiple times.

Mel shook herself. "We've got a good arrangement going," she said. "I don't want it to change."

Daniel paused the movie so that Rick and Louis were frozen in the middle of witty repartee. He turned his head to grin at her. "Mel. Do you . . . *like*-like this woman?"

Mel crossed her arms over her chest, resting them atop Daniel's shins. "Don't be so juvenile."

"You're the one turning down a sleepover at Casa Bebe because you're afraid of catching feelings."

"I am not catching—!"

"Like you always do," he added with a nail-in-the-coffin sort of finality.

Mel felt her teeth grinding. She hated being a stereotype, but what else could you call a lesbian who married the first woman she'd ever slept with? Dating someone at seventeen and marrying them at twenty-two had been a bad idea in hindsight. Mel knew she should have waited; should have done a lot more growing up before settling down. But even as a little kid, Mel had pictured herself as an all-in, always-and-forever, till-death, etc., kind of person. At the time, she'd thought marriage was as aspirational as it was inevitable.

Now? "I've got bigger fish to fry," she informed Daniel, taking another fistful of popcorn as recompense for his jab. "The competition, for one."

Daniel munched on more popcorn, too. "Have you heard back about your application?"

"No, not yet. But I'm going to assume I'm in and work on my cocktail in the meantime. Hopefully that will give me an extra edge." She made a face. "I need all the help I can get after that Marinara Mary." The pizza-flavored Bloody Mary she'd concocted for Daniel last week had not been her best work. Herby tomato/vodka sauce in a glass? Way too muddled, and not in the fun way.

"Come on, it wasn't that bad. I still think you could shove a garlic knot garnish on that thing and call it a day." Daniel mimed taking a photo with an invisible phone. "Very 'grammable."

Mel pretended to gag. "I'd rather drink broken glass than have *that* be the reason I win. Play the damn movie."

They watched the last half of *Casablanca*, Daniel falling asleep before the airport scene like he always did.

The next day, Mel left early for her shift, eager to try out some ideas she'd jotted down in her ratty notebook. She'd been thinking about fat-washing some bourbon (which was just a fancy way of infusing a spirit with something oily) and was wondering if apples would be the right way to introduce fruity notes. Plenty of the contestants were probably going to do some play on the Big Apple, in keeping with the New York theme, so Mel was determined to do something different to set her drink apart. The two thoughts collided in her head while she was walking to T&V: apple butter.

It was a play on words, since real apple butter didn't have any fat, but that didn't mean Mel couldn't make a compound butter with the requisite apples, brown sugar, and spices and use that for her fat-wash. She quickened her pace, dodging slow walkers and tiny dogs so she could get to work.

Terror & Virtue boasted top-of-the-line equipment in the back for making all kinds of cocktail ingredients, which was a real blessing. The blast chiller could work its magic on the bourbon in under two hours instead of the twenty-four-plus it would take for a normal freezer. Mel was able to stew some apples, make the compound butter, brown it, mix it with the bourbon, and get it separated before the rest of the staff showed up for the evening shift. She was in the middle of straining the mixture off when Daniel appeared in the back, shucking his coat.

"Whoa." He stopped in his tracks instead of heading for his locker. "What is that? It smells like an orchard in here."

"Taste this," Mel ordered, pouring out a small dram of the finished bourbon. "Tell me what you think." She held out the measure for him.

Daniel took it, gave it an appreciative sniff, and sipped at the amber liquid. "Oh my god." He stared down into the glass.

Mel watched his face nervously. "Oh my god, good? Oh my god, bad?"

"Oh my god, you could serve this to the judges with a fucking *straw* and nothing else." He took another sip, downing the remainder and surfacing with a satisfied *ahhhh*. "You know me, I'm a piña colada girlie, not a whiskey drinker—but this is amazing."

Mel felt her lips stretching into a wide smile. "Thanks, but I don't think I can get away with serving bourbon neat at Food Fest. It'll just be one component of the drink."

"Are you sure? Because I think she's perfect as is." Daniel held out his empty glass and waggled it in the universal gesture for *refill, please*.

"Sorry, bud, I need to save the rest of her for more tests." Mel capped the bottle and wrote out a label that said MEL'S APPLE THING—DO NOT TOUCH. Her mind was already awhirl with possibilities. She could use the bourbon in an old-fashioned, something that screamed Central Park in the autumn. Warm and spicy and crisp. Damn, Mel couldn't wait until she saw Bebe again so she could tell her about it. She was going to be all over it.

Mel paused in the middle of placing the handwritten label on the face of the bottle. Shit. That was not the reaction of a chill person having no-strings-attached sex with their—not-girlfriend. That was the reaction of a very unchill person who was chomping at the bit to show their not-girlfriend the cool thing they'd made.

"Hey," Daniel said, startling her from her reverie, "you okay?"

"Yeah. Fine. Just . . . thinking." Mel gave him a weak smile.

"Well, don't let me stop you." He unwound his scarf and headed for the bank of lockers, calling over his shoulder as he went, "If you keep this up, you're a shoo-in for that prize money."

Right. The competition. The money. That's what mattered, not her fling with Bebe. Mel finished smoothing the label on the bourbon. She needed to focus. Bebe was like training wheels. Mel could practice dating someone, sleeping with someone, sharing meals and walks and laughs with someone—while not falling in love. As long as she did that, she'd be fine.

CHAPTER 10

Sometimes, Bebe made it very difficult not to love her.

Take now, for example. It was another Monday night, their usual date night. They were having dinner at some old-school red-sauce joint complete with fresh mozzarella made in-house and cranky waiters who barked to each other in Italian. Bebe was listening intently as Mel yammered on about nascent ideas she had for the cocktail competition.

"So there's kind of a Wall Street boardroom thing going on there that might be fun to play with in a whiskey drink. Except I don't want it to be super spirit-forward. Accessible, right? Something T&V would never put on their menu because we 'want to attract a certain clientele.' I want people who wouldn't normally drink bourbon to try it and say, 'Damn, that's a good drink!' And if T&V won't let me do it at work, I'll do it for this weird contest." Mel gestured wildly with her fork to underscore her point.

Bebe's eyes flicked down to her chest. "Oh, Sweetheart, you've got something on you." She pointed to the blob of marinara on Mel's heather-gray shirt.

"Ah, shit." Mel put down her saucy fork and picked at the stain. "Every time."

"Not to worry." Bebe produced a Tide pen from her purse with a triumphant cry. "*I* always come prepared." She leaned over the table and scribbled the tip of the pen across the stain, right over Mel's sternum. The tip of her tongue poked out of the corner of her mouth as she concentrated. "Almost . . . there. All gone." She capped the pen and smiled, still leaning close.

Mel had no choice but to kiss her right in front of a busboy.

Afterward, they strode down a Chelsea avenue arm in arm, their breath misting in the air. "Where to now?" Mel asked. They'd been taking turns choosing date-night activities, and tonight was all Bebe.

"That depends," Bebe said. Her arm squeezed Mel's in the crook of her elbow. "We can hop on the subway and go back to my place . . ."

"Love your place," Mel said, then bit her tongue. She had to stop using the L-word for every damn thing. It was starting to look suspicious. "It's very convenient." Great save.

Bebe kept talking like she hadn't heard Mel, though she gave her a sly sideways glance. "Or we could go to your place . . ."

"That is also a great place." They'd had two sleepovers at Mel's apartment so far, and Mel was getting better at hosting. She'd even bought real hand soap for the bathroom instead of her usual move: filling the old dispenser with water, swishing it around, and praying for the best.

"Orrrrrrr . . ." Bebe drew out the word like a purr. "We could go look at some art. Any interest?"

Mel tried not to make a face, but she couldn't help it. She screwed her mouth to one side. "It's hard to beat going back to my place. Or yours." She paused. "What kind of art are we talking about?"

"Kade's," Bebe said.

"Oh." Mel was getting used to the fact that Kade was not some uncredited bit player in Bebe's life. In the beginning, she had tried to forget the fact that she was dating a married woman, but Kade was as much a part of Bebe's life as her job or her jokes or her opinions on restaurants. It was impossible to expect their name to be completely excised from conversation. Still, Mel wasn't sure how to act when they came up, and she certainly didn't know if viewing their art was an appropriate date idea. "So it's, like, on display somewhere?"

"Yep," Bebe said. "At a gallery not far from here. Tonight's the opening night, and I thought, you know." A shrug. "Free drinks if nothing else."

"Hold on." Mel stopped in the middle of the sidewalk to goggle at her. Bebe had to stop, too, since their arms were linked. "Your wife is having a gallery opening tonight? And you're on a date with me instead?"

Bebe waved her free hand airily. "I've been to dozens of their opening nights and I'll probably attend a hundred more. Kade doesn't need me at every single one, honestly." She caught Mel's doubtful look and elaborated: "We've spoken about it. They genuinely don't mind. They're always overwhelmed with people they need to talk to at these things, so it's not like they'd have much time for me, anyway. You don't have a lot of free nights, so when we were scheduling this date, Kade told me to go ahead."

Mel frowned. "I can't imagine being married and not having my wife at an important event like that."

"Well, you're not Kade," Bebe pointed out.

Mel's brow bounced upward. "That is very true." She couldn't think of anyone she was less like than the aloof artist.

Bebe shrugged. "Look, I thought you might find it interesting, but if you'd rather not go, that's fine. There's always my place. Or yours." She swayed closer, their hands joined together between them, breath misting in the cold.

Mel stole a quick kiss, then bit her lip in thought. She felt kind of guilty for taking Bebe away from Kade's opening night, even accidentally. On the other hand, extending her date with Bebe into Kade's domain felt like the kind of thing you'd do if you were serious about integrating yourself into someone's life. Decidedly un-casual.

She was overthinking this. Kade was Mel's metamour—the paramour of her paramour, a word that Daniel had gleefully taught her—and she should have at least a civil relationship with them. And their art was fucking cool, so why not drop in? Might earn her some brownie points with Bebe, show how chill she could be about worlds colliding.

"Or we could go back to my place *after* we look at some art," Mel said in what she hoped was a smooth way.

Bebe squealed in delight but managed to muffle most of it in the thick scarf around her neck. "That sounds perfect. Come on, it's this way." She tugged Mel by the hand down a narrow street.

Mel was only familiar with art galleries from her time as a freelance events bartender. It was customary for a gallery opening to have an open bar—usually very brief and very cheap, but the temptation of free sauvignon blanc and vodka sodas was enough to get asses in proverbial seats. People would stare at the ugliest paintings in the world as long as they had a complimentary drink, in Mel's experience.

The gallery Bebe led her to was much like the ones Mel had worked at in the past: glass storefront, white walls, and a lot of people milling around with plastic cups clutched in their hands. Mel held the door open for Bebe, and together they entered the warm, crowded space. A kid wearing a black vest with a *he/him* pin took their coats and hung them on a rolling rack that served as coat check. There was a small table set up in a corner with a beleaguered bartender slinging drinks to patrons five deep.

"Do you want something?" Bebe asked, indicating the long, messy line of people waiting.

Mel grimaced at the selection of middling wine lined up at the table's edge. "I'd rather sip on my own spit," she muttered. Then, realizing that was probably not the classiest thing to say on a date: "Uh, I mean—if you're going to have one, sure."

But Bebe was already cracking up, her smile wide enough that her polite fan of a hand couldn't cover it. "I hear they do a great cup of saliva here, actually," she managed to say between giggles. "I take it you have experience with these open bars?"

"Yeah, from the other side of the rail. Not my favorite era." She grimaced. "Sorry, I can turn off the bitchiness, I promise."

"Are you kidding? Why would I want that?" Bebe turned her head to check out the room, which gave Mel a chance to hopefully get over her blushing without being seen. "I think we should start over here," Bebe said, pointing at a wall and using her free hand to hold Mel's. "Work our way through the exhibit chronologically."

Mel craned her neck to try to spot a head of red hair in the crowd, but she couldn't get a fix on it. "You don't want to say hi to Kade first?"

"Nah," Bebe said, leading her confidently through the room. "They'll have their hands full with schmoozers. We'll find them when we find them." She paused in front of the first frame, a small square only slightly larger than a cocktail napkin.

It was a sketch of what might have been a round area rug. Or a pizza. Mel tipped her head to the side and squinted at it. She felt completely out of her depth. It was hard to appreciate something when she didn't know what it was supposed to be. She read the tiny white card pinned to the wall next to it, but it was no help. The title was *Hers*, and it was a print from a copperplate etching, whatever that meant, made this year.

"You know," Bebe whispered in her ear, "I didn't get this stuff at all. Not at first."

Mel turned her head. "Really?" Bebe seemed so cosmopolitan, so put-together. "I kind of assumed you must have been born with an innate understanding of, I don't know, all the postmodern artists and their seminal works."

Bebe laughed. "No, I was born with an innate understanding of the Comstock Laws. Art came later." She faced the etching again, smiling faintly. "Kade was very patient with me. They explained it in a way I could understand."

Mel looked back at the tiny picture. "Mind passing along the info? Or is it top secret?"

Bebe laughed. "Not secret in the least. Look." She pointed at the picture. "See how the lines are a little janky? That's because Kade didn't draw this directly onto paper. It's a print. They took a piece of copperplate and coated it with this—I don't remember what it was called, exactly. Black stuff."

"Black stuff." Mel nodded sagely. "The professional term."

Bebe grinned. "Then they scratched this design into it. Did you ever do crayon art as a kid where you layered a bunch of colors over each other, then used the end of a paper clip to scratch a picture into it?" She pretended to scratch with an imaginary tool.

"Yeah," Mel said slowly. The distant memory from elementary school came flooding back. "I'd always do a black layer on top. It made it look cool, like rainbows underneath."

"Same principle. Except then Kade takes the plate and gives it an acid bath."

"Definitely didn't have access to acid baths in first grade."

"Pity. The acid eats away at the copper that's been exposed, and Kade's left with essentially a stamp. They can ink the stamp and make prints like this one." She indicated the artwork with a little twirl of her hand. "What we're looking at is the product of all that work, not the work itself. They are intentionally showing us the print without its matching plate." Her face softened as she regarded the etching, her head cocked to the side. Mel was transfixed by her and it in equal measure. "It's the culmination. The child, not the parent. The parent is somewhere else, invisible to us."

"Hers," Mel said, finally understanding. She looked at the etching again, now that she had some background clues. The roundness of it could have been a belly or a breast. "Is Kade's mother—?"

"They're estranged," Bebe said, quiet and a little angry.

"Literally not in the picture." Mel felt that with her whole self, thinking of her own parents over in Jersey. The tiny cocktail napkin of a drawing seemed larger now. It encompassed a feeling so complicated, so huge, Mel could easily see herself in it. "Is all art this good once you learn a thing or two about it?"

"No," Bebe said in a lighter voice. "Some of it gets worse."

They shared a laugh, Mel's hand seeking Bebe's. Their fingers twined together and squeezed. They might have stayed there in front of the print the whole night, delighted with each other, but a loud bang from the other side of the gallery interrupted the moment.

Mel looked over at the bartending station and saw the staff member rushing to grab a bottle of red wine that had fallen onto the floor. It hadn't shattered, thank god, but there didn't seem to be enough paper towels in the world to stem the tide of cheap merlot. The staffer looked overwhelmed, eyes puffy and red, lower lip trembling, frantically mopping up the mess on their hands and knees. She was young, no more than twenty-three, with a blunt blond bob and a *she/her* pronoun pin on her black vest.

"Oh, goodness," Bebe whispered, full of sympathy. "Poor kid."

Mel's heart twinged. That had been her, ten years ago: overworked, underpaid (in some instances, totally *un*paid), tired, hungry, and on the verge of having a nervous breakdown because her life was a mess and so was her station. Someone had to give the kid a hand.

Ah hell, Mel thought.

She looked at Bebe, already cursing herself for what she was about to do. "I'm really sorry about this, but can I press pause on our date? Just for a few minutes? I'm having a great time, but—" She gestured helplessly at the red wine mess.

Bebe blinked. "Oh!" She tucked her lips in and nodded sharply. "Yes, of course. Go ahead."

Mel let out a relieved breath. "Thanks." She pressed a quick kiss to Bebe's knuckles before letting go and approaching the disaster zone. Dozens of guests were standing around the bar, vulturelike, unwilling to give up on their free drink even though the bartender was clearly in crisis.

"Hey." Mel went to one knee next to the wine puddle and gently took the roll of paper towels from the bartender's shaking hands. "What's your name?"

"What? Uh. Dahlia," she said, sniffing.

"Dahlia, I'm Mel. Here's what's going to happen: we're going to get this cleaned up, then you're going to take a twenty-minute break. Get some air, walk around the block, whatever it takes to calm down.

I'll cover for you, okay?" She mopped up more merlot and stuffed the soaked paper towels in the small trash can hidden beneath the bar.

"Huh? But—" Dahlia's eyes filled with more tears. "Sorry, I'm fine. Really."

"You're not fine," Mel said. "You're dead on your feet. You probably worked a wedding or some bullshit earlier today, then had to run over here to set up all on your own, right? Because the events company you freelance for is run by morons who are always short-staffed."

One tear ran down Dahlia's cheek. "I haven't even had time to eat anything today," she whispered.

Mel shook her head. This fucking business. Sometimes she couldn't stand it. "Seriously, go. Take the twenty." She finished cleaning up the last of the wine. "I can handle things while you're gone."

"I don't think I'm allowed to do that," Dahlia said. "I'm not supposed to leave the setup unattended—or, like, with a stranger."

"What's the worst that can happen? I make off with thirty bucks of shitty wine while you're gone? I steal the"—Mel glanced at the sad jar on the bar top—"two dollars and change you got in tips? Trust me, your boss isn't here, and no one's going to tattle on you."

Mel could see the wheels turning behind Dahlia's red-rimmed eyes, the calculus of the exhausted. "Okay," she said. "Just twenty minutes, though."

Mel stood and offered her a hand in rising. "Take however long you need."

Now the kid really looked like she was going to start sobbing and never stop. Another tear rolled down her face, hurriedly wiped away. "Thank you? I don't know what to—"

"Don't say anything. Beat it." Mel shooed her toward the door and then took her place behind the makeshift bar. One quick glance at her wares—ugh, even worse than she'd imagined—and then she pointed at the guest closest to the front. "Red or white?" she barked.

The crowd pressed closer, growing now that some of the people who'd had the decency not to loom while Dahlia was flailing came back. Mel lost herself in the act of pouring scant measures of wine into clear plastic cups over and over again. A couple bills found their way into the tip jar, which Mel acknowledged with a grin, knowing they'd all be Dahlia's at the end of the night.

After a few minutes, the worst of the mob died down, and Mel took a moment to check for any sign of Dahlia through the gallery windows. There she was, standing on the sidewalk in a heavy down coat—with Bebe. Mel watched as Bebe pressed a round foil-wrapped packet into the kid's hands, her head bent close as she spoke. Mel couldn't hear what she was saying to Dahlia, but the kid was nodding through tears. She unwrapped the thing Bebe had given her—a bacon, egg, and cheese, it looked like—and tore into it. Bebe put a hand on her shoulder, still murmuring what could only be an inspired pep talk, because the kid stood a little taller as she chewed.

Had Bebe overheard them talking about Dahlia's shitty day? Or had she known somehow what the kid needed to feel better?

Mel's chest filled with warmth. God, that woman was a marvel.

Mel paused in the middle of unscrewing the cap off a fresh bottle of shitty Chablis. She examined with great trepidation the quality of the warmth inside herself. It wasn't unfamiliar. In fact, it felt very much like—

Oh. Great.

She *like*-liked Bebe.

This wasn't supposed to happen. These were supposed to be her training wheels, her practice run to get back into dating. This wasn't supposed to be anything serious. And even if it could be, it was way too soon. Way too fast. For god's sake, Bebe was married to—

A redheaded figure appeared directly in front of the bar. "Kade!" Mel yelped.

"Hello, Mel." Kade was wearing fuchsia eyeliner, a sleeveless black jumpsuit, and a frown. "Do you . . . also work with the catering company?"

"No, no! I'm just pitching in for a minute." She glanced back at the window, but Bebe had disappeared. Dahlia stood alone, polishing off her BEC. "Long story. Can I get you a drink?"

"I'll have some water, please, if you have it," Kade said.

Mel dug a bottle of Fiji—oh, sure, splurge on the fucking *water*—

from an ice chest. "Congrats on the show, by the way. Your stuff is pretty cool." She winced, still wrist-deep in ice. "Sorry. Probably not the most enlightened review you've ever gotten, huh?"

"Well," Kade said, accepting the water bottle with regal poise, "I've had worse." It was hard to tell if they were being facetious or not.

Before Mel could form a response, Bebe appeared at Kade's side. "There you are, Darling!" she said, embracing them with a happy bounce. "I was showing Mel your etchings. They're so wonderful." Without missing a beat, she dug a fifty-dollar bill from her purse and dropped it in the tip jar. She winked at Mel, quick as a flash. "Dahlia's had a rough time of it, poor lamb. I think she'll be back shortly, though."

"Who's Dahlia?" Kade asked.

"I'll tell you later. Now go mingle." She gave her wife a gentle push, and Kade went with minimal grumbling. Bebe turned back to Mel. Her eyes were as bright as a thousand streetlights. "You're a hero, you know that?"

"Eh." Mel busied herself with pre-pouring a few more cups of wine for people to grab. "It's not a big deal. What's twenty minutes of my time?"

"To some people, everything." Her face softened into something Mel could hardly look at directly, it was so affectionate. It made her want to blurt out things she couldn't possibly share, not now. Not ever. "Absolutely everything. That's why I like you so much, Mel Sorrento."

Mel was screwed. There was nothing she could say to that that wasn't dangerously close to the truth, so instead she said nothing. She watched the soft look on Bebe's face slide into concern. Possibly disappointment. Definitely that.

"I'm back," Dahlia announced, reappearing at the bar. "Thanks for the coverage." She looked much better, albeit a little embarrassed.

Mel sent a silent prayer to whatever saint oversaw huge fumbles. At least the awkward moment was interrupted. "No worries. Take it easy, okay?" She gave up her spot and moseyed back to Bebe's side. Bebe's hand dangled there, and Mel considered clasping it and dragging her deeper into the gallery, but it felt like the moment for that had passed. She tipped her head toward the back wall instead, feigning an upbeat tone. "Want to show me more of this art stuff?"

"Yeah," Bebe said, her voice edged with the same strained bubbliness. "Sure thing."

CHAPTER 11

MELANIE SORRENTO:
After reviewing your submission materials, The Beverage Outreach Committee of Food Fest, Inc., is pleased to welcome you as an official competitor in the inaugural contest celebrating The New Era of New York Mixology. Once your cocktail recipe is finalized, please complete the attached form to request the necessary ingredients, tools, and glassware so they can be provided on the day of the competition. You will also find attached the official schedule and rule book. If you have any questions, please don't hesitate to reach out. We are looking forward to seeing you and your fellow competitors shine a well-deserved spotlight on the dynamic and innovative New York cocktail scene.

Mel read the email a third time to make sure she wasn't hallucinating. She was in. She wasn't magical-thinking her way through the waiting period anymore; she was actually in. This was real.

She put her hands over her mouth and gave a muffled scream of happiness.

Mel put her battered laptop to the side and searched through her twisty bedsheets for her phone. This called for a celebration. Mel couldn't wait to tell Bebe, who would surely know the perfect fabulous-yet-unknown restaurant for the occasion. When her fingers finally closed around the phone, Mel remembered: she'd probably ruined things with Bebe last night at the gallery.

She thought "probably" because it had all been so fucking weird. Bebe had acted like her normal effusive self, but there was a pall hanging over the rest of their date night. Once they finished taking in Kade's art, they'd lingered awkwardly on the sidewalk. Mel hadn't waited for Bebe to do the rejecting. She'd made some excuse about needing an early start the next morning. Their plans for spending the night together were put aside. It was the first time one of their dates hadn't involved sex of some kind. Bebe didn't seem upset about that, exactly, but there had been a strange tension in her when she kissed Mel good night.

Maybe Mel should have just returned the sentiment when Bebe had said she liked her. Except she couldn't say that because it was too true.

She tossed her cell onto her nightstand with a groan. Better to leave it for now, give them both some breathing room. She could tell Bebe the good news later. After all, she needed her "early start" excuse to hold water, and it wouldn't if she started texting Bebe first thing.

She'd have to be content with telling Daniel when she saw him at work. He'd spent the night at Jackson's and wasn't home yet. Mel dragged herself out of bed and into her clothes. Might as well *actually* start early, especially now that she seriously needed to refine her competition drink.

She headed into Terror & Virtue and spent several hours behind the bar messing around with her apple butter old-fashioned idea. Maybe it was the stilted way she'd left things with Bebe, but she felt off her game. Amateur mistakes, measuring out the wrong amounts, forgetting to chill what needed chilling, shaking what should have been stirred. Still, she kept at it because that was what she did.

Mel brought the glass under her nose and sniffed its contents. The aroma was close to what she'd been aiming for, a combination of herbaceous, spicy, and fruity. She held the glass up to the light, taking in the cocktail's rosy color. That was also on point. Secretly, Mel was pleased to have captured the essence of Bebe's cheeks in a postorgasmic flush.

Not that this drink was about Bebe.

Mel had merely . . . taken Bebe's tastes into account while building this recipe.

The fat-washed bourbon was paired with high-grade maple syrup, a dash of cinnamon candy bitters, and a skewer of cherries stewed in Finger Lakes Riesling. Very Bebe, but also very New York. Mel had spent hours combing through boring state government websites to learn about upstate agriculture so she could showcase local products in the drink. She hadn't realized before that New York had the largest population of tappable sugar maples in the country (suck it, Vermont), but once she found out, she subbed the usual sweet element with maple syrup. Mel gave her glass one final, proud look before she took a sip.

And recoiled.

It was sickeningly sweet, cloying to the point of frying every taste bud she had. Forget New York and its exciting nightlife; this cocktail's inspiration was closer to overindulging on candy corn. Mel swallowed, but the harsh flavor remained in her mouth. "Ugh. Bleh." She worked her tongue around, then chugged a glass of ice water to cleanse her palate.

She put both hands on the rail and let her head hang heavy between her shoulders. Her groan echoed. The fat-washed bourbon had tasted great on its own. Every element, in fact, had tasted great individually. Why did it suck so bad in combination? It didn't make any sense.

Maybe, a voice whispered in Mel's head, *some things are better off alone.*

She shoved the thought away. "Back to the drawing board," she muttered to herself, and dumped the too-sweet cocktail into the sink. It swirled pinkishly down the drain.

Daniel swished up to the bar, looking harried. His hair was unusually messy, but given his night spent at Jackson's, that was possibly a good thing. "Hey, did you hear about this bullshit?"

Mel held up a palm. "Wait, I have something to tell you first."

His expression fell. "Can't my thing be first?"

"No, let's do my thing. It's a good thing." She shook off her disappointment with the test-run drink and her squishy feelings for Bebe and tried to bask for a moment. She struck a pose, hands on her hips. "You're looking at an official entrant in the Food Fest cocktail competition."

"Really?" Daniel's face lit up in genuine joy. "Mel, that's amazing!" He tried to reach over the bar, but the distance was too much, so he ducked under the leaf and wrapped her up in a bear hug. "I knew you could do it."

Mel squeezed her arms around his waist. "This is only step one, though. Still got to win the damn thing."

"Well, yeah, but step one is done. You crushed step one." Daniel bounced up and down on the balls of his feet a couple times, and Mel joined him, laughing.

When they broke apart, Mel made a rolling gesture with her hands. "Okay. Now tell me your thing. What bullshit?"

Daniel's good cheer slipped away. "Jessica told me that Kathy Ellen told her that Brent said we're going to be sold."

Mel's head swung up. "What do you mean, sold? Why? To who?"

T&V was one of the top five, if not the absolute top, cocktail lounges in the tristate area in terms of profitability. Why would the owner ever sell? Her thoughts were in a jumble. Maybe the current owner, a retired bartender who'd made it big-time with a series of bestselling mixology books, had stopped covering the rent. Maybe he'd embezzled Terror & Virtue's profits and left the bar drained. Maybe the new owner was some shady investment conglomerate that was going to fire everyone and replace them with AI.

"I don't have any details yet," Daniel said. "Brent's in his office, but no one's had the balls to ask him what's going on."

Mel wiped her hands on a bar towel. "Let's go."

"Wha— Now? The both of us?" Daniel's mouth trouted open and shut. "Do I really need to be there? I'm more of a post-confrontation debriefer."

Mel opened the leaf at the end of the bar with a sharp smack. "Front row seat, Danny. Strap in." She headed straight toward the back, where the managerial office's discreet door blended into the wallpaper.

Daniel fast-walked to catch up. "Okay, but I am only here as a witness."

Mel rapped on the door, turning the knob even before she heard Brent's belated "Come in." The shift manager was sitting behind his desk in the cramped room, working at a laptop. He was middle-aged, white, bearded, and milquetoastedly pleasant in a way Mel supposed was good for dealing with guests, though it personally grated on her nerves.

Brent glanced up from his laptop screen. "Oh, Mel. Daniel." He returned his gaze to the computer, tapping away at the keys. "What can I do for you?"

Mel crossed her arms over her chest. "Who's buying us?"

That got Brent's attention. He looked back up at her and shut the lid of his laptop.

Behind her, Daniel slowly closed the office door with a soft click.

"The news is spreading like wildfire, huh?" Brent smiled, but it was brittle, the kind he wore when denying someone a night off. "Yes, it's all very exciting. I'm sure you've heard of the Sunspot Group?"

"Oh, sure, the Sunspot Group," Daniel muttered under his breath. "Everyone knows the Sunspot Group." He leaned closer to Mel. "What the fuck is the Sunspot Group?"

Mel turned her head toward him. "Huge hospitality conglomerate. They own about two-thirds of the most profitable restaurants in
this town. Del Pucci, Café Vivori, City Kitchen, The Rare Parrot. And
now us." She turned back to Brent. "*Why* us? I don't think Sunspot's
ever invested in a cocktail lounge before."

Brent raised both palms in the air. "Look, at this point, I know
about as much as you do. It's all lawyers and contracts and negotia-
tions. Above my pay grade."

Mel's lips thinned. Lawyers and contracts? Bebe might know what
the deal was. Mel made a mental note to ask if she'd heard anything
the next time they got together.

Her silence must have made Brent uncomfortable because he
forged ahead: "If you're worried about the future, don't be. Nothing
will change for us. Same business, same menu, just a different name
on your paychecks. And if things do start evolving down the road,
everything'll be positive. Sunspot is a fantastic outfit. They'll make
sure we're a finely tuned money-making machine, better than ever.
That's all."

Mel didn't like the sound of that one bit. Terror & Virtue was
already packed every night, so the only ways she could see the bar
making more money was cutting corners, raising prices, and under-
staffing. Guests weren't fools—well, for the most part. But even the
fools would notice a decline in quality; they'd start going to newer
bars that offered a better experience. She'd seen it happen again and
again in this town. The T&V name was only as good as its current
level of service.

"The staff might appreciate updates," she said stiffly. "You know,
as everything develops."

Brent gave her a double thumbs-up. "You got it. As soon as I
know more, you'll know more. You have my word."

Mel didn't put much stock in Brent's word. He'd also promised
to replace the ragged floor mats behind the bar months ago, and the
torn-up black plastic honeycomb was still there, tripping up bartenders at least five times every shift.

Still, Mel gave Brent a nod in thanks. "Yeah. Keep us posted." She turned back to the door, a hand on Daniel's arm, but Brent spoke up again, causing her to turn back.

"Oh hey, Mel, while you're here, can I have a word?" He looked pointedly at Daniel. "You can close the door on your way out, Dan."

Daniel gave Mel a look, which she silently answered with a tilt of her head. *Go ahead, I'll give you all the gossip later.* Daniel nodded, a small gesture that clearly stated, *You better*.

Once Daniel was gone and the door was shut, Brent gestured to the battered chair in front of his desk. "Sit, sit! I hardly ever have a chance to catch up with my MVP of bartenders. You carry every shift, you know that?" He smiled wide and fake. "A real asset to the T&V family."

"Thanks," Mel said, taking her seat with more than a little trepidation. She'd never bought into the whole "We Are Family" crap that Brent peddled. If they were a family, where was her damn health insurance, for starters? Her paid sick leave? Family was supposed to take care of each other, not expect unending sacrifice from select members.

"I want to talk about your little science project," Brent said. "I saw some containers in the blast chiller? With your name on some Post-its?"

Mel stared at him. While he was making it sound like a question, she wasn't really sure what he was asking. The bartenders at T&V had always been allowed, even encouraged, to use the high-grade equipment to experiment with new flavor profiles and techniques. As long as their pet projects didn't interfere with their regular work—and they gave their best results to Calvin, the head bartender, to consider incorporating into the strictly curated menu—it was all kosher. The Post-it system was simply their low-tech way of keeping things organized. "Yeah?" she finally said.

"In the future, we're going to streamline things a touch," Brent said, still smiling that creepy smile. "The next time you want to make something off-book, come run it by me first."

"Why?" Mel couldn't keep the note of distrust out of her voice. "I thought tinkering in the back was okay as long as we were off the clock."

"Yeah, of course. No doubt, no doubt." Brent bobbed his head, then leaned over the desk like he was sharing a secret. "It's just that the new guys with Sunspot are already asking us to find ways to get costs down, and one thing we can do is try to keep the experiments to a minimum. Very eco-friendly, actually. Less waste all around."

Mel felt her jaw ticking. "But developing new drinks—"

"Is Calvin's job," Brent said. "And if I'm remembering right, Calvin and I haven't given any of your drinks the green light before, right?" His voice held a pitying note that made Mel want to smash his face in with his Chrysler Building paperweight.

"No," Mel said, all ice. "Not yet."

"Right! Exactly. Not yet. Love that optimism." Brent held up one finger. "But with the way we're streamlining now, we're going to have to give priority to the folks with an existing track record. You understand, right?"

"So I'm never going to have a real shot at getting something on the menu because you only want people with menu experience to make new stuff?" Mel barked out a harsh laugh. It was a snake-eating-its-own-tail situation.

"No, no," Brent cooed. "Of course you'll have opportunities. You'll just need my sign-off first before taking up valuable resources, that's all." He paused, looking regretful in a carefully practiced way. "And if the rumors are true, whatever you're working on right now isn't for the Terror & Virtue menu. It's for some competition, right?" He shook his head. "It's not really fair to the other bartenders if you're using stuff for personal reasons."

There were a million arguments on the tip of Mel's tongue. Snappy lines about professional development and needing to feel the backing of her "T&V family" in this competition. Ideas about how raising her own profile meant raising the profile for Terror & Virtue itself, being an ambassador, showing the world that the best new ideas in mixology were coming out of their bar and nowhere else. A metric ton of bullshit corporate-speak when what she really wanted to say was, *Fuck you, no one else was using the chiller! Don't piss on me and tell me it's raining, you smarmy sack of shit.*

But Mel did not say that. She didn't say any of it, even the more reasoned stuff. She could see, in the glint of Brent's eye, how it would go: she would protest, he would shoot her down, all while pretending to be her best buddy, and nothing would change. There was no winning. Brent was like a managerial killbot. He had his orders and wouldn't deviate. That much was clear.

"Sure," she said, feeling pathetic and defeated. "Message received."

"I knew you'd understand. Smart girl like you." He opened his laptop, the dismissal clear in the gesture. "Well, I won't keep you. We've got a shift to crush, yeah?"

Mel pictured setting him on fire. It was a strangely soothing image. She didn't bother giving him an answer, just left the office and stalked back to the bar.

Daniel swanned up alongside. "What did the bearded wonder want to talk to you about?"

"Nothing," Mel grumbled. "He wanted to rap my knuckles for wasting company resources on the competition."

"You're kidding. What's next? Telling me I'm not allowed to take bar olives home?"

Mel squinted at him. "You take home olives? When? How?" Those commercial jars of olives were about the size of a terrier; Mel was certain she would have noticed Daniel lugging one home after a shift.

"I have a system. It involves a lot of Ziploc bags. But we're not talking about me right now." Daniel stuck a finger in her direction. "You weren't buying what our good buddy Brent was selling, were you?"

"About everything being hunky-dory, yellow-brick-road with the new ownership?" Mel sighed. "Yeah. I'm skeptical. Which reminds me—" She pulled out her cell phone—her shift didn't start for another forty-five minutes, so Brent couldn't complain—and texted Bebe.

> Hey Bee have you heard anything about the Sunspot Group? Looks like they're buying t&v

Mel stared at the screen, smiling when she saw the tiny Read checkmark appear. Maybe she was too in her own head about last night. Bebe wasn't the kind of person to hold a grudge over something like that. The dots that indicated Bebe typing a reply undulated right beneath. Then they stopped. Mel's smile slipped. She thought she saw the dots appear again, but they disappeared so fast she thought she might be mistaken. She waited for what felt like the longest minute of her life. Still nothing.

"Huh," she said. "That's weird."

Daniel looked up, frozen in the act of spearing an olive from Mel's garnish tray with a cocktail stick. "What's weird?"

"Bebe. She left me on Read. She never leaves me on Read."

Daniel shrugged and jabbed his stick through a plump olive. "She could be going into a courtroom or something."

"Yeah. That's probably it." Were courts open this late in the afternoon? No sense dwelling on it. Mel slipped her phone into her back pocket. Technically she was supposed to keep it in a locker during her shift, but she wanted to feel the vibration if and when Bebe texted her back. No harm in that. "Hey, quit eating my back-up work! Don't you have your own prep to do?" She shooed Daniel away from her tray.

Daniel popped the olive in his mouth, maintaining eye contact the whole time. "Ziplocs," he said before floating away to do whatever a server did before a shift.

CHAPTER 12

Mel stood in front of Bebe's condo door, working up the courage to knock.

She'd become such a frequent visitor lately that the doorman merely nodded to her when she entered. She'd texted earlier in the day, mentioning that she wanted to stop by, but Bebe had been weirdly silent in response.

In fact, Bebe had been uncharacteristically incommunicado for the past couple of days. Whereas Mel had come to expect at least a text or two daily from Bebe—scheduling their dates required constant back-and-forth, not to mention the banter—she hadn't heard a peep from her since Monday night. Bebe hadn't responded to Mel's question about T&V's new ownership. Not a single sympathetic emoji following Mel's frustrated string of messages about how Brent was watching her like a hawk at work. When Mel sent her an extremely funny video of a small dog trying to carry a big stick? Nada. It was like Bebe had dropped off the face of the earth.

Mel would have asked Kade if everything was okay, but she didn't have their number. It was worrisome enough that Mel decided to stop in to check on Bebe's well-being.

Even in casual arrangements, there was a certain level of care required, and Mel figured that making sure your—girlfriend? The guidelines didn't cover what to call each other—was alive and well was the bare minimum.

She let out a breath and knocked. Bebe answered the door.

She looked fine, was Mel's first, relieved thought. Maybe a little tired, a little strained around her expressive eyes. But otherwise, Bebe looked absolutely normal, standing in the doorway.

"Mel!" Her eyes were wide with surprise, like she was coming out of a daze and the last thing she'd expected to see was Mel in her hallway. Then her gaze softened into that bright, beaming happiness she so often exuded. "That's right, it's Monday. Did we have plans tonight?" She opened the door wider, ushering Mel inside.

"No," Mel said, pulling her winter hat off her head, "no plans. Just wanted to see you." Then, because that sounded too sappy, she shoved her hands in her coat pockets and rocked on her boot heels. "Couldn't seem to raise you on the horn, so I thought I'd check in. See how you're doing."

She took in the sight of Bebe's home while Bebe closed the door. Some documents were spread out on the kitchen counter, not an uncommon sight in Bebe's domain. Her job involved about a metric ton of paperwork. Piles of folders littered the floor of Bebe's spare bedroom/office on the regular, and now it seemed the avalanche had migrated to this room, too.

Bebe followed Mel's gaze and gave a harried sigh. She hustled over to the counter and shuffled the paperwork into a stack before squirreling them away in one of the kitchen drawers. "I'm so sorry. I've been snowed with work, plus Kade and I had to meet with Callen about some boring financial things . . ." She slammed the drawer shut and braced her hands on the countertop, shaking her head. "I meant to answer your texts, really. It's been one of those weeks."

Mel felt she had to justify showing up uninvited, so she cleared her throat and said, "You usually text back no matter what time it is. I was worried." Then, because that sounded too honest, she added, "I thought you were, like, stuck in a coma somewhere, *While You Were Sleeping*–style. Seemed to be the only logical explanation."

Bebe went soft as pudding, her eyes swimming in fondness. "Oh, you absolute sweetheart." There was something melancholy in her voice that bothered Mel. But then Bebe cleared her throat and took Mel's coat, and everything seemed normal again. "Here, make yourself at home. Sit! I haven't seen you in ages. Catch me up on everything I've missed because of my stupid job."

It shouldn't have been that simple, but Mel felt mollified by Bebe's easy manner and quick apology. Of course she'd been busy. Of course she wasn't ignoring Mel on purpose. They were keeping everything so casual, a few days without word was absolutely fine.

Mel threw herself into the cushy embrace of the sectional and sighed. Her whole body felt swallowed by the luxurious cushions. "My work's been a real pain, too. Terror & Virtue got sold to this batshit conglomerate a few days ago and—oh, okay." She stopped her complaining as Bebe slid atop her lap, pressing Mel further into the sofa. Mel's hands found the soft swell of Bebe's hips automatically, and her eyes met Bebe's.

Bebe leaned over Mel, her long hair spilling over her shoulder to tickle at Mel's collarbone. She pulled at the hem of her tailored skirt until it was bunched around the tops of her thick thighs. "Oh, I'm sorry," she said, sounding not sorry at all. "I didn't mean to interrupt. You were saying?"

Mel sat up, Pavlovian to a T. "I was saying something?" She slid her hands up Bebe's legs, mapping acres of her peaches-and-cream skin. "Wasn't me. I've never said anything in my life."

Bebe gasped happily as Mel's mouth closed over her throat. A distant worry tapped at the back of Mel's brain—were they alone, or was Kade home? She tried not to care; either way, she wasn't doing anything wrong. She had the sign-off. Besides, it had been a whole week since she'd last tasted Bebe. She deserved a little fun.

Still—it would be more fun in the privacy of Bebe's bedroom. One thing Mel had quickly learned from dating Bebe: she and Kade did indeed maintain separate bedrooms. The room Mel had assumed was Kade's home office was actually where they usually slept.

Mel stopped kissing Bebe's neck to say, "Should we take this upstairs?" Bebe enthusiastically agreed. They clattered up the staircase, dropping Bebe's clothes like breadcrumbs in their eagerness.

A few hours and orgasms later, Mel was wide awake and unable to sleep, which wasn't unusual. Mel had only ever lived in squat walk-ups in the city, so the comparative quiet of Bebe's condo was jarring. Here, high above the streets, the sounds of traffic were muffled to a whisper. Mel couldn't even hear a single persistent car alarm. It wasn't natural.

She sat up in Bebe's bed, her back cushioned by the upholstered headboard, her knees making a tent under the bedclothes. Next to her, Bebe was asleep with her long hair spilling over her silk pillowcases. She was a deep sleeper; the car alarms and midnight arguments on the street never seemed to bother her when she stayed over at Mel's. Mel listened closely to the sounds of Bebe's lungs working, the sweet sigh of her breath. She had worn a lacy nightgown to bed, and the thin silk of the strap had slipped down her arm, making her look like a pinup model. If pinup models made the occasional charming backhoe-like snore.

Mel reached for a strand of honey hair, twining it around her finger. God, the hold this woman had on her. And she didn't even know it.

Couldn't know it, really. Mel had been the one to establish the "keep it casual" rule, and here in the dark of the night, she could admit to herself that she was failing at sticking to it. She was more than fond of Bebe, more than attracted. She was so into her, it hurt. That was a complication Mel wasn't prepared to deal with. The whole point of dating Bebe was to *not* get too involved too quickly. She scrubbed a hand over her tired face. Fuck, trying to sleep at normal-people hours was a useless exercise. She needed a glass of ice water and a Bogart flick.

There was no real reason to be quiet since nothing short of an airstrike would wake up Bebe, but Mel was careful anyway. She slipped out of bed, finding her black boxer briefs on the floor and tugging them on. Her shirt had disappeared somewhere in the night, so Mel grabbed Bebe's diaphanous blue robe from where it was slung over the upholstered vanity stool. She stumbled out of the bedroom, tying the robe's belt into a half-hearted knot at her hip.

She found her way down the floating staircase and into the living area. Ambient light from the city streamed in through the huge glass windows, casting strange shadows around the room. Kade's sculptures looked ghostly like this, and Mel found herself staring at the shapes they threw on the walls as she padded toward the kitchen.

She was so distracted, she nearly jumped out of her skin when she heard a softly spoken, "Good evening."

"Fucking—" Mel clutched a hand over her heart, looking wildly to the kitchen island, where Kade was sitting still as a statue with a mug cupped between their palms. "You scared the shit out of me."

"I'm sorry," Kade said, though they didn't sound it. Their eyes were barely visible in the gloom, tracking Mel as she drew closer. "I thought you'd notice me eventually, and when you didn't, I wasn't sure how best to announce myself."

"It's your house. You don't have to announce anything." Mel stood awkwardly, glancing down at her half-dressed state. The robe, designed for Bebe's voluptuous proportions, gaped at her chest in a way that threatened to show Kade a lot more boob than they probably cared to see. Mel's hand grasped the edges of it and held it tightly closed at the base of her throat. "If I'd known this was a party, I would've dressed up. Or, you know, put on actual clothes." The last thing she wanted was for her girlfriend's wife to think she was parading around half-naked to stake a claim or some bullshit like that.

"I'm not bothered by what you're wearing." That, at least, sounded sincere through and through. Kade leaned away from the island and gestured to their own midnight ensemble: a mostly unbuttoned striped pajama top paired with spandex bike shorts. It was the most casual outfit Mel had ever seen on Kade. "I'm not exactly dressed for company either," they said.

"Well, I'll"—Mel pointed with both hands over her shoulder at the stairs—"leave you to it," she finished. Barging in on Kade's late-night solo brooding was not among her top ten ways to spend an evening.

"No, please." Kade reached out one long, bare leg and kicked out the stool next to them. "You're not company. You're Mel."

Even in Kade's bloodless monotone, that was the most welcoming sentiment Mel had ever heard from them. She took the offered seat, feeling awkward but eager to make a good impression. She still hadn't figured out where she stood with Bebe's wife. Some part of her considered them to be kind of like . . . coworkers? Except Bebe was not a job, so that didn't really wash. They were like ships passing. Or maybe moons made a better metaphor; celestial bodies orbiting around a shared planet, always on separate paths.

"You usually aren't around when I stay over," Mel said, unable to keep her curiosity at bay. "Do you go hang out with, um, other partners or . . . ?"

"No, I don't have any others. Not at the moment." Kade turned the mug between their hands. "Those few times you've stayed over, I tend to pull all-nighters at my studio."

"Ah." Mel nodded. "That's really cool of you. To give Bebe that kind of space, I mean."

"It's more for my benefit than hers. My wife has a"—they smiled to themself, staring down into their mug—"far greater capacity for social interaction than I do. I need lots of time to myself. We're lucky that our lives fit together like they do." Kade lifted the mug in their hands. "Herbal tea. Would you like some?"

Mel licked her dry lips. "Uh, I could actually go for a glass of water if it's not too much trouble."

Kade got up and moved around the kitchen on silent feet, collecting a glass from a cabinet and filling it at the fridge's built-in dispenser. "So you're a night owl, too, I take it."

"Yeah." Mel listened to the ice cubes clinking, then the low shush of water filling the glass. "The hours they have me working, hard not to be." She accepted the cold glass from Kade, fingers brushing in the dark. "Thanks."

"It's nothing." Then, "I often have trouble sleeping, especially when I'm in the middle of a project," Kade said. They retook their seat and held their mug again. "It's one of the reasons Bebe and I sleep apart sometimes. She needs her rest, and I need space to ramble around on nights like this." They stared into the depths of their tea, then took a serene sip. "There's nothing more romantic than allowing your partner what they need, I think."

"You don't miss sleeping next to someone—her—at night?" Mel asked. She remembered how hard it had been after her divorce, getting used to a bed that felt empty and lopsided without her wife in it.

Kade shot Mel a calculating look. "If one of us is in the mood, we'll sleep in the same bed. Usually hers. That mattress . . ." They shook their head in wonder.

"Oh my god, I know. It's like a cloud made of angel breath," Mel said. Was it weird to rhapsodize about high-quality memory foam with your metamour? She chugged her water to keep from saying anything more.

Kade seemed unfazed, though. "Nothing but the best for our girl." A small, almost sweet smile appeared on their lips before it was locked away. "I've been meaning to ask—how are things with you two?"

Mel froze in the middle of wiping her wet mouth with the back of her hand. That question and all its potential answers seemed like a minefield. Especially since lately, Bebe had been so distant.

Kade must have sensed her hesitation, because they rushed to add, "We don't—it's not a requirement for us to discuss this. If you'd rather not. It's only—" They took a deep breath and started again. "Our situation is unique. I thought you might not have many people you could speak to comfortably. If you'd like, you could speak to me. I love Bebe and I want her to be happy."

"Do you have reason to believe she's not?" Mel swallowed around the lump in her throat. *With me*, went unsaid.

Kade tipped their head to the side, contemplating their mug of tea like it held state secrets. "Please understand, I know her better than I know myself. She has seemed . . . agitated lately." They paused. "Then again, it could be I am painting her with my own worries."

Mel bit her lip. "I don't think you're off base. She's been a little—distracted, I guess?" She wondered how much she should share with Kade. No way was she going to tell them she had ended up liking Bebe more than she'd planned, but she did want to exchange pertinent information about their mutual partner. The thought of Bebe sleeping upstairs with her hair spilling over the pillows pushed Mel to say, "I came over tonight kind of uninvited because I was worried about her, actually."

Kade sat up straighter at that, their face taking on a thoughtful cast. "And did she tell you what's been bothering her?"

"Uh, not really. We kind of—" Mel felt her face flaming. "Got distracted. By other—stuff. Sorry." Whether the apology was for her lack of fact-finding or mentioning doing unmentionable things to their wife, Mel wasn't sure.

A rueful almost-smile stole across Kade's lips, though it could have been a play of the shadows. "No need to apologize. I am intimately familiar with the ways Bebe can distract an otherwise levelheaded person." Looked like they were taking it as the former. "I'm glad it's not just me who thinks something is off, though."

"Definitely not just you. It's almost like—I don't know, did I do something wrong?" She looked at Kade, feeling her face pinch. Maybe Bebe had mentioned the moment at the gallery to Kade. Maybe she had taken it harder than Mel had thought, when Mel hadn't returned the offered affection.

But Kade shook their head. "I don't think you're the problem. When Bebe talks about you, she glows."

Mel felt an absurd amount of relief sweep through her. She almost slumped off the high stool with the force of it. "Really?"

"Of course." Kade said it like it was a fact, a given, an immutable law of nature. "Don't you know she—?" They stopped. Their mouth clamped shut with a click.

"She what?" Mel asked.

Kade ignored the question like it had never been asked. "I suspect it's some issue at work."

"That class action lawsuit. She told me how messy it was," Mel said.

They nodded. "The likely culprit, although normally she would talk to me if work was overwhelming. As much as she's allowed, anyway, given the legal constraints around client confidentiality." They stood and placed their mug in the sink with a dull thud. "I wonder if she might confide in you. You wouldn't have to tell me the details, but I'd like to know she's speaking to someone. Bottling it up will do her no favors."

Mel made a considering noise. "So, what, we're on the same side now? Team Get Bebe Out of Her Funk?"

Kade stilled at the sink, their hands bracing on either side of it, their back a taut line. Mel wished she could see what their face was doing, because she couldn't parse the tone of their voice when they finally said, "You and I have always been on the same side. Haven't we?"

"Um, sure. Same is fine," Mel babbled. "We're all here. On the same—yeah." Maybe it was the insomnia making her punchy, but Mel felt warm at the notion. Kade wasn't all dryly raised eyebrows and pursed lips. Somewhere under that reserve was the soul of an artist.

Mel was glad they were on the same team, at least when it came to Bebe.

Kade turned then, their gaze tracking to the windows. "It's very late. I should at least attempt to get some sleep." They gestured to the expansive kitchen before heading toward the floating steps. "Help yourself to whatever you need. What's mine is yours."

"Ha, good one," Mel said with a soft snort. "Poly humor."

Kade just stared at her. Right. They'd never stoop so low as to crack a joke.

"Never mind. I mean—thanks. Good night." Mel drank more water, hoping it would wash away the embarrassed heat in her cheeks.

Kade gave her a bemused nod, then headed up the stairs. Mel listened to their soft footfalls on plush carpet overhead, and finally heard the click of a door.

She folded herself over the kitchen island, pressing her forehead to the cool marble with a groan. Why did every interaction with Kade make her feel like she'd failed a standardized test? No, not only failed—like she hadn't even brought the right pencil. She hoped they realized how hard she was trying to be respectful and polite in this three-way relationship.

Mel drained her glass of water, then placed it in the sink next to Kade's mug. She was still keyed up, no way she'd get any sleep if she went back to bed now. A late-night poke around the kitchen might get her out of her head. With a fridge and pantry as well stocked as Bebe's, maybe she could get some inspiration for the next iteration of her competition cocktail.

A wine rack was bolted to the kitchen wall, filled with all kinds of bottles. Mel noticed that at least four of them were the same Bordeaux, and she wondered whether Bebe or Kade was a fan of that vintage. She pulled one free and scanned the label, recognizing the winery. T&V maintained a small selection of beer and wine on their menu for customers who didn't like the hard stuff, and she knew this to be a solid red, not too expensive, and readily available.

A New York sour with the traditional red wine float could be just the ticket to win the competition. They'd fallen out of fashion a few decades ago, but Mel recalled someone at work saying the Savoy in London had put one on their menu this year. Could be time for a resurgence. Plus it fit the brief perfectly.

Well, Kade *had* told her to help herself to whatever she wanted. Mel placed the wine bottle on the counter and went hunting for other ingredients.

The kitchen was solidly Bebe's domain, and Mel felt strangely close to her pawing through it. Even with Bebe sleeping a flight of stairs away, Mel could sense her in every meticulously organized cupboard. The sugar was in a space-age airlock container with SUGAR stenciled on the front, for Christ's sake. A wealth of lemons sat nestled in a clear plastic bin in the fridge right next to the limes and oranges. Mel smiled to herself as she plucked one from its nest. Leave it to Bebe to always keep fresh citrus on hand for a rainy day.

A small roadblock loomed: Mel needed a corkscrew to open the wine. She opened what felt like it should be a utensil drawer but found only tea towels in different vibrant prints. "If I were Bebe's corkscrew," she muttered to herself, "where would I be?"

Another drawer: forks and spoons. Another: every kind of spatula under the sun. Mel opened a fourth drawer, certain that it would contain what she needed, but deflated when she saw it was filled with nothing but random bits and pieces. Even ritzy people had a junk drawer, she supposed. Mel dug through it hoping to turn up a cork-screw, but only encountered loose AA batteries, a ruler, receipts, spare keys, and paperwork.

Right when she was about to slam the drawer shut and move on, some papers in particular caught her eye. Mel vaguely remembered Bebe putting them in the drawer earlier in the evening, before they'd gotten distracted with other things. The top page was on company letterhead—Bebe's company, Kipling and Beech—and Bebe's name was repeated up and down the document, her full name, Blair Blanche Murray. Bebe's handwriting was also all over it, the same handwriting that appeared on their relationship guidelines. Cramped into the mar-gins, squeezed between the lines of type.

Mel thought about leaving it alone. For half a second. But she'd promised Kade she'd try to figure out what was bothering Bebe, and this seemed like a good place to start.

She removed the paper and started reading. Then she read it again. And again.

"Oh," she said out loud. It echoed in the empty room. "Fuck."

At least now she knew what was wrong with Bebe.

CHAPTER 13

Mel was sitting motionless on the sectional sofa when Bebe finally descended the stairs around six in the morning. Mel hadn't slept a wink. She hadn't even tried. Her mind was spinning like a washing machine in its final cycle, and it would not slow down. The papers she'd discovered in the drawer sat like a loaded gun on the coffee table in front of her.

Bebe paused on the second-to-last stair as she spotted Mel. She was working an earring into her left ear, head tilted to accommodate. "There you are, Sweetheart," she said with an easy smile. "I thought you might have let yourself out."

"No," Mel said. Her voice was very scratchy from long hours of disuse. "I'm still here."

"Coffee?" Bebe finished with her earring and dismounted the staircase. She was wearing a pantsuit the color of eggplant, paired with a creamy blouse. Her hair was up, showing off the bright silver discs that dangled from her ears. She was gorgeous, as always.

Mel averted her eyes. "None for me."

"All right," Bebe said slowly. She changed course, heading to the sofa instead of the kitchen. "Are you feeling okay? You sound—" Mel knew the exact moment Bebe's gaze landed on the papers. There was a sudden heaviness to the air, like the moment between a flash of lightning and the crack of thunder. A moment where the world held its breath.

"You were not," Bebe said, "supposed to see that." She came closer, her heels clicking on the floor, and picked up the company letterhead with a quiet whoosh of displaced air.

Mel stopped studying the corner of the room and turned to her. "I didn't go looking for it, if that's what you're thinking," she snapped. "Shit, Bebe, I was just trying to open a fucking bottle of wine. Why can't you keep a corkscrew somewhere sensible like everyone else?"

"I'm sorry. Corkscrews are one of those things that's always getting away from me." Bebe wasn't looking at her. She was instead studying the letter, her eyes skimming over it like she was overly familiar with its contents and was rereading it from a novice's perspective. Her face went paler and paler. "I know this must look bad to you—" she began.

"Yeah." Mel shot to her feet. Her borrowed robe ballooned around her, and she wrapped it tighter around her frame. "It looks real fucking bad. Because unless I'm reading this completely wrong, you're being blackmailed. Because of me."

The paper—an interoffice memo from the partners at Bebe's law firm—was meant to inform Bebe that Gary Willis, he of the strip club scotches, had contacted them on behalf of his client. And that client was the Sunspot Group. The same Sunspot that "happened" to buy Terror & Virtue recently. Willis had, as a professional courtesy, apprised Kipling and Beech, LLP, of the fact that Blair Murray, Esq., was romantically involved with an unnamed person employed by his client. He told the partners he looked forward to hearing from them regarding "the handling of the situation," which he hoped "wouldn't necessitate involving the judge." Mel, whose knowledge of legalese began and ended with half-watched episodes of *Law & Order*, could still see what it meant. Bebe's frantic handwritten scribbles confirmed it: it was a conflict of interest for Bebe to date someone who worked for the company she was taking to court. They were fucked.

Bebe sighed through her nose. "'Blackmail' is a bit much. Technically it's just a professional heads-up."

"Feels like more than a heads-up." Mel crossed her arms over her chest. "Reads more like a 'heads will roll' type of situation. Your bosses sound really unhappy." She hesitated. "You've been working on the case against Sunspot for a while now. Did you know that they were going to buy T&V? Is that why you were avoiding me?"

Bebe's eyes went wide. "Of course not. I only found out about the sale when you texted me about it. The whole point was to sideswipe me. Gary clearly had this plan in mind from the moment he saw us on our first date. I guess I should be flattered that he was so scared of losing to me—again—that he convinced his client to drop a couple mil on a new investment." She stopped and put a fingertip to her chin in thought. "Sunspot must have a ton of skeletons in their closet that they don't want to come out in discovery. If I lean on them harder right now, I bet they'd—"

"Listen to yourself." It only came out as a hiss instead of a scream because Mel didn't want to wake up Kade. She jabbed a finger at the letter Bebe still held. "All this and you still only care about winning?"

Bebe shook her head and placed the papers back on the table. "Sweetheart . . ."

"You said we would be honest with each other," Mel spat. "That was the golden rule, right? Honesty."

"I was going to tell you as soon as I could." Bebe grabbed up both of Mel's hands in her soft ones and squeezed. "I needed to get some things straightened out before we discussed it. You don't understand how complicated this stuff is."

Mel stared at her, then pulled her hands out of Bebe's lax grip. "Don't tell me I don't understand. Don't talk to me like I'm stupid."

"I wasn't—!" Bebe closed her mouth forcefully. Mel could see her jaw working and distantly wondered what her dentist would say at the next checkup. "I'm sorry. I shouldn't have phrased it that way. What I meant was, I wasn't sure what our options were, legally, and I had to work that out before bringing this to you. And I was going to, I swear I was."

"Why couldn't you have just told me from the beginning? There's no law against telling your—me—about your—whatever they call it. Conflict of interest."

"No, but depending on what I—*we* decide to do about it, there are laws about that. And since we're not married, you can't plead the Fifth if something goes sideways."

Mel snorted. "Oh, I see. So you're actually protecting me by keeping me in the dark. That's what I'm supposed to believe?"

"I can't help what you believe." Bebe threw her hands in the air. "If you'd rather tell yourself some story, I can't stop you. I can only tell you that I . . . care for you and I was trying my best." She wrapped her arms around herself. "I'm sorry I didn't come to you sooner. I wanted to, but I also didn't want to put you or myself at risk."

Mel eyed her warily. She sounded so convincing, but Mel didn't want to be soothed. "Well, it's a bit late for that, isn't it? Because as I understand it—as an uneducated layman—"

"Mel," Bebe said with a heavy sigh.

Mel ignored her. "—we have three choices." She held up three fingers in a fan. "One." She pressed down her ring finger. "I quit T&V. Conflict gone. Two." As much as she wanted to leave her middle finger in the air, she pressed it down next. "You quit the case. Conflict, again, gone. And three." The final pointer finger remained straining upward. "We quit each other. Not a speck of conflict to be found. Have I covered all the bases, Counselor?"

Bebe's whole posture deflated. Normally she seemed taller than she was, though she and Mel were around the same height. Now she looked smaller, her shoulders rounding forward and her gaze on the ground. "We don't have to talk about this now," she said. Her voice was wooden in a way Mel had never heard it before. "I haven't even had my caffeine yet. Why don't we both take a moment to cool off?"

"I think we've wasted enough time. I want to get this over with." Mel folded her arms over her chest. Her heart was beating so fast, she worried it was going to break free through skin and bone. "You never back down from a case. That's what you told me. So is that option off the table?"

"Sweetheart, I—" Bebe looked up at last. Her face was stricken, pinched. "It's not only my ego on the line here. I have an obligation to my clients, the employees who got screwed over by Sunspot. Remember the pregnant ones? They've got *kids*, Mel, and this lawsuit might be the difference between those kids going to college or not."

"Lots of people don't go to college! I didn't go to college." Mel pressed her hands to her chest.

"That's not the point!" Bebe said. "The point is, if word gets around that all it takes is a little light maneuvering to get me off a case, then the bad guys win."

"And you can't stand to lose." Mel wasn't sure why she was surprised. Cold ice spread through her veins. She forced her voice not to shake. "I'm the one who should give up something, is that it? I have to quit my entire job—not just a piece of it, like you'd have to—while you get to sail onward, doing your *important work*?"

"I'm saying there are *levels* of importance—" Bebe began.

Mel held up her palm. "Do you have any idea how I worked my ass off to get where I am?"

Bebe scoffed. "You complain constantly about your job," she argued. "It's not a crime for me to point out that option."

Mel's mouth hung open. "Complaining about my job and quitting it outright are two very different things." She snatched the paper out of Bebe's hand and tossed it back on the coffee table. "Sure, T&V might not be perfect, but it's the best bar in the city by a lot of measures. There's nowhere to go but down if I leave."

"That is not true," Bebe said, heated. "You could open your own place. If you'd just let me help—"

"I don't want your money," Mel said. "Even if I did, I don't have the wherewithal to start something from scratch right now. And that is a totally separate discussion from this."

"So what discussion are we having?" Bebe asked. She actually looked at her wristwatch. It made Mel want to scream. "What do you want me to say?"

"I want—" Mel bit the inside of her cheek hard enough to bleed. She stared at Bebe, her face pink with frustration, her soft hands in fists at her sides. What did it matter what she wanted? It was her own fault for ever believing this could work. For ever thinking she could have anything approaching real. "Nothing," she finally said. "You don't have to say a damn thing."

She brushed by Bebe and headed up the stairs. Bebe stood at the bottom, calling up to her. "I need to head into the office now. Early meeting. But can we—can we please talk about this later?"

Mel didn't answer. She went to Bebe's bedroom and collected her things. Threw on her own clothes and discarded the pretty robe. Shoved her feet into boots without bothering to lace them. When she went back downstairs, Bebe was standing exactly where she'd left her, though her eyes—they looked suspiciously red.

"Mel?" Her hand clutched the handrail of the staircase. "I said, can we talk about this later? Please?"

"I have to go," Mel muttered, and grabbed her coat from the rack. If Bebe was going to stop her, it would be now, while Mel was preoccupied with jamming herself into the black, heavy cocoon of her duffel coat.

But nobody stopped her at all. Mel was already gone.

CHAPTER 14

Mel was not miserable because she wouldn't let herself be. In fact, she didn't feel anything. When she returned to her apartment in those early dawn hours, Daniel was in the kitchen eating cereal, still dance-club sweaty from his own late night.

"Hey," he said, "how's Bebe?"

"She and I are over," Mel said, and shut herself in her bedroom where she planned to sleep until her shift. She spent hours staring at the ceiling, but she'd once read an article that said the mere fact of lying in bed meant your body and brain were getting some kind of scientifically measurable rest even if you couldn't sleep. When her alarm blared, Mel crawled off the mattress and into her work uniform, ignoring all the notifications that crowded her phone screen.

She worked her shift on autopilot. It was busy—Terror & Virtue was always busy, even on a freezing Tuesday night—so she didn't have to spend a second alone with her thoughts. She poured and shook and stirred and chatted and smiled and smiled and smiled some more. Brent deigned to swing by the bar to point at her and say, "Gold star tonight, MVP." If she showed any outward signs of distress, no one seemed to notice. Mel was absurdly proud of that.

"Want to grab some tacos?" Daniel asked after they'd closed up for the night. He wound his scarf around his neck, a long cherry-red line that made Mel think of Bebe's lipstick.

"No thanks," she said, shrugging on her coat. "I should really work on my competition drink tonight." Especially if T&V was going to take the downturn she predicted it would. No sense in focusing solely on her job when the prize money beckoned. She'd barely spared a moment to think about the competition the last few days, her attention consumed by worrying about Bebe.

Daniel's fingers paused in zipping up his jacket. "You just spent nine hours mixing drinks and . . . you want to go home and mix *more*? You need to rest at some point."

"I will." She jammed her hat on. "When I'm dead."

They went home. Mel holed herself up in the kitchen, trying to come up with a new idea for her competition cocktail. The apple butter old-fashioned wasn't going to work. It was too sweet, too fruity, too—Bebe. Everything was too Bebe.

Mel reached for the tequila. Not her good, small-batch stuff, but the regular old Jose Cuervo. She sloshed some into a lowball glass, forgoing ice. Daniel poked his head into the kitchen.

"I'm here if you need me to taste anything," he said. His gaze fell pointedly to the glass. "What are you working on?"

"Oh, it's a real winner," Mel said, capping the bottle. "I call it 'nothing but straight tequila because fuck everything.'" She raised the glass in a mocking toast and tossed it back, grimacing at the taste. No lime, no salt, no ice; nothing but the burn.

Daniel drew in a long breath. "Okay," he said, and grabbed another glass from the open cupboard. He placed it next to Mel's, exhaling deeply. "One for me, please."

Mel shook her head at him. "You don't have to join the pity party."

"Come on, with your tolerance? You'll drink every drop of liquor in the house before you even get tipsy. No way am I letting you do that." A beat. "At least half of it's mine, and that's not fair."

A snort of bitter laughter left Mel's throat. It took a lot to get her drunk, true, but she wasn't superhuman. "You can't get hammered with me tonight. You've got that hookup tomorrow—what's-his-name. Who schedules a morning booty call, anyway?"

"Gays who both work nights," Daniel said with a shrug. "I can cancel on what's-his-name. But I can't let you drink alone." He nudged his empty glass toward the bottle. "Pretend we're twenty-two again, m'kay? Wreck my shit."

Mel rolled her eyes and poured him a scant measure. "All right. Catch up, Quince."

Daniel drank the shot, then made a series of wheezy gurgles, sticking his tongue out and curling it back in.

Despite the shitty day she'd had, Mel smiled. A tiny one, but still. "You okay?"

"I'm amazing," Daniel said, sounding like he'd gargled with barbed wire. He slammed his glass back onto the counter. "Hit me again."

They did another shot together, then another. It was enough to make Mel feel a tad floaty in her limbs, being on an empty stomach and at the end of a long shift. Daniel, on the other hand, looked ready to keel over on the linoleum floor.

"So wha—? Bebe. Your—girl. Friend? Fling-friend. What happened with her?" he slurred, waving his empty glass at Mel.

Mel frowned down at her own glass, turning it in her fingers. "I don't know if I'm drunk enough to talk about it."

Daniel bent at the waist, arms crossed on the counter to pillow his head. He watched Mel with a watery gaze. "I fuckin' am. Doesn't that count for anything?"

Mel felt the faint prickle of tears behind her eyes. She didn't deserve Daniel. She didn't deserve—most things.

"She, um." Mel worked her tongue over her teeth. "She's working on a case against Sunspot." The whole story spilled out: the weird radio silence, finding Bebe's paperwork, the fight they'd had that morning. How it was probably all over between them, now that they were at this impasse. "I don't know why I'm so upset about it," she said through her tears. "It's not like I expected to be—important to her." She sounded like a little kid, one who'd stayed up too late and was so exhausted there was nothing left to do but dissolve into a crying jag.

"Oh, sweetie." Daniel swayed upright and wrapped her in a hug.

"I fucked up," Mel said, muffled into Daniel's solid shoulder. "I let her become too important to *me*." She sniffed hard, trying her best not to get snot on Daniel's work shirt. "I was falling for her, and now—"

"I know." He put his chin on the top of her head. "It's okay. I know."

It wasn't okay, and he couldn't have known, but Mel let the ounce of comfort wash over her in their tiny kitchen, her fingers tequila-sticky where they clung to Daniel's shirt.

CHAPTER 15

Three days.

Mel made it through the next three days. It wasn't all a fog; it didn't all happen in a blur. But most of it did. She clung, though, to those moments of clarity—fleeting seconds in the shower or lacing up her boots where she would think, *Oh well.*

I went for something, and it didn't work out. Oh well.

I was on the verge of trusting someone again and now I won't. Oh well.

I tried and I failed. Oh well.

It would take time, she knew, before she felt better, but that would happen eventually. How long had Bebe been in her life, anyway? Two, two and a half months? That was an eyeblink compared to a marriage of nearly a decade. Mel had survived one earth-shattering heartbreak; she could survive this tremor.

Except she was starting to understand that there was no Richter scale for relationships. Losing Bebe didn't hurt less simply because they hadn't been together for years. It only hurt differently. It was a loss of possibility, of what could have been. In some ways, that was worse than the slow decline with her ex-wife. At least in that case, when the marriage ended, Mel was ready, on some level, to be done. Things with Bebe had just begun.

It was easy to stay busy, at least. There were new cocktail recipes to create for the competition, experiments she conducted at home for hours on end, though Mel discarded all the results as either too derivative or too obscure. She showed up to every one of her shifts at T&V, scoffing at Daniel's suggestion that she call in sick. Being behind the bar was a mixed blessing: it kept her from wallowing, but she never seemed to have a moment's peace to really process what was happening. For that reason, she'd been declining Bebe's calls, leaving her texts unread. Mel wasn't ready to talk to her about what had happened. She barely knew how she felt about it.

There had been one text, though—an unknown number—that Mel had read:

> This is Kade. Contact me if you want to talk. Ignore this if you don't.

Mel hadn't responded. But she had saved the number in her phone under *St. Cloud, Kade (Bebe's Wife)*.

She tried to ignore the surge of warmth, remembering their late-night conversation in the condo. Plenty of reasons to keep the number. You never knew, she told herself. Might need an artist someday.

Mel shook water droplets from her freshly rinsed mixing tin as she surveyed the bar and lounge. Busy as usual, despite the handful of new Yelp reviews blasting the recently implemented reservation policy: credit card required, plus a one-hundred-dollar deposit. Sunspot was really putting the "hostile" in hospitality.

Her eyes landed on a familiar face at the other end of the bar.

Bebe lifted a hand in greeting. Mel had never known her to be tentative, and she still wasn't, but there was an uncertainty to the set of her mouth, like she didn't know if she was going to be thrown out. She didn't look bad, exactly—her clothes were as polished and pressed as they'd always been, and if there was any hint of darkness under her eyes due to lack of sleep, her makeup covered it flawlessly. And yet Bebe lacked something in her bearing that Mel found herself missing.

Her eyes, she realized. They weren't dancing. Not even a single twinkle.

Mel set down her shaker. Her hands were steady. That made her feel better. The typhoon of emotion had to stay internal. She strode over to where Bebe was sitting, even though it wasn't her assigned section of the bar. Jessica gave her a curious look, but Mel waved her off.

She stood in front of Bebe and leaned in so she wouldn't be heard by the other guests over the clamor of a Friday night. "What are you doing here?"

"I was hoping we could talk," Bebe said. Her cheeks were pink, but her chin was tilted up.

"I'm working."

"I know. I can wait."

"You'll be waiting a long time," Mel said. It gave her a kind of smug satisfaction to give such a dry dismissal. Then she registered the real hurt in those un-sparkling eyes and she felt like a real asshole.

Bebe collected herself, the pain in her expression smoothing away, then nodded once. She reached for her purse on the hook under the bar. "I'm sorry. I shouldn't have come. I'll leave you alone."

She rose from her seat, and Mel saw in an instant what life would look like if she let Bebe walk away from her now.

She'd always wonder. And she would regret it.

"Hey." Mel rested her hand on the crook of Bebe's elbow. "I have a break coming up in about an hour." It was unpaid, and Mel hardly ever took it even when her shift stretched into the nine-hour range like it was liable to do on a Friday. But these were special circumstances. "If you want to talk, meet me outside then."

A little of Bebe's old shimmer returned. "Okay. I'll be there." She didn't stay like Mel half expected her to; she picked up her coat, shot Mel one last hopeful look, and made a beeline for the door.

Good thing, too. There was a waiting list a mile long for that single free seat at the bar. A patron gestured for her, and she was right back in the thick of it, mixing a martini dirtier than a subway floor. The hour went by so fast that Mel didn't have any time to worry about why Bebe wanted to speak to her.

Mel had calculated the ebb and flow of service perfectly. The guests at the bar were settled into their second or third cocktails, lingering in that perfect spot where a bartender had no credit cards to run or new orders to fill. A lull like this was as good a time as any to step away.

Mel wiped her hands on a dry bar towel. "Hey, I need a break. Are you going to be okay for a few minutes?" she asked Jessica.

She looked surprised but recovered admirably. "Yeah, of course." She glanced toward the shut door to the manager's office. "Go quick. Before Brent comes back."

There was an exit through the back that staff were expected to use during business hours, and Mel went that way so she could grab her coat. She made her way down the narrow alley to reach the street that fronted T&V. There were still tons of people lining the (definitely not ADA-friendly) sidewalk in front of the bar, dressed to the nines, hoping to get inside one of the best-rated bars in the city. The social media–ites were shooting video of themselves standing in the freezing cold. Couples were huddling together. Mel stepped neatly through their ranks.

There was a small traffic island situated between the bike lane and the rest of the street. In recent years it had been spruced up by the city with a spindly tree, though its branches were winter-bare. Beneath it sat a green park bench. Bebe was on that bench, blowing into her gloved hands. Her eyes were riveted to the front door of T&V, clearly expecting Mel to come from that direction instead of the one she had.

Mel watched her for a moment, unseen. Had she waited there the whole hour in the cold?

No sense prolonging this. Mel approached with her hands stuffed in her jacket pockets. "Hey."

Bebe's head whipped to the side at the sound of her voice. "Mel! Hi." She struggled to stand, but her joints must have been frozen solid, making it difficult for her to get off the bench.

"Don't get up. I'll sit, it's fine." Mel claimed the far end of the bench, putting as much distance between them as possible. The minute she sat, throbbing pain shot up from the soles of her feet toward her knees. Mel ignored it, used to the sensation after so many years of long shifts. "I can give you fifteen minutes before I have to go back to work," she told Bebe.

"I won't waste your time, then." Bebe turned her whole body to face Mel, shivering in her camel coat. "I've recused myself from the case."

Mel stared at her.

Bebe swallowed. "That means—"

"I know what it means," Mel said. It was one of those words they tossed around on *Law & Order* pretty often. "I thought you never quit when it came to your work."

"Well." Bebe shrugged one shoulder. "First time for everything." She pursed her lips like she was disappointed in her own flippant response. "It was the right thing to do. One of my colleagues took it over. He's good. The client will be well served, just not by me."

Mel mulled this over. "Why are you telling me this? Your problem was solved when we broke up."

Bebe inhaled sharply like she'd been struck. "Is that what we've done?"

"I stormed out of your house. We haven't spoken in days," Mel pointed out. "It's over, right?"

"Are you asking me?" Bebe's eyes went wide. "Because that's not the answer I would give."

Mel rubbed her tired eyes. She was so confused. "So you quit the case to get me back? Is that what's happening here?"

"No! Mel, I—" Bebe frowned down at the chipped green paint between them. "I should have recused myself regardless."

Mel furrowed her brow. "Why?"

"Because." Bebe lifted her eyes and stared miserably at Mel. "The standard for having a conflict of interest is any personal investment in the outcome. And I am absolutely, beyond a shadow of a doubt, personally invested in you." She sighed through her nose. "Whether we're together or not."

Mel looked away and forced out a laugh. "You make it sound like you're in love with me or something."

Only silence came from Bebe's side of the bench.

Mel glanced back at her. She looked wide-eyed with guilt.

"You told me not to tell you," Bebe whispered. "You specifically said you weren't interested in that. I was trying to respect your wishes."

"What?" Mel could barely speak.

Bebe reached across the bench and put her hand on Mel's arm. Her eyes were liquid. "I love you, and I love your kindness, and I want to be around you because maybe some of it will rub off on me if I try hard enough." Her lips shut into a thin line like she hadn't meant to say quite so much. "But it's not about what I want, not really," Bebe said quietly. She looked down and away. "And if you say you want to end things, that's your choice. I can't argue with that, as much as I want to."

That wasn't right. That was all backward. Mel slipped a naked hand out of her coat pocket and touched the soft leather of Bebe's gloved one where it still rested on her arm. Mel squeezed her hand over Bebe's. Despite sitting out in the freezing winter air for an hour, the heat of her was palpable. Mel could feel it through her glove, from across the insurmountable-seeming foot-and-a-half of bench. She'd be able to feel it halfway around the world. If she tried to hold on to it.

Her throat clicked as she spoke. "I don't mind if you argue."

Bebe's gaze rocketed back to hers. "No?"

Mel sighed. "I love you, too," she said.

Now that the secret was out, it felt like a two-ton weight had been lifted from her shoulders. She could catch her breath, which she hadn't been able to do properly since Bebe had waltzed into her life and took it away.

A smile bloomed on Bebe's lips. "I know," she said. "A girl can always tell."

Mel ducked her head with a snort. "I was hiding it pretty well, I thought."

"Nah, you did a bad job." Then, smile faltering, Bebe said, "But that's just one slice of the pie. The love part. Thrilled we have that squared away, don't get me wrong, but what about—?" Her hand tightened on Mel's arm, and Mel lifted it to finally, finally invite her closer. Bebe scooted right up against her side, ducking under her arm and generally being a perfect warm weight along her ribs. "Are you okay with this being more than casual going forward?"

With Bebe's head tucked under her chin, Mel could let her face go through a series of squishes and creases as she thought. "I think I have to be," she eventually said. "Ever since I met you, I've been trying to maintain a distance between us, but that isn't working, clearly. I wouldn't have been so pissed at finding that paperwork in your kitchen if I didn't give a shit about you. But I do give a shit. A massive, steaming—"

"You know what I love most about you?" Bebe sighed. "Your romantic soul."

Mel pressed her lips to the cold earmuff band that was nestled in Bebe's hair, shaking with silent laughter. "Sorry."

"No, *I'm* sorry." Bebe lifted her head from Mel's chest to look her in the eye. "I should have recused myself from the jump. It was the only real answer, and I was too stubborn to accept it. Or discuss it with anyone." She squinched her nose up. "I've been so good at keeping my work life from interfering with my personal life up to now. I guess I wanted to handle it by myself like a big hero."

"I'm sorry I blew up at the first sign of trouble," Mel said. "If you had come to me and said, 'Hey, there's this problem at work and you're a part of it,' I couldn't have been mad. But I was probably looking for any excuse to bail."

Bebe ran a gloved hand over the back of Mel's head, tickling the shorn hair there. "Because you were falling madly in love with me?"

Mel rolled her eyes but smiled. "Yeah. Because of that."

Bebe cuddled up close again. Her gloved hands slid into the opening in Mel's unbuttoned coat, her arms winding around her middle.

"We'll have to have a long talk, you know. Not casual anymore. Big step. Dare I say, serious."

"You love negotiating, though," Mel said. Her arm settled heavily around Bebe in turn.

"It's one of my favorite things." Bebe kissed her neck, right where the sprig of rosemary was tattooed. "But don't worry. You're high on the list, too."

They sat there together for another minute or so, enjoying their closeness, the seismic shift they'd just been through.

Mel spoke first: "By the way, I made it into that competition."

"Seriously?" Bebe sat bolt upright, twisting so she could face Mel properly. "Food Fest picked you for the contest? Why didn't you lead with that?"

"It's not a big deal," Mel lied.

"Oh my god, I'm so proud of you." Bebe took her face in her hands and kissed her so thoroughly, a couple passersby whistled. "You're going to destroy all comers," Bebe said when they parted.

"Exactly how high is winning on that list of your favorite things?" Mel asked, breathless.

Bebe gave her a knowing look. "Guess you'll have to win and find out."

<u>Updated</u> GUIDELINES FOR POLY LIVING
WITH BEBE & MEL

1. Communication in everything. <u>Even when it's hard.</u> (THIS IS HARD.)

2. New partners may be added to anyone's personal roster so long as all in- volved are informed beforehand with an open discussion in mind.

3. Be respectful of boundaries. Everyone gets to decide for themselves what they want to hear about their partner's other partners and what they are willing to have shared of themselves.

4. For the health and peace of mind of everyone involved, we all agree to be tested regularly.

5. Though a married, cohabitating couple will naturally have some joint ob- ligations that cannot be avoided, all involved agree that there will be no "power ranking" of couples in the arrangement, i.e., one partner will not

be held as superior or more important than the other when it comes to
scheduling, distribution of affection, etc.

6. ~~Bebe agrees to keep the arrangement with Mel casual, as defined by:~~
   Mel agrees to see where this goes as a committed couple.

     a. ~~No commitments more than three weeks in the future~~

     b. ~~No use of the L word for any reason~~ Use of L word
encouraged for any reason

     c. ~~No endearments except for "sweetheart." Variations on
"sweetheart" not permitted~~

PART TWO
CORPSE REVIVER

CHAPTER 16

Bebe lounged naked on her stomach on top of Mel's bedsheets, paging through an old cocktail recipe book Mel kept on her bedside table. Terror & Virtue opened late on Sundays, so Mel had an extra hour to spend in bed with Bebe. She'd been doing that more often, hanging out for no real reason, now that they had talked through the logistics of their not-as-casual, more-serious relationship.

The radiator hissed and spat under the window, turning the room almost tropical with its steam. It clanked loudly, making Bebe jump in surprise. She pressed her hand flat to her chest, laughed at herself, and then glanced over at Mel, who watched her from her pillow with a smile lingering on her lips.

"That thing sounds like there's a man trapped inside and he's banging away on the pipes with a monkey wrench," Bebe said.

"I can promise you there's no man," Mel said.

"Better not be." Bebe turned back to her reading with snooty primness. "I don't mind voyeurism, but I insist on being consulted first."

Mel hummed. She reached out to skate a hand along the smooth, sweat-dappled skin of Bebe's arm. "Got to make sure you're working your good side?"

Bebe shot her a grin. "Sweetie, all my sides are good."

Mel leaned over so she could kiss Bebe's shoulder, where a deep purple love bite the exact dimensions of Mel's teeth was already taking shape. Bebe liked being marked, a development that had thrown Mel for a loop at first. She'd assumed, apparently wrongly, that a buttoned-up professional would want to be free of hickeys, lest nosy colleagues spotted the evidence of her personal life on her neck. Bebe had assured her she had plenty of turtlenecks.

There was also Kade, of course. Mel had thought they would want their wife returned in pristine condition. The first time Bebe had bossily ordered Mel to suck a bruise onto her skin, Mel had reared back and said, "Kade won't mind?"

But Bebe had laughed and said, "No. They won't mind," all while guiding Mel with a firm hand to the back of her head, bringing her mouth to the pale vulnerability of her throat.

Now, though, when Mel was working her way up to round two, Bebe pulled away. Her gaze was thoughtful, her fingertips tracing loops along the open book. "Hey, I had this idea—" Bebe chewed on her bottom lip for a moment, her eyes heavy on Mel. "And you can totally say no if you're not interested."

Mel perked up. Bebe was probably unraveling yet another sexual request, and Mel had liked the sexy stuff she'd proposed so far. "What is it?"

Bebe smiled. "Do you like skiing?"

For a second, Mel's brain tried to figure out which fetish might go by the moniker "skiing." Was it slang for fucking while doing coke? Because Mel was not into coke. It made her itchy. Then she realized—

"Like, on skis? In the snow?" Mel blurted out.

"That is traditionally where one does it, yes." Bebe was glittering now, her amused smile growing wider.

Mel flopped on her back and crowed with laughter. She could feel her ribs shaking with it. The whole bed, too. She hoped Daniel wasn't home, and if he was, that he knew better than to listen.

"What's so funny?" Bebe asked.

"You!" Mel sat up, her bare breasts heaving with the last of her giggles. "It's like you're from another planet. Are all rich people like this?"

Bebe's smile slipped. Mel felt only a little guilty about it. "What do you mean? What did I say?"

Mel rolled her eyes. "When the fuck would I have ever gone *skiing*, Bebe? That's yuppie territory. It's 'no, not that Jag, let's take the *other* Jag' behavior."

Bebe bristled, propping herself on one elbow so she could face Mel more fully. "Well, excuse me! I didn't want to assume either way."

"I think you can safely assume a girl like me has never climbed into a snowsuit or—whatever the hell those things are. Snow pants?" Mel snorted. "I couldn't even afford the outfits, let alone the equipment."

"Okay. Fine. You've never skied. It was silly of me to ask," Bebe said, barreling onward, "but would you be *interested* in going on a ski trip?"

Mel stopped laughing. "With you?"

"No, with the King of England and his royal—yes, with me!" Bebe huffed, blowing a strand of loose hair out of her eyes. "And Kade as well. We go up to this beautiful spot in Canada every winter. A friend lets us use his cabin. I thought you might want to join us. Maybe." She paused for another moment. "Do you have a passport? I didn't think about that, sorry."

"Yeah, I have one, though I have to check if it's still valid." Mel sat up straighter against her rickety headboard. "But—you really want me to come along on your couples getaway? Wouldn't that be weird?"

Bebe rolled her eyes and propped her head on one hand. "No weirder than having two lovers. Whom I love." She grinned. "I thought it might be nice for all of us to spend some time together. Plus, when's the last time you had a vacation?"

Mel wondered if her wedding counted. They'd stayed upstate for a long weekend for it, but there'd been no honeymoon. She and her ex couldn't afford the time off. Not that she was going to tell Bebe about that right now and ruin the good vibes.

"A really long time," Mel finally admitted. "Maybe I am due for one." She had a strong work ethic, but what with T&V's new, shittier ownership, she didn't feel obligated to show up for every possible shift. As she'd feared, Sunspot bigwigs were cracking down on costs, urging the bar to use inferior ingredients, opting not to hire a new server when an old one gave notice. Little things, but they added up. Could be time to start looking for something new—definitely time to request some vacation.

Bebe gestured grandly. "Picture it! The bracing cold. The beautiful powder. Me, teaching you how to go down the bunny hill."

"Haven't I gone down that hill plenty?" Mel asked, her hand slipping low over Bebe's soft stomach.

Bebe caught her wandering hand and held it to her lips. "Not to mention, it would give you time to work on your competition ideas. They always keep the liquor cabinet at this place filled to the brim. You could play around to your heart's content."

That was a good point. Mel hadn't made a ton of progress on that front lately. A long weekend in a relaxing atmosphere would be perfect. She could try out some new ideas and hammer out her plan for the cocktail competition.

Although—

"How would vacationing together, you know, work?" Mel asked. "Would you and Kade share a room while I crash on the sofa?"

"I guess that's up to you." Bebe tilted her head in thought. A strand of honey-blond hair fell into her eyes, and she tucked it behind her ear. "There's two bedrooms, so if you want your own space, that's not an issue," she said.

"Right, okay, but which one of us would you . . . ?" Mel trailed off.

"Sleep with?" Bebe hummed. "Do you have a preference?"

Mel felt like she was treading on thin ice. The fact that she and Kade shared Bebe's time and her life was something she could usually—not forget, exactly, but not examine too closely. A new environment, say, a shared vacation home, threw all of that into stark relief.

"Shouldn't Kade get—" Mel paused. "Dibs" sounded extremely juvenile. "To decide?"

"Well, when I asked them if I could invite you, they were very enthusiastic—"

"*Kade* was?" Mel boggled. "What does that even look like?"

"—and said they were flexible on the sleeping arrangements. And since I am legitimately fine with whatever, that leaves it up to you." She reached over and booped Mel on the nose with her finger.

Mel rubbed her nose. "I guess Kade and I could . . . take turns spending the night with you?" That was fair, right? Democratic.

Bebe beamed. "So you'll come?"

"Yeah, I'll come," Mel said, "though I'll need to borrow a skiing outfit." She mimed covering her whole torso with some invisible force.

"I bet you're Kade's size. Closer than my size, anyway. I'm sure they can lend you something."

Mel quirked a brow. "Will they be pissed if I get stains on their designer clothes?"

"What stains? There won't be anything but snow and—" Seeing Mel's bouncing, goofy eyebrow, Bebe gave her a whack in the arm with a pillow. "The mouth on you!" She laughed.

"The mouth on me," Mel agreed, and then became preoccupied with showing Bebe exactly how much mouth she had.

CHAPTER 17

On the day of the departure, Mel ran around her apartment, throwing whatever was clean into a duffel bag. She'd always been a last-minute packer. "Daniel!" she called. "Have you seen my biker boots?"

Daniel popped his head into the room, looking unimpressed. "Aren't you wearing them?"

"These are my studded boots. I'm looking for the ones with the O-ring at the ankle. Ugh, why can I never find what I need in this place?" She slammed her closet door shut in frustration.

"How can you be so goddamn unhappy when your rich girlfriend and her wife are literally taking you skiing in Banff?" Daniel demanded, making Italian bouquets with his fingertips.

"I'm not unhappy. I'm just stressed. Travel is stressful." Mel stuffed another pair of socks in her bag to be safe. "Plus this is the first time

I'll be hanging out with Kade for any real length of time. They're intimidating, you know? Not in a scary way. In, like, a sexy artistic way."

Daniel rolled his eyes. "Well, enjoy your nonproblem," he said as he turned to leave.

Mel paused in peeking under her bed to look for the errant boots. "Hey," she called after him, "you okay?"

"Peachy!" he yelled back. "Go catch your plane."

Mel considered pushing more, but she really needed to get a move on. She threw an extra winter hat in her bag and zipped it shut. When she got back from this trip, she'd have a talk with Daniel. He'd been crabby ever since she and Bebe had gotten more official. Mel wasn't sure what his problem was, but she didn't have time to figure it out at the moment.

She showed up early to Bebe and Kade's condo. The plan was to take a cab together to the airport, but when Mel let herself in with her new key—commitment!—she found the downstairs empty. Two suitcases were lined up beside the breakfast bar, but their owners were nowhere to be seen.

Mel closed the door behind her with a frown. "Hello?" she called.

Kade popped into view at the top of the stairs, their loose clothes swishing with every movement. Today's ensemble was a shade of gray that looked almost iridescent when it caught the light. "Bebe isn't here," they said. "She went into the office early, said she had one or two things to wrap up before we left. Should be back any minute." Kade looked like they were about to say something else, but they were interrupted by the sound of a cell phone vibrating across the breakfast bar right next to Mel. A grinning picture of Bebe lit up the screen. "Can you speak to her?" Kade said. "I still need to find my passport." They darted out of sight, leaving Mel alone.

Mel picked up Kade's buzzing cell and answered it. "Hey, it's me."

"Mel! Listen, I'm really sorry—" It sounded like Bebe was in the Holland Tunnel, muffled one moment, breaking up the next.

Mel shoved the phone between her ear and her shoulder so she could wriggle her backpack straps off her arms. "I can barely hear you.

Where are you? We need to hustle if we want to get to the airport on time."

"Something's come up," Bebe said through the crackling connection. "My newest case just hit the fan. I can't get away at the moment."

"Okay," Mel said slowly. She set her backpack on one of the dining chairs. "So should we try and get a later flight out?"

There was a long pause. Mel was almost certain the call had dropped, but she looked at the screen and saw the call time still ticking upward. She put the phone back to her ear. The faint sound of many voices echoed in the background.

"Bebe? Are you still there?" She turned to face the kitchen wall, hoping for better reception.

"Yeah. Sorry." Bebe sounded even more stressed than that week she'd recused herself from her big case. "It's an emergency, all-hands-on-deck kind of deal." Another pause in which Bebe's voice mingled with others in a distant sort of way. Bebe was likely pressing her cell phone against her chest while tossing out arguments and counter-arguments with her team. When she finally came back on the line, she sounded tired. "Mel, I don't think I'm getting on a plane today. I'll spare you the details, but the team and I are going to be up all night working on this."

Mel clutched Kade's phone so hard, she feared she might crack the protective case. "What about our trip?" She hated how much disappointment leeched into her voice. What a silly thing to get butt-hurt over. She switched the phone to her other ear. "I mean, if it's an emergency, I can call the airline and cancel everything."

"No, no! Don't cancel the tickets." Bebe was either snapping her fingers at a coworker to get their attention or she was walking very fast down a marble floor in her heels. Both seemed equally likely culprits for the harsh staccato sounds coming down the line. "You and Kade go ahead. I'll take the first flight out in the morning."

Mel's stomach flopped over. "You want me and Kade to leave without you?"

A low whisper came from behind her. "What's happening?"

She spun to find Kade standing there with a blue passport in hand. Their face was its usual impassive mask, though Mel thought she detected a hint of a wrinkle down the center of their forehead. Maybe that's how they showed concern.

Mel placed her hand over the phone and hissed, "There's some problem at work. Bebe's saying we should go without her and she'll catch up later. That's a little—I mean, that would be weird, right?" Without her girlfriend, Mel would be making the trip with—her girlfriend's wife. Which was a sentence she'd never imagined she'd be thinking.

Kade held out a hand. "Let me talk to her." Mel gave up the phone, and Kade put it on speaker. "Love? It's Darling."

"Darling! Listen, you and Mel should go ahead and get on the flight. I told her, I'll come as soon as I can. You'll see me at breakfast tomorrow. Lunch at the latest." Her voice brimmed with optimism.

Kade flicked their gray eyes up to Mel's face but gave away nothing. She had no idea how they felt about this last-minute change of plans. "Are you sure?" they asked the phone. "You wouldn't rather we all wait and go together when you're done putting out fires?"

"There's no reason for you two to waste a whole day of vacation because of my little work drama. Go! Hit the slopes! Soak in a hot tub! Take advantage of the cabin while you can."

Mel cleared her throat before chiming in. "And you're sure you can come up tomorrow?"

"Absolutely! I'm already rebooking my ticket." More snapping sounds, which Mel guessed were orders to Bebe's underlings and not her high heels after all.

Mel looked back at Kade, lifting her shoulders in question. "I guess if Kade doesn't mind hanging out with me . . ."

Their stony face showed no hint of excitement at the prospect, but there was no outright disgust either. "Our bags are already packed. We're ready to go, so we may as well stay on schedule."

Not the most resounding endorsement, but okay.

"All right, then!" Mel said with a thick layer of cheer in her voice toward the phone. "Go get 'em, tiger. Don't worry about us. We'll see you tomorrow."

Bebe sighed happily. "Thank you both for being so understand-ing. Travel safe! I love you."

Mel fought the funny tingle that wound through her at those words. Even now, it surprised her to hear Bebe say it out loud some-times.

"We will. Love you, too," Kade said. They paused and waited, lifting an eyebrow at Mel. Their thumb hovered over the disconnect button on the phone screen.

"Bye," Mel said, cringing at her lackluster farewell. She couldn't be sure what was an appropriate amount of affection to show in front of Kade.

Kade hung up and then checked their phone. "I suppose we should get a taxi now." They sounded, if not dejected, at least fairly bummed. The crease between their brows was deepening by the second.

It only got deeper as they lugged their suitcases downstairs and got into a cab. The whole way out to Queens, Mel and Kade sat si-lently in the back seat. Mel kept shooting Kade appraising glances. Finally, when they emerged from the Battery Tunnel, she couldn't take it anymore.

"Look, I know this sucks," she said, "but we're only stuck together for a day and a half. It's not that bad."

The crease softened as Kade looked at her. "I didn't say it was."

"Yeah, because you never say anything." Mel spread her hands out in front of her. "Look, this is a good opportunity to—chat. Right? Get to know each other a little better?" Or at all. The only things Mel re-ally knew about Kade was they were an artist, they had insomnia, and they would die for Bebe. Mel could vibe with at least two of those. There was common ground between them, surely.

"Okay." Kade turned on the squeaky black taxi upholstery to face Mel more fully. "Let's—chat." They looked uncomfortable with small talk, but managed to say, "How has work been?"

"Eh, not great." Mel frowned. "T&V's going downhill, slowly but surely. Don't get me wrong, we're still doing big numbers every night, but some of my regulars are noticing the new ownership changes. The other day, one asked me why we weren't using organic cucumber in the Pimm's Cup anymore. Can you believe that? I didn't think anyone would taste the difference, but there you go."

"Oh," Kade said. They seemed at a loss to add anything to the topic of cucumbers. Which was fair.

Mel tried to pick up the slack. She gestured to Kade's steel-gray outfit underneath their puffy snow jacket. "I really like your, uh, kilt. Thing."

Kade looked down at the swishy fabric that covered them from waist to mid-shin. "It's a skirt," they said.

"Right. Sorry. Skirt." Mel grimaced. She hoped Kade didn't think she was passing judgement on their presentation. She hadn't been sure what words Kade liked to use for certain things. "It's cool. Looks comfy."

Kade stared at her. "It's Ferragamo."

"Oh." That . . . kind of ended her line of questioning. There wasn't much Mel, in her black sweatpants and ratty White Zombie tee, could add to a conversation about haute couture except: "Nice."

It must have occurred to Kade to return the compliment, but their eyes bounced over Mel in silence, unable to find some sartorial detail they could endorse. "You look comfortable, too," Kade finally said.

Mel supposed a backhanded compliment was better than nothing.

"You know what?" Mel pulled her earbuds out of her backpack. "Maybe we can just chill until we get on the plane."

"Fine," Kade said. Before long, the cabbie let them off at the terminal.

"Thank you, sir," the driver said when Kade paid. Kade, for their part, grabbed the handles of the two massive rolling suitcases and maneuvered them inside and up to the ticket counter. It was all Mel could do to keep pace.

When she reached the counter—the one dedicated exclusively to the fancy airline members—Kade was in the middle of checking their bags and making a request. "—wondered if she could join me in the lounge if that's possible." They glanced over at Mel.

"Of course, Mr. St. Cloud," said the airline staffer in the crisp hairdo. "Your wife can certainly accompany you." A smile was then aimed at Mel, who panicked at the implication.

"Oh, we're not—" She wagged a thumb between her and Kade. "Like, not at *all*. We're more like, um. Coworkers."

Kade gave a small sigh and closed their eyes.

"I see." The staffer's eerie smile didn't waver. "Any guest of Mr. St. Cloud's will be permitted in the lounge, including his coworkers. Do you need my assistance with anything else, sir?"

"No, thank you." They accepted a baggage claim ticket with great dignity.

Mel prickled at all the 'sirs' and 'misters' that were being thrown around, but when it came to the misgendering stuff, she knew she should take her cues from Kade. So far, they seemed largely unbothered. Though it was hard to tell when a person didn't show any expression.

After security—and several more rounds of people looking at Kade's ticket and passport and calling them "sir"—Mel cleared her throat. "So. The lounge, huh? Sounds fancy." She stooped to get her boots back on her feet.

"It's more comfortable than waiting at the gate. I fly a lot for work, international exhibitions, foreign clients. That's why I have access," Kade said—a little defensively, Mel thought. "This way." They headed down one of the terminal wings to a discreet door Mel would have never noticed otherwise. The brass plaque next to it announcing the frequent-fliers' lounge location was miniscule.

"It's like a speakeasy," she murmured.

Kade glanced at her. "Yes, except the drinks are free."

That perked Mel up considerably. She held the door for Kade since they were, in a sense, the one treating her. A buttoned-up concierge greeted them at the hosting podium.

"Thank you for flying with us today, sir. May I see your ticket?"

Kade's jaw twitched, but they handed over their phone with the screen open to the ticket app for inspection.

"Your flight is experiencing a slight delay, so please relax. I will make sure you're alerted when boarding is about to begin." The host handed the phone back. "Can I offer you anything in particular while you wait?"

"They could use a drink," Mel broke in, "and so could I." She hoisted her backpack strap higher on her shoulder.

"Of course." The host gestured toward the left with an upraised palm. "Rita is our bartender this morning. She will take good care of you and Mr. St. Cloud." Mel's use of Kade's pronoun must have flown over the host's head.

Kade murmured their thanks and stepped through a pair of automatic sliding doors, making a beeline to the left. Mel followed, her mind occupied with what she should order. Did she dare try a Bloody Mary? Those could be really hit or miss, as her own failed experiments had shown.

The bar turned out to be a sprawling horseshoe of zinc-top that offered a panoramic view of the tarmac. At this early hour, only one other guest was seated at the very end, a suit sipping an Irish coffee. Mel wondered if time zone differences meant some guests were drinking hard at all hours, or if most seasoned travelers stuck to local time when choosing their cocktails.

Kade slid onto one of the high swivel seats near the middle of the horseshoe, and Mel sat next to them. Rita the bartender approached, her name tag glinting as she walked. She was young, brunet, and way too perky for the hour. "Good morning, ma'am," she said to Mel first. "What can I get for you?"

"A paloma, please." It was Mel's go-to when she didn't trust a bar. Even a bad paloma was good. Kind of like pizza.

Rita turned to Kade, her smile incandescent. "And for you, sir?"

"I'm not a 'sir,'" Kade said. Their voice was tight, like they were trying to hold themself in check.

"I'm sorry." Rita passed her eyes over Kade, taking in their Ferragamo outfit. "Pardon me. Ma'am?"

"I'm not a 'ma'am.'" Mel could see Kade's nostrils flare. "And I'll have a gin and tonic."

"Oh!" Rita seemed completely off-track now, mouth opening and closing. "I didn't—I thought only women were nonbinary."

Kade closed their eyes and breathed out like they were gathering strength. Or deciding whether it was worth it to prolong this interaction any more than was necessary.

Mel couldn't sit quietly on the sidelines any longer. She leaned across the bar, palms flat on the zinc surface. "The fuck is wrong with you? You can't say that to a guest."

"Mel—" Kade touched the back of her arm, but Mel ignored them.

"You work in hospitality. Where's the hospitality?" she demanded. At the far end of the bar, Irish Coffee looked up at the commotion and then pointedly stared down into the drink.

"I have to greet guests by calling them either 'sir' or 'ma'am.' That's the rule!" Rita said, wide-eyed.

Mel snorted. "It's a shitty rule. Fucking ignore it. Otherwise you're rolling the dice every time, hoping someone like Kade won't show up in this joint. How do you think that makes them feel? Not welcome, I'll tell you that much."

"Mel." Kade's hands, thin and strong, were on her shoulders now. Mel hadn't realized how close the two of them were; she'd been too pissed to notice. "It's fine."

"No, it's not. It's the opposite of fine," she snapped. Then, because Rita looked like she was about to burst into tears, Mel backed up an inch. "Look, I know you've probably been on your feet for ten hours and they're probably not paying you half of what they should, but you can't talk to people that way. That wouldn't fly at my bar, and it sure as shit isn't acceptable here."

"I—I'm sorry. Really. Please." Rita's big, wet eyes darted between them. "Let me make you something from the top shelf. Normally that's not complimentary, but if you could please accept it with my apologies—"

"That's very kind of you," Kade said, their voice dropping to its usual flat calm, "but I'd actually prefer some water now." They cut their eyes at Mel, clearly expecting her to go along with the new plan. She supposed adding alcohol to an already tense situation was not the best idea.

She sighed and held her fingers up in a V. "Make it two."

Rita presented them with the most elaborate ice waters ever served in the western hemisphere, highballs of crushed ice with perfect wheels of lemon and bamboo straws sticking out from the top. "Again, I'm very sorry," she said, misery leaking from her every word. "But—I'll get in trouble if I don't follow the rules."

Kade stood and placed one hand palm down on the bar top. "I understand," they said in a way that sounded like they also could not condone it. "Thank you for the water." They took their glass and swept out of the bar area and into a more casual space filled with couches and wingback chairs.

Mel followed, but not before giving Rita a wary look that said, *You're getting off easy.* She had all the sympathy in the world for her fellow service workers, but "just following orders" was not something she could swallow. She flopped into a cushy chair next to the one Kade had chosen and sipped at her water. The weight of Kade's gaze made her look up. Their eyes were examining her placidly—no, calculatingly.

"Okay." Mel put her water glass down on a side table with a click. She worried at the frayed hem of her T-shirt. "So I might have overstepped back there. Sorry I made such a scene. It's—well, I get a little worked up when bartenders do that kind of shit. Call it professional pride."

Kade only stared at her.

Mel winced. Yeah, she'd fucked up for sure. "I wouldn't have said anything, but you looked like you were pretty fed up with, you know, all that."

They drew a line through the condensation on their glass with a fingertip. "Today has been stressful. Normally I can ignore the constant inaccuracies from strangers. I would never leave the house, otherwise. But on days like this, it's difficult. You didn't—" Kade paused, then said slowly, deliberately, "I would never do what you did."

Mel nodded, pursing her lips. The cabbie and the airline desk and security and all the rest—Rita must have been the last straw for Kade's raw nerves. Still, Mel had been out of line. Now Kade was probably going to hate her the whole weekend, possibly longer. "Message received," she said, and turned to her phone, pretending to check her nonexistent text messages.

Kade opened their mouth, then closed it, frowning. "Fine." They retrieved a copy of *Frankenstein* from their carry-on and cracked it open.

Mel drank her water, and Kade drank theirs, and they waited in stilted silence for their boarding announcement. Mel stared down into her melting ice, hoping this vacation wasn't completely cursed by bad vibes.

CHAPTER 18

They were definitely cursed.

Their flight was delayed an hour. Customs took forever. The rental car company had lost their reservation. It was kind of comical, how bad of a start they'd gotten off to. Mel tried to get through the annoying travel issues with good humor, but by the time they wrangled a Land Rover out of the rental place, she was out of juice. Kade had been quiet since takeoff, every attempt Mel made at conversation bouncing off them Teflon-like. Maybe that was normal for them, though. Mel couldn't get a read on the stone-faced artist no matter how hard she tried.

Mel loaded the bags into the car while Kade signed the rental agreement. God, she wished Bebe were there. She would know what to do in this situation. It would probably be something horny, but that was infinitely preferable to whatever flailing Mel was doing.

"Do you want me to drive?" Mel asked as she shut the back door.

Kade froze in the act of opening the driver's side door, key fob in hand. "I believe only I can. The reservation was made under Bebe's name. Spousal benefit."

"Oh. Right." There was no hierarchy in their own poly guidelines, but out here in the real world, Kade trumped her every time.

They stood there for an awkward beat. "It's a foolish rule, though." Kade held out the fob. "Please. I insist."

"No, no." Mel held up her hands. "The way our luck is going, I'd probably drive us into a ditch. Let's just go." She headed for the passenger side.

They drove in silence for hours, leaving the city behind and heading into the mountains. Mel considered asking if she could stream some music through the car stereo, but when she checked her phone, she saw she had no reception. Silence it was, then.

Soon the mountain highway turned into a bumpy gravel road that was lined with towering pines. Mel resisted the urge to press her nose to the window and stare at the pristine, wintry nature. New York got the occasional snowstorm, but it never looked like this. The best the city could hope for were disgusting slushy puddles at crosswalks and grimy, salted paths across the Manhattan grid.

Here, though, everything was untouched. The snow had been pushed off the roadway, but fluffy white banks remained on either side. Mel watched as a tall pine tree, its boughs bent under the weight of the snow, finally shed its burden in a shower of flakes. She twisted in her seat so she could catch the whole thing as they passed. It was strangely quiet, hardly a sound but the *shush* of snow hitting snow. The black shape of a bird flew between the trees, its call muffled by the cold.

"I've always liked this area." Kade's voice was as hushed as the forest that surrounded them. "Peaceful."

Mel turned to regard them. They seemed intent on the road, cautiously navigating the Land Rover around a muddy pothole. Mel relaxed against the heated leather seat. Maybe this trip wouldn't be a total bust after all. How bad could it be, hanging out in a rustic cabin for a few days, sipping cocoa and watching the snow slide off the pine branches? Kade wasn't the worst travel companion one could ask for. Even with their initial plans ruined, they could still have a nice time.

"We're here," Kade said.

Mel jolted out of her daydream, surprised to see the Land Rover was turning off the road onto a narrower, bumpier one. More of a driveway, actually, that snaked up a hill toward a brightly lit building. It looked like a jewel in a crown, the way it sat centered on the hilltop.

"Where's the cabin?" Mel ducked her head to get a better view through the frosted windshield. "Is it behind that huge house?"

"No." Kade gave her one of their Looks. Mel mentally updated her hazard sign: it has been zero minutes since our last bitchy eyebrow. "That *is* the cabin."

"What?" She looked at the building, which was getting even larger as they got closer, then looked back at Kade. "Are you sure?"

"I've stayed here on four previous occasions," Kade said. They brought the Land Rover to a stop at the foot of some steps that led to an elevated deck and tugged the parking brake. "I'm sure."

Mel gaped out the window some more. The "cabin" was nothing like Mel had been picturing. Instead of rough-hewn logs and a pointy-hatted chimney jutting out of the roofline, the building before her was all glass and sleek steel. Its high A-line peak was one huge, continuous window that spanned two floors. She could see the modern comforts within: a spacious open kitchen, the upstairs loft that held a sprawling bed, the funky fireplace that was suspended from the ceiling in the middle of the sunken living area. A postcard-perfect lean-to filled to the brim with firewood was situated several hundred yards away against the side of an outbuilding.

"Um, okay. So this is massive," Mel said, popping her seat belt off while still staring at the vacation home. Christ, was that a wet bar in the corner?

"What were you expecting?" Kade's tone was bland as they unbuckled themself and opened the driver's-side door. "A one-room hovel à la Abraham Lincoln?"

"No! Well . . ." Mel exited the vehicle as well, her boots crunching into the snow, making deep impressions that rose past her ankles. "I definitely wasn't expecting a mansion. In a place like this, you and I could rattle around all weekend and not cross paths even once."

She felt this was a very witty observation, so she was disappointed when Kade rounded the Land Rover wearing a distressed look. The corners of their mouth pulled downward into a frown.

"If that's what you'd prefer," they said as they brushed by.

Mel blinked at their retreating back. "That's not what I meant. I was making a joke about—ugh, never mind." She busied herself with opening the back of the Land Rover to retrieve the bags. "You take things a little too literally sometimes, you know that, Kade?" She raised her voice to be heard while her entire upper body was inside the car, groping for the bags that had shifted out of reach during the drive. She stood on tiptoe in an attempt to snag the handle of a suitcase. "I'm looking forward to spending time with you one-on-one, really," she said, hoping that none of her anxiety was audible in her voice. "Bebe is obviously a fan of you, and I think Bebe has excellent taste, if I do say so myself. Maybe we have stuff in common, you know? Maybe we could even be—friends." Of course, the inscrutable Kade gave no answer to that. Mel huffed and stretched as far as she could, finally yanking Kade's bag toward her. Success. She extricated herself from the Land Rover and looked around. "Kade?"

They were gone. The front door had been left cracked open. They hadn't stuck around to hear any of that heartfelt shit. Mel let loose a frustrated groan and closed the tailgate. The slam echoed through the quiet, snowy woods. A pair of crows cawed in annoyance and took flight, leaving the trees to become blotches against the gray sky.

Inside, the house was warm and pine-scented. Everything had a veneer of elegant coziness. Even the unlit mid-century-modern fireplace was homey in its own weird way. It dominated the sunken living area with its sectional sofas built into the walls of the sunken part.

"Oh wow, this is nice." Mel set down the bags with a dreamy sigh. "Daniel's going to be so jealous when I tell him about this place."

Kade took a seat on one of the sofas and examined a small card on a side table that listed the Wi-Fi information. "Is Daniel your . . . ?" They trailed off, glancing up at Mel.

"Best friend. And roommate." Mel threw herself on the sofa opposite Kade, laying on her belly in the cushions' soft embrace.

"I see. Why would he be jealous?"

Mel propped herself up on her elbows. She wondered if this was Kade's attempt at chitchat. "Are you kidding? *I'm* jealous of me right now. Completely normal to be jealous of this. Well, normal for—you know." She grimaced. "Other people. Not you. I know you don't get jealous."

"I don't get jealous?" Kade's eyebrows did something complicated.

Mel frowned. "I mean, you're okay with Bebe dating other people. You wouldn't be if it made you jealous, right?"

Kade tipped their head to the side, considering. "Jealousy isn't a failing. It's a feeling like any other. I would have to be some kind of robot to not ever feel jealous."

Mel's eyes went wide. "So you do get jealous?"

Kade shrugged one shoulder. "Sometimes I look up from my work and want to tell her something, but I remember she's with you or at the office. I miss her in those moments. And yes, in those moments, there's a part of me that wants to monopolize her time. But that part is not the whole of me."

A twinge of regret worked through Mel's chest. "I guess I thought you were above stuff like that." She worried her lip. "I don't like the idea that you're sitting at home seething while Bebe and I are out on a date."

"I don't seethe." They sounded offended at the very notion. "There are other ways to cope. If I see a dead bird on the sidewalk, for example, I am sad, but I don't let that sadness derail my entire day. I mourn, I reflect, I move on."

"You feel sad about birds?" Mel blurted out. "That's so cute."

Kade gave her a look that somehow managed to convey an eye roll without their eyes moving at all. "Anyway, there's a difference between feeling something and letting it consume you." They cocked their head to the side much like a bird itself. "Unless I need the artistic inspiration and my schedule is free, of course. Then I suppose I can pencil it in."

Mel stared at them in growing awe. "Was that . . . a joke?"

Kade gave a haughty sniff. "I can joke," they said severely.

"No, yeah, totally—I just didn't think you had a sense of humor." Mel put her thumb and forefinger close together. "Even a tiny one."

She thought her observation might set off another round of banter, but Kade's whole face shuttered. They stood abruptly. "I should get our things upstairs. Could you call Bebe and see how she's progressing, please?" Without waiting for an answer, they moved down the hall that presumably led to the stairs, toting a suitcase and one of Mel's bags.

Great. Now Kade hated her again. Mel sighed and rolled onto her back with her arms flung above her head. She was making too many missteps with her metamour. Every time she thought they were warming to her, she made things awkward. Maybe she should give up on trying to forge a deeper connection. Be content with plain civility.

No, she told herself firmly. Bebe was joining them tomorrow, and she'd be thrilled if she arrived to find her two partners getting along. Mel owed her that much; Bebe had probably been assigned this new urgent shitstorm of a case because she'd recused herself from the last one. Mel had the entire rest of the day and some of the morning to figure out how to be more friendly with Kade. They might never consider Mel a bosom buddy or anything, but surely with a little persistence, the two of them could have a healthy working relationship.

Mel pulled out her phone and frowned at it. Still no reception. She levered herself off the couch and snatched up the little card with the Wi-Fi password. Once she got connected, her phone pinged relentlessly with about a million missed calls and texts from Bebe. Mel smiled to herself. Sweet of her to check in. She called Bebe on video chat, and Bebe picked up within seconds.

"Oh, thank god." It looked like she was standing in a nondescript office hallway. She was perfectly made-up, as usual, though two strands of hair had escaped her businesslike bun to hang in her eyes. She brushed them away with a swipe of her hand. "Are you okay? Are you still in Calgary?"

"Uh . . ." Mel held her phone out at arm's length and moved in a circle so Bebe could see her surroundings. "We're at the cabin. Mansion-cabin. Why would we still be in Calgary?"

The Wi-Fi must have had its hands full with the video call because Bebe's face froze for a long moment, her voice cut off into garbled robotic nonsense. "—the storm?" was all Mel caught.

"Storm? What storm?" She moved around the room with her arm outstretched, hoping to find a spot where the signal was stronger. "Sorry, you're breaking up."

Bebe thankfully resolved after a moment. "The blizzard!" she said with an exasperation that meant she'd probably repeated it several times. "You haven't heard?"

That sounded . . . not good. "Kade!" Mel called over her shoulder. "Can you come here for a second?" Then, turning back to Bebe's worried face on her phone, she hissed, "No, I haven't heard. I haven't had cell service since we got into the mountains."

Kade appeared at that super opportune moment, poking their head over Mel's shoulder to see the phone. "Hello, Love."

"Darling, there's a massive blizzard headed right for you," Bebe said in lieu of a greeting.

Kade's reaction was infuriatingly nonplussed. "I see," they said. "That is unfortunate."

Mel's head spun. "Wait, how massive are we talking?" she asked Bebe. "Are you still flying out tomorrow?"

Bebe gave a miserable huff. "All flights in and out of Calgary are canceled. I can't book a ticket." She checked her wristwatch. "I called the company our friend hired to maintain the cabin—"

"Mansion," Mel muttered under her breath.

"—and they told me the best thing for you to do if you're already there is to hunker down."

"Leaving is not an option?" Kade squinted out of the plate-glass window. Mel could see ominous gray clouds blotting out the sky, but it wasn't snowing or anything. "The weather doesn't look too terrible at the moment."

"The weather channel says the blizzard is moving fast. If you leave, you could get stuck on the roads," Bebe said. "Sit tight. That's all you can do at this point."

Mel's heart sank into her Docs. A long weekend trapped in a luxury cabin alone with Kade? The thought made her more panicked than the threat of a storm. Weather, she could understand. Kade St. Cloud? Not so much.

"I wish I could be there with you," Bebe said, as if reading Mel's mind. She forced some cheer into her voice, though the janky Wi-Fi connection cut off some of what she was saying. "—the worst might miss you. If not—" Another lag. "—for a snowplow to dig you out."

A snowplow? Oh, hell no. "Uh, Bebe, can I talk to you alone for a minute? I'll be right back, Kade." She hustled upstairs with the phone still in hand, looking for some privacy. Kade had placed her backpack in one of the two bedrooms, so she entered that one. It was a very nice room with a picture window facing the woods. Outside, the wind howled like barflies who'd been told it was last call. Fat flakes of snow were falling one by one, picking up speed. Mel shut the door behind her and addressed Bebe on the phone in a low whisper. "Are you absolutely sure Kade and I can't make a break for it? Because if we get trapped on a mountain alone together, we might murder each other."

Bebe laughed. Laughed! At Mel's potential demise. "What on earth are you—?" The call glitched briefly. "—can't be that bad."

"It is," Mel said, piecing Bebe's point together as best she could. "I'm ninety-nine percent sure they hate my guts."

"What makes you say that?" Bebe asked.

Mel blew out a breath. That morning at the airport lounge loomed large in her mind. "It's a long story, but I kind of blew up at someone who kept misgendering Kade and they told me"—Mel adopted a chilly monotone for her best St. Cloud impression—"'I would never have done that.' Or something."

Bebe stared at her for so long, Mel was convinced the screen was frozen again. "I don't think they meant it in a bad way."

Mel groaned and scrubbed her face with her free hand. "Yeah, right. That must be why we've barely spoken two words to each other the whole way here." And those that had been spoken only seemed to rub each other the wrong way. "What are we going to do all weekend alone?"

Bebe's eyebrows did a little dance. "I have a couple suggestions."

"Bebe. Be serious."

"What? It's cold, you're snowed in—if you two wanted to spend the time getting to know each other, biblically or otherwise, you have my blessing."

Mel shook her head. She couldn't begin to imagine being biblical with Kade. "They would rather walk into the woods and disappear forever. They hate me."

"That's simply not true." Bebe's face softened on the screen. "Look, I'll be the first to admit that it takes a certain amount of . . . practice to communicate effectively with Kade. But I promise you, they don't—" The picture froze with Bebe's eyes in a half blink. "In fa—"

Mel shook her phone like it was an Etch A Sketch, hoping it would help somehow. "Bebe? I'm losing you."

"—told them I wouldn't say anything to you, but—" She cut out again.

Mel's eyes went wide. "Say what to me? Bebe!"

The call dropped. Mel tried to redial but couldn't get through. The Wi-Fi, her phone helpfully informed her, was gone.

CHAPTER 19

"Hey, quick question: Are we going to starve to death?" Mel tried to sound upbeat about the whole experience, but it was difficult to put a positive spin on what could easily become a Donner Party situation. She paced along the confines of the sunken living room with her arms folded tight across her chest. Outside, the sky was turning black from more than just the setting sun. She stopped to look out the huge window-wall. The storm was getting worse, snow falling in great, gusty sheets now.

Kade opened the fridge in the sleek kitchen and peered inside. They had changed out of their Ferragamo ensemble and into more practical winter clothes: thick trousers and a wooly sweater with a wide neck. "There's plenty of food." They closed the fridge and turned their attention to the pantry. "We should try to make it last, though. If we get snowed in, who knows how long it will take to dig out."

Mel wrapped her arms tighter around herself and shivered. "Not

sure I could eat anything right now, anyway. My stomach's in knots."
With the Wi-Fi down and no reception, they didn't have any up-to-
date information on the stormfront, but the last piece of info Kade
had seen on their phone before everything went to shit wasn't promising. It looked like they were right in the path of the blizzard. Canadian news said to expect up to three feet of snow and high winds.

"People around here have dealt with worse storms than this,"
Kade reminded her. "We'll be fine as long as we stay inside."

It was exactly then that the power went out.

Every light in the house snapped off with a frisson of electrical
power giving up the ghost. Deep in the guts of the cabin, something
gave a mechanical *ca-chunk*. Mel stood blinking in the pitch-black
darkness, where not a speck of light was around to help her eyes ad-
just. She got out her phone and turned on its flashlight. Kade stared
back at her from the shadows, a box of pasta in their hand, looking
startled.

"Oh yeah," Mel drawled, "I'm feeling *absolutely* fine."

"Sarcasm will not help the situation," Kade said. They smacked
the pasta box onto the counter.

"Okay, so what will?"

"Candles." Kade began the painstaking journey through the
house in the dark. "Or flashlights. They must keep something around
for emergencies."

She moved her phone in front of Kade, trying to light their way.
"Does this place have one of those binders? The ones hotels and rental
places have sometimes? 'Check out time is blah blah blah; here's how
you use the coffee maker; in case of emergency, candles are located
here' type stuff?"

"Yes. That makes sense. There should be a binder." Kade swept their
hands over the surface of the kitchen counter and, finding nothing,
moved on to accost the living room's coffee table. "Do you see one?"

"No, but—" Mel swished her light around the room and landed
on the empty fireplace. "We could build a fire."

"Excellent idea," Kade said. They bumped into tasteful mid-
century-modern furnishings as they picked their way over to the

hanging fireplace. It looked like a huge black smokestack that ran from the ceiling to a few feet above the floor, where it ended in a widened mouth of a grate. Kade crouched beside the spacey-looking circle of iron that held a handful of logs. "I'll hold the light and you can start the fire," they said.

Mel made a doubtful noise. "I don't know how to start a fire."

Kade's head snapped up, their mouth a distressed oval. "What do you mean, you don't know?"

"I mean I don't know! I've never had to light a fire before."

"You've never been camping?"

"I wasn't exactly Girl Scout material growing up." It had been more of a tarot-and-witchcraft vibe at that age. She shifted on her feet. The light bounced along Kade's arms. "Can't you do it?"

Kade's lips thinned into a line. The look on their face said more than a biography.

Mel nearly dropped her phone. "You've got to be fucking kidding me. You don't know either?"

"I'm not an outdoorsy type," Kade said defensively. "Bebe's always been the one to light the fire here before."

Mel rubbed a hand over her face. "Well, we can't exactly ask her how to do it, now, can we?" What kind of tops were they? Completely useless, the pair of them.

Kade peered into the fireplace. "I remember she needed paper to get it started last time. Or cardboard?"

Mel snapped her fingers. "I'll dump the pasta out. We'll use the box." She picked her way carefully toward the kitchen. "What about the flue?"

"What about it?" Kade asked.

"I don't know. Shouldn't it . . . do something?" Mel set her phone down so she could tear open the box of ziti. "All I know is that it's part of the whole chimney setup."

Kade hesitated, then said, "Maybe it's not crucial?"

Turned out, it was crucial, which they only discovered after many false starts: lighting the cardboard box with the gas stove. Running it over to the fireplace to stick on top of the stack of logs they'd arranged

in the grate. Realizing the logs would never catch without more en-
couragement. Finding some bamboo skewers in a kitchen drawer
that could act as kindling. Cheering when the fire at last caught the
wood. Watching in horror as the living room filled with a huge puff of
smoke. Then—finally—turning the knob on the fireplace to open the
flue as wide as it would go so they wouldn't cough up a lung.

"See? That wasn't so hard," Mel panted as they both collapsed
onto the carpeted floor in front of their hard-won flickering fire.

"Child's play," Kade agreed. They had a smudge of soot across their
cheek. Mel thought about wiping it away, but she was too exhausted
to move. Also, Kade would probably shy away from her touch.

Outside, the wind howled. In the firelight, Mel could see the
storm pounding away at the windows, whorls of fat snowflakes
turning everything outside the cabin into a blank canvas. It was a
total whiteout. She was glad they were safe inside a sturdy and well-
appointed mansion.

"How long will the fire burn, do you think?" Mel asked.

Kade shrugged, then reached over to grab the last fresh log from
the holder, tossing it on the roaring fire. "All night, I imagine." An
uncharacteristically optimistic estimate, but Mel didn't know enough
about logs to argue.

There were two sofas arranged at a right angle, so they claimed
one each and settled in for the night. It seemed an unspoken fact that
they weren't going to wander far from their only light source. The
firelight was too unsteady to read by, so Kade gave up fairly quickly
on the novel they'd brought.

"We could—talk," Mel suggested. She herself had done nothing
for the past hour except watch Kade try to read. They were kind of
pretty when they were frowning at a book, all perfect skin and freckles
on their neck. She picked up one of the sleek throw pillows and held
it across her stomach like a shield. "There's not much else to do."

"How gratifying to know speaking to me is slightly preferable to
doing nothing," Kade muttered.

Mel rolled her eyes but was not deterred. "Can I ask you something?"

"If I say no, will that stop you?"

Mel barreled onward, not caring in the least that she was proving Kade's point. "Why does Bebe call you her wife? You're gender neutral about most things, but not that."

They pursed their lips in thought before answering. "I like the word 'wife.' It appeals to me in a way the other words for 'spouse' never could," Kade said. "Bebe and I have imbued it with a kind of magic, I think. Words are just symbols, and a symbol can mean whatever you ascribe to it. I don't think you need to be a woman to be a wife. Even men could be wives, if they tried hard enough." They cast a dry look in Mel's direction. "Most of them don't. But there's always hope."

Mel pursed her lips to keep from laughing. "So you're not the biggest fan of men?" Finally, something they had in common. It wasn't like Mel hated men—Daniel was a man, after all, and he was one of her favorite people in the world—but she had never been attracted to them. It was like how some people didn't like cilantro. She'd never begrudge anyone for it, but she didn't get the appeal.

"Some of them are all right in small doses," Kade said. Then they hesitated, which seemed strange for them. "Sawyer and I—you met him at brunch, didn't you? We used to share a bed off and on. But that time has passed."

"You're just friends now?" Mel asked.

Kade thought about this; Mel could tell the gears were turning because they had caught their bottom lip between their teeth. She filed away the tell in an imaginary box marked KADE. "'Just' friends makes it sound like something lesser. Easier. I don't think it is. It's still a garden that needs tending, even if it's growing something else. In some other season."

"Hm." Mel mulled that over. A garden that needed tending—maybe her friendship with Daniel, the only person who'd stuck by her through the divorce and everything that had followed, required more attention. And not just bullshit fertilizer. No one else had been there when she and Bebe were rocky. She made a mental note to set aside some time when she got home to sit down with Daniel. Really get to the bottom of what was eating him lately.

She lifted her head and realized Kade was staring. Right, this was supposed to be an exercise in getting to know her lover's lover. "And, uh, what about now? Any updates on your love life since we had our late-night tea session?"

That got a hint of a whiff of a smile from them. Their eyes tracked down to the floor. "No, I'm not currently involved with anyone but Bebe."

Mel's curiosity wouldn't let it lie at that. "How come?"

Kade didn't do the intense eye contact that Bebe did, but their fleeting glance was no less affecting. There was a vulnerability there, Mel realized with a start. There was something that had been hurt. "It hasn't been the right time," they said, cryptic as ever.

Mel opened her mouth to ask more probing questions, but she paused with her lips parted. She could see her breath frosting in the air.

"Are you getting cold?" she asked, rubbing her hands up and down her arms. The fire was settling into a glowing ember-ish state, but even so, it should've been throwing off plenty of warmth. Especially when coupled with the house's heating system.

Oh shit. Mel froze. The heating system.

Kade's voice sounded a million miles away. "I'm a little chilly, yes. I'd put another log on the fire, but we've used up the ones in the rack." The artsy geometric firewood holder next to the fireplace was indeed empty.

Mel levered herself off the sofa and headed to the far wall that met the A-frame of glass. She could feel the cold seeping through the window. Her breath was even more noticeable this far from the fireplace. She went to one knee and put her hand on the metal bar of the baseboard heater that ran along the bottom of the wall. Stone cold.

"Uh, Kade?" she said. "The cabin's heating system is electric."

The couch springs creaked as Kade sat up very slowly. "What?"

"It's out. We're not getting any heat." Mel slapped her hand against the heater, producing nothing but a hollow ringing sound. She looked over her shoulder and saw that Kade's face had gone pale.

"We're going to get very cold. Very fast." Kade gestured to the A-frame's glass feature wall, which soared two floors high. "This place isn't exactly designed for efficient heating. It takes a lot of power to get a huge open space like this up to a comfortable temperature."

Mel gnawed her lip. "We could wear a couple extra sweaters?" They could also cuddle for warmth, she thought dimly, but she didn't see Kade leaping at the chance to be her little spoon.

"It's likely in the negatives outside," Kade said. "We can't put on extra layers and hope for the best. We need heat." They got to their feet and went to the glass wall, peering into the torrent of snow. "We have to get more firewood."

Mel stood and stared up at the beautiful timber ceiling. She sighed, hands on her hips. Every cell in her risk-averse body was telling her not to do this. "Fuck me, I guess." She looked at Kade. "I'll go."

"Mel—" Kade began in that grating, reasonable tone of theirs.

"Look, of the two of us, I'm the one who has the most experience with blue-collar shit, right? Lifting heavy things is in my job description." She pointed out the window in the vague direction she remembered seeing the lean-to. "And as the butchest person in residence, I should haul the firewood."

"Absolutely not, Sorrento," Kade said. The use of her last name was new. Kind of funny, like they were in the same platoon or something. "I'm going." They moved to their suitcase that still sat nearby, opened it, and pulled out a second pair of thick socks.

Mel boggled at them. They weren't exactly willowy, but they weren't built either. "Why you? I'm the most logical choice."

"Because if anything happens to you—" Kade shut their mouth with a click, jaw working furiously. "Bebe would kill me," they said in a more sedate voice.

"And what do you think she'd do to me if I let you freeze to death?" Mel groaned, and scrubbed a hand over her face. "We could both go."

Kade pulled on the socks, standing on one leg then switching. "So we can *both* die a horrible icy death? How is that better?"

"I am trying to come up with equitable solutions!"

Kade cast around as if looking for something. "We could flip a coin."

"Do we even have a coin?"

Kade strode to the sofa and plucked their discarded book off the cushions. "We could toss this in the air. Front cover, I go. Back cover, you go. Deal?"

Mel eyed the tattered copy of *Frankenstein*. "Fine," she said, "but I'm doing the tossing, St. Cloud."

"If you insist." Kade shoved the book into her hands.

She threw the book so that it spun end over end near the high ceiling before flopping back to the floor. The front cover of *Franken-stein* stared up at them.

Mel winced. "Best two out of three?"

"I'm going," Kade said, pulling on a pink-and-yellow ski jacket that looked like it had been plucked directly from 1985. "You should stand by the window with your cell's flashlight on. That way, I can follow the light if I lose my bearings. How's your phone charge?"

Admitting defeat, she checked her phone's screen. "Half battery. Should be fine. I'll put it on low-power mode now. You know where the firewood is stacked?"

"Yes, I saw it when we arrived." They jammed a hat on their head and snapped on a pair of ski goggles. "It's not that far. I'll move briskly but carefully. The last thing we need is a twisted ankle." They stepped into a pair of ski boots and began fastening them.

Mel stood there, feeling helpless and rubbing her arms to ward off the creeping chill of the house. Outside, the wind was whipping through the trees and around the house. The walls shook, picture frames rattling. "I don't like this. I should be the one going."

Kade looked up at her, a wry eyebrow raised. "Look at it this way. If I don't come back, you'll have the house to yourself."

"Don't fucking joke about that," Mel snapped. "That's not—don't even think it, for fuck's sake."

"Sorry." Kade adopted a shamed look. They stood to their full height, which was the same as Mel's. "Bad time to attempt humor."

"I'll say. You can crack wise all you want once you're back here safe and sound." Mel looked them up and down. They looked like a neon marshmallow, bundled from head to toe in flashy colors. It didn't feel right to send them into the blizzard without some gesture of gratitude or—something. "I'm going to hug you." She opened her arms. "Can I hug you?"

"Oh." Kade blinked behind their already-foggy goggles. "Yes? Yes. If you like."

Mel wrapped her arms around them, squeezing tight so they could feel her through the puffy layers. Her chin hooked over their shoulder, and she felt theirs settle atop hers in turn. Kade smelled a little like Bebe, plus woodsmoke and a hint of panic sweat. It wasn't bad, actually. Tentatively, like they weren't sure if it was allowed, they wound their arms around her waist.

"I'll be back soon," they said, and then peeled away.

Mel went with them to the mudroom. With one last nod, Kade wrenched the door open. The snow was flying sideways in torrents of sharp, stinging pellets, so different from the earlier fluffy flakes. They ducked into the storm, and Mel slammed the door closed, fighting the wind the whole way.

She ran back to the huge window and turned on her phone's flashlight. Kade's neon shape moved across the snow drifts, obscured more and more by the snowfall the farther away they got. Mel slapped her phone light-side out to the glass. If Kade could see it, they made no sign, trudging single-mindedly toward the outbuilding. Within moments, they disappeared completely into the white.

"Come on," Mel whispered to herself. "Come on, Kade." She counted the seconds to herself, trying to gauge when they would come back into view. Sixty seconds went by; they had to be coming back soon. Another sixty. Surely it didn't take so long to grab a few pieces of wood. Sixty more. Should they have agreed on a time frame? Mel couldn't be expected to sit here all night with Kade out there in the barren arctic wasteland. She lost track of how much time had passed. Too much, she decided. She dragged a side table closer to the window and propped her phone up against a decorative bowl so that the light still shone like a beacon.

Kade's bag held the extra winterwear they'd brought to lend her. If she suited up, just to be safe, Kade would probably make it back by the time she was done. Mel tore through the suitcase and began donning every piece she could find, miles of Patagonia fleece in dark, staid colors. Kade was still nowhere to be seen. How long could someone safely be outside in this kind of weather?

Mel heard a crack in the distance. A terrible whoosh and a thud. A tree had fallen under the force of the icy wind. Close enough for the house to shake.

"Screw this," Mel said, and went out the door.

CHAPTER 20

Kade was not happy to see her. Kade was also still alive, so Mel didn't really give a shit about the other stuff.

"What are you doing?" they shouted when they saw her dragging herself through the snow. They were a pink-and-yellow smear next to the outbuilding, which was frosted completely white. The entrance of the lean-to was covered with a blue tarp to protect the firewood, and Kade was struggling to release the myriad bungee cords that held it in place. "You're supposed to be inside!"

"Well, I'm here, so let's get this done." Mel could barely speak, the cold wind taking her breath away whenever she opened her mouth. Her nose stung; her lips felt like they were on fire. She wished she'd thought to craft a sweater into a muffler of some kind because even a few inches of exposed skin was too much.

They communicated in clumsy ski-glove gestures more than words, since the wind whipped them away as soon as they were spoken. Kade pointed frantically at the bungee hooks. The damn things had frozen together, locked in ice and refusing to come undone. Kade struggled with them, but they only managed to dislodge a clump of snow from the top of the lean-to, cursing as it fell down the back of their neck. It took Mel several whacks of her gloved fist to get one hook loose and by then, the icy chill was inching its way into her body. She'd never been as bone-achingly cold as she was out there. Kade smashed their doubled-up hands into another set of hooks.

At last, after endless strong-arming, the plastic tarp fell away. Kade mimed folding it into a sort of carrier that they could use to drag the firewood back to the house. Mel flashed two thumbs up. *Pretty soon*, she thought wildly, *we'll be unbeatable at charades.* They loaded up a couple dozen split logs and started dragging their prize, parachute-like in the tarp, back to the cabin.

It was slow going. The snow was almost up to Mel's knees. At one point, she put her foot down and the earth wasn't where she thought it would be. She stumbled forward, but Kade caught her by the arm before she fell face-first into a drift. Their eyes were wild behind their goggles.

Mel nodded her thanks and kept pulling her designated tarp corner.

Tumbling back inside the house felt like reaching the pearly gates. Mel wanted to weep with happiness at the relative warmth indoors. She struggled to shove the door closed, then sat heavily on the mud-room floor. Kade made it to the step that led up to the main floor and all but collapsed onto it. The harsh sound of their combined breathing, heavy and desperate, was the only counterpoint to the noise of the storm.

"Fire," Kade said after long minutes had passed and their breathing was somewhat stable. "We should get a new one going." The fireplace's embers were nothing but glowing coals, throwing off very little light. If not for Mel's propped-up phone, they wouldn't be able to see their hands in front of their faces.

"I can do it." Mel groaned as she rose to her feet. "You should get out of those clothes, you're soaked."

Kade looked down at themselves. Their ski jacket and pants were indeed caked in ice that was slowly dripping onto the floor. "I suppose you're right."

Mel did the preliminary work of stripping off her outer layers, then got to work on the fire. She realized—belatedly, but better than never—that the knob that opened the flue didn't need to be opened fully, and that in fact, by keeping it only partway open, it would release the smoke but not eat up the firewood as fast as the first attempt had. It was all about airflow control. Same concept as creating smoke bubbles on cocktails, a trend that Mel hoped to god would die already.

She raided the pantry for more cardboard (*sorry, Triscuits, you live in a salad bowl now*) and lit a new, hopefully longer-lasting fire.

"There we go." She stood, dusting bits of bark from her hands and watching the logs catch in the grate. "Should be plenty of light and warmth for tonight, although we might want to—" She turned around and stopped short as she caught sight of Kade.

Kade was standing with their back to her, in the middle of tugging their thin, silky thermal layer over their head. Their tousled red curls popped free, leaving them naked from the waist up. Mel had never seen them in any state of undress unless you counted the removal of dramatic overcoats and capes. And she'd certainly never seen Kade like this, down to the skin, the smooth expanse of their back bunching with lithe muscle.

That was shocking enough by itself. But even more shocking—and delightful—was the discovery that Kade, like Mel, was covered in ink. She saw the dark swath of it roiling up Kade's spine and across their left shoulder blade before she could register what the shape was. By then, Kade had turned toward her so they could rummage through their suitcase for dry clothes.

"We might want to what?" They looked up and caught her staring, freezing in the act of pulling out a jade cable-knit sweater.

Mel couldn't stop herself from scanning Kade's arms and chest, looking for more tattoos, but their front was bare save for a smattering of body hair. *Must have just the one back piece*, she thought. *Unless there's something more below the waistline.*

Which was not an appropriate thing to wonder about your girl-friend's wife.

She shook herself. It felt like she'd been standing there with her mouth open for a solid hour. "Sorry, I was surprised. I didn't realize you had—" She pointed over her own shoulder.

"Oh." Kade peered over their shoulder as if they'd forgotten the tattoo's existence and was mildly confused to be reminded of it again. "Yes. I do."

"It's a lot of ink," Mel said in what she hoped was an interested yet respectful voice. "Can I take a look?"

Kade looked at her, their eyes dark in the flickering firelight. Only a couple yards separated them, but Mel felt it as an ocean gulf. She couldn't detect any clues from Kade's face, whether they were insulted or intrigued, so she had to assume the worst.

"Never mind." She held up her hands like she could stop the very idea. Kade didn't need her all up in their business, checking it out. "Forget I asked."

"It's fine," Kade said. "You can look."

Mel's hands lowered. "Really?"

"I should warm up by the fire anyway." They crossed the distance and turned around, presenting their back to Mel. Their head turned slightly so that Mel could view them in profile. That sharp nose. That delicate jaw. They stood, silently waiting, patient and still.

"Okay." Mel swallowed. "Uh, thanks." The word came out in a whisper. It seemed only right to speak softly when the only other sounds were the distant whistle of the wind against the chalet and their combined breathing. She fastened her gaze ahead and got her first real eyeful of Kade's tattoo.

It wasn't some abstract shape like she'd assumed at first glance. It was a tree branch, she realized. The gnarled length of it began in the center of Kade's spine, artfully shaded so the viewer could easily imagine it attached to a strong tree trunk that might follow the knobs of their vertebrae. The branch twisted upward and out, across Kade's shoulder to end in a twiggy point right where their arm met its socket. Whoever had inked it had done a fantastic job getting the texture of the tree bark just right; Mel's hand lifted of its own accord, aching to touch it to see if, by some magic, it felt as rough as it looked.

She curled her hand into a fist and dropped it to her side. A harsh squeeze, her fingernails digging into her palm. She'd gotten permission to look, not to touch.

And there was still so much to look at. All along the length of the branch, tiny bits of plant life were sketched curling in on themselves like brown, brittle feathers. Mel caught sight of a small splash of green at the very end of the branch. One plant was still alive, brilliantly alive among the shades of black and brown and gray. It stretched upward toward some unseen sun, its miniscule leaves defiant.

"It's an oak tree," Kade said. They were whispering, too. "A live oak."

"And the little plant things?" Mel asked, unable to tear her eyes from Kade's back. She traced the shape of the branch with her gaze again and again, each time finding some new detail: a bole in the wood, a tattered swag of Spanish moss.

"Resurrection fern. In a drought, it dries up and looks dead, but when it rains, it comes back to life." They reached their right hand over their left shoulder and tapped the single green speck at the end of the branch.

"It's beautiful." She was closer to Kade's skin than she meant to be; her breath ghosted along the nape of their neck. Gooseflesh pebbled under her gaze.

Kade drew a shaky inhale.

Mel took an abrupt step backward. "Sorry. You're probably—it's freezing in here, you must want to get dressed." She stared down at her double-socked feet, scratching one hand through the stubble on the back of her head. Very casual, very cool.

Kade turned around. They did not, Mel noticed, put on the sweater they held in their hands. She was a casual, cool person, so she looked away from their chest as soon as she realized she was staring.

"Maybe you could—show me some of yours," they said. "I've never had a chance to see your tattoos up close."

"Oh, mine are nothing special." Mel shook out her hands, the nautical stars flashing on the backs of them. She smiled in self-deprecation. "Your piece is clearly thought out. Meaningful. Most of mine were just something to do."

"Does that make them any less meaningful?" Kade's brow furrowed. "It's still art, even if it's idle."

Mel's smile grew. "You've always got to say the most poetic shit possible, huh?"

She meant it as a compliment, but Kade ducked their head, murmuring, "Sorry. That must annoy you." They shoved their head into their sweater and pulled it on.

"No, it's fine, it's—" Mel clamped her mouth shut. She reached for the hem of her oversized hoodie. "Let me show you mine. It's only fair."

"You don't have to."

"Shut up. I'm doing it, aren't I?" Mel's words were muffled inside her fleece and double-layered shirts as she struggled to work them over her head, but finally she popped free. She tossed the clothes onto the sofa, leaving her in a black sports bra. "Okay." She planted her hands on her hips to showcase her arms. "Look all you like."

Kade stayed where they were for a moment like they thought the invitation might be a trap. Only when Mel gave an impatient huff did they come closer, their eyes running over Mel's skin with the cool detachment of a professional. Mel tried not to fidget under that gaze. She knew her left arm was a mess, a smattering of small tattoos arranged in a haphazard jumble along her biceps and forearms. They were older, the first ones she'd ever gotten, inked before she'd had the money for something bigger: the stick-and-poke laughing skull near her elbow; Italy on the inside of her forearm; the long line of a bar spoon running along the outside; a pinup's legs kicking high from the depths of a coupe glass; a spread of tarot cards a fortune-teller had once drawn for Mel to cover a bar tab; a devil sticking out his tongue. Mel wasn't particularly proud of any of them, but she also wasn't ashamed—that is, until she noticed Kade pause and lean down to get a better look at the inside of her biceps.

"What is this?" they asked.

"It's nothing." Mel crossed her arms over her chest and shivered. It really was chilly even right by the fire.

Kade straightened and looked Mel in the eye. "It looked like numbers. A date?"

It was a date. Mel's wedding date. A terrible, impulsive, romantic decision to get it tattooed on her arm the night before the ceremony. She'd invited their favorite tattoo artist to the wedding, of course, and he'd offered it as a wedding present. Mel had been so certain she'd want it on her skin forever. Now every time she looked at it, she cringed. She'd been such a tool. And yet she still hadn't found the time to schedule a cover-up. She told herself she didn't have the time or money to waste on it, but on some level, she wondered if she felt she deserved to carry the reminder of her mistakes around forever.

"Can you please admire the actual artwork now?" She waggled her right arm, with its carefully composed sleeve showcasing a waterfall of citrus fruits and fresh herbs tumbling out of a Boston shaker. The image was studded with ice cubes and cherries skewered on shiny chrome cocktail sticks. It had taken weeks to complete the piece, and months for Mel to save up for the cost, but it was worth it. She'd wanted a tattoo that celebrated everything she loved about being behind the bar since she'd mixed her first milk punch.

Kade admired the piece, brows raised and chin lifted. "It's all artwork," they said. "All of it." They shook their head. "What were you going to say before? About the fire . . . ?"

"Oh! Yeah." Mel grabbed up her shirt and tugged it back on. "We should probably spend the night out here where it's warmer. Try to conserve as much wood as we can. Use up the milk and whatever else is in the fridge before we eat the pantry stuff. Who knows when the storm will clear?"

Kade nodded. "I'll get the pillows and blankets from the beds. Excuse me." They headed upstairs, using their phone to light the way.

Mel stood there staring into the flames, thinking about plants that came back to life and listening to the sound of snowfall.

CHAPTER 21

"You're a gin drinker, right?" Mel asked. Now that they had eaten a hearty dinner of perishable food—cold cut sandwiches and milky hot chocolate—she was behind the wet bar, doing what she would have done hours ago if there hadn't been an unending series of crises to deal with: taking stock. Whoever was in charge of outfitting the cabin was no cheapskate. Mel pulled out a jewel-tone blue bottle and gave the label an approving nod. She could work with that.

Kade didn't look up from the sketchpad on their lap. "That's my preferred spirit, yes." They'd set up shop on one of the sofas with their art supplies, blankets, and pillows. The firelight danced along Kade's hair, which was now dried in astonishing ringlets around their head. "I'll try anything, though."

"Okay, my adventurous friend." She dug through the cabinet under the wet bar and, with a cry of triumph, retrieved a dusty green bottle of absinthe.

"Everything all right?" Kade called from the sofa.

"Just peachy." Mel twisted the cap off and gave it a sniff. The smell of lush anise seed filled her nostrils. Good, it hadn't turned. There was no fortified wine—no one's luck extended that far—so she scrounged a dry vermouth from the bar instead. No triple sec, but there was a weird little bottle of French origin that styled itself as ginger liqueur. Close enough. She took her treasures to the kitchen, where she found a lemon in the still-chilly fridge.

The ice. The shake. The strained pour. The delicate twists of lemon peel twirled around the rim before sinking into their cold bath.

Mel brought the drinks into the living room and shoved one glass under Kade's nose. "Here," she said, "try this."

Kade hastily slammed their sketchpad shut and sat up straight. They peered into the rocks glass, the only kind Mel had available. "What is it?" they asked, taking the glass from her hand like it might be filled with nuclear material instead of cloudy liquid.

"A Corpse Reviver Number Two," Mel said, flopping onto the other end of the couch. "Like all the best classic cocktails, it was invented at a fancy London hotel for fancy artists and writers who needed something for their fancy hangovers." There must have been something in the water at the Savoy in the early twentieth century. Mel made a mental note to look it up as soon as they had internet again.

"Why's it called 'Number Two'?" Kade quirked an eyebrow at her. "What happened to the first one?"

Mel shrugged. "No one drinks that one anymore because it's fucking gross. Unless you like cognac." She paused. "Do you like cognac?"

"I have no feelings one way or the other about cognac," Kade said.

"Well, trust me. This version blows the cognac one away. It's not often the sequel is better than the original, but in this case? Forget about it." She sat down in the armchair across from Kade and lifted her own glass. "To staying alive."

Kade returned the gesture. "Cheers."

They sipped their drinks. Mel watched Kade over the rim of her glass as the flavor washed over her tongue: juniper, citrus, sweetness, dryness, and the barest hint of anise. She gave a small shiver as the combo hit her right in the jaw. It was not for the faint of heart.

Kade, for their part, sat up even straighter. Their eyes widened comically as they stared at their drink, then at Mel. "That's . . ." They took another, deeper sip, sighing as they swallowed. "That's exactly what I needed after the day we've had."

"It'll sure wake you up in the morning," she murmured.

"Or in the middle of a dreary night." Kade glanced out the floor-to-ceiling glass windows that faced the white-encrusted woods. The snow was still falling, the bastard. "I'm sorry about the storm, and Bebe, and—everything, I suppose. This is not the relaxing vacation I had envisioned for the three of us."

Mel lifted her glass again. "Hey, not your fault. Sometimes plans get fucked up."

Kade made a neutral noise in the back of their throat. "I suppose there are worse ways to spend a weekend." They turned their glass between their nimble fingertips, watching the pale liquid catch the light from the fireplace. "This really is delicious. Are you going to make this for the cocktail competition?"

"What, a little Corpse Reviver riff?" Mel snorted. "Too British for the brief, too bitter overall. Not exactly the kind of thing they're serving in trendy spots these days. Plus, no offense, but it's kind of— divisive." She smirked. "It's the absinthe rinse. That black licorice flavor. Most people either love it or hate it."

"And you?" Kade looked up, their eyes boring into Mel. Must've gotten lessons from Bebe. Hand to god, these two could stare down a charging rhino. "Are you the kind of person who . . . loves it?"

Mel shrugged and took another sip. "I'm one of those rare people who don't mind it either way. In the right circumstances."

The answer seemed to mollify Kade, who relaxed back into the sofa cushions with a feline smile on their lips. "So many things in life," they said, "come down to circumstances."

"Ain't that the truth." Mel's gaze fell to the sketchpad in their lap. She gestured at it. "Can I see what you've been working on?"

Kade pulled the pad protectively to their chest. "I'm not finished. It's still very rough."

"Hey, I showed you my rough draft." She lifted her glass and took another sip. Yeah, it was way too sharp. It made her mouth pucker. She swallowed, then said, "Come on, one peek."

Kade looked at her through narrowed eyes. Their shoulders were practically hugging their ears. Then, all at once, the fight seemed to leave them, making them slump down against the arm of the sofa. "Fine." They flipped the sketchpad open to the page they'd been working on and passed it over.

Mel put her cocktail aside on the coffee table and took the thick pad carefully in both hands. Kade took their art seriously, so she wanted to be delicate.

Then she looked at what Kade had drawn—really looked—and her lips parted on a soundless *oh*.

It was her. It was Mel, her face and body, picked out in whorls of black and gray. The image showed her standing with her back to the viewer, her head turned to the right to show her face in profile. The lines of her shoulders and spine somehow looked like architecture, like a dependable shelter. It was rough, as Kade had warned her, just a collection of charcoal swipes that gave a sense of her form, no details like clothing. The tattoos of her right arm were denoted only by a vague tumble of lines that suggested the sleeve's shape. Her closely shorn hair was picked out in tiny ticks along the delicate curve of her skull. Without having to be told, she knew that this illustrated version of herself was in the cabin's kitchen. In fact, she could tell the precise moment the drawing was meant to show: a few minutes prior, when she'd been mixing their drinks. The sketch made her look beautiful, graceful. Strong.

This was how Kade saw her.

This was how Kade saw her?

"Uh." Her stomach shifted inside her. Her throat was suddenly dry. She reached for her glass and took another sip to buy herself some time. "It's—nice." *Wow. Real nuanced take, Melanie.* She glanced at Kade, and they seemed as unimpressed with her response as she herself had been. Though she noticed they were having a hard time meeting her eyes.

"Thank you," they said, curling up into an even tighter ball in the sofa's embrace. Their gaze wandered over to the fireplace to stare into the flickering flames. "Like I said, it's still rough."

Mel licked her lips and tried again to express what the drawing moved inside her. "I knew you were talented. But I mean, wow . . . look at how good you made me look." She wanted to trace her finger-tips along the line of her drawn body, but she stopped herself at the last moment. She didn't want to smudge it. Her hand hovered over the paper, a millimeter away. Less.

Kade huffed, not a laugh, but definitely more breathless than a scoff. "As if you don't know," they muttered into their drink.

"What?"

"What?" Kade's face took on an innocent, blank look.

Mel shook her head. She might never understand Kade. "What else have you been drawing?" she asked, and flipped back through the sketchpad to look at the earlier pages.

"Oh, those are all very old—" Kade leaned forward as if to take the sketches back, but they stopped and seemed to deliberately lower their hand to rest on their thigh. "You can look, though. If you want."

Mel did want. She didn't know much about art, but she knew she liked Kade's, and she wanted to learn more about it. She started at the beginning of the sketchpad, flipping through the first few pages in quick succession, then slowing down to appreciate them more lei-surely. They were beautiful, these rough studies of a nude form. After a few pages, Mel realized it was the same form, over and over in dif-ferent poses.

"Who is this?" she asked. "A model?"

"No." Kade drank deeply from their cocktail. "A former lover of mine."

Mel waited, but Kade seemed to have hit a verbal roadblock. She nudged their leg with her foot. At some point, they'd gotten cozier on the shared couch, turning to face each other and stretching out a bit. "What's their name?"

"Blue. Her name was Blue."

"Pretty name." Mel flipped to another page: Blue laughing, head thrown back. "Where'd you meet?"

"At a gallery in Milan. He was showing his paintings. There was a connection between us right away, like—" Kade snapped their fingers. "I'd never experienced something like that before, and I doubt I will again. Bebe and I needed time to figure out how we fit together, you see."

Mel looked up from the pages. "Sorry to stop your story with a pronoun question, but—?"

"Blue used all pronouns. They used to say it was the closest they could get to describing the infinite spirit inside them." That brought a small, sad smile to Kade's face, one that Mel had to really search to find.

"Gotcha." Mel dreaded where this story might be headed; Kade's use of the past tense made her wonder if something horrible had happened. But it was Kade's story, and she got the impression they hadn't told it to many people. In a way, she felt honored to hear it, even if it was scary and sad. "Sorry. Continue."

"There's not much more to tell. We were together. Now we're not." Kade drank the last dregs of their cocktail, throwing their head back to catch the final drops.

Mel pointed to their empty glass. "Want another?"

"Dear god, yes." Kade handed the glass over, and Mel traded it for the sketchpad.

While Mel was in the kitchen measuring out the second round, Kade slouched down so their head was resting on the arm of the sofa, their long legs stretched out before them. "Have you ever met someone," they said, "who seemed to know you so thoroughly, like they understood you down to the smallest atom? And then—poof." They made an exploding gesture with their long fingers. "It's like they never saw you at all. It was just a grand mirage, a lie you told yourself."

Mel filled the shaker with ice and thought about her ex. Kade's words pulled that old pain out of the cabinet in Mel's chest, dust motes and all. "Yeah," she said. "I have." She swallowed. "My, um. My ex-wife. Lynn."

She hadn't said—hadn't even thought—Lynn's name in so long, it felt like the syllable would set a barb into her throat as she said it. But it didn't. It slipped out like any other word. Saying it aloud seemed to dispel its power. Mel was taken aback by how easy it was, after it had been so hard for so long.

Kade must have noticed her shock. They said, quiet and low, "You don't talk about her much, do you?"

"No, I guess I don't. It's kind of embarrassing. Like, a total cliché." Mel poured a scant amount of absinthe in each glass and swirled it around before pouring the excess into the sink. "We were barely more than kids when we met. Got married way too young. We both worked in the industry, which didn't help. Time and money—never enough. Jesus, what was I thinking?" She shook her head. "I didn't even know what kind of martini I preferred at that age. What made me think I knew who I'd want to be with forever?"

"Is that what marriage is to you?" Kade's voice, for once, held no tinge of judgement. "Being with someone forever?"

"I mean—that's the idea, right? Why? Is it different for you and Bebe? More loosey-goosey?"

Kade considered this for a moment. "I think it's strange to define a good marriage as one in which two people stay together until they—what? Both die simultaneously? It's a lot of pressure, not to mention statistically unlikely." They raised their arms above their head and let them flop over the side of the sofa. "'Forever' is a lofty goal. My only goal is happiness, and I don't pretend to know what that will look like in the future."

"See? That's really fucking smart. You can't even begin to comprehend shit like that when you're twenty-three." Mel clapped the tin on and started shaking, raising her voice to be heard over the noise. "You only know what you see in sitcoms and movies, and you think your relationship should follow that story. Which, by the way, are all stories about straight people!" She felt the metal shaker frost in her hands as cold as the blizzard outside. "So we got married young. Moved to the city. Made friends, or rather she made friends. She'd always been the more approachable one so—why are you laughing?"

Kade's shoulders shook as they stared up at the ceiling. They bit their lip in suppressed mirth. "You literally chat with strangers as a job. How much more approachable can a person be?"

"You never met Lynn," Mel said as she strained the drinks into their glasses. "I'm good with people as long as there's a bar between us, but she could make friends with anyone over anything. Which meant that when we split, all my so-called friends chose her side."

"I'm so sorry."

Mel shrugged. "It wasn't anyone's fault. We—grew apart. I was a different person at thirty than I was at twenty, you know?" She cut new twists from the lemon, the peel separating neatly from the pith. "I think I stuck it out for so long because I believed I was a failure if I couldn't make my marriage work. That love could solve everything, so I just had to love her more. Oh, and that all lesbians have perfect relationships and if I didn't, I was a traitor to the cause."

"Lesbians are supposed to have perfect relationships? Is that a thing?"

"Yeah, don't you know? We're all conflict-free, like good diamonds." She rubbed the twists along the rims of the glasses, one in each hand, and dropped them into the liquid. "Anyway, after the divorce, I felt like the biggest loser. I'd fought so hard and still came up empty-handed. I thought I was on track to be alone for the rest of my life."

"Until you met Bebe," Kade murmured.

Mel nodded. "Until I met Bebe." It felt weird talking about her girlfriend without her present. She brought the finished cocktails back to the couch. "It's not—are we gossiping if we talk about her now? I don't want to pole-vault over a boundary or anything."

"I think it would be odd *not* to speak about Bebe. She is, after all, the one thing we have in common." Kade shifted their legs to give Mel room. "That and heartbreak, I suppose."

Mel smiled at that and handed over Kade's drink. "True. She's probably told you how prickly I was at first. I was really invested in my sour grapes–idea that love wasn't real and everyone who thought it was must be kidding themselves and yadda yadda yadda. But Bebe—"

She sat down with a smile on her lips. "She makes you feel like anything is possible, doesn't she?"

"She certainly does." Kade paused, then raised their glass. "To our girl."

Mel let her smile take over her mouth. "Our girl." She clinked the rim of her cup to Kade's.

They both drank, Mel watching Kade's throat as they swallowed.

"So," she said once an appropriately friendly amount of silence had passed, "what happened with Blue?" She watched Kade's face go elastic with trying to form an answer, the tip of their tongue touching their upper lip in thought. "If that's too personal—"

"It isn't," Kade insisted. They slouched further down into the cushions. Their socked feet brushed Mel's knee. "Bebe and I share a deep bond. I love her more than I can say. But we are very different people."

"I've noticed," Mel said, dry as her favorite martini.

Kade's eyebrow hooked up in a way that Mel now saw as good-humored. "Yes, well. There are times in my life where I have felt very much the outsider. Not just because I'm genderqueer, although that is part of it. But I'm aware that—" They made a gesture beside their ear, like they were turning a dial. "My mind doesn't always follow the same lines as other people's."

"Nothing wrong with that," Mel said with a shrug. Daniel had told her years ago that he suspected he had undiagnosed ADHD. Sometimes he focused on a new hobby or topic to the exclusion of all else or had trouble doing a small chore because the stars weren't in alignment. Mel didn't see it as a problem so much as another part of his personality, and she liked his personality.

"I agree. And for the most part, the people I've surrounded myself with have learned to embrace it, or at least tolerate it. But Blue—she worked the same way I do."

Mel nodded. "There's a big difference between being embraced and someone fucking getting it, huh?"

"Exactly." Kade's face softened in relief. "Blue and I were—not inseparable, we both had other partners and responsibilities—but when we were together, it was like—" They paused to worry their bottom lip. "This might sound terrible, but it felt like we were one person instead of two."

"That's not terrible," Mel said. "That's what I had with Lynn. Or, I thought it's what I had. It's definitely what I wanted." There was a certain kind of comfort in being absorbed almost literally by someone you loved. They had been together for so long, they had adopted each other's habits and patterns of speech. They had their own language. It had tickled Mel, the way they'd created their own country of two.

Maybe there was some lesson there about borders. What they were good for, at least when it came to this.

Mel focused back on Kade; they were the one spilling their guts. "So what happened?"

"They were offered a residency at an institution in Australia." Kade ran their fingertip along the rim of their rocks glass. "I was happy for them, of course. A fantastic opportunity. But I thought we would discuss it, at least, before Blue made any decisions." A wry look from across the short distance. "Their bags were packed before they even told me the news."

"Shit," Mel said. "I'm sorry. That sucks." It was such a useless thing to say about losing a piece of your heart, but she couldn't think of anything else that encapsulated the situation.

"I couldn't stop thinking, 'It's not anyone's fault. Blue doesn't owe me anything. He certainly shouldn't toss aside this chance to move their art forward for me.' But that didn't change the fact that—" Kade shook their head. "I could conceive of nothing that would make me leave Blue's side. I would never have done that willingly. And yet—he didn't feel the same way about me." They raised one hand, palm up, as if to say *there it is*. "The oldest story in the world. Feelings not returned. Sorry to be so boring."

"Hey. Shut up." Mel leaned forward and smacked her hand atop Kade's knee. "Doesn't matter if it happens every day. It still hurts when it happens to you." Memories of Lynn sitting at their kitchen table with a stack of paperwork in front of her, already written up by some lawyer who shared office space with a travel agency on their block—

we need to talk. She squeezed at Kade's knee before letting her hand fall away. "Thank you. For telling me. I know this shit's not easy."

One corner of Kade's mouth lifted. "Thank you for listening. And for not immediately telling me, 'Well, at least you had Bebe.'"

It hadn't even occurred to Mel to say something like that. "Wait, did people really say that to you? What the fuck?" She groped for the words that would encompass her anger. She hadn't had another partner during the divorce, obviously, but she couldn't imagine anything or anyone that would have made it hurt any less. "That's bullshit."

That made Kade almost laugh. Or at least huff a breath out through their nose in a way that was very close to laughter. "You'd be surprised how many people assumed I had no reason to be upset because I had a wife to quote, unquote, 'fall back on.'" They took a sip of their Reviver. "Bebe is an amazing source of support and I love her, but she's not Blue. Just like how Blue isn't—wasn't—Bebe."

"Right! It's like, has meeting Bebe changed my life? Yes. Is she the reason I've learned to love again or whatever? Of course. Does our relationship make the pain from what happened with Lynn disappear?" Mel gestured wildly, nearly spilling her drink but catching herself at the last moment. "Absolutely not. It's apples and oranges. If the partners you have throughout your lifetime are interchangeable, then that's a fucking red flag."

Kade sat up straighter, nodding emphatically at Mel. "Yes, thank you. You understand." They looked at Mel with something like relief, like joy, suffusing every inch of them. Then a measure of that happiness faded away, their brow knotting. "I should tell you something."

"Sure, go ahead. We've already covered all the major traumas. Everything else is gravy." Mel took an unconcerned sip of her cocktail.

"I like you."

Mel didn't spit out her drink, but it was a near thing. It went down the wrong pipe instead, meaning it took her almost a minute to form an answer. "What?"

"Bebe calls it a crush," Kade said with a roll of their eyes, "but

that sounds so pathetic. I just—I feel drawn to you. I can't explain it."
They looked down into the depths of their drink. "Not only are you
devastatingly attractive—"

"I am?"

Kade ignored her. "—but you have this sense of justice that makes
me weak. Bebe told me what you did for the bartender at my show.
And when you defended me at that airport bar . . ." They looked up at
her. "I am stunned every time I look at you. In every sense."

Mel swallowed. "And here I thought I'd blown it with that stunt
at the airport. You seemed so upset with me."

Kade's brow furrowed. "I was upset about the situation. When I
said I'd have never done what you did, I meant I was thankful."

Wow. Okay. Kade liked her. How bizarre. Or, wait—was it?

Everything she knew about Kade so far pointed to the simple fact
that they weren't as cold or stony as they first appeared—that their
aloofness was only what people saw on the surface. Kade wasn't an
emotionless robot. They actually felt very deeply—what they'd described with Blue was not the mark of someone who couldn't feel
love and loss and pain. They were—and Mel could scarcely believe it,
though she knew it to be true—a big, beautiful romantic.

Kade must have taken her stunned silence as rejection, rushing to
say, "This doesn't need to change anything between us. I only wanted
to be honest with you because—I've gotten closer to you in the last
twenty-four hours than I thought I would in a lifetime. I don't expect
anything from you in return."

"I like you, too," Mel blurted out. Because it was true, and because she couldn't not say it. "I mean, I kind of thought you hated
me—"

Kade's eyes widened. "I've never hated you!"

"—and I kept kicking myself for always getting it wrong when it
came to you, but"—she smiled—"you're something else, Kade. Something I'm really fond of."

"Yes." They relaxed slightly from their affronted posture. "That's
the perfect word. I have an unending fondness for you."

"And you think I'm hot." Mel felt it was important to make sure she'd heard that part right.

"Yes. Despite my best efforts not to," Kade said with a tiny, growing grin.

"See, now I get it! This is you being funny." Mel wagged a finger in their direction. "You're funny. In addition to being aggravatingly sexy. *And* talented? Fucking pick one, leave some for the rest of us."

Kade dropped their gaze but not their smile, then looked up again at Mel. It was a look designed to do something to her, and damn if it wasn't working. "Before we left, Bebe suggested to me that you and I might—have some fun in bed together. On this trip. I told her she was being silly, of course."

"Of course," Mel said. "She tried to tell me the same thing on the phone. I think. The connection was pretty choppy."

"If we did do anything, she'd be very annoying about it," Kade observed.

"Downright insufferable," Mel agreed. Her own grin was broadening to Cheshire dimensions.

Kade stared at her for a beat, then swayed forward, reaching out with nimble fingers to pluck Mel's glass from her hand. They set both Mel's and theirs on the coffee table, not even half-empty. Their gaze never left Mel, serious and delighted all at once.

They met in the middle, their mouths searching hungrily. Teeth and clawing fingers, Kade's hands holding her head, Mel reaching under their sweater to scratch lines up their back. There might be something to Bebe's pet theory, because she was right about Kade: they were a totally different animal like this. Needful and frantic and rough.

And loud.

Really loud.

Mel was stunned by the noises Kade was making, the range of snarls and whines, as uninhibited as could be. The volume alone was enough to rattle Mel down to the bone, but the desperation—that made her feel like something powerful.

Kade broke first, tearing their lips away from Mel's to pant for breath. "We don't have to—" they began to say.

"Do you want to, though?" Mel asked. Her hands were already dragging the hem of Kade's sweater up to their armpits.

Those dark eyes flashed in the firelight. "Yes. I do."

"Another thing we have in common." Mel tugged the sweater off, flinging it to the floor. "We're just racking them up."

CHAPTER 22

They made a nest on the floor of the sunken living room in front of the fireplace. The fluffy duvets and luxury pillows from the bedroom were pressed into service. In the grate, the fire crackled gently, providing enough warmth to be comfortable without layers upon layers of clothing.

Which was really lucky, because Mel was wearing exactly zero clothes.

She reclined naked against a mound of pillows, content to watch Kade strip out of their trousers. They were gorgeous. Completely different from Bebe's voluptuous femme fatale routine, but just as easy on Mel's eyes. They weren't skinny, exactly, but delicate around their joints. Torso-wise, they were built along the lines of a cello, with a soft stomach and compact shoulders. Kade's fashion sense often gave them an androgynous, ethereal quality, but like this, wearing nothing but firelight, they looked even more like some otherworldly being.

She reached out and ran a hand over the muscle of their calf, tickling through the hairs there.

Kade smiled down at her. "Sorry, I usually shave them," they said, holding their leg out for Mel to better grope. "Not in the winter, though."

"Do I look like I care whether you have leg hair or not?" Mel flexed her toes, showing off her own unshaven legs. "Just get down here."

Kade did so, but in that catlike way that made it look like they were doing it because they wanted to, not because they were told. "What can I do for you?" they asked against Mel's throat. "Tell me." They moved on to her lips, nipping with teeth.

Mel hummed. "I thought you'd be the one issuing orders here. According to Bebe, at least."

Kade moved from their position, laying mostly on top of Mel so they could look her in the eye. "Bebe said that?"

"Well, she said you're—different from how you usually are, when you're like this." Mel dragged her fingernails up Kade's arms, watching the skin shiver. "More aggressive."

That tiny smile—Mel was getting better at spotting it—flashed across Kade's lips. "I am . . . more active than not," they said with strange delicacy, given that their hard cock was idly grinding against Mel's hipbone. "But only because I like doing for others. There's nothing more erotic to me than bringing pleasure."

"Oh." Mel felt her whole body expand, like it wanted more space between her cells for something new. "Are we secretly a *service top*, St. Cloud?" She'd never met one before in real life. It was like meeting a unicorn. Or the tooth fairy. A real live person who got off exclusively on getting other people off? Hallelujah and pass the plate.

"It's not much of a secret." They bent to kiss her, but Mel held a finger to their wet lips, arresting the movement.

"You're not going to believe this—" she said.

"You'd be surprised what I'll believe," Kade said right against her finger.

"—but I'm also into being a certain way when it comes to sex. At least, I am lately." She owed Bebe so much. When she saw her again, she was going to make sure she thanked her thoroughly. "And I think my thing combined with your thing is actually *very* interesting."

"Wait, Bebe told me about this." Kade's eyes narrowed to slits. "Isn't your thing . . . ?"

Mel pulled their hair until they gave a soft cry, head tipped back and throat exposed. "Being a little mean." She set her teeth to their throat and sucked a pink mark into the skin.

"Oh fuck," they whispered. "Sorrento, if what you really want is for me to submit, I can. I may not be the best at it, but—"

"Where's the creativity in that?" she demanded. The grin on her face was positively wolfish; she could see it reflected in the fireplace's glass. "Come on, think. What's the meanest thing you can do to a people pleaser?"

". . . . Don't let them please anyone?" Kade said after a long pause.

"Ding ding ding." A thrill of power coursed through Mel. She was flush with it, she was hot as hell, she could do anything she wanted. "I don't think you should be allowed to touch me."

Kade ran their tongue over their teeth, regarding Mel with an impressed look. "If that's really what you want."

"Oh, it is." Mel could feel herself warming to the theme. She put her palm flat on Kade's chest and pushed. "Off."

They went willingly, the frustration on their face at odds with the eagerness of their movements. Push and pull. Mel liked that. "Here?" Kade asked, lying on their side right next to Mel.

"Nice try. Scooch over." Mel shooed at them. "And no touching."

With a performative grumble, Kade wriggled about a foot away, not a single part of them brushing against Mel. She missed their warmth, but more than that, she was excited to experience delayed gratification. With Bebe, gratification was pretty swift. Here, they had all the time in the world.

Mel crossed her arms over her chest in an X, palming her small breasts. There was a lush slickness already building between her thighs, but this wasn't about getting herself primed. This was about putting on a show for Kade, who was watching her from across the scant distance like she was dinner.

"You're so fucking hot," they murmured. Their eyes were getting glassy, losing that intelligent sheen in favor of something single-minded. They stretched one long, naked arm along the ground and pillowed their head on it, staring at Mel intensely.

"Thanks." Mel plucked at the barbell piercings in her nipples, tugging them upward, knowing the movement would give Kade a prime view of the tattoos under her breasts, a pair of gray bird wings. "You're not so bad yourself." Her right hand stole down between her legs, teasing but not giving herself anything more.

Kade's breath hitched. It was loud in the quiet room. They couldn't possibly see Mel dipping her fingers in and out of her wet cunt from their position, but they had an artist's understanding of anatomy that clearly filled in the gaps. As Mel watched with her head turned to the side, Kade's own hand traveled down their torso to seek out their own need.

"Buh-buh-buh!" Mel held up a glistening finger in warning. "I said no touching. And I mean it."

Kade seemed hypnotized by the fluid on her finger and took longer than usual to form a snappish reply. "I can't even touch myself? What am I supposed to do, then?"

"Absolutely nothing." Mel thrust her hand back between her thighs and gave her clit a luscious sweep of her thumb. "Though if you behave, maybe I'll let you put on a show for me."

"You're cruel." Kade's eyes were like molten fire. "I like that about you." They sat up and very deliberately laced their hands together, then brought them to rest behind their head. It was the kind of pose that made Mel think of handcuffs. Ooh, maybe someday she could invest in some props. "Is this sufficient?"

"Perfect." Mel dipped her fingers through her folds, her hips shifting without her say-so. Her whole body felt heightened and warm.

"What about talking?" Kade asked. Their pose forced their shoulders and upper arms into such an intriguing shape, Mel was too distracted to understand the question.

"What about it?"

"Am I allowed to talk?"

"Uh, sure." If Sexy Kade was more talkative than Normal Kade, Mel was curious to hear them. "Chatter to your heart's content." She dipped one finger deeper inside herself and let her eyes close with the pleasure it gave her.

"Bebe told me you were glorious," Kade said. Their voice was a dark rumble in the shadowy room, so unlike their usual flat affect. "But this—I wasn't prepared, not even a little. You're a force of nature, aren't you?"

Mel opened her eyes and shot them a smirk. "Bet you say that to all the girls." She gripped her left hand into the soft down of the duvet she was laid out on, seeking purchase as her hips worked.

Kade's arms flexed like they wanted to help her, but they held themselves in check. Their muscles quivered with the strain of it. "You know I don't."

Oh, that *zinged* through Mel. She'd thought, on some level, that the most poly of people would shy away from bestowing any special favor on one person or another, but she was thrilled to see how wrong she was. Because apparently, she liked being the specialest gal in the world, if only to Kade, if only in this moment.

"How could I possibly know that?" she said, all innocence. Another breathy sigh left her as she crooked her finger just right. "I'm way over here. Minding my own business."

"You think this is funny?" Kade said, sharp and edging toward desperation. "I'm sitting here watching you fuck yourself, and you're laughing?"

Mel slowed down a moment, casting a questioning glance over at Kade. If they were actually angry and not playing around—

Kade gave her a subtle look, licking their lips and tipping their chin in Mel's direction as if to say, *Go ahead. Don't stop.*

Well, as long as it was done in fun. Mel grinned and added a second finger. "I think it's hilarious."

Kade gave a whiny scoff. "I'm getting all filthy because of you." They weren't lying; Mel could see the sheen of fluid smeared over their belly.

"Not my problem." Mel gleefully planted her feet on the floor and lifted her hips, panting as she found the perfect angle. "If you can't control yourself, that's on you."

Kade's shaking arms dropped from their raised position. They sat with their legs crisscrossed, hands on their knees. Mel could see Kade's fingertips digging into their kneecaps to keep themself in check. "Let me touch you. I promise I'll make you feel good," they purred.

"I'm feeling great as is, thanks," Mel said, and demonstrated it thoroughly. She writhed against her hand, her release so close, she could feel the shape of it looming inside her. "But"—she panted for air—"go ahead. Touch yourself. Let me see."

The shift in the air was immediate. Kade dove forward so they were on hands and knees, their hand wrapping around their hard cock and stroking it in a tight fist. They crawled until their mouth hovered over Mel's, the both of them breathing hard into each other.

"Can I taste you?" Asked in a breath that was hot against Mel's skin.

She pursed her lips and blew Kade a kiss. "Not yet."

Kade groaned, their eyes sliding shut in what could have been frustration or pleasure. Probably both. "Mel—"

"Oh, we're doing first names now?" Mel put her tongue to the corner of her mouth. She was almost there, almost. Her hand hastened against her, into her. She pressed one breast into the cage of her free hand, fingers kneading flesh. "Wait until I'm coming. Then you can do anything you like."

Their eyes snapped open, pupils blown so wide only black showed. "Anything? Can I make a mess out of you?"

Mel smiled. They already had, but she could do the more literal version, too. "Fuck yes."

Kade pressed their forehead to Mel's shoulder, hot skin to skin, their moan a sweet counterpoint to Mel's quickening movements. They whispered shattered bits of nonsense, things Mel could barely parse. Her cold marble statue, reduced to whimpers. It was enough to make her body clench and her orgasm roared right over her. A fire that consumed and cleansed.

"Oh—" Her spine went stick-straight, her toes splaying.

She watched Kade swing a leg over her. They propped themself up on one hand, the other jacking their cock. Their gaze was fixed on her, roving over her face, her heaving chest, her stuttering hips, her twitching stomach.

"Now?" The heat in their voice was incandescent.

Mel shut her eyes and tossed her head back. "Yes, fuck, do it."

A strangled cry, and then Kade was coming, too. Hot splashes landed on Mel's navel, her hip, in the triangle of her pubic hair. It seemed to go on for a long time until finally Kade went still, hand wrapped around their cock, the only motion in their body their lungs moving like bellows. Mel looked down at herself. Her flushed skin was shiny with Kade's come. It was a new sensation, one she liked. She slowly pulled her fingers free of the clutch of her body with a sigh and dragged a fingertip through the pool on her belly. It was tacky, like syrup.

"You better pray there's still hot water in this place," she murmured, fond.

Kade blinked at her like they'd forgotten how to speak English. Then, giving up on saying anything, they lowered their mouth to Mel's.

The kiss was indulgent, slow compared to their earlier frantic make out, though no less heated. Kade's tongue swept over Mel's like a promise, and when they pulled away, their eyes held it, too. They shifted down Mel's body and fucking *licked* her, lapping up the fluid on her belly.

Mel dug her clean hand through their hair with a hysterical laugh. "You're going to clean me up yourself, huh? This is a full-service experience."

"I aim to please," Kade whispered into her skin. They kissed her hip, nosed into her body hair, catching every drop. Moving lower and lower, they settled between her jellylike spread legs. "Shall I clean up the mess *you* made while I'm here?" They rubbed their cheek against her thigh, right above her own slick wetness.

Mel hummed and petted her fingers through their hair. "As long as you don't expect me to come again so soon after that. I can't really do multiples." One and done was her lifelong MO, anyway.

Kade lifted their head and looked at her. "Have you ever tried?" They licked their lips like a wolf.

Well. No time like the present. "Okay, St. Cloud." She guided them by the hair toward her cunt. "Show me what you got."

CHAPTER 23

It took two days for the power to come back on and would take another two for the road to get plowed. It was the longest vacation Mel had ever had, and she appreciated every minute with Kade. Besides the sex (fantastic), they made time for eating meals of plain noodles (boiled on the gas stove) and s'mores (roasted over the fire). There was also plenty of time to mix new concoctions for Kade to taste.

"What's this one?" Kade asked, hooking their chin over Mel's shoulder as she added various things to a blender.

"It's a play on a Last Word. There's no Chartreuse in the liquor cabinet, so I'm making a kind of green juice. Thawed spinach from the freezer with fennel seed and dill from the spice rack." She ran the blender on high, blitzing the veggies into a verdant pulp.

"Sounds healthy," Kade said.

Mel hummed a doubtful note. "Probably reads more SoCal than

New York, huh?" She strained the green liquid into a cup and added a judicious measure to the gin, maraschino liqueur, and lime already waiting in the shaker.

"I think it could still meet the brief." They stepped away to give Mel the space to shake. "You're taking this competition seriously, aren't you?"

Mel finished shaking and strained the frosty contents into a waiting glass. "Lot of money on the line. You bet your ass I'm taking it seriously." She pushed the glass down the counter toward Kade. "Try that."

Kade took up the glass and sipped at it. They waited a moment, then took a second sip. Mel waited as patiently as she could; she'd come to understand that Kade needed plenty of time before voicing their opinions.

"It's weird," they finally said. No punches pulled there. They took another drink. "It's gin-based?"

"Yeah," Mel said. "Why?"

"You've been making a lot of gin drinks this weekend."

"Well, you like gin, don't you?"

"I do. But—" They set their half-empty glass on the counter with a thoughtful click. "When I'm working on a commission, I often find myself trying to find a balance between what my patron wants and what my own vision is."

"Balance." Mel frowned. "Sounds tough." She picked up the glass and took a swig of her own. Not her best work. It tipped too much into the medicinal, even the sharpness of the citrus fading against that vegetal taste.

"It can be," Kade said. They swayed forward, dragging a kiss across Mel's lips.

Mel pulled back, determined not to be distracted. "So you don't think I should make a gin drink for the competition? Ten years ago, no way, but now gin's having a moment. There's potential for mass appeal if I just—"

Kade kissed her again, lingering this time in a way that thoroughly distracted her. "Balance," they said against her mouth at the end of it. "You'll get there. I know you will."

Mel hiked them up to sit on the counter and got somewhere else entirely.

That night, Mel curled up in the nest they'd made on the floor in front of the fire. She was dressed in her most comfortable, rattiest pajamas and playing with Kade's hair. Their head lay in her lap. They were wearing a blue silk smoking jacket because they couldn't even do nightwear like a regular person. Which was good, because Mel liked them as irregular as they could get.

"So," Mel said, looking up at the ceiling beams, "what happens when we go home?"

Kade yawned behind their hand. "What do you mean?"

"I mean, do we . . . keep this up? Somehow?" She tried to keep her tone casual, but it was becoming clear to everyone, Mel included, that she was no good at casual.

Kade must have sensed her question's import. They sat up slowly, their elbows hooking around their upturned knees, and turned to regard Mel. "When you say 'this,'" they said, "I assume you're not referring solely to sex. You mean this, too. The intimacy, the closeness. Am I right?"

Not a single punch pulled again. Mel scrubbed a hand over her shorn head and sighed. "Yeah. That stuff. All of it."

Kade smiled. Invisible, except Mel knew how to look for it now. "I would like to keep that up," they said. "Would you?"

Mel tried to imagine going back to New York—the real world, their normal lives—and never kissing Kade again. Never playing silly, sexy games with them, never talking late into the night about things they couldn't tell anyone else. She didn't like how that looked. She didn't like it one bit. Only a few months ago, Mel had been convinced she would never be interested in anyone but Bebe, but now? Now she was feeling very grateful for the freedom their guidelines gave her.

"Yeah." She raised both brows, surprised at herself for saying it so easily. "Yeah, I would." Her knee nudged into the small of Kade's back. "Have you and Bebe ever shared someone before?"

They shook their head, still smiling. "No, not really. It presents a unique challenge, but I'm prepared to try if you are."

"And if she isn't?" Mel asked.

Kade waved a hand through the air. "She will be."

"Oh?" Mel sat up, too, her hands propping her up from behind. "How can you be so sure?"

"Because I know her," Kade said. They leaned over and kissed her, a quiet, reassuring press of lips and teeth against Mel's. "And I know you. And I know she knows you, and she knows—"

"Okay, yep, we all know each other." Mel laughed. Her gaze fell to Kade's mouth. "Or at least, we're getting there." Kade swayed close again, but Mel stopped them with a single fingertip poked into their chest. "What do I call you now? Are you my girlfriend?"

Kade made a face like they'd smelled something awful. "Please, anything but that. It sounds so . . . juvenile."

"Metamour-turned-amour?"

"That's quite complicated, don't you think?"

"How about 'associate'? That's suitably grown-up." She nodded to herself. "Kissing associate. Senior smooching associate."

"I can't believe I'm this attracted to you," Kade muttered almost to themself.

On the fifth day, the snowplow arrived. Actual Mounties came to the cabin to escort them safely out of the wilderness. They weren't dressed like cartoons or riding horses—much to Mel's disappointment—but they assured her they were the modern-day version. Mel and Kade were back in Calgary before they knew it.

Once they returned to the land of cell reception, Mel answered about a million texts from Daniel, asking her where she was and why she hadn't come home as scheduled. She made a mental note to give him Bebe's number for any future emergencies—Kade's, too, come to think of it. It was nice to know Daniel still cared, at any rate. She texted him an explanation from the Calgary airport, to which he'd only responded:

Glad you're safe. No emojis, not even one heart. Yeah, she was going to have to do some gardening with that one.

She also texted Bebe with updates, as did Kade. Mel wanted to save the details for an in-person conversation, so she only gave the vaguest, broadest strokes. They were both fine. Their flight was leaving soon. She missed Bebe so much. She couldn't wait to see her and talk about—stuff.

Mel lifted her head from where she was hunched over her phone, waiting to go through airport security. "Hey, how much are you telling Bebe about what happened?" she asked.

Kade merely held up their phone to show Mel their last message to Bebe:

> You're right. She can be very mean when she wants to be.

Bebe had responded with about six hundred exclamation points and one emoji of water droplets.

The flight home was blissfully uneventful. When Bebe opened the door of the condo for them, she was wearing a smile on her face and a faded NYU T-shirt hanging to mid-thigh and nothing else.

"I knew it!" she crowed, pointing at Mel and Kade in turn. "You kissed! You did more than kiss! Your faces say it all."

"So would my mouth, if you waited one second for me to tell you," Kade said with regal patience.

Bebe ignored them, instead doing a kind of victory dance in the doorway. It looked suspiciously like the lawn mower. "Score one for me! You both owe me a Coke."

"I never made a bet with you about this," Kade said. They turned to Mel, their eyes wide and scandalized. "I wouldn't do something like that."

"You didn't know," Mel said to Bebe as she brushed past to enter the condo. "You couldn't have known! *We* didn't know." She dumped her backpack on the floor and flung herself face-first onto the sofa. Why was it so exhausting to sit in an airplane for a few hours?

"Au contraire, darling sweethearts." Bebe welcomed Kade inside and shut the door, divesting them of their winter overcoat. "You're both too alike. Attraction was bound to happen."

This was met with a veritable wall of hollering.

"We are nothing alike!" Mel cried, sitting up on the sofa.

Kade went right into threats: "You take that back."

"If anything, we're polar opposites."

"Not true." Bebe shook her head and held up a single, perfectly manicured finger. "You're both cranky bitches—and I say that with all the affection in the world—but secretly you're also sensitive artists brimming with hidden passions."

"Please stop." Kade massaged their temples with their fingertips. "I will give you money to stop. Name the price."

"I hate this," Mel said. She mock-pouted, her arms crossed over her chest. "I take it back. I want a refund."

"No you don't," Bebe singsonged as she traipsed up the stairs.

Kade looked at Mel with an apology in their eyes. They came to stand right in front of her, leaning down to give her a kiss. "She can be a handful."

"Well, that's what we love about her," Mel said. She curled her fingers into the weird asymmetric collar of Kade's shirt and pulled them down to join her on the couch.

NEWLY Updated GUIDELINES FOR POLY LIVING WITH BEBE & MEL + KADE

1. Communication in everything. Even when it's hard. (THIS IS HARD.)

2. New partners may be added to anyone's personal roster so long as all involved are informed beforehand with an open discussion in mind.

3. Be respectful of boundaries. Everyone gets to decide for themselves what they want to hear about their partner's other partners and what they are willing to have shared of themselves.

4. For the health and peace of mind of everyone involved, we all agree to be tested regularly.

5. Though a married, cohabitating couple will naturally have some joint obligations that cannot be avoided, all involved agree that there will be no "power ranking" of couples in the arrangement, i.e., one partner will not be held as superior or more important than the other when it comes to scheduling, distribution of affection, etc.

6. ~~Bebe agrees to keep the arrangement with Mel casual, as defined by:~~
   Mel and Bebe agree to see where this goes as a committed couple.
   a. ~~No commitments more than three weeks in the future~~
   b. ~~No use of the L word for any reason~~ Use of L word
      encouraged for any reason
   c. ~~No endearments except for "sweetheart." Variations on~~
      ~~"sweetheart" not permitted~~
7. Additionally, Mel and Kade agree to also being a committed couple.
   d. No endearments (LAST NAMES ARE NOT
      ENDEARMENTS)—yes, they are!
   e. Mel's caveat: Though all involved will be expected to
      communicate, a degree of separation should be maintained
      between the pairs to preserve each unique relationship. E.g., no
      third wheels on date nights.

"So we can't grab dinner together?" Bebe asked, her pen poised above the much-revised paper.

"A quick dinner is fine if it's just about eating," Mel said, "but my point is, I don't want to horn in on your and Kade's alone time. You wouldn't want to disrupt ours, right?"

"But we all enjoy each other's company." Kade sipped at their cocktail—a Mel-crafted G&T. They were lounging on the floor with their head pillowed on Bebe's knee while the two women pored over the guidelines between them on the sofa. "I thought we might—spend more time together, the three of us." They tipped their head back and looked warily at Bebe, that silent communication that Mel couldn't hope to understand.

All the more reason why they needed this rule. Everyone had to know their place, most of all her.

"I would feel more comfortable if we kept everything organized in a way that makes sense. Bebe and I make sense; you and I make sense; you and Bebe make sense. Simple. No need to complicate things."

Bebe drew in a quiet breath. "If that's how you feel . . ."

"It is." Mel tapped the paper with her fingernail. "Make sure it's underlined. So we don't forget."

PART THREE

THREE PARTS TEQUILA

CHAPTER 24

Mel assumed that being polyamorous, like anything else in the world, could be mastered through careful study.

She had studied her way to better bartending jobs, after all. Those long nights spent with old cocktail recipe books and self-quizzes had paid off. It was simply a matter of retaining information and ensuring she could put it into practice.

But a couple of weeks after Mel returned home from the ski trip with Kade, her self-education was not going well. She'd ordered about five different books—used, of course; thank you, Al Gore's internet— filled with advice on poly relationships, but she couldn't make heads or tails of them. They all seemed to have different theories about how a poly person should approach their poly-ness, one book contradicting another. Sometimes the contradiction was the whole point, an entire tome written in response to someone else's, written years earlier. The authors seemed to be talking among themselves, and Mel felt a little left out.

She skimmed the sections on attachment theory but didn't see herself reflected in any of the options. Was she a mix of two or three different styles? Mel flipped back and forth between the pages, squinting at the tiny font that academic books were apparently required to use. It was like a Rorschach test, she thought, or those times in her twenties when someone would pull out an astrology book at a party and go around the room, reading people's horoscopes. Was Mel attracted to people physically? Emotionally? Intellectually? Who the fuck could say. Didn't it all depend on the person and the circumstances?

Her feelings for Bebe, for example, were very different from her feelings for Kade. She was attracted to them both on a physical level, of course, but as far as connecting went, her two lovers were like night and day. When Mel came down with a cold so awful that she called out of work for the first time in years, Bebe was the one who showed up at her apartment with a take-out container of matzo ball soup as big as Mel's head. She'd puttered around Mel's bedroom, tucking her in, tidying laundry piles that had been neglected, and refilling her water bottle once every hour to ensure she was hydrating. She was all sweetness and light.

Kade, on the other hand, was the opposite. Sure, they accepted every cocktail Mel pressed into their hand, but their opinions could be harsh. Kade wasn't a coddler. They cared for Mel in other ways; when Mel complained about the dearth of quality citrus at the markets this time of year, a box of fresh Indian River grapefruit showed up at her building the very next morning. No card, no text giving her a heads-up. She only knew it was from Kade because she asked, to which they gave a bewildered, "Yes, who else?"

Both relationships worked for her, though they were totally different. It seemed impossible to quantify it in a way that made sense. Mel wasn't about to give up, though. She flipped to a graph showing the differences in several types of "nontraditional" relationships arranged on an X-Y axis. This was the kind of thing that made her eyes go blurry around the edges and her brain emit a low-level static. She was getting flashbacks from her time in high school math classes, which she'd hated passionately. Not math itself—she was a natural at certain types of math: geometry, financial calculations, *fractions*. She kicked ass at fractions. Probably why she was such a good mixologist, a field that relied heavily on understanding ratios and proportions. But slapping some information on a graph and expecting her to get it? A losing proposition.

She stared at the different names and values assigned to the relationship types in the boring poly book. Stuff like "polyfidelity" and "poly-intimates" were shapeless blobs to her, defined by dry word salad.

"Relationship anarchy" sounded pretty badass, though. She ran a highlighter over that one so she would remember to come back to it later. When her brain wasn't melting.

Daniel shuffled out of his bedroom in his boxers, scratching at his chest. He wasn't wearing his glasses, so he had to really squint to make out the scene. He then squinted at the wall clock. "Did you stay up all night with this stuff?"

"Couldn't sleep." Mel grabbed another book and flipped through the introduction. Why on earth did people put introductions in books? *Ooooh, here's the story before we actually get to the story.* Fuck off with that shit. "Thought I'd get some reading done." She had to figure this stuff out now that she was seeing two people. Mel hadn't even had time to have that serious talk with Daniel yet, and since he was not his best in the morning, she figured this wasn't a good time to try.

Daniel lurched toward the coffee table, still yawning. "Okay, are those . . . flash cards?" He reached for the stack.

"Don't mess those up! I have them in the exact order I want them." Mel uncurled from her spine-ruining ball on the sofa, but she wasn't fast enough to stop him.

An offhand hum from Daniel, which meant he was pretending to have heard. "'Compersion,'" he read off the front of the card, then flipped it over. "'Definition: the feeling of happiness when your partner is happy, especially when they are enjoying another partner.' What's all this for?"

"Learning the vocabulary is important," Mel said. She had the names, origins, and flavor profile of almost every edible fruit in the world memorized. Surely this would be a cakewalk by comparison.

"Wow, nerd. Are you expecting to be tested on this?" Daniel asked, winging one eyebrow high.

Mel's face went hot. She scrambled to her feet and swiped her flash cards out of Daniel's hands. "I'm trying to put in a little effort, okay?" Now that she was officially dating not one, but two people who were way out of her league, she had an obligation to give it her best shot. And if that meant poring over dry academic works with a bunch of charts and diagrams—none of which were the least bit sexy—Mel would do it. "Bebe and Kade are already, like, poly black belts. I'm the little kid at the back of the dojo with the orange belt."

"Hold on." Daniel cocked his hip to one side and placed his hand on it. "Are you really comparing being poly, even metaphorically, to the martial arts?"

"Why not?" Mel snapped. "You have to learn how to defend yourself, right? Keep yourself safe? Same with relationships."

"Okay, Little Miss Avoidant Attachment Style," Daniel muttered under his breath.

Mel threw the dog-eared book onto the carpet, where it landed with a dull thud. "This is what I'm talking about! It's like you people all went to the same college and read the same books and have the same secret little language."

Daniel silently mouthed the phrase "you people" into thin air.

Mel ignored him. "And by the way, when I was married, I was the most clingy, 'let's talk about our feelings until sunrise' partner you've ever seen. Now, clearly, things are different. People change. But I'm supposed to have some style ingrained since childhood? I don't get this stuff!" She crossed her arms over her chest and gave the book a light kick, sending it a few inches across the shag pile. "I couldn't keep a relationship with *one* person going. How am I going to handle having two?"

"If these books aren't doing it for you, why are you looking to them for answers?" he snapped.

"Where else am I supposed to look?" Mel snapped right back.

"Me!" Daniel flattened his hands against his chest. "You could look to me, your best friend who is also going through a similar thing!"

"Yeah but—" Even as Mel held up one of the advice books, she knew her point was weak. "I thought, experts? I don't know, do you really want me bothering you with this stuff?"

"Oh, Mel." Daniel motioned her to scooch over so he could fall onto the couch beside her. "No one's got a PhD in polyamory. Most people in nonmonogamous relationships are just—fumbling through. Figuring it out as they go." He cocked his head to the side in thought. "Exactly like most monogamous people, actually."

She steeled herself and said something she'd been meaning to say since returning from Canada. "Hey, if I've done something to piss you off, you'd tell me, right? Because I feel like you've had a chip on your shoulder ever since Bebe and I, like, got together-together." She hesitated. "Do you think I'm making the wrong choice being with her? Or Kade, for that matter?"

Daniel blew a breath out through his nose. "No, I—that's not it. I'm sure they're both great for you. It's only—" He sighed and turned more fully toward her, one arm on the back of the sofa, his feet tucked up beneath him. "You've been so busy ever since you got into this relationship. I feel like we never hang out anymore unless there's some huge personal crisis. And tequila." He grimaced.

"Shit." Mel put a hand on his knee. "You're right. I'm sorry, Danny. I've been so focused on Bebe, and Kade, and this cocktail competition, and work, sometimes I forget to make time for you. I'll try to be better at that, really." She thought hard. "What if we had a standing BFF date? Brunch on Thursdays? If you don't mind waking up at a decent hour like a normie."

Daniel blinked. "But you have all that other stuff on your plate."

"Yeah, and I'm making room on the plate for you," she said. "We can go to the diner for pancakes and bitch about Brent's ugly ties. What do you think?"

He sniffed, looked away, then flashed her a smile. "Okay. Sure. Thursday brunch. We can do that. Should probably be hashing out an escape plan, anyway, now that T&V is looking shaky. I'm getting, like, ten percent less in tips since the last menu update."

It was true; they hadn't even made time to complain about the changes at work or plot out their next step. "Let me text Ronica. I ran into her recently. She might know who's hiring. Hell, she might want to get in on the lottery dream with us."

"Good idea. I've always liked her." He knocked his shoulder against hers. "Too bad Sal's is getting sold. We could all get jobs there."

They both laughed at that absurd idea, quieting into their own thoughts.

Daniel broke the silence first. "Thanks for the brunch invite, Bud. I know you're busy as hell these days."

"It's the least I can do considering how much I've been talking your ear off about my drama." Mel's gaze landed on the stack of note-cards and books spread out on the coffee table. "Sorry about that," she said quietly.

There was a long moment of silence before Daniel spoke again. "Listen, most of the time, I love hearing about the drama. And don't beat yourself up about Bebe and Kade," Daniel said. "You clearly adore these people. You're putting in the effort. For what it's worth, I think you're doing a great job."

Mel groaned. "No I'm not." She couldn't even get through her reading list without a pep talk from her BFF.

"Yeah, you are. You pulled two extremely hot, interesting people who want to be with you." He held her hand and jiggled it a little. "You must be doing something right."

Mel's phone pinged loudly from its spot on the coffee table. It was a photo from Bebe: a selfie in some nondescript boardroom. She was making a silly face, her tongue sticking out and her eyes all googly.

"Sorry, I should—" Mel pointed with her free hand.

"No worries," Daniel said. He smiled, a genuine one, and gestured for her to get the phone.

Bebe had sent a text:

> Work is wild today! I can't wait to
> see you tonight. Looking forward to
> unwinding . . .☺

Right, today was Monday. Mel smiled to herself. As exhausted as she was, she was glad she had plans with Bebe. Tonight's date was exactly what she needed. She could soak up Bebe's charm and beauty, eat some delicious food at the no-doubt excellent restaurant Bebe had chosen, see a sold-out Broadway show that Bebe had miraculously snagged tickets for, and fuck her wonderful girlfriend on her wonderful mattress before getting a great night's sleep. A deep sigh thrummed through her.

Her phone pinged again. Anticipating another update from Bebe, she checked it immediately, but it was a text from Kade.

> Six o'clock, right? Meet you at yours.

Mel's blood froze in her veins. "No, no, no." She checked her calendar app. Kade must have gotten their dates mixed up; they'd made plans with Mel to see a special exhibit at the Botanical Garden up in the Bronx followed by dinner at a hole-in-the-wall Indian place that was supposed to be the best in the city—but that was next week, surely?

Her calendar loaded the current day. She had apparently blocked off the entire afternoon and evening and labeled it DATE NIGHT. Her thumbs hastily swiped to view next Monday's schedule, but it was a complete blank.

Oh, fuck.

Mel had double-booked her dates. With her two dates. On the exact same date.

She flung her arm out and let her phone slip out of her hand to land on the carpet with a thump. With her other hand, she grabbed a throw pillow from behind her head and shoved it over her face. Her scream of anguish was only slightly muffled by the lumpy poly-fill.

"Bad news?" Daniel asked with all the delicacy of a sledgehammer.

"I'm the worst girlfriend ever," she moaned into the pillow.

Daniel didn't miss a beat. "You double-booked yourself."

Mel tossed the pillow aside and scrambled off the sofa to grab her phone. "I've got to fix this."

Daniel craned his neck to call after her. "Just tell them you made a mistake!"

"No! Then they'll have to draw straws to see who gets to go out with me tonight, or I'll have to pick, and—ugh." Mel spun in a circle, staring up at the ceiling like god or Mrs. Goldman in 6E had all the answers. "What if I rebooked them both for dinner at the same restaurant tonight? I could make a reservation for two tables in different areas and kind of—jump between them?"

"You're describing the climactic scene from *Mrs. Doubtfire*," Daniel drawled. "Need I remind you, that plan did not work out for Robin Williams. RIP." He pointed a finger and his gaze upward as a sign of respect.

"RIP," Mel repeated, doing a quick sign of the cross. Sure, the flick was full of problematic cross-dressing, but still. What a legend.

Focus, Sorrento.

Mel shook herself. "I can figure this out. Kade doesn't work a day job either, so we can . . . move our plans up a little earlier in the day." She tapped out a text to Kade.

> why don't you
> come around noon
> instead?

There. Not a lie. Merely a suggestion for a new time.

Kade replied almost immediately:

> ? The exhibit is after-hours.

"Oh, screw the exhibit," Mel hissed at her phone.

"So how would you describe your communication style, Mel?"

Daniel picked up one of the discarded polyam self-help books and flipped through it. "Slightly evasive or wholly dishonest?"

"Shut up." Mel typed out a response that intimated they should forget the Botanical Garden and instead indulge in some afternoon delight. A smattering of eggplant emojis and one mistyped taco—that would drive her point home. Kade never turned down a chance to service Mel sexually. She sent the text and stared at the screen, waiting for Kade's enthusiastic agreement.

Her phone rang. A photo she'd taken of Kade on their not-skiing trip sprang onto her screen: they were bundled in a sweater and sleeping open-mouthed on the cabin floor, hair disheveled.

"They're calling. Why are they calling? Who *calls* anymore!?" Mel shook her phone at Daniel like it was his fault.

"As your trusted adviser, I think you should answer it" was all Daniel said. He was mostly preoccupied with filing away a hangnail with the manicure set he kept within easy reach of the sofa.

Mel groaned and picked up. "Yes, St. Cloud?"

Daniel turned away from his nails to mouth at her: *St. Cloud?*

Mel turned her back to him so she could listen in relative privacy. Kade spoke slowly and deliberately down the line. "Why don't you want to go to the Botanical Garden tonight?"

"Oh, I mean, I'd love to go. Really. Plants—art—arty plants, I'm sure they're awesome. I was only thinking"—Mel paced the short length of the living room and went into the kitchen for privacy—"why go out when we can stay in?" She tried to inject a salacious note into her voice, but it came out sounding more high-pitched and anxious than sexy.

Kade was silent for a long beat. Then they sighed and said, "You're double-booked."

"What? Pfffft. Noooooo."

"I just checked the calendar I share with Bebe," Kade said. "She has tonight set aside for dinner and a show with you."

Mel squeezed her eyes shut, unseen in the kitchen. Motherfucker. Of course they had a shared calendar. Why wasn't she on the shared calendar? Did she have to prove herself first before she could be calendar-worthy? If so, she was probably failing that test, hard.

"Okay, yes," Mel finally confessed in a whoosh. "I double-booked myself. But it was an accident! I really thought the plant thing was next week."

"So instead of explaining this to me, you tried to reschedule me for afternoon sex to make room for your date with Bebe tonight?" Kade asked. They didn't sound angry, exactly, but it was hard to tell with them. The only time Mel had heard them raise their voice was in the bedroom, and that was a very welcome volume.

Mel winced. "Well, Bebe's tickets were really hard to get, so I figured—"

"Mel, it's not the order of importance you arrived at that bothers me—although it is slightly annoying to only rank a midday quickie—"

"I was going to set aside four to five hours, so not that quick."

Kade continued like she hadn't spoken, which was probably for the best. "—it's that your first course of action was to obfuscate."

The words hung heavily on the phone line between them. Mel leaned back against the kitchen counter and shook her head. "I'm trying not to let anybody down," she said, quiet and strained. "I didn't know what else to do."

"You could tell me. Or Bebe. Or, ideally, the both of us." Kade's tone was almost . . . gentle. It was weird. "What did you think would happen if you did?"

Tears sprang to Mel's eyes, burning against the backs of them. They came so suddenly, she was startled. Probably a lack of sleep making her punchy. She wiped at her eyes with the back of her arm, glad that Kade hadn't called her on video chat. "I don't know." She sounded miserable and small, and she hated it.

There was a long pause where Mel fought to keep from sobbing by biting the inside of her cheek, and Kade said nothing. At last, they said, "All right. Why don't we cancel our plans? Both of them."

Mel's heart plummeted. "No, don't do that—"

"Mel, listen to me." The first name stopped Mel in her tracks. Kade continued, "The three of us should talk tonight. Don't take this as a rejection because it's not. You're upset. I want to help, and I know Bebe will, too. Will you let us?"

"But the tickets . . ."

"Tickets are things. You're our *person*." Kade sighed down the line. Mel could picture them clearly, probably wearing something fabulous while stalking around their studio with paint spatter on their hands. "Bebe is better at these kinds of conversations. I'm sorry."

"No, you're fine," Mel said. She actually did feel calmer now. "So. I should come by your place tonight?"

"We could come to yours, if you'd rather." That was as near as Kade could come to being sappy, Mel knew. They were offering her a chance to have this big, important talk on her own turf. In case that made her feel steadier, more in control.

She shook her head, then remembered this was a phone call. "I'd rather come to you." Between recipe trials and work, she hadn't had a spare minute to clean. The apartment was . . . not looking its best, her room especially.

"I'll let Bebe know. And Sorrento?"

"Yeah?"

"Wear comfortable clothing." They hung up without saying goodbye, which was par for the course for Kade. Mel would've been more worried had they dragged it out.

She stared at her now-black phone screen in her hand. Comfortable clothing? What were they going to do, aerobics?

CHAPTER 25

Mel decided to walk to Bebe and Kade's instead of taking public transit. It was meant to be an act of efficiency, not self-flagellation—the subway was a mess after a breakdown somewhere in Brooklyn; the M22 bus was slow as hell and never seemed to be around when she needed it—but it didn't turn out that way. Three blocks from her apartment, it started to snow.

It was late in the year for snow in the city. By rights, spring should've been right around the corner. Yet the flakes floated through the air, fat and fluffy. They stuck to Mel's shaved head and melted against her skin. She could have gone back home for a hat, or better yet, an umbrella, but three blocks was just far enough to be a hassle. It wasn't too much farther to the condo. She could tough it out.

When she at last appeared at Bebe and Kade's door, she was soaked to the bone. It wasn't easy to look waterlogged and bedraggled when you had less than an eighth of an inch of hair on your head, but

Mel managed it. She knew she looked pitiful; even the doorman had given her a concerned grimace in greeting.

Bebe opened the door with a strangled cry. "Oh, Sweetheart, get in here! What happened? Did you get tsunamied by a truck on the way?" Being a pedestrian in New York meant constantly braving the walls of water traffic sometimes sprayed on the sidewalk. But Mel didn't even have that excuse.

"N-no," she said through chattering teeth. "I'm just an idiot."

"Oh, shush. Darling! Can you find Mel the comfy robe?" Bebe shouted up the stairs.

"Coming," Kade called back. Mel could hear their footfalls on the floor above her head.

Bebe spun Mel around and grabbed the collar of her sodden coat. "Let's get you out of these wet things. Do you want something warm to drink?"

"I thought I was supposed to discuss—you know, how I fucked up," Mel said, "not get babied."

"We can do both," Bebe said, and shucked off Mel's coat and scarf. "Sit down."

"Bully," Mel muttered, but in a pleased way. She sat on the sofa as ordered.

Kade appeared with a robe Mel had never seen before. It smelled like both Bebe and Kade and felt like angel kisses when she put it on, like the fabric only existed to feel good against skin.

"It's for hard days," Kade explained as they tugged the lapels over Mel's throat. "Do you want fuzzy socks, too?" They said this so seriously, so stone-faced, that Mel had to bite her lip. If she started laughing, she might crack a rib, between that and the shivering.

"I already have socks." Mel kicked her feet in demonstration.

Bebe gave Mel's mismatched, worn socks a dubious look. "I'm getting you fuzzy ones," she said, and ran upstairs.

Once Mel was suitably bundled up in soft things, her two lovers pulled her off the couch.

"Bebe's bed is big enough for the three of us," Kade said. "More comfortable than cramming onto a sofa."

"Oh?" Mel felt a nervous zing go through her. "What are we going to do that we'll need to be comfortable?"

"Talking, obviously." Bebe led them all into her room. It was as luxuriously appointed and slightly disorganized as ever, and the bed beckoned.

Mel crawled into its familiar, fresh-smelling sheets and pressed her face into a pillow. She breathed in and out slowly, feeling her body deflate like a used-up balloon. She was no stranger to feeling tired—six night shifts a week will do that to you—but this was an exhaustion that crept deeper than bone. It felt like her soul was out of juice.

"Are you okay to talk about what happened today?" Bebe removed her blazer—she must have come straight from the office—and hung it on a velvet-covered hanger in her closet.

Mel sighed, a tremble through her lungs. "Guess so." She flipped onto her back so she wasn't speaking to Bebe's pillows.

Bebe joined her on the bed, slipping in on Mel's right side and nosing her way under her arm so she could lay her head on her chest. Kade nuzzled up against Mel's opposite shoulder. They both seemed content to wait for Mel to start. Mel stared up at the ceiling, feeling their bodies breathing together.

"I'm sorry I double-booked," she finally said. "I don't have any good excuses. Work's a mess, but it's been a mess since those new owners took over. I completely spaced."

"Everyone makes mistakes. Bebe once triple-booked herself," Kade offered.

Bebe lifted her head to say to them, "Oh my god, remember how for a second there it looked like I was going to try and have all three of you show up at the same restaurant but at different tables like—"

Mel's brows rose as she stared straight up. "The climactic scene in *Mrs. Doubtfire*?"

Kade snorted. "See, Sorrento? At least you weren't grasping at straws like this one here." They gave Bebe's arm a teasing prod where it lay across Mel's waist.

"Yeah," Mel muttered, "what kind of weirdo would do that?" She shook her head. "Regardless. It won't happen again. I'm not going to make the same mistake twice." She squeezed her arm around Bebe's plump shoulders and let Kade hold her free hand.

Bebe gave a doubtful hum. "It's not the end of the world if it happens again. That's—not really my main concern."

"You're our main concern," Kade said. Their breath was warm against Mel's neck. "Why didn't you tell us when you realized what you'd done?"

"Because—" Mel swallowed. She wondered if her two favorites had chosen this position, cuddled up in bed like this, specifically so she didn't have to make eye contact with anyone. She wasn't sure she could've forced the words out otherwise. "I thought you'd both be angry, and I don't want you to break up with me."

For a long moment, no one spoke, but Bebe and Kade clung harder to Mel, burying their faces against her.

"Do you really think we'd end our arrangement with you over something so trivial?" Kade asked.

"More importantly," Bebe said, "if we did, don't you think you'd be well rid of us?"

That made Mel laugh, a harsh, wet sound forced out of her chest. "But I don't want to be rid of you," she said. It was meant as a joke, but it was true. That was the whole reason she was in this mess. Quieter and more seriously, she said, "I don't want to lose you." Didn't one of those self-help books warn against the dangers of possessive behavior? Mel licked her lips. "Not that I own you. Not that you're objects that I can—ugh. I *suck* at this."

Kade sat up at that, looking down at Mel with a determined cast to their jaw. "You do not suck."

"Well, she does," Bebe said, her head still cuddled beneath Mel's chin, "but in the good way. I have the bite marks to prove it."

Kade stifled a laugh. "Love, please, I am trying to make a point." They turned back to Mel. "You are an amazing human. You are a joy to be around." Their face softened. "I can't promise you and I or you and Bebe will be together forever. I don't know what the future holds. But if, for whatever reason, our paths diverge, I know you will be all right. Because how can someone so wonderful need anyone or any-thing else to be whole?"

Mel blinked, and she was surprised to find her lashes wet. "I don't feel whole. Sometimes," she confessed.

Bebe sat up then, and because she didn't want to be the odd one out, Mel sat up, too, leaning back against the upholstered headboard. She held Bebe's hand in her right and Kade's in her left.

"Kade mentioned that you two talked about your ex-wife when you were stuck in Canada," Bebe said, her eyes fastened on Mel.

Before Mel could respond, Kade jumped in. "But that's all I told her. No details. I know it's very personal for you."

"It is." Mel nodded. "But—" She looked at Bebe, who was glow-ing with sincerity, and at Kade, who was—well, like they always were. A little hard to read. But their hand was gentle where it held Mel's. "I don't want it to be this secret thing that hangs over my head anymore. It's been years. It needs to be dealt with." She straightened, shoulders back. "For the longest time, I thought Lynn left me because I was a shitty wife. I worked too hard. We never had enough money. I never spent enough time with her."

"Fucking capitalism," Bebe said with narrowed eyes.

Kade rolled theirs. "Love, please let her speak."

Mel shot them both a grin. "I mean, yeah, some of our problems were normal stuff everyone has to deal with. But I took it personally. Like *I* was the problem. And Lynn seemed to agree." She shrugged. "You grow up, thinking, 'If only I can find the one person I can be with for the rest of my life, if only I can get a house with a yard, as long as I am living the most normal, blameless life, then that will show 'em. You know? You think you have to tick all these boxes. That your relationship has to look a certain way. Even if you're—no, *espe-cially* if you're queer. There's so much pressure to do the right thing."

"Even if it's not right for you," Bebe said. Her voice was unchar-acteristically quiet. She shared a look with Kade, then focused back on Mel. "I get that. I really, really get that."

"Your divorce made you question what it was all for," Kade, the gender-neutral king of leading statements, said.

"Exactly! What was the point of trying so hard to fit this mold if Lynn was going to turn around and say, 'You know what? It's been real, but after nine years of this, I'm out'? Why bother being in a relationship when it can all blow up at any moment for any reason?" Mel dragged a hand over her shorn head, dislodging a few long stray hairs (Bebe's) that she flicked toward the floor. "That's why I was so anti-romance when we met. That's why I try to—I don't know—compartmentalize everything. Keep it in separate areas. Like how the *Titanic* had those emergency doors to shut off certain parts of the ship to save it from taking on water."

Kade made a face. "Need I remind you how that shook out, historically?"

"We all saw the film!" She gave them a whack on the leg, a friendly one. "But that's the principle I've been using. I figured if I messed things up with one of you . . ." She trailed off, unable to finish the thought. Instead she stared down at the knot of hands in her lap.

"Oh, Sweetheart." Bebe pressed herself to Mel's side, her head coming to rest on Mel's shoulder.

Kade didn't say anything, but their hand tightened on Mel's and they cleared their throat meaningfully.

Bebe exhaled. "What my wife is trying to say is that we should probably discuss something I've been wanting to ask you."

Mel tried not to panic. Her voice only shook a little when she said, "Oh?"

"The thing is," Bebe said, still not lifting her head, "you're not on a doomed ocean liner. You're here, with us. Yes?"

"Yes," Mel said, not sure where this was going.

"Do you think you might ever want to"—Bebe waggled her head like she was trying to shake the right word out of her brain, then lifted it so she could look Mel in the eye—"stop keeping us in separate compartments?"

Mel furrowed her brow. "As in . . . ?"

"You, Bebe, and me," Kade said. They shifted their hand, still joined with Mel's, so that they covered up Mel's other hand where it held Bebe's. "The three of us, together."

"I know it's a big step," Bebe said in a rush, "so no pressure if you need some time to consider it."

"You'd want that?" Mel looked between the two of them, the best kind of tennis match. "I mean, you'd be okay with that?"

"That is why we are bringing it up, yes," Kade said very slowly.

Bebe reached over with her free hand and pinched their arm, grinning at their high yelp. "Mel's sarcasm is rubbing off on you, Darling. Along with other things, I'm sure." She gave Mel an exaggerated wink. Then, sobering, "But seriously. We'd love to be the Three Amigos instead of two-by-two. If that's something you want."

Mel bit her lip. She'd be lying if she hadn't fantasized about Bebe and Kade together, but she had written that off as a purely sexual thing. She hadn't allowed herself to think about what it might be like to form a triad with them. It was like flying too close to the sun. It seemed like an invitation for disaster.

Mel's gaze tracked along her lap, then caught sight of her left arm, the one covered in the random piecemeal tattoos. The boot shape of Italy stared back at her, reminding her of Pompeii. She had roots in a disaster zone; she'd been born into it. Maybe, instead of running from it, she could stand still, face the eruption, and embrace whatever came.

It was scary. It was hard. But she wanted to do it anyway because— what were the odds of finding two people like these in the whole wide world?

"I don't really know what the three of us together would look like," Mel said. "I've never done that before. Obviously."

"Neither have we," Bebe reminded her.

Kade nodded. "It would be new ground for all of us."

"We'd . . . have to update the guidelines." Mel looked at Bebe with something like shyness.

Bebe smiled. "My favorite activity," she said.

Mel swayed forward and kissed her. She couldn't stop herself, and she never wanted to. Bebe tasted of lipstick and coffee. She tasted perfect.

On Mel's other side, Kade made a sound, a small, happy sigh.

They were very patient, so Mel thought it only right to reward them with a kiss of their own. Kade responded with a fraction of their usual primal need, but it was there in the way they nipped Mel's lip. They tasted like nothing at all, which was also perfect.

"Oh." Mel pulled back, remembering. "We never ate dinner."

Bebe pulled her hand free from Mel's and clapped. "Here's what's going to happen," she said, shifting into Leader Mode. "I am going to order our favorites from the Chinese place. We are going to eat dinner in bed—"

"But the crumbs," Mel protested.

"Spring roll crumbs," Kade muttered.

"I'll put everything on a breakfast tray, oh my god." Bebe reached over to her nightstand and grabbed her phone, tapping away rapidly. "Where was I? Dinner in bed, followed by the best sleep of your fucking life, cuddled between the hottest people you know." Bebe looked up from her phone briefly. "Do we want dumplings? The hell am I saying, of course we want dumplings."

Mel gave Kade's hand one last squeeze, then let it go. "Cuddled." It wasn't a question, more of a statement of disbelief. "Do you mean naked cuddling?" She fiddled with the belt on her cozy robe, trying to figure out the knot Kade had put in it.

"You're exhausted," Kade said. Their hands covered hers on the knot and gently brought them back down to her lap. "One thing at a time: nourishment, then sleep, then we'll amend our terms—"

"And then sex?" Mel was already thinking of the variations the three of them could get up to. Damn, why hadn't they tried this sooner?

Oh yeah, because of the trauma.

"I'm getting crab rangoon, too. Wait, is that too much?" Bebe paused in her tapping, then shrugged. "Eh, we'll have leftovers for tomorrow."

Kade brought their hand up to cup Mel's cheek. They looked near enough to smiling to count. "One thing at a time," they repeated.

Later, stuffed full of moo shu pork and dumplings (and spring rolls and crab rangoon and various bites of Kade's kung pao chicken and Bebe's veggie lo mein), Mel found herself lying in the center of Bebe's bed, staring up at the dark ceiling. On her left, Kade lay close with an arm flung over her waist. Their breathing had finally evened out, their night-twitches calming down. On Mel's right, Bebe was zonked out atop Mel's arm, snoring like a bear. Mel knew her arm would be numb soon, but she didn't care. She fought sleep for as long as she could, wanting to imprint into her memory every detail of her two people holding her.

Then she remembered this wasn't the end, only the beginning, and more nights like this were in her future. Who knew how many? But that wasn't the point.

The point was, she was loved twice over. Her life was a long, continuous corridor of love that she was going to walk through. Maybe it wouldn't look the way she thought it would, and maybe it would change as she went, but it was hers.

She fell asleep to the sounds of her lovers being alive in the dark, and she was happy.

<u>Even Newer</u> NEWLY <u>Updated</u> GUIDELINES FOR POLY LIVING
WITH BEBE & MEL + KADE

1. Communication in everything. <u>Even when it's hard.</u> (THIS IS HARD.)

2. New partners may be added to anyone's personal roster so long as all involved are informed beforehand, allowing time for open discussion.

3. Be respectful of boundaries. Everyone gets to decide for themselves what they want to hear about their partner's other partners and what they are willing to have shared of themselves.

4. For the health and peace of mind of everyone involved, we all agree to be tested regularly.

5. Though a married, cohabitating couple will naturally have some joint obligations that cannot be avoided, all involved agree that there will be no "power ranking" of couples in the arrangement, i.e., one partner will not be held as superior or more important than the other when it comes to scheduling, distribution of affection, etc.

6. ~~Bebe agrees to keep the arrangement with Mel casual, as defined by:~~ Mel and Bebe agree to see where this goes as a committed couple.

    a. ~~No commitments more than three weeks in the future~~

    b. ~~No use of the L word for any reason~~ Use of L word encouraged for any reason

    c. ~~No endearments except for "sweetheart." Variations on "sweetheart" not permitted~~

7. Additionally, Mel and Kade agree to also being a committed couple.

    d. No endearments (LAST NAMES ARE NOT ENDEARMENTS)—yes, they are!

    e. ~~Mel's caveat: Though all involved will be expected to communicate, a degree of separation should be maintained between each pair to preserve each unique relationships. E.g., no third wheels on date nights.~~ Fuck it. We ball.

CHAPTER 26

Sunday night. A little under two weeks until Food Fest. Crunch time.

The deadline for submitting her final recipe's ingredient list was Wednesday, which meant Mel needed to hustle. No more wacky experiments, only decisions. She'd taken the day off work to finalize her competition drink, which needed to be perfect: something that screamed New York; batchable for high-volume events; and accessible enough that a wide range of guests would enjoy it.

It was all hands on deck. Bebe and Kade were already ensconced on her sofa, ready and willing to imbibe whatever she handed them. Daniel had claimed the threadbare armchair. Even Jackson, Daniel's boyfriend, was there, crammed in the narrow slice of floor between the armchair and the coffee table so he could rest his head on Daniel's knee.

"I really appreciate everyone doing this," Mel said as she distributed glasses of ice water on the coffee table. Her test subjects would need to stay hydrated and as sober as possible if she wanted helpful feedback and not a series of drunken thumbs-ups.

"Are you kidding?" Jackson grinned at her. He was Afro-Cuban and had model-perfect cheekbones. He was also (as Mel was discovering, now that she was bothering to interact with him when he came over) as sweet as a Shirley Temple. "When Daniel told me you wanted to make free craft cocktails for us tonight, I was like, 'Did we hit the jackpot or something?'"

"We're all excited to try your creations, Sweetheart," Bebe assured her. "What have you got for us?"

Mel shifted nervously on her feet. "I thought we could start with something vodka-based."

"Weren't you working on some old-fashioned variation?" Daniel said. "Or was it a Corpse Reviver? I can't remember everything you've had me drink in the last couple months."

"The old-fashioned was too sweet. The Reviver was too—everything," Mel said, glancing at Bebe and Kade. "I need something that has a chance at actually winning." She retreated to the kitchen. "Which means we're going to use the most inoffensive spirit possible."

Since the apartment was the size of a postage stamp, they could all continue conversing without raising their voices. Mel even had a line of sight on everyone, sort of, if she looked to the side.

Kade leaned to the left so they could see Mel more clearly as she gathered her tools and ingredients at the kitchen counter. "I don't think I've ever known you to mix a vodka drink outside of work," they said.

Mel shrugged. It was true; even the best vodka was not anything she'd write home about. By its very nature, it faded into cocktail recipes, providing very little taste, color, or body. That was why vodka drinks were a staple on so many menus: they could be dressed up any which way to please any number of people. Fruity, spicy, sour, savory—vodka didn't care what you did to it. It got you drunk one way or another. It was the mixology equivalent of shooting fish in a barrel. Mel usually avoided it simply because it bored her. But now—

"This is a competition. I'm trying to appeal to the judges and a broad spectrum of potential customers. Remember, this is a drink that's meant to be served at official city functions." She plucked a couple of fruit shrubs from her lineup and eyed them critically. "Plus it has to embody the spirit of New York, whatever the hell that means."

"You could serve it in a hollowed-out pigeon," Daniel said. "That would fit the bill."

Mel pulled a disgusted face. "Okay, you're officially banned from making suggestions." She grabbed a fresh lemon and started slicing off a series of twists. Her ratty notebook was open before her, all the notes she'd made scrawled across the page: a foolproof combination of citrus, berries, and fizz. A grown-up vodka soda, an ode to the simple concoction that the working girlies and FiDi boys were drinking in the 2010s, when Mel had first come on the bartending scene. Refreshing, uncomplicated, quick, inexpensive, universally pleasing.

It came together in under five minutes: a heaping spoonful of berry compote at the bottom of the highball, ice cubes up to the brim, equal parts vodka and soda water, then a dash of lemon juice, some maraschino cordial, and a quick stir with a cocktail spoon to encourage the compote to mix with the liquid. To finish, she balanced a shiso leaf on top of the ice so it could hold a twist like a raft. She stuck metal straws into each of the five identical drinks, lined up like soldiers on the counter.

"Okay, insta." Jackson snapped his fingers, craning his neck to watch Mel load the glasses onto a serving tray. "That looks delicious."

Daniel made a slashing motion across his throat. "She doesn't like stuff that's too 'grammable. Style over substance, that kind of thing."

"At this point, I'll do anything if it'll help me win." Mel carefully approached the living room with the tray in hand, taking pains not to slosh. How did Daniel practically jog around T&V without spilling a drop? Finally, she doled out the glasses into her friends' and lovers' waiting hands. "Tell me what you think." She left her own glass untouched on the coffee table for the moment; she wanted to get everyone else's opinions before she formed her own. It was too nerve-racking to stand around and watch everyone take their first sips, so Mel hustled back to the kitchen and busied herself with wiping down the counter.

Finally, Daniel let go of the straw with a slight pop of his lips. "Okay. It is delicious," he said.

"Really, really good," Jackson piped up.

"Great." Mel grabbed up her notebook, eager to write down everything she'd done so she wouldn't forget.

"But." Daniel held up a finger. "I don't think this is your competition drink."

"What? Why? What's wrong with it?" Mel stalked over to the coffee table, grabbed up her glass, and took a sip. The sweetness of the berries and the tang of citrus, it was all on point. The fragrance of lemon and shiso was pleasant, but not overwhelming. And it went down easy, which was the most important thing. It was fine.

"I agree with what Daniel's saying," Bebe said, not unkindly. She took another drag from the straw, then shook her head. "There's no Mel in it."

Mel made a face. "What do you mean? I made it. I'm in there. There's tons of me in there."

Kade set their glass on the coffee table with a click, having only consumed a scant inch of liquid. "Anyone could have made that drink. It's good, but it's also nothing special. I know you, and when I drink something you've made from the heart, I can taste the difference."

Mel took another, more thoughtful sip of her vodka soda. "But this drink isn't for people who know me. It's for strangers. No one's going to care if there's a piece of me in it or not. My style isn't that distinctive anyway."

"Bullshit," Daniel said amiably. "When your heart's in something, I could taste it blindfolded." He made a shooing motion toward the kitchen. "Make us something else. Something different."

"Different?" Mel groaned and slumped toward the couch, drink still in hand. Kade and Bebe scooted over to make a space between them, and Mel squeezed into it. "There's nothing new under the sun! All the great drinks have already been invented." She took another sullen sip. "You're right. This sucks. If I show up at Food Fest with something like this, I'll embarrass myself in front of the whole in-dustry."

"Okay, first of all, there will almost certainly be a white guy with dreads at this thing, so you won't be the most embarrassing no matter how hard you try," Daniel said. "Second, you don't have to reinvent the wheel here. Try to have fun."

"Fun?" Mel scoffed. "Fun doesn't win awards."

Kade put a hand on her knee. "It's actually good that this is so hard for you. It means you care."

"Yeah." Bebe snaked her arm along the back of the couch to rest across Mel's shoulders, a comforting weight. "Look at those dime-a-dozen bartenders slinging drinks in tacky tourist traps, charging twenty bucks for something that tastes like motor oil. They don't have any pride in their work. You do."

Mel grimaced. "I would rather not have any pride. That would be easier," she said miserably.

A chorus of protests rose from the group.

"Don't say that!"

"You can do this, girl."

"We're here to support you." Bebe dropped her head to Mel's shoulder and gave her a squeeze.

Kade took the vodka drink from Mel's slack fingers and placed it out of reach on the coffee table. Their eyes bored into Mel. "This is your craft. You can't turn your back on it now."

"Come on, St. Cloud." Mel rolled her eyes. "It's a drink, not the fucking *Mona Lisa*."

"The *Mona Lisa* is only paint on a piece of wood," Kade said. "Music is just random sounds in a particular order. Dancing is simply moving around. All art is just *something*. It's the meaning behind it that makes it great."

That took Mel aback, but she recovered after a moment. "You're being dramatic. A cocktail is a nice little thing, a luxury. It's not going to change the world."

Jackson spoke up from the floor. "I don't want to live in a world without nice little things. Do you?"

"Damn it, Mel, with the world we're living in?" Daniel shifted in his armchair so his legs were thrown over one arm and he could gaze fondly in Mel's direction. "Some of us could really use a fucking drink."

"*Hell* yes." Bebe momentarily broke away from cuddling Mel to give Daniel a high five. Jackson and Kade offered their own murmurs of agreement, with Jackson raising his glass to the sentiment.

That got a smile out of Mel. Her three favorite people were behind her (plus Jackson, but she was only now getting to know him, so it wasn't his fault he wasn't in the official tally). She could do this.

"Right." She slapped her thighs and got up from the sofa. "I'm getting the tequila."

Daniel made a distressed noise, his cheerful confidence slipping away. "Are we sure about that? I still haven't recovered from the last time."

"This time will be different," Mel called over her shoulder as she darted into the kitchen. She leafed through her notebook's foxed-edged pages, looking over her piecemeal notes. There was an idea in there, one she'd been toying with for ages. "I'm going to make something I'd want to drink."

"What, a paloma?" Bebe asked.

That was Mel's usual, simple and clean. When she made it at home, she used grapefruit Jarritos from the bodega down the street, a squeeze of lime, and a hit of homemade rosemary syrup if she had some on hand. The bones were there. She could build off them.

She rinsed out her shaker in the sink. "Well, a version of it. A paloma is more Tex-Mex than New York City. I need to make one that embodies . . ." She trailed off, staring down into the shaker but not really seeing its damp metal interior. Her thoughts were a million miles away in the Rio Grande, in Pompeii, in the thousand points along the globe where so many people had moved like one singular animal toward a beacon in a harbor. And she—she had moved with them, across time, across the Hudson, to come here. A tiny island that was bigger than the sum of its parts.

Manhattan had seen a lot of things—violent displacement,

colonizers coming in waves and with different wars, lifetimes of struggle and joy and marchers in the streets, a million rebuildings and reinventions. The only thing that had no place here was stagnation.

"Everything changes," she said to herself.

"So?" Daniel said, breaking into her thoughts. "What are we changing?"

Mel turned to the four of them sitting in the living room. They stared back with a range of eager, encouraging expressions. She felt feverish with excitement, like she was on fire. "What's the number one cocktail sold across America? The thing basically everyone who drinks will order if they see it on a menu?"

"Uh, I don't know," Jackson said. "A beer?"

"Beer isn't a cocktail, babe." Daniel reached down and patted the back of his neck.

Mel grabbed up a bottle of Cointreau and held it aloft. "A margarita!" At everyone's blank stares, she lowered the bottle. "Seriously. Easy to remember the ratios, easy to drink. It's the number one seller in the country."

"Oh, really?" Kade frowned. "Interesting. I wouldn't have guessed that."

"Okay," Daniel said slowly. "But if you're worried about a paloma being too Tex-Mex for the competition, isn't a margarita . . . ?"

Mel shook her head. "It came from a place that I didn't, and I got to respect that. But it's been changed and remade so many times by so many people. Same as me." She set down the Cointreau and began picking through her extensive array of tequila, examining labels and remembering flavor profiles. "I'm thinking a marg-paloma mash-up. I'd want to drink it, at least. And what's more New York than combining two things to make a new thing?"

"Like the Cronut." Daniel nodded in thought. "Or that roti taco place in the Village."

"Or the Cajun pizza place," Jackson offered.

"Or that restaurant that does the mac and cheese spring rolls." Bebe wiggled her shoulders in delight. Kade snapped once and pointed at her in agreement.

Mel hefted a bottle of her favorite small-batch blanco in her hand. "Let's give it a shot."

Once she got going, it all happened organically. There were always a few stems of rosemary in the fridge. The herb released a pine-ish aroma into the air as she crushed the sprig in her hand. Mel was briefly reminded of the cabin she'd shared with Kade, and it brought a smile to her face. She hunted in the back of a cabinet and found an unopened jar of Luxardo cherries that cost more than a cocktail at T&V. Their rich red color was classy and refined, like a certain pinup model she knew.

Next she had to work in the grapefruit and a hint of lime. Luckily, Mel had three fat grapefruits in the fridge, courtesy of Kade's gift box. She washed one and started peeling the rind away in thin strips with her paring knife for garnishes.

"Daniel?" she called. "Would you mind running to the bodega? I need some Topo Chico." The plain seltzer in the fridge wouldn't do; Mel wanted that mineral tang in the background.

"I can go," Jackson said. "I love being helpful."

Mel turned to look at him, blinking. He was already on his feet, getting his coat on. "Thank you," she said. "You're the best."

She caught Daniel's eye, sharing a silent conversation: *Okay, I guess he's good enough for you*. Daniel gave a pleased tilt of his eyebrows. *Told you so*.

Jackson let himself out, and everyone else's voices faded into the background as Mel focused on her drink. The hum of conversation and laughter floated from the living room, warming her as she muddled the rosemary in a saucepan with some sugar and water. She juiced the grapefruits and some limes, too, while the syrup worked on the stove. While she waited for the mixture to boil, she readied her glasses, chilling a set of lowballs in the freezer. Jackson returned, triumphantly carrying a six-pack of the requested seltzer, which Mel thanked him for profusely.

Everything in balance, Mel repeated to herself over and over as she measured out the components. She wished there was more time to steep and cool the syrup, but she reminded herself this was a test run; she could tweak things as they went. By the time everything was boiled, strained, cooled, shaken, poured, and topped with bubbles, Mel's mouth was flooded with anticipation. The final touch on the lush orange liquid was a single Luxardo cherry, sweet yet tart, skewered on a gleaming silver cocktail stick and balanced on the spice-salted rim of each drink. She carefully placed the filled glasses on the serving tray.

"Okay, here we are," she called as she slowly made her way out of the kitchen and into the living room.

The friendly conversation died down, giving way to *ooh*s and *aah*s at the steadily approaching drinks. Well, Bebe, Jackson, and Daniel *ooh*ed and *aah*ed. Kade nodded knowingly, which Mel understood was their version of being excited.

"That looks divine, Sweetheart," Bebe said.

Daniel rose an inch off the armchair. "Do you need help?"

"No, no, sit. Relax. I've got it." Mel shuffled closer and began passing out glasses. "Now, be honest. I want your undistilled feedback." She took the final glass for herself before collapsing on the sofa between Bebe and Kade once more. That had been tiring. And—fun. So fun she almost didn't care what her friends and lovers thought of the result.

Almost.

She watched everyone take their first sip. Bebe's red lipstick left a print on her glass. Kade closed their eyes and worked their jaw, seemingly trying to taste every note. Daniel blinked down at his glass with wide eyes. Jackson took one sip, then chugged nearly half the rest in a huge gulp.

"Well?" Mel could hardly stand it.

Daniel smiled up at her. "It's perfect."

"The best one yet," Bebe said, taking another healthy swig.

"That's dangerous. I could have twelve of those." Jackson smacked his lips.

Kade lifted their glass, a proud, tiny smile on their lips. "Balanced."

"Seriously?" Mel took a sip from her glass and felt the flavors sweeping through her mouth. The smooth assertion of the tequila, the sharp spike of three kinds of citrus, the woodsy rosemary, the mineral fizz of the seltzer, even the sweet cherry. It was her. It was her in a glass.

"Take a bow, Mel," Daniel said. "You made something beautiful."

"Thanks, I—" It was on the tip of her tongue to blurt out all her insecurities: the citrus was on the verge of overwhelming; the proportions needed fiddling; the syrup might be more interesting if she added jalapeño; she'd probably shaken it with too much ice; the garnish could be more elaborate, befitting a special occasion. But then Mel looked into the depths of her drink and let it go. "Thanks, Danny," she said with real warmth.

Mel sipped at her cocktail and listened to her favorite people—romantic and not—chat with each other about things they loved, joking and laughing and, in Kade's case, nodding pleasantly. This was it, the drink she was going to bring to the competition. And these were the people she was going to win it for.

CHAPTER 27

Hell was empty. All the devils were at the Javits Center.

It was Mel's worst nightmare: tightly packed crowds surging in random directions and blocking the way to the escalators; lots of first-timers staring open-mouthed at the crystal ceiling suspended hundreds of feet above their heads; the sense that everyone was coughing on everyone else; and general confusion as people peered at the various signs and maps posted at odd intervals.

Mel clutched her mini cooler to her chest as yet another person who wasn't watching where they were going jostled into her. She'd be damned if she lost the competition because her carefully crafted syrup ended up spilled across the convention center's floor. It had already taken her about an hour to get through security, with the rent-a-cops inspecting every single bottle despite the fact she had a letter confirming her status as a bona fide cocktail competitor. They'd taken one look at her freshly shaved head and septum piercing and apparently decided she needed the third degree. And after Mel had dressed semiprofessionally for the occasion! Her patent Docs with unripped black jeans and a crisp black button-down telegraphed "fun undertaker," if anything.

"Mel! There you are." Bebe weaved through the sluggish crowd, a fast, bright spot in her butter-yellow dress and turquoise flats. She was clearly taking to the first warm days of spring like a champ. Her guest pass bounced at her chest on a bright pink lanyard. She held a tiny paper boat in one hand, which contained the remnants of what looked like a banh mi. "I was about to send a search party." She popped the last bite of the sandwich in her mouth.

"Security wanted to sniff my stuff," she said, hefting the cooler in her arms. "Is Kade—?"

"Right here." Kade was already right at Mel's side, which she was getting more used to lately. She hardly jumped at all. "Good luck today," they said, and pressed a kiss to her cheek. They smelled like charcoal and bergamot, and they were wearing a pretty staid ensemble, for them—flared black pants and a navy tunic. Their pass was peeking out of a breast pocket, no garish lanyard for them.

"Thank you both for coming." Mel sidestepped another slack-jawed attendee with no spatial awareness. "This isn't how I'd want to spend my Saturday if I were you, so I really appreciate it." The competition was only one piece of the massive circus that was Food Fest, far from the biggest draw, but there would be an audience to watch the proceedings. Having two friendly faces in the crowd was going to be a big confidence boost, Mel was sure of it.

"Are you kidding?" Bebe snagged another bite-sized sample from a vendor passing through the entry hall. "You know I love a good graze. This is pretty much heaven for me." She popped the colorful morsel into her mouth and chewed. "Mmm, mini ramen burrito," she said with her hand politely in front of her lips.

"And we want to support you," Kade said, also snagging a snack and taking a bite.

"Yes, obviously that. But the nibbles are a nice bonus." Bebe leaned in and brushed a kiss over Mel's cheek. "Do you have to get going right away?"

Mel juggled the mini-Igloo so she could check the clock on her phone. Even with the security delay, she still had some time before she was due to report to the cocktail competition's staging area. "I can do one quick lap of the floor. I should probably eat something, anyway." Her stomach had been too jumpy for breakfast, but passing out in front of the biggest names in the beverage world was likely worse than being sick in the ladies' room before it was her turn to present her drink.

Bebe lit up. "Want me to carry your cooler?" She reached out for it, but Kade intercepted her.

"I can carry it," they said. They took it from Mel's arms and tucked it under one of their own.

Bebe's painted lips opened in preparation for a protest, and Mel—she couldn't help it. She laughed long and loud. "Are you two really going to fight over who gets to carry my books?" She preened, pretending to toss an imaginary length of hair over her shoulder. "I'm the luckiest gal in school."

Mel took Kade's free hand in hers, threaded her arm through Bebe's, and led them into the sprawling exhibition hall, feeling like Dorothy traipsing down the yellow brick road with her beloved companions.

Inside the main floor, Food Fest was a swirl of activity. The smell of a thousand kinds of cuisine all melded together into a cloud of savory confusion. A maze of booths in a rainbow of colors tempted attendees with promises of great product. The noise was akin to a hurricane roar, with vendors blasting music and people shouting to each other to be heard over other people shouting. Mel knew instantly there was no way to walk three abreast through such chaos, so she dropped Kade's hand and Bebe's arm so they could move in slow single file through the hot, close crowd.

"Maybe a whole lap was too optimistic," she called over her shoulder to Bebe. "It'll take us a week to see everything at this rate."

"We've been browsing for hours. Let us show you a couple highlights, then you can go do the thing." Bebe nudged her way in front of Mel, taking the lead. Mel was glad her girlfriend was wearing such a bright dress. It made keeping track of her in the mass of bodies so much easier.

She followed Bebe with Kade right behind her all the way to the westernmost wall of the convention center, where a massive booth sat like a monolith in fuchsia. A rotating sign the size of Madison Square Garden bore the name CompCo, a food service company Mel was familiar with. They supplied semi-prepped stuff to half the bars and restaurants in Manhattan: gallons of hard-boiled eggs, buckets of pickles, garlic-stuffed olives by the pound, number ten cans of cocktail onions, things like that. Currently the booth was offering platters of simple apps constructed from their products. Mel caught sight of some deviled eggs topped with a sprinkle of paprika and a slice of cornichon.

"Oh, hell yeah." She was a sucker for a deviled egg. With a quick nod to Kade and Bebe, they made a beeline for the food. When she finally got within snatching distance, Mel grabbed up three perfect halves and distributed her winnings to her partners.

"Why don't I make these for dinner parties more often?" Bebe said as she examined her piece. "They're so good." She popped it into her mouth, moaning appreciatively.

"Because they're a pain to make," Kade observed before eating theirs.

Mel bit her egg in two, savoring the taste. She swallowed and said, "If I ever open my own place, we'll definitely have fancy deviled eggs on the menu." Cheap to produce, filling, salty—the perfect bar snack. Especially when you had a professional line cook in the back to do all the fiddly work for you. She turned her back on the booth, excited to tell Bebe and Kade exactly what flavors she envisioned.

"Mel?" a voice behind her said.

A very familiar voice.

Mel nearly dropped her egg on the floor. She whirled around and saw a face that matched the voice. "Lynn!" There was no way to keep her shock out of the name.

It was the first time she'd seen her ex in almost two years. She was wearing her hair differently, the brown curtain loose to her shoulders.

Her old punk attire had been replaced by a CompCo-branded polo shirt, though the sinewy black lines of her tattoos peeked out from the short sleeves to snake down her pale arms. Her blue eyes were as wide as Mel's probably were.

"I—I didn't expect to see you here," Lynn stammered.

"Yeah! No. Same. I didn't expect—this." Mel tried to shake off her initial surprise. Sure, running into her ex-wife hadn't been on her official agenda for today, but she didn't have to be weird about it. "So you're with CompCo now?" Made sense. Like Mel, Lynn had always worked in the industry.

Lynn nodded, a tentative smile spreading across her face. "Sales. Nice and stable." Right. Lynn had always wanted that. "And you? Are you here with . . . ?" She looked over Mel's shoulder with undisguised curiosity. "Another company?"

"Oh! No, we're—" Mel turned to Bebe and Kade, who were politely waiting behind her, Bebe with a wide grin on her face and Kade with a blank look that was, for them, a good effort at being friendly. Mel hesitated, wondering how to make introductions. What was the etiquette for your ex-wife meeting your polycule? Miss Manners never covered shit like this.

Before Mel could cobble together any words, though, a new challenger entered the scene, also wearing a CompCo polo. Mel recognized the petite blond from back before she'd deleted her Instagram account. It was Lynn's new girlfriend—although Mel supposed she wasn't exactly new anymore. "Hey, Honey," the girlfriend said, pressing a kiss to Lynn's cheek. "What's all this?" She smiled aggressively in Mel's direction.

"Chris, this is Mel. You've heard about her," Lynn said with great tact. "Mel, this is my partner, Chris. She works here, too."

"Coworkers! That's cute." Mel tried not to sound sarcastic, but it was hard when her voice came out sounding like that naturally. She tried to salvage things by offering Chris a hand to shake. "It's nice to meet you, seriously."

Chris seemed to take it in stride, shaking Mel's hand heartily. "Likewise."

"So, Mel. How are you these days?" Lynn's eyes were like a cartoon kitten's, all sad and pitying. "You doing okay?"

"Yeah, actually." Mel released Chris's hand and put a palm on the small of both Bebe's and Kade's backs. Despite the press of the crowds, it felt like they were in their own little world, the five of them. But even if everyone in the Javits Center had been staring at Mel in that moment, she wouldn't have cared. She wasn't going to mince words to make Lynn more comfortable. "These are my partners. This is Bebe"—she nodded at the gleeful ball of energy waving hello on her right—"and Kade." A nod to her left, where Kade was lifting a hand in a less-enthusiastic greeting. Mel couldn't help but smile at the sight.

When she turned back to Lynn and Chris, she saw both women were standing stock-still, with their mouths slightly open. Kind of thrilling, Mel had to say. Chris recovered first.

"Ah, business partners?" she asked, though it came out as a high squeak.

"No," Kade said. Flat as an old bottle of soda water.

"Romantic partners," Bebe clarified. She looped one arm around Mel's waist to drive the point home. "Mel is going to compete in the cocktail showdown later, so we're here to be the cheering section."

"Well, that's fuuuuuuun." Chris latched on to the more familiar topic of convention goings-on like a lamprey. "I heard about that competition. I'm so glad they started doing it this year! Good luck with that, Mel. Fingers crossed that you take home the big prize."

"Thanks," Mel said. She couldn't help but notice Lynn was still struggling to rejoin the conversation.

Lynn saw Mel's glance and seemed to shake herself back to the present. "So is this, um, a new thing?" She pointed between— among—all three of them on the other side of the table.

"Well, parts of it are?" Mel said at the same time Bebe said, "We started dating last year." Technically true since they'd met in December, but clearly phrased to be contrary. Bebe was so hot when she was contrary.

"Sounds complicated!" Chris said in an upbeat way.

Kade smirked. "Not really."

They were also a very hot contrarian, Mel realized.

Lynn stared at Mel like she didn't recognize her. "I . . . never pictured you as that kind of person," she said.

"What kind of person is that?" Mel asked. She was a mature adult without a petty bone in her body. She was not enjoying this. Okay, maybe she was enjoying it a little. But she bit her tongue to keep herself from adding, *A happy one?*

"I don't know." Lynn laughed at herself, shaking her head. "Don't mind me. My brain must be fried from Food Fest."

Bebe made a noise of sympathy. "It *is* a lot, isn't it?" The queen of the double meaning.

"Right, exactly," Lynn said. She looked at Mel and smiled, a little strained, but not insincere. "It was good to see you. I'm glad you— I'm glad." Clearly she wanted to wrap things up and leave on a high note, a sentiment Mel agreed with wholeheartedly.

Mel nodded to her. "Yeah, great seeing you. And nice to meet you," she said to Chris, giving her a little wave.

"Yes, nice meeting all of you," Lynn rushed to add, smiling at Bebe and Kade. "Have a good time at the competition."

"Take more deviled eggs," Chris suggested. She nudged the serving platter across the table.

Bebe scooped up another three. "Oh, twist my arm, why don't you?" She gave Mel's ex-wife an exaggerated wink.

"Bye, Lynn," Mel said, and together with her two paramours, she left the orbit of the booth like she was walking on air instead of the battered convention floor carpet. None of the daydreams she'd had about seeing Lynn again had ever ended up like that. A sense of peace curled in her belly as they shuffled through the mass of bodies.

"That could have gone worse," Bebe said once they were out of earshot of the CompCo booth.

"Yeah," Mel said, more than a little shocked at the truth of it. Sure, the pain of her divorce wasn't erased because of that one interaction, but Mel felt it from its proper distance of years. It was as if, now that she was where she was, she could put that part of her life in a box, not to hide it away, but to store it on a shelf along with all her other memories, all her achievements, all her highs and lows. "It's kind of goofy to say it out loud but—I feel like I've already won? In a way?" She grinned. "Anything else will be the cherry on top."

Kade nodded. "A healthy attitude."

"Very," Bebe said, "although I do want to see you crush your opponents into dust."

Mel side-eyed her. "Jesus, Bee."

"What? I'm being supportive!"

CHAPTER 28

They wove through the heaving crowd, making their way downstairs where different seminars and offshoot events were being
held. Mel located the room for the cocktail competition easily. A
banner that read THE NEW ERA OF NEW YORK MIXOLOGY hung across
a pair of massive doors along with a photo of Adam Lavender serving
up his iconic forest-themed cocktail. Mel stared at the picture, feeling
a frisson of her earlier nervousness run through her. Nerves were fine.
She welcomed those butterflies. They were a symptom of giving a shit.

A person wearing a headset and holding a clipboard—the
kind of person you deferred to as your god in situations like this—
approached. "Are you here for the cocktail competition?" they asked
Kade, presumably because they were still holding Mel's mini cooler
full of ingredients.

"I am. Melanie Sorrento." Mel took the Igloo back from Kade
with a whispered thanks.

A quick check of the clipboard, then Headset nodded. "Come with me, please." They headed toward a smaller door in the middle of the long hallway.

Mel got twin kisses goodbye and dual wishes for luck from Bebe and Kade before following at a fast clip.

It was the first time Food Fest was holding something like this, and despite the big cash prize and legendary judges, cocktails were still an afterthought in the grand scheme of the weekend, taking a back seat to food and wine. Mel figured she'd be competing against a handful of people, a dozen at most, mostly locals who wouldn't need to shell out a ton of money for travel.

There turned out to be way more than a handful. Mel found herself herded into a holding area with nearly twenty other bartenders of various ages and origins. Her ears picked up chatter in English, Spanish, French, and a smattering of what sounded like German. It wasn't long before they were all given a lineup number and told the order of events: they'd be brought onto the stage one by one to mix their cocktail and serve it to the judging panel. They were expected to explain the recipe as they went, and if time allowed, the judges would offer comments. Once everyone had had their turn, the scores would be tallied and the winner announced. This information had been laid out on the entry forms, but Mel listened to each detail like she was hearing it for the first time.

Mel was positioned toward the back of the lineup for reasons that weren't clear to her at first, but when the guy in front of her introduced himself as Xavier Saldana, she realized they were in alphabetical order by surname. She wished, not for the first time, she'd been born an Andersen or an Abbott. It was going to take forever for the dozen or so people in front of her to show the judges their stuff. She alternated pacing around the small room and sitting jiggly-legged in one of the metal folding chairs until it was Xavier's turn. Then Mel waited as close to the curtained exit as possible, listening to the smatterings of applause and the muffled microphoned words from the people onstage.

At last came a final round of applause for Xavier. Headset pointed at Mel and motioned her forward. "Your turn."

Mel took a deep breath and made the long walk onto the stage.

There was a freestanding bar set up in the center, very much like the kind freelance caterers used at events. Stagehands in all-black outfits swapped out the used bar tools for a clean set and placed Mel's name-tagged cooler behind the work area as she approached. Before she climbed the steps that led onto the stage, she looked out over the audience. Damn, it was standing room only, a veritable mob lined up against the back wall. Maybe next year Food Fest would add some more cocktail content; the interest was clearly there. Mel spotted Bebe and Kade in the front row, Bebe's outfit like a bright flag. She was waving in frantic excitement while Kade held her free hand.

Mel also spotted the judges' table, which was set up on the far side of the stage, angled to give the audience a clear view. She recognized each face and could put it to a name. Hell, she'd practically made whole dossiers for the panel during her months of prep. There was Vivian Carlyle, the godmother of the Black American cocktail movement and owner of the hottest bar in Atlanta. She was in her fifties, with neon-green eyeglasses and close-cropped hair. At the other end of the judging table sat Ray Lyton, who'd founded a craft beer label uptown a few years back. They were young, white, nonbinary, and apparently a fan of every beverage ever created, because as hard as Mel looked, she couldn't find any evidence of flavors they didn't vibe with. And in the middle, looming large, was Adam Lavender with his sharp goatee and piercing eyes.

Mel took her spot behind the bar and cleared her throat. *Pretend this is just another shift at T&V*, she told herself as she grabbed the clean Boston shaker. *No, even better: pretend you're mixing a drink for Bebe and Kade in your apartment. No one to impress, nothing to prove. You already know they love this.* She lifted her head and blew her two lovers in the front room a kiss, a simple silent pucker of her lips. *You already know they love you.*

"This cocktail is called the Rock Dove." Her lapel mic caught every word and projected it in ringing tones across the room. She knew how to tell a drink's story. This was what she was good at. "A rock dove is another name for a pigeon." Ice shoveled into the shaker, tinkling like gems. "And there's nothing more New York than a pigeon," she said. That got a laugh from the crowd. She didn't need to crack jokes onstage, but an element of showmanship was expected. All bars were a stage, in the end. All service was a production.

"My drink of choice is the paloma, which is Spanish for dove, so the Rock Dove is a riff on that, with heavy influence from the margarita, America's favorite cocktail. Sure, New York isn't America's favorite city, but we like to pretend we are. Live here long enough and you start to forget there *are* other cities." She measured out the tequila and triple sec as she talked. "We make our own way here, and we like it like that. This is a rosemary-lime syrup, by the way." Mel held her mason jar with the golden liquid sloshing within. "Made it myself. In she goes." A measure added to the ice. She tried to maintain eye contact with each judge the way she would for any guest in her section. Their expressions were inscrutable, for the most part, although Lyton smiled encouragingly.

She clapped her tins closed and started to shake. Once Mel began straining the cocktail into three chilled rocks glasses, she said, "Top with seltzer." A deft splash of Topo Chico on each. "Garnish simply with a cherry, Luxardo if you got it." They were already skewered, and she dropped them in like coins in a fountain. "Italian, like me. The whole thing is me, actually. Top to bottom. My whole bartending career in a glass. Cheers." She presented the tray with a flourish, and the audience clapped politely. Bebe even stuck her fingers in her mouth and whistled.

It was nerve-racking to stand in the wings and watch the judges sip her cocktail from afar. Mel wrung her hands in front of her. The adrenaline that had powered her through was starting to wane, leaving her feeling lightheaded. Probably should have eaten more than a couple deviled eggs. She thought she caught the shape of the word "good" on Vivian Carlyle's lips, but she couldn't be sure. The other judges had their heads bent over their scorecards so that Mel couldn't see their reactions at all.

A headset-wearing organizer made a wrist-tapping gesture to Adam Lavender. He nodded and said into his mic, "Moving right along to our next contestant." Mel's heart sunk as some bartender named Watkins was brought onstage. There hadn't even been time for feedback? She hoped that wasn't a reflection on her cocktail's performance.

She was ushered back into the holding area to wait out the last couple presentations, and then it was time for the mixologists to gather onstage to hear the results. Mel stood in the lineup, not sure where to put her hands, while Lavender gave a nice speech about how blown away he was by the talented showcase, and how hard it had been to decide a winner. At least, Mel was pretty sure he said something to that effect. His voice was mostly a muffled buzz that went in one ear and out the other. Like a Canadian version of the adults from *Peanuts*. Mel concentrated on clasping her hands totally naturally in front of her and not looking too weird.

She nearly missed the actual announcement, tuning in just in time to catch Adam Lavender say, "—of the grand prize is . . ." The room held its breath. "Alejandra Hernandez and her Everything Bagel Boozy Egg Cream."

Mel's first thought: *Well, shit.*

Her second, close on its heels? *Not the everything bagel seasoning rim!* Kade was going to be so smug that their prediction so many months ago, as sarcastic as it had been, had come true. Mel made eye contact with them in the front row, and sure enough, the dry humor in their eyes was already there.

And finally, Mel thought, *I need to fucking clap so I don't look like an asshole.* She joined the rest of the contestants and the audience in applauding for Alejandra, a short kid with a Bronx accent who was stammering her thanks into a provided microphone and accepting her comically overlarge check. There were a few closing remarks by Adam, and then it was all over. The audience began rising from their seats and heading for the doors. Contestants milled around on the stage, chatting with each other and waiting for their chance to congratulate the winner personally.

For something that Mel had spent months preparing for, the end was decidedly anticlimactic. She was disappointed about losing, but that was a distant ache compared to the profound relief she felt. It was over. She'd done the best she could.

She saw Bebe waving to her through the throng of people coming and going. Kade was right next to her, looking quietly proud. Mel smiled at them.

Even if she hadn't won, she was still going home after this with the hottest people in the room. So who was the real winner here? Well, Alejandra, obviously—but Mel was happy for her. Boozy egg cream, that was actually kind of genius. Not Mel's style, but she could respect the vision.

She gestured to Bebe to wait for a moment and was about to head backstage to collect her empty cooler when Adam Lavender himself stepped in front of her. He wasn't as tall as she thought he'd be. His smile seemed genuine, which was nice.

Oh, he was talking to her.

"—wanted to say, it was really close. I mean it, your drink was right up there in our top scores. I thought it was delicious, well-balanced." He held out his hand.

Mel shook it, dazed. "Thank you. That means a lot."

"Your entry materials said you're tending bar at Terror & Virtue?" It was less of a question and more of a request for confirmation.

"Yes?" Mel cleared her throat. "Yes. Been there several years now."

"Have you ever thought about opening up your own place?" Adam asked. "Because what you put out today—it should be on a menu somewhere."

The adrenaline kicked in again. "I've absolutely thought about it," Mel said. "Hopefully I'll do more than think someday soon."

Adam broke off their handshake and pulled a matte-green business card from his pastel suit jacket. "Keep in touch. I'm always looking for new ventures to support."

"Oh wow." Mel stared at the card. Adam Lavender's card. It was like she'd been handed the contact info for the King of Spain: unlikely and pretty awesome. "That's very generous, thank you."

He shrugged. "It's a little selfish. I want to have another Rock Dove at some point, and I know T&V doesn't allow much mixologist input on the menu." With one last smile, he moved down the line to chat with someone else.

Okay. Mel slipped the card into her jeans pocket and tried not to scream out of pure joy. Adam Lavender, the inventor of the For-est Floor, wanted to support her? His advice would be invaluable to someone like her. Or did he mean—financial support? As in seed money?

Mel could hardly wait to get home and spend way too long com-posing an email to the address on the card.

She turned around, looking for Bebe and Kade, but a tall, lanky shape stopped her in her tracks. It was one of the other judges, Ray Lyton.

"Hey, loved your drink, seriously," they said. "It was in my top three for sure."

"Thank you, thank you so much." Mel's head was spinning from all the thanking she'd done today.

"Listen, normally I wouldn't assume but . . ." They leaned in closer so they couldn't be overheard by the people surrounding them. "Any interest in an invite-only queer afterparty? Me and some of the other gays on the bev side are having a little get-together after the Fest wraps tonight."

"Uh." Mel blinked. "Yeah. Totally. Can I bring my paramours? It's a plus-two situation." She motioned to the edge of the stage, where Bebe and Kade were still waiting for her. Bebe was pointing emphat-ically at Ray and saying something urgent into Kade's ear, but when she saw that she'd been spotted, she grinned and waggled her fingers in Ray's direction.

Ray waved back amiably. "No problem," they said. "The more the merrier." They handed Mel a small, photocopied flyer with a picture of a coupe glass and a disco ball on it along with a time and place. "See you all there."

When Mel finally rejoined Bebe and Kade, she was welcomed with a barrage of hugs, forehead kisses, and in Bebe's case, the third degree.

"What did Ray Lyton want? That baking show they host is my absolute favorite. I have the biggest crush on them. Did they give you their number!? Oh my god, my girlfriend has so much *game*."

"Not a phone number." Mel held up the flyer. "We're going dancing tonight."

CHAPTER 29

Nobody partied harder than people in the beverage industry. And nobody did it better than the queer ones.

The drag club that had been rented out for the night was already packed with all kinds of folks, their Food Fest badges and lanyards still wagging around their necks as they danced and drank and shouted over a Beyoncé track. Mel spotted Ray holding court in one of the booths toward the back, a curvy brunet perched on their lap. The woman's whole attention was taken by them, laughing at something they'd said, oblivious to anyone else.

"Maybe she's more open than she looks," Bebe said into Mel's ear. "Do you think I have a shot?"

Mel gave her a mock-stern glare. "Let's not get kicked out *right* away."

Kade snorted and led the way to the open bar, where plenty of beer, mixed drinks, and mocktails were on offer. Once they had secured their preferred poison (a gin and tonic for Kade, a standard old-fashioned for Bebe, a paloma for Mel), they found a free booth in the corner. Mel tried to usher Kade into the U-shape, but Bebe stopped her.

"Sit in the middle," she said as she plunked herself at the far end of the booth. "We haven't had a chance to heap praise upon you yet!"

Mel grumbled but did as she was told. "Praise? For what? I didn't even win."

"But you did an excellent job," Kade said, sliding in behind her. "You didn't see all the other presentations. We did. Yours was superior to the vast majority."

That meant a lot, coming from someone as critical as Kade. Mel gave them a kiss in thanks. And because she could.

"Not to mention, you made inroads with Adam-fucking-Lavender," Bebe said. "Plus got us an invite to hang with the cool kids." She spoke the next part into her rocks glass. "And now I can watch my cooking show crush make out with their girlfriend in the middle of a drag club."

"Wait, really?" Mel swiveled her head to try to get a glimpse of Ray Lyton.

Bebe smacked her on the arm. "Don't stare. You'll get us thrown out."

"No one is throwing us out," Kade intoned.

"Yeah, I would love to see someone try to throw you out, St. Cloud." Mel leaned into their space with a leer. "You'd just glower at them until they shrank into the fetal position."

"My point is—" Bebe broke in.

"I don't glower," Kade said, glowering.

"—we are here to celebrate," Bebe finished firmly. "A toast." She lifted her glass. Mel copied her with a good-natured eye roll, and Kade did as well with more gravitas. "To Melanie Sorrento, the bravest, hottest, most kick-ass lady you'll find behind a bar. And the easiest to love."

Mel did not tear up. There was simply something in her eye. They clinked their glasses together and settled into a relaxed sprawl, not caring who saw them sharing a booth that was way bigger than they pretended it was. Pure contentment washed over Mel as she sipped her drink. She watched queer bodies of all shapes and sizes moving on the dance floor. Then the music changed to something slower, something more romantic. The dancers started pairing off into couples, pressed together and swaying. Mel hummed along to the first strains of Cyndi Lauper singing about love.

Kade tilted their head and looked at her. "Do you want to dance?"

"With you?" Mel grinned. "I never took you for a dancer."

"I'm a superb dancer," they said, nodding to the other side of the booth. "So is Bebe."

Bebe nodded, biting her lip in clear eagerness.

Mel looked between them both, hesitating. It felt wrong to choose. Maybe— "Can we all dance together? Is that weird?" The only people currently dancing were couples, but Mel didn't much care what everyone else was doing.

Bebe clapped her hands over her mouth and squealed. "I thought you'd never ask! Come on." She started wriggling out of her side of the booth, her hand closing around Mel's wrist to tug her along. "Can I be the Alan Cumming in this *Romy & Michele* reenactment?"

"Who? This what?" Mel let herself be pulled to her feet.

Kade was right behind her. "It's a film from the nineties. Bebe has made me watch it many, many times."

"Alan is a bisexual icon," Bebe declared, which cleared up precisely nothing for Mel, "and that movie is poly culture."

"Sure, okay, you can be Alan Cumming," Mel said. She couldn't deny Bebe anything—unless it was within very specific, sexy parameters.

Bebe took her hand and Kade's and led them onto the dance floor. It wasn't too crowded; the slow song had scared away more dancers than it tempted, so there was plenty of room for the three of them. At first Mel felt awkward, not knowing what to do since they weren't dancing in the usual pair, but Bebe took charge. She twirled Mel and Kade, one on each side, and took turns dipping them low. Kade was achingly graceful, moving their limbs with the poise of a ballet dancer. Instead of feeling self-conscious with comparisons, Mel tried to channel some of their confidence, moving like her feet weren't that of a Clydesdale. She caught Kade's secret smile as they whirled by her. There was so much joy bubbling inside her, she threw her head back and laughed.

She and Kade orbited around Bebe like planets around their sun. They met and parted; they took Bebe for a spin of her own, but then returned; they made a ring with their joined hands and spun until they were dizzy. Mel was sure they looked downright unhinged. She didn't care.

When the song faded to a close, Bebe beamed so brightly that Mel had to kiss her. Smoky whiskey flowed over her tongue, the soft curve of Bebe's waist fitting into her hands. Then, because she couldn't leave it at that, she reeled Kade closer with a grip on their sweater and kissed them, too. Herbaceous gin, the tang of quinine and lime. They wrapped their arms around Mel and drank her in, too.

Mel surfaced from the kiss, only vaguely aware that people were clapping. "Let's go home," she whispered against Kade's cheek.

They went as fast as the Uber could take them.

They ended up in Bebe's room, since her bed was the only one big enough to hold the three of them comfortably.

Bebe made a beeline for her dresser drawer and retrieved a fistful of intriguing seafoam-green lace that Mel couldn't identify. "I'm going to do a quick rinse," she announced. "All that dancing has me sweaty. Why don't you two make yourselves comfortable?" She bounced her eyebrows up and down while glancing meaningfully at the monstrous bed.

"Take your time, Love," Kade said.

Mel was already shucking off her black button-down. "But not too long."

While Bebe disappeared into the en suite, shower running in a muffled way, Mel crawled into the luxurious softness of the bed. She starfished in the very center of the mattress and let her sore, aching body be cradled by it. For a moment, Mel could close her eyes and drift.

Then the bed shifted, and Kade's weight came to rest atop hers. Mel cracked open one eye to see them looming above her, looking ethereal and lovely in the low light.

"Can I help you, St. Cloud?" she asked with faux archness.

"You were brilliant today." They tugged the hem of her undershirt up until Mel raised her arms, the bare minimum needed for Kade to work it over her head. "You were on fire. It was stunning to witness." They tossed the undershirt onto the floor.

"I didn't win," Mel pointed out once again. "I couldn't have been that stunning."

"I don't mean the competition," Kade said with a curl at the corner of their mouth, "although I believe you did extremely well. I meant when you danced with us." They lowered their head and placed a kiss at the edge of the tattoo that decorated Mel's collarbone. "And when you introduced us to your ex." They moved lower, kissing between her breasts, nosing at the sleek line of her black bralette. "When you stood at my side and did not care who saw us together."

Mel dug her fingers into that thick ginger hair and tugged. Kade made a noise at that, but it was a good one, and they allowed Mel to drag them up until they were nose to nose. "I did care who saw us together." She waited one half beat, long enough for a tinge of worry to appear in Kade's dark eyes. "I want the biggest possible audience. I went through hell to get you. May as well show you off."

Kade's eyes narrowed, though they also glittered with good humor. "You are incorrigible, Sorrento."

"What are you going to do about it?" Mel lifted her hips to grind against Kade. They moaned, already halfway hard. It made Mel grin like mad.

Distantly, Mel registered the sound of the shower shutting off, but she was currently preoccupied with kissing that prissy pout off Kade's mouth. Kade was a welcome weight on top of her, unhurried as they kissed, their nimble fingers tracing invisible designs along Mel's ribs.

The bathroom door opened. "Did you start without me?" Bebe's voice, despite her efforts to sound affronted, practically dripped with delight. "You're both so impatient."

Kade pulled away from Mel's mouth to share a long-suffering look with her, then rolled off to the side. Mel propped herself up on her hands to get a good look at Bebe. She stood framed in the doorway, leaning against it like a classic femme fatale. The seafoam lace turned out to be a sheer teddy that clung to every curve of Bebe's soft body. It was a sight Mel could have stared at for hours, but luckily, she could do more than stare. She scrambled upright to tuck her legs under her and beckoned Bebe with one finger.

"You. Over here. Now."

Bebe tossed her hair. "Not even a 'please'?"

Kade gave a huff that bordered on a snort. "Love, would you *please* get over here so that Mel and I can play with our favorite toy?" They gave Mel a quick glance. "I have an idea. If everyone is amenable."

"Boy oh boy, mark me down as amenable for sure," Bebe said. She clambered onto the bed with less grace than usual for her, but her enthusiasm was contagious.

Kade gave their wife an admonishing look. "You don't know what it is yet."

Bebe situated herself on her side between Mel and Kade, wriggling happily. "I know how your brain works. No details necessary. Sign me up."

Mel wrapped her arms around Bebe's otherworldly hips and pulled her back against her chest. "I'm still working on my poly-telepathy. You're going to have to spell it out for me," she said over Bebe's shoulder. One of her hands drifted up to play with Bebe's nipple beneath the soft lace, making Bebe giggle.

Kade wedged themself closer to Bebe and kissed her once, hard. "Shush, Love," they said when they pulled away. "Mel and I are talking." They addressed Mel with their head propped on one hand, conversing over Bebe's flushed neck. "I am not trying to . . . flex, if I understand that slang correctly," they said, "but do you agree that I know Bebe better than anyone else does?"

"Please don't ever use slang. It sounds wrong. And also yes," Mel said. "You know her best." That was simply a fact. They'd had almost a decade head start on Mel.

Kade's hand cupped the side of Bebe's jaw, drawing her into a deep kiss. Kade, meanwhile, did not break eye contact with Mel. Mel swallowed, feeling want and need pool low in her body. She'd never thought of herself as much of a voyeur, but hearing Bebe whimper between them made her reevaluate.

When Kade broke the kiss, it was to say, "I'd like to tell you what to do to her. I'd like to show you how I have her. Would you like that, too?"

"Oh, please please please," Bebe chanted, pressing kisses along Kade's neck and chest, their arm, any part of them she could reach.

Mel licked her lips. Her breath was coming like a steam engine. "Hell yeah."

Which was how Mel found herself flat on her back with Bebe sitting on her face. Mel's hands gripped at the round flesh of Bebe's ass, pulling her harder against her mouth. Her tongue worked over her as Kade, curled on their side right next to Mel, purred in her ear.

"Slow, that's it, slow at first. Can you see how pink she is? She's so close already, we don't want to finish her yet."

"We don't?" Bebe gasped out from her seat atop Mel's chin. Mel gave her a hard swipe of her tongue in retaliation, and Bebe yelped. The thighs on either side of Mel's head trembled like an earthquake had struck.

Mel couldn't see Kade from her position buried under Bebe's slick heat, but she could hear the raised eyebrow in their voice as they said, "Her eyes are bigger than her stomach, you know. She wants to come two, three, four times before we're through with her, but she turns to jelly as soon as you give her one."

Mel grabbed Bebe under her hot thighs and lifted her cunt an inch off her lips. A strand of spit connected them still. "I don't see why that should stop me," Mel murmured, then let Bebe fall back to earth. She kept at it, licking into her and making her rock back and forth.

Kade hummed as if in thought, pressing a kiss to Mel's shoulder and running their hand along her flank. "That's good thinking. I bet she'd enjoy being forced to come even when it's too much for her. And you'd like that—you're so cruel. It's fascinating." The mattress shifted, and Mel felt Kade leave her side, leaving goose bumps along her arm in their wake.

Bebe let loose a desperate cry, grinding down harder on Mel's face. "Darling," she said. "Sweetheart! Please."

Mel wondered what she was begging for, but then she remembered: Kade would let her know. It was all in their capable hands.

"A moment, Love. You have to be patient." Those very hands ticked at Mel's ankles. She couldn't see what Kade was doing, but she could figure it out from touch alone. She could hear the clank of buckles, the supple slide of leather straps caressing Mel's legs as they dragged upward. Kade was outfitting her with the harness she kept stored under Bebe's bed. Mel squeezed her eyes shut in bliss. It was one of her favorite things, using this on Bebe.

"Lift your hips," Kade said as they reached the tops of her thighs. Mel did, trying to keep her concentration on pleasuring Bebe, even as Kade took advantage of her spread legs to give her own clit a swift lick. The harness settled into place, and Mel lowered her hips back to the bed. The heavy weight of the strap-on dick bobbed against her pubic bone.

When Kade spoke again, it was to Bebe. "Enough of that." Mel felt the weight leave her face as Bebe was lifted free. She worked her damp jaw back and forth, hearing the hinge click. When she peered down the length of her torso, the sight that greeted her was worth dislocation: Kade with their arms wrapped around Bebe from behind, their gaze fixed on Mel as they positioned Bebe over Mel's bright pink cock. "Look how wet you made her." With the lace shoved aside, their clever fingers spread Bebe's lips, showing Mel the steady drip of fluid. They kept Bebe spread open and lowered her down onto the toy.

Mel's eyes rolled back, and she lost track of the sight for a moment. "Oh, fuck." This strap-on was one of Mel's favorite toys for a reason: the base of the dildo was equipped with a clever little vibrator that gave off a short buzz every time it pressed against her body.

Bebe made a noise that forced Mel to get her eyes working again. She was seated in Mel's lap with her arms held over her breasts in a posture of helplessness. Kneeling to one side of her, Kade tugged at her nipples through the teddy, lips on her ear. "Are you just going to sit there on Mel's cock, Love? Or can you be motivated to move?"

"I can, I can," Bebe babbled. She planted her toes against the mattress and rose up a few inches, then dropped back down. The spike of pleasure that went through Mel was mirrored in Bebe's rapturous face. Mel's hands went to her hips, their favorite handhold.

"Do you know what she loves me to do when I'm fucking her like this?" Kade asked Mel with a deep-throated rumble.

Mel could barely speak, she was panting so hard. "I have a feeling you're going to tell me."

Kade gave her a smile, almost a normal-sized one, and licked their lips. "She likes me to touch her." Their hand disappeared from Mel's view, behind Bebe's backside. "Right here."

Bebe's spine straightened, her eyes going wide. Through the lacy teddy, Mel could see her creamy skin going bright red. "K-Kade, please—"

"Please what, Beautiful?" Mel thrust up into Bebe, feeling her bounce in her lap.

"Fuck her harder," Kade directed her, and Mel sped up. Over Bebe's kittenish cries, they clicked their tongue, impressed. "I can feel you inside her, too. She likes that, being filled up."

"Jesus Christ," Mel said almost to herself.

"I'm only stating facts." Kade removed their hand, making Bebe's mouth go into a tight O. "Put her on her hands and knees," they said, wiping their fingers, shiny with lube, on the bedclothes.

Bebe whined at being moved, but it was all for show. She clearly liked the position, given how much her thick thighs quivered under Mel's touch. "Come on, Sweetie," Mel cooed as she worked Bebe back onto her cock. "There you are."

Kade shuffled on their knees to the head of the bed, where Bebe's own head hung between her shoulders as Mel fucked her from behind. "Very good," they said, thumbing along Bebe's cheek. "Want something in your mouth, Love?"

Bebe moaned and nodded, her lips already parting to receive Kade's hard cock. Mel braced a hand flat on Bebe's back. She kept her eyes locked on Bebe's bobbing head, then flicked her gaze up to meet Kade's.

They blew her a kiss.

Mel laughed, a huff of shocked air leaving her lungs as her orgasm ripped through her. She hadn't realized how close she was until it was too late. The force of it tipped her over Bebe's lace-covered back, hips stuttering against Bebe's ass.

"That's right. Come in her. She likes how it feels." Kade was pumping their hips lazily, one hand on Bebe's head. Bebe groaned in agreement.

"Holy—fuck." Mel thrust in one last time, as deep as she could go. One of her hands stole down between Bebe's shaking thighs to rub over her hard clit. She heard more than saw Bebe reach her finish, her high whine punctuated with fine tremors across her skin. It took a few more minutes for Kade to come, time that Mel spent chewing on Bebe's earlobe.

At last they all stilled into sweaty quiet, only their harsh breathing punctuating the silence.

Bebe was the first to clear her throat. "Again?" she asked sweetly.

"Love, your eyes are already closing," Kade said, stroking her cheek with deep fondness. "You're asleep on your feet. Well, hands and knees." They drew Bebe down so that she could sprawl more comfortably atop the bed.

Bebe rubbed her face, catlike, against one of the silk pillows. "Maybe a quick nap."

"Maybe it's time for bed," Mel said, unbuckling her harness and tossing it to the carpet with a wet *THWAP*. "If Kade and I are able to get to sleep tonight."

Kade gave her an arch look. "I think my insomnia has been counteracted by the fact that I just came so hard, I saw stars."

"Slumber partyyyyy . . . ," Bebe mumbled into her pillow. "I'm so happy."

"You're dead to the world," Kade told her gently. Then, to Mel: "There's plenty of room for us to all fit."

They were right.

Mel fell asleep in the middle of the sandwich, Kade in her arms and Bebe snoring against her back. And there was nowhere on earth she would've rather been.

EPILOGUE

A year and a bit later

The text from Daniel lit up Mel's phone on the marble bar top. Movinggggggg dayyyyyyyy!!!, it said with his characteristic flair. Mel groaned at the reminder. She'd been looking forward to this day for weeks, and now that it was here, she didn't feel prepared. She still had so much work to do, and not just at the apartment.

Her bar needed her attention, too.

It was the hottest day of the summer, and the AC had crapped out. Mel had called about six different repair companies, all of whom said they couldn't possibly get out to her before next Monday. She rubbed at her gritty eyes and tried to think. The soft opening was supposed to be in three days. How was she going to get this done before then?

"Hello, stranger."

Mel dragged her hands off her face to find Bebe sitting across the empty bar from her, having claimed one of the stools that was still covered in a plastic sheet. Kade was taking another spot right next to her.

"What are you doing here?" Mel leaned across the bar to steal twin kisses hello. "I thought you were in court the whole day. And you"—she wagged a finger at Kade—"are supposed to be getting ready for your show next week."

"The guy settled," Bebe said brightly, "and Kade is ahead of schedule on their pieces."

"We thought you might appreciate some company," Kade added.

Mel looked around the space that had once been Sal's. Almost everything from the old dive bar had been ripped out or refurbished, transforming what had once been a dank armpit of a bar into a cozy, laid-back lounge. There were tables in intimate alcoves along the wall and secondhand chandeliers (handpicked by Daniel) hanging mismatched from the stamped tin ceiling. A rolling garage door was flung open at the front of the lounge to let in a warm breeze and the smells from the bakery down the street. A permanent ramp had recently been installed at the front door, which was also propped open. It was the kind of place Mel had always dreamed of owning.

Which she did, now. Sort of. She owned a 10 percent stake in it, at least. Collective Spirits had many owners. Some of them were silent partners—Kade, Bebe, their financial guy, Callen. Also, Adam Lavender himself. Though Mel had welcomed his input in the venture alongside his money, Adam had insisted the vision remain with the not-so-silent partners: Mel, Daniel, and Ronica.

It had taken over a year to get the financing and the sale of the property in order. Staffing had been quicker: Mel didn't feel at all guilty about poaching some of the best people from Terror & Virtue. Brent was going to be operating with a skeleton crew in a few days—if Mel could figure out how to cool down the ninety-four-degree lounge before the opening.

"Plus it's moving day!" Bebe waved her hands in celebration. "Are you excited?"

Mel grinned. Despite the stress of getting CS ready, she was. "I think this is going to be a good change," she said.

"You're sure you won't miss being Daniel's roommate?" Kade quirked a brow.

"I mean, yeah. A little." Mel nodded to herself. "But I won't lie—I'm looking forward to having the place to myself."

Daniel was finally moving in with Jackson. They'd chosen a roomy condo three blocks from Collective Spirits, their own little love nest. Mel had agreed to take over the rent-controlled apartment. Keeping it in the family, Daniel had said. The arrangement had worked out perfectly: for the first time in her adult life, Mel would have a place to call her own. She needed that. One day, she might want to move in with Bebe and Kade—they'd offered—but for now, she was eager to put her own touch on the LES apartment. With Daniel's blessing (and the judicious use of his storage unit), she had grand plans for changing out Granny Quince's museum pieces for some of her own.

But she had to figure out how to fix the AC at the new bar before she could worry about what kind of art to put up on the walls of her apartment.

"Do you happen to know anyone who works in HVAC repair?" she asked her two paramours. It was meant to be a dry joke—why would the classiest people in Manhattan have an HVAC dude on speed dial?—but once again Bebe surprised her. She pulled out her phone and started tapping away.

"Sawyer's older sister's ex-husband—we like him—is some kind of contractor on Long Island. Let me see if he knows anybody."

"How do you always have a guy?" Mel muttered.

Bebe didn't stop typing. "The poly social network, Sweetheart."

"Hey." Kade's soft voice arrested Mel's attention. "You seem tired."

Mel gave them a shrug that was half fond, half *tell me something I don't know*. "I can sleep when we're open," she said.

"You'll sleep tonight if I have to hold you down and make you," Kade said mildly.

"I thought tonight was my alone time with Bebe." Mel pulled up their shared calendar on her phone. Even though she was working her ass off trying to get this wild idea off the ground, her partners always made sure she was taking plenty of breaks. Their regular dates, in pairs and as a threesome, were as much a part of Mel's life as Collective Spirits was. "Yep, says so right here."

"Fine. But the offer stands." Their gaze shifted to the bottles already lined up in the mirrored case behind the bar. "Now, how about a relaxing drink?"

"That I'll need to make, huh?" Mel was already reaching for her shaker despite her complaining. The ice machines had been installed earlier in the week, and she was eager to see if they were producing the correct size and shape.

"Love you," Kade said with their version of a winning smile.

Mel almost fumbled her shaker. Sometimes she forgot they said that to her now. Still felt a little like a dream. Kind of like the new tattoo on her biceps, the one that covered up an old date: a fat, happy pigeon strutting along, all puffed up. "Love you, too, St. Cloud," she said fondly.

"Aha!" Bebe tapped enthusiastically at her phone. "Samson does know someone. Sending the details to your work email."

"Thanks, Bee. Why don't you two head out to the back patio and I'll bring you something nice and summery?" Mel scooped ice— perfect pebbles—into her shaker.

"The patio is finished?" Kade raised an impressed eyebrow. "The deck wasn't even laid the last time I was here. Come on, Love." They took Bebe, who was still preoccupied with her phone, gently by the elbow and guided her to the back door that led out onto the brand-new, linen-shaded, fairy light–draped outdoor area.

"Oooh, the guy might even give you the family-and-friends discount," Bebe said as she followed Kade's lead. "Let me see if I can talk him down a little more."

Mel shook her head, smiled down into her shaker, and reached for a bottle of her best tequila.

ACKNOWLEDGMENTS

This book would not exist if not for all the sluts, slags, and dirty girls (gender neutral) who are there for me when I drop an unhinged idea into the group chat. Thank you for yes, and'ing me, always.

Thank you, Dana, for your no-nonsense corralling and for lending me your dog's name for Mel. Ren, thank you for all your guidance and cheerleading. Francis, thank you for your wonderful generosity. Thank you to my wife, as usual, for everything.

My unending thanks to my editor, Lara Jones, for letting me tell yet another kind of love story. A giant heap of gratitude to my agent, Larissa Melo-Pienkowski, whose advice is invaluable and whose tastes are impeccable. An avalanche of flowers to everyone at Atria who has touched my books. A special glass of something nice for every bookseller and librarian who's put my book in someone's hands. A knowing salute to every bartender who has ever taken care of me.

And finally, a soft, tender, well-deserved forehead kiss to everyone who loves in their own way, with their whole heart, in defiance of anyone who tries to tell you otherwise. Cheers, my loves.